WHERE THE LIGHTS LEAD

WHERE THE LIGHTS LEAD

L . H . BLAKE

Author's Note:

This book contains on-page intimate scenes and mature content and is intended for mature audiences only. For more details on the content warnings for this novel, please visit: www.lhblake.com

This story, while fictional, is set in Canada. As such, it is written in Canadian English which is a combination of American and British spelling, sometimes without any particular rhyme or reason. As such, you may notice a lot of Us and Zs and double Ls, as well as some words which end in an "re" instead of "er". There are also a handful of references to Canadian culture and landmarks.

To Phil, my soulmate.

I'm sorry for all the nights I didn't come to bed because I was writing this book.

Toronto

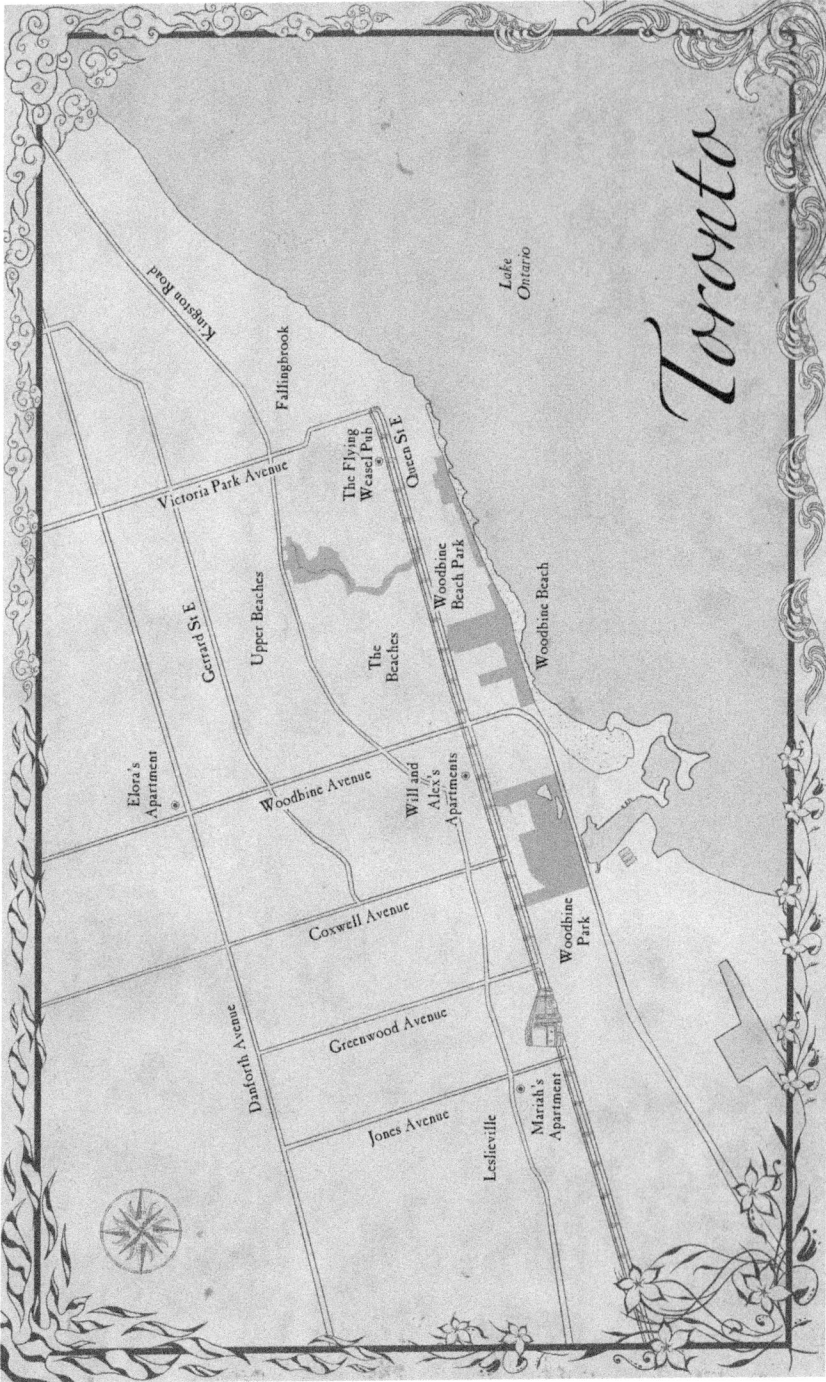

Kingston Road

Fallingbrook

Victoria Park Avenue

The Flying
Weasel Pub

Queen St E

Lake
Ontario

Gerrard St E

Upper Beaches

The
Beaches

Woodbine
Beach Park

Woodbine Beach

Elora's
Apartment

Woodbine Avenue

Will and
Alex's
Apartments

Coxwell Avenue

Woodbine
Park

Danforth Avenue

Greenwood Avenue

Jones Avenue

Leslieville

Mariah's
Apartment

WHERE THE THE LIGHTS LEAD

L . H . BLAKE

PROLOGUE

T he smell of bleach and bandages is something I don't think I will ever get used to, and at this point, the scent of death is preferable. My stomach roils as I take a deep breath, wrapping my stethoscope around my neck before reaching for my coffee and heading out of the locker room. I hook my pager on the waistband of my scrubs and push through the double doors of the Emergency Room toward the nursing station. I flick my wrist to light up my smart watch. It's almost seven in the evening and time to check in with the hospital staff who are coming off shift.

The ER seems relatively quiet tonight, but I have worked enough shifts in emergency medicine by now to know that it can fill up in a matter of minutes. I take a sip of my coffee as I come up to the nursing station. I nod at several familiar faces, most of whom smile back. The meeting is mercifully brief, then a pile of charts is dumped in my lap as I sit down at the desk. Sighing, I flip through them, sipping my coffee and keeping distanced from the nurses who dash to and fro with practiced ease.

The few charts I look at seem relatively straightforward: a broken ankle from a tumble down some stairs, another with abdominal pain, and a young man with a large cut who needs some stitches.

"Dr. Stevens?"

I look up to see Tabitha, a young nurse I've worked with on several occasions.

"Yes?"

"Intake is starting to fill up so we're trying to free up some beds. There are two patients who were brought in this morning. I recall Dr. Shafiq saying they should probably be moved up to long-term care. Can you have a look over their charts and see if we can move them?" Tabitha holds out two medical charts across the wide desk.

"Of course," I say. "Would you mind accompanying me? I see here that vitals haven't been checked in a while."

Tabitha nods and grabs the rolling vitals cart from a few feet away. "I believe the first patient is in room 131."

"All right."

Tabitha leads the way down the cluttered hallway, the steady squeak of our non-slip shoes on the terrazzo floor is loud amidst the rare quiet of the ER. I pass several urgent trauma rooms, most of them empty for now, but that likely won't last. At the end of the hall, Tabitha pushes open the large door into a dimly lit room, the heavy metal door swinging shut behind us. The familiar sound of the heart and oxygen monitor beeps steadily, the noise filling the room as Tabitha flicks on the overhead lights. A dark-haired, young man lies propped up in the bed. His face is badly bruised and swollen, and there is a long section of stitches above his right eyebrow.

"It was a car accident," Tabitha says as I look over his face for any signs of infection. "He hasn't woken up yet."

I prod at him, checking his pupils for dilation, turning his head back and forth. His breathing remains steady, the monitors beeping along at an appropriate rate. "Age?"

Tabitha scans the chart. "Twenty-two."

I take the chart back while Tabitha wheels the vitals cart closer to the side of the bed. Scanning over his paperwork, I feel a sense of dread sweep over me, my stomach churning at the words on the page.

"He was burned…" I say softly. Noticing for the first time that the man isn't wearing a white t-shirt under the sheets, but his entire upper body is covered in white gauze. The sight of the bandages triggers my gag reflex and my hand lifts toward my mouth on impulse, but there's no smell. That nauseating dirty bandage smell doesn't hang in the air like it should. I take a deep breath and think maybe I've finally gone nose blind to it after all.

"Yes," Tabitha says while taking his temperature. "The paramedics told us the car caught fire during a crash up north somewhere. Haliburton, I think they said. They airlifted him in, but his parents died in the crash."

I look at her with a frown, my heart aching for the young man lying before me. I try to compose myself, pushing the sorrow down to keep my mind clear and professional. "That's awful."

Putting on a pair of gloves, I brace myself, then pull back a section of the gauze on his chest. Oddly, the bandages are still fresh, even though the skin underneath is blistered and angry. My lips press together, perhaps this is why it doesn't smell. It is strange though, a burn like this is sure to leave the gauze bloody within a matter of minutes, but it looks as though it was just changed. Maybe it was, but I missed the note on the chart.

"Are we providing pain management for this?" I ask.

The nurse points at the IV pole where several bags of fluids are hooked up, including a morphine drip.

"Good," I say, "when he comes to…he'll need it."

Tabitha nods as she continues.

Checking the chart again, I scan the pages. "I see here an MRI was ordered to check for any brain damage. Do you know where the scan is?"

Tabitha pulls an iPad out from the vitals cart and flips through until she finds what she's looking for before passing it to me. I stare at the images for a few moments, but they make little sense.

"This is the MRI scan?" I ask.

She nods. This can't be right. It's just pure white light in the shape of a body.

"Are you sure—"

"Yeah, Dr. Shafiq couldn't figure it out, either. I guess the machine is faulty. It shut down and won't come back online."

I blink. "Our MRI machine is down?"

Tabitha presses her lips together and moves around the bed to switch one of the bags on the IV pole. "Yeah, they've had a nightmare rescheduling things upstairs."

I blow out a long breath and put the iPad down. I take another peek at the mangled flesh of his chest beneath the bandages, checking for any signs of infection. The shape of a letter V indented in his skin catches my attention. I take a step forward to get a better look.

"What is this?" I ask.

"What's what?" Tabitha asks, coming to stand by my shoulder.

I point to where the V is clearly visible in his skin. I push back more bandages, there's an I there too, and a circle.

"These marks, right here," I say.

My eyes turn to look at Tabitha, but after she takes a long look, she glances back up at me, her eyebrows pulled together. "All I see is a big blister."

I lose my grip on the bandages, which slide back into place. "You don't see letters?"

Tabitha shakes her head. "Uh…no."

My fingers pull at the bandages again, but the marks are gone, an angry blister in their place. I blink rapidly and shake my head. "Sorry. I thought I saw something. I guess I haven't had enough coffee yet."

Tabitha relaxes and chuckles. "I hear that. So what do you think? Vitals look good?"

I check the name on the chart. "Willan Reed," I say quietly. "Unusual name, Willan."

Tabitha shrugs her shoulders. "I kind of like it. It's unique."

"Well, I think everything looks okay to move him to long-term care." I jot down a few final notes and snap the chart shut to tuck it into the bottom of the bed.

"I don't envy who has to tell him about his parents when he wakes up," Tabitha says.

My heart aches again. I've had to have that conversation too many times before, and it always breaks my heart.

"Come on," Tabitha says, pushing the cart. "There's one more to see."

I follow her out through the heavy door into a hallway in utter chaos. Nurses are running up and down the hall, pushing patients on stretchers into every corner of free space.

"Melanie!"

I look over the commotion to see the on-call internal medicine doctor jogging toward me.

"Anthony? What's going on?" I ask.

He shakes his head in disbelief. "What? What do you mean? Where've you been?"

I look around, utterly bewildered. "I was just checking in on a patient to see if he's been cleared to move to long-term care. I've only been gone fifteen minutes max."

"We've been paging you for over an hour," he says, annoyed.

My mouth falls open and I grasp the pager on my hip where I'm horrified to discover twenty unanswered pages. "What the hell?" I mutter.

I flick my watch—the face lighting up to see that it's almost nine o'clock. Almost two whole hours have passed since I started my shift. I turn and look back at the room I just left. Through the small window, I can see the young man still resting on the bed. I rub at my temple, wondering how I could've possibly taken so long with only one patient. It only felt like a few minutes, not hours, that I was in there with Tabitha. How could this have possibly happened? I look down at my pager again—the flashing missed messages screaming at me, and I feel a flush of heated embarrassment flood my cheeks. I've never missed a page before, let alone this many.

I look back through the window, the air shimmering around the young man, the light distorting as though through water. I rub my eyes and look again, but the temporary optical illusion has dissipated. Perhaps I haven't gotten as much sleep as I thought.

"I'm so sorry, Anthony, I'm not sure where the time went. I didn't realize it has been so long. I'm trying to free up some beds."

He shakes his head. "Well, at least that's one good thing. We need them."

"I have one more patient to see who I think we can move out of here," I say, feeling flustered.

"Do it then," he says before turning and walking away. "But do it quickly."

I grip the second chart in my hand and look down at the room number. 133. Right next door. Tabitha has disappeared with the vitals cart, but I quickly stop by the nursing station.

"Patient in 131 can be moved to long-term care," I say.

The nurse picks up the phone and makes arrangements to move the young man while I head over toward room 133. I push the door open to find Tabitha quietly changing the IV bags for a young red-headed girl asleep in the bed.

"Hey, Tabitha?" I call, closing the door behind me.

She looks up. "Yeah?"

"Let's be quick with this one, all right? Anthony is pissed at me."

She narrows her eyes. "Why?"

I walk over to check the print-out from the steadily beating monitors. "Because we took so long with that last patient."

Tabitha checks her watch. "What are you talking about?"

I look up and openly gape at her. "It's almost nine o'clock."

Her lips pull into a frown, and she checks her watch again, then looks back at me. "It's only seven-thirty. Dr. Stevens, are you feeling all right?"

I drop the chart onto the bed and flick my watch again. Sure enough, in bold digital numbers: seven twenty-eight.

"What the—" I mutter.

Tabitha shrugs and continues doing the vitals check. "Maybe your watch is glitching?" she offers as a reason before moving around the bed.

I shake my head. "Yeah…maybe." Picking the chart back up, I scan for the patient's name. "Elora Green. She's being treated for hypothermia?"

Tabitha nods. "Yeah, she was pulled out of the lake this morning."

I nearly drop the chart again. "What?"

"Oh, yeah, you didn't hear about that?" Tabitha asks. "She was found by a couple of guys ice fishing out on the lake. No one knows how long she was under, but miraculously her heart seems fine and she's still breathing. And," she pauses to take her temperature, "her body temperature is back to normal, it seems." Tabitha jots down a few numbers on the chart next to the bed.

I feel the shock on my face as I roll down the heavy blankets covering the girl. "That's wild." My eyes travel down the girl's slender, freckled arms. There's some strange scarring from her wrists to her elbows. Jagged cuts that look like they've been made and healed time and time again. "What happened here?"

Tabitha sighs. "She has quite a bit of scarring on both forearms."

"From self-harm, maybe?" I suggest, having seen similar scars on patients in mental health treatment facilities during my residency. Although not quite to this extent.

She nods. "That would be my guess. Perhaps that's how she ended up in the lake in the first place."

"What?"

Tabitha frowns. "You know, like Ophelia in *Hamlet*. I suppose for some people, drowning could seem like a romantic way to die."

I blink, trying to ignore that nonsense, and look down at the chart. "She seems stable enough to move, but I'll arrange to have someone from Psychology in to assess her when she wakes up." I pull on a new pair of gloves and lean over to check her pupils. "Has she gained consciousness at all since she was brought in?" I ask, my light shining into the most shocking pair of blue eyes I've ever seen. Her pupils contract as the light shines down, her eyes practically neon with intensity. I look back down at her wrists, picking up one of her arms to examine the crisscross pattern of cuts and scars that cover every inch of skin on her forearms.

"Poor girl," I say. "Were we able to get her an MRI to check for internal injuries before the machine broke down?"

Tabitha shakes her head. "No. She came in right after that Willan Reed patient."

My latex-covered thumb runs along the raised scars on Elora's arms that spread out toward her palm. There is something painful but mesmerizing about the pattern of despair written on this girl's skin. The lights overhead flicker, and the monitor that drums out the steady pattern of her heartbeat spikes then flicks off—a loud, glaring alarm sounding at the loss of power.

"What was that?" Tabitha asks.

A painful zap of electricity shoots through my fingers, up my arm, and I instinctively drop Elora's hand with a jerk. "Ouch!"

"What?"

I shake my head. "Nothing, just a spark. Will you make the call into psych for me? I have a million things to catch up on, it seems, and we need the bed. It's crazy out there."

"Sure thing."

I sign off the bottom of the chart and tuck it into the end of the bed as Tabitha reboots the monitor. Taking a deep breath, I push my way back through the heavy trauma door toward the nursing station to see what they need attending to first. But the halls are quiet again and everything is calm, cool, and collected at the nursing station. When I reach the desk where I've left my coffee, I'm surprised to find it still warm.

An orderly passes and I wave him down. "Sorry, have you seen Dr. Anthony Commisso?"

The man tilts his head. "He hasn't come in yet, he's not due to start his shift for another," he glances at his watch, "half an hour or so."

My stomach turns uncomfortably. "What? That's impossible. I saw him only ten minutes ago. Also, it was packed in here. Where did everyone go?"

"It's been quiet for a while now. Are you feeling okay?"

I check my pager, but there are no missed messages. What the hell is going on? The orderly continues on and I drop into the chair at the desk, my fingers tapping against the warm sides of the paper coffee cup. There's a loud bang, and I look up to see the first patient, Willan, being wheeled out of room 131 toward the elevators. As he disappears behind the steel doors, I see another orderly pushing Elora in the same direction. The overhead lights flicker again, and I look down at my computer to find it rebooting.

"Are we getting some kind of storm?" a nearby nurse asks as she groans at her blank screen.

"I didn't see anything in the forecast," another nurse answers.

A custodian passes, and the smell of bleach hits me like a punch to the gut. I grab my coffee and stand up. "I'll be right back. I just need some fresh air."

The nurses nod and I walk briskly toward the ER exit where the ambulance bay is. The doors open, and I'm surprised to see an absolute downpour of freezing rain—the paramedics slipping on the black ice covering the pavement. With the smell of bleach giving way to the scent of rain, I take a long sip of my coffee. My breath rising in little clouds in front of my face.

Maybe I should schedule a visit with the psychologist myself because nothing seems to make much sense tonight. I think about the two patients I just saw. One is going to wake up to find out his family is gone. That he'll forever carry the reminder of that awful accident on his skin wherever he goes.

And the red-headed girl, whose eyes radiated energy even while unconscious. I think about her scars and how she nearly drowned. What happened to that girl to make her feel like there was no other way out? If that is really how she wound up in that lake. Perhaps she has a personality disorder. Perhaps someone has broken her heart. But drowning? Tabitha's words echo in my mind. *I suppose for some people, drowning could seem like a romantic way to die.*

But I know better. There is no romantic way to die. Death is messy and hard, and often painful. Drowning in a freezing lake? What a terrible way to want to go. A violent shiver races down my spine. My hip vibrates and I pull the clip off to look at the page. I take one last sip of my coffee then toss the cup into the trash by the entrance and head back to the nursing station.

TWO
YEARS
LATER

1

T he loud crash of the garbage truck outside my bedroom window makes me jump. I sigh loudly, realizing I forgot to close the window last night. At seven in the morning every Thursday, the city waste department makes it their personal mission to wake up as many residents as possible, or at least that's what it seems like to me. I pull the pillow over my head, but I know it's pointless now. I'm awake, and so my eyes open slowly to the early April sun shining through my wide bedroom window.

I reach my hand blindly toward the small table next to my bed, feeling for my glasses, squinting through the blurry haze and bright sunlight. Finally, my fingers latch onto the thick frames and I pull the glasses onto my face, pressing them up on the bridge of my nose. I blink rapidly a few times, trying to adjust to the strong lenses. The world grows more focused than before. My glasses have been such an irritating conundrum, and it still puzzles the doctors when I go back for checkups every few months, the prescriptions changing wildly each time.

One doctor mentioned it could be a symptom of some kind of neurological damage from the accident that killed my parents two years ago. They called me lucky. Lucky to survive the devastating crash and subsequent fire that engulfed that car. Sometimes, I wish I didn't make it out. At least then I wouldn't feel so alone all the time.

Rolling my shoulders to work out the kinks and swallow down the gloom, I push myself out of bed, my bare feet coming into contact with the cold wooden floor. I cross the room to shut the window which is letting cold spring air filter in. The moment the window shuts, the noise almost completely extinguishes.

"Fucking garbage trucks," I mutter before shivering and heading for the bathroom.

I turn on the shower, busying myself with my morning routine as I wait for the water to heat up. The pipes in this building are old, so they often take at least a few minutes to get to any temperature above freezing. I catch sight of myself in the mirror, my reflection fuzzy around the edges of my frames. I push my curly hair off my forehead. The fluffy black strands fall back down, some falling below my eyebrows, skimming the tops of my glasses and tickling my eyelids. Maybe it's time for a haircut.

I trace my finger along the long scar above my right eyebrow and the tiny one on my lip that is a result of the accident, but nothing compares to the absolute atrocity that is my torso. I take a long steadying breath as I pull my t-shirt up and over my head, tossing it onto the tile floor. My entire upper body, all the way to just above my elbows, is covered in hard, jagged, scarred skin. I usually do my best to avoid looking at it for too long, but today, I lean toward the mirror to study it as the steam rises out of the shower. I touch my fingertips to my collarbone, feeling the rough texture underneath. Sometimes I swear the scarring looks different from day to day. I mentioned it once to the optometrist who follows me for my eyes and they said that could simply be because the skin sheds and regrows, but I don't think they quite understood what I meant.

I stare at the stretch of skin just above my heart and it swirls before my eyes. When I blink, it stops. Perhaps it is a combination of skin regrowth and my completely fucked up eyesight working together to drive me insane. Or maybe it is simply that I can't accept myself, accept what happened, the loss. My heart starts to race, and the scars itch fiercely until I can barely breathe. I hurriedly flick my eyes away, noticing the beads of condensation dripping down the walls. I step out of my boxers and under the warm water, placing my glasses carefully on the edge of the sink.

My hair falls into my eyes as water splashes down on me, invigorating me from my short sleep. I've only had a few hours of rest after getting home from work at nearly two thirty in the morning last night and the water is helping to wake up my body.

Afterward, I towel off and quickly get dressed, once again avoiding that horrid reflection in the mirror, then make my way into the small kitchen, grabbing a box of cereal and pouring myself a bowl. My apartment is small, but at least it's mine. It's not overly crowded with stuff, the walls mostly bare with only the absolute necessities. My kitchen with only one of everything and the almost nonexistent living room with an old sofa I'm sure is straight out of the seventies and still smells a bit like cigarettes even though I'd sprayed it a hundred times with upholstery cleaner.

It was such a strange turn of events after the accident. I woke up in the sterile hospital, beeping and rushing footsteps greeting me as I crawled up from the darkness. Someone with a kind voice told me my parents were gone. Everything changed in that moment. The bad dreams I was plagued with while sleeping in that hospital now seemed preferable to this new nightmare. And on top of all that, we were getting ready to move. At least that's what the police officer told me when I inquired about my belongings. I don't even remember packing.

It is like everything before the accident got lost, tangled in my mind, forgotten.

During those three weeks I was unconscious—the moving company discarded all of our family possessions, auctioning them off to the highest bidder. My entire life for two-thousand dollars. I recall thinking I should be angry, sad, terrified, but there was just nothing. It seemed ironically fitting. My parents were dead. Gone. Why not everything else? I am on my own, completely. Sometimes it's hard to remember them at all. Just a blurry image of them in my head. Trying to remember the details of a past life as they slipped through my fingers like water. In fact, because I have no pictures of them, I can barely remember what they looked like anymore. Whatever phone I had before the accident has been lost as well. Thankfully, I have my wallet and I.D. which was the only way the hospital knew how to identify me and the bodies of my parents.

I crack my knuckles to pull myself out of my thoughts, pouring some milk into my cereal bowl and sinking down into my sofa, turning on my TV in order to spend far too long scrolling through Netflix, deciding on what to watch. When I finally settle on some new Korean horror show, my pocket vibrates against my thigh as the screen of my phone lights up. I pull it out and look at the notification. It's a text from my manager at work.

Heidi:
Can you come in a bit earlier today? Brandon is doing a few interviews so he won't be able to do the prep.

I let my head drop back and let out a long sigh. Today was my only shift at the pub this week that I wasn't scheduled to start early, but at least it would be a few extra hours in the bank.

Will:

Sure, I'll be there at 2.

Heidi:
Thanks a bunch.

I toss the phone onto the sofa next to me. Who am I kidding? It's not like I have a life outside of my job at the pub anyway. Other than the weekly trip to the laundromat and the grocery store, my entire social life revolves around working at the Flying Weasel Pub on Queen Street East. I don't have any friends outside of it and even within the pub, only a few of us are close.

It's lonely though. On the days I have off and the others are still working, it's like drowning in an empty void. Nothing to do and no one to talk to. Those are the moments where I fall into the abyss of my mind, trying to retain the details of my parents, memories, anything. But every time I search, I'm left with nothing but fuzzy, barely there images. Then, the misery speaks in a dark, dangerous voice. *It would have been better if you died in that wreck.*

I scroll for a while through my social media, trying to distract myself from the boredom that presses in on me like a fog. The sound of screams from the show in the background fades away, and before I know it, my eyes start to feel heavy.

· ——— ✳ ——— ·

IT'S DARK, *the smell of damp rotting earth floods my senses as I look around. I blink hard, forcing the blurry surroundings into focus behind my glasses. There are trees all around me and I spin around to gauge my direction, but there is nothing. Nothing except more trees and more darkness. My hands shoot out in front of me, trying to discern the clearest path so I won't stumble.*

Then, there's a flicker of light—bright blue and pulsing through the trees in the distance.

It calls to me. Like a song. Like the feeling you get when a loved one calls your name. Some familiar, urgent sensation sweeps through my chest, and suddenly the place seems so familiar. Like I've been here many times before. My body understands as I step swiftly over the uneven ground without trouble. The light blinks again, as if unstable or moving farther away beyond the trees.

"Wait!" I call, and my voice cracks.

A shadow moves to my right, and I turn to look at it. There's a flash of red, then a voice calls back to me out of the darkness. "Willan."

I'm jarred awake by a loud knocking on my door. I pick my head up off the couch, my glasses sliding down my nose.

"Will? Hey, man, you decent? I'm coming in!" a voice calls from outside my door.

Shit, I fell asleep. I straighten my glasses and slowly stand before the door is thrown open. The tall, dark frame of my neighbour Alex strolls into my apartment kitchen.

"Nice to see you," I say, rolling my eyes.

He pulls open my fridge. "Got any milk?"

I yawn and nod. "Yeah, help yourself."

"Planned on it," he says, taking a gulp out of the carton.

I close my eyes in exasperation. "Dude, I meant like pour yourself a glass, not get your fucking germs on my carton."

Alex smirks. "Since when do you care about germs? Weren't you all up in Priscilla's business only a few nights ago?"

Heat floods my cheeks. I didn't know that Alex knew about that. I shrug. "It was her last day at the pub. Thought I should give her a memorable send off."

Alex grabs a pack of crackers out of my cabinet and smiles.

"My God, Will, how you get so much ass, I'll never understand. I'm way prettier than you."

I roll my eyes, but it's true. Alex is a good-looking guy. His dark flawless skin and green eyes are downright TV star worthy. We were hired at the same time two years ago after I was released from the hospital and moved to the Beaches area of Toronto. We found apartments next door to each other that same day. I often thought out of all of my friends from work, if I ever left, maybe Alex would be the one who'd stick with me. I tilt my head as I watch him stuff crackers into his mouth.

"Yeah, well, it's not my fault you can't please the ladies," I tease.

Alex rolls his eyes back at me. "You must be packing something under there because your reputation is starting to precede you at the bar."

"Fuck off," I say, sitting back down on my couch and checking the time on my phone. "What time are you heading in?"

"Going in for opening. You?"

I nod. "Same. Heidi asked me to come in early. Apparently, Brandon is interviewing some new blood."

Alex's face turns positively giddy. "Really? What do you think? New servers or new line cooks?"

I shrug indifferently. "No idea. If I have to wager a guess, probably a new server to replace Priscilla."

"Think she'll be hot?" he asks, coming to sit on the couch next to me with the box of crackers.

"Who says it'll be a she?" I ask, raising an eyebrow.

Alex offers the crackers to me. "You know Brandon as well as I do. He hires women for the floor. To be honest, I wonder what he says when guys apply to work up front."

I chuckle. "No idea."

"So how was it with Priscilla?" Alex asks.

"Oh," I say, "it was good."

Alex narrows his eyes. "Just good?"

I scroll through the Netflix menu for something to watch, avoiding the question. It's true, the sex had been good. It was always good, and not to inflate my ego, but Alex was right. I have managed to obtain a certain reputation at the pub. The girls I bring home with me always leave satisfied, but sometimes I feel like it's an out-of-body experience. My mind is in it, but my body is on autopilot. I know how best to touch to provoke a moan of pleasure from their lips, but when they touch me…it's that same muted, empty feeling. My whole body is almost numb. Perhaps it's another side effect of the accident, like how my eyes are all screwed up.

That's the other problem. I remember how a certain touch should feel. It's the only thing I really know for certain. But when I try to recall my sexual experiences prior to the accident, it's the same as everything else, blurry and nearly non-existent. It's infuriating.

The alarm on my phone beeps, letting me know I have an hour to get to work.

Alex pours some more crackers into his open mouth. "Meet you in the hall in twenty?"

I nod. "Yeah, all right."

·———✳———·

THE FLYING WEASEL pub has a black storefront with large windows and a blood red door that's scraped and worn around the edges and the door handle from years of patronage. It's a place I've come to recognize as a second home of sorts. With my apartment being so barren and impersonal, I've grown to enjoy the personality of this place, and I often feel like it helps me fill in the gaps in my own life.

The door's locked, but I see Heidi, one of the managers at the hostess' desk. She smiles when she sees us through the window of the door and jogs over to let us in.

"Hey, guys." She backs up, then relocks the door. "Thanks for coming early, Will. I really appreciate it."

I give her a quick, dismissive wave of my hand. "Anything for you, Heidi."

She smiles at me. "Free dinner tonight? On me?"

I smile at her. "You're the best."

Alex spins around. "What the hell? What about me?"

Heidi places her hand on her hip. "When have you ever agreed to come in early when I've asked?"

Alex feigns outrage. "I would more often if I knew it meant free food."

She rolls her eyes and shoos him toward the kitchen. "Away with you."

I slap Alex hard on the back as I steer him toward the kitchen and notice the office door is ajar as we pass it. I spot Brandon, the owner, speaking to someone out of sight, likely the person being interviewed.

Alex notices me glancing at the door. "Bet you it's another blonde."

I shake my head. "Nah, the last few have been blondes. I feel like Brandon's due for a brunette, just to shake the system up."

"Care to put money on that?" he asks, jutting his chin at me as we continue into the back where the lockers are.

I laugh. "Don't have much money to spare."

"What about your free dinner?" he says, wiggling his eyebrows at me.

I twist my lips, considering. "Fine, but what do I get?"

Alex smirks. "Enough beer to make an embarrassment of yourself."

I snort out a laugh. "Deal."

✴

HALF AN HOUR PASSES and we still don't catch any glimpse of the person being interviewed, but as three o'clock draws nearer, the other staff members arrive. My eyes blur after chopping lettuce for a while and when I look back up, Mariah, with her chocolate coloured skin and tight curls, is bouncing her way over to me.

"Willan!" she calls, and I cringe at the sound of my full name.

"Am I ever going to not regret showing you my I.D.?" I ask as she rocks up onto her tiptoes to plant a glossy peck on my cheek.

She leans back, pretending to be thinking hard. "Mmm, probably not. Sorry not sorry. What are you doing here so early? I thought you were closing tonight."

I turn back toward my lettuce. "I am. Heidi needed a favour."

I point the knife in my hands toward the office door, which I realize now is wide open but empty. I lean forward through the pass-through, but there's no sign of Brandon or the new hire.

"Where'd the person Brandon was interviewing go?"

"To replace Priscilla? Oh exciting! A new victim to torment." She claps her hands excitedly backing up toward the changeroom.

Jenni, an impossibly pretty blonde with long legs, one of Brandon's more recent hires, walks through the swing door. "Oh please, your form of torture is baking cupcakes and handing out friendship bracelets," she says to Mariah, who smiles then disappears. "Hi, Will."

"Hey," I say, simply offering her a friendly smile.

"You closing tonight?" Jenni asks me. "I thought I saw you on the schedule."

"Uh, yeah, I am."

She smiles, her brilliantly white teeth gleaming at me. "Me too." She twists her shoulders then turns to head toward the back changing area.

Not a moment later, I feel Alex slide in beside me along the stainless steel counter. "She likes you."

I take a deep breath in through my nose. "Yeah. So?"

Alex drops his mouth open. "What do you mean? Do you need my permission to hit that? Because please do. I'll even write you a permission form."

I shake my head, laughing. "No, no way. She just started a few months ago. Don't want to make it weird."

"Why does it have to get weird?"

I shrug. "Women don't exactly like it when you sleep with them and then don't call them again."

Alex elbows me in the ribs. "Why does it need to be a one-time thing? She's smart, funny, ridiculously hot, and most importantly, into *you*! Why can't she be someone you, you know, date?"

I grab another head of lettuce and continue chopping. "If she's so smart and funny and hot, then what the fuck would she want with someone like me?"

Alex sighs and leans back. "Oh my God, Will, you're killing me."

Jenni passes by in her black flats and skin tight black cocktail dress, her hair pulled back in a low ponytail. She gives me a little wave and I smile back at her before she disappears through the swing door to the dining area.

"What was that all about?" Mariah asks, wrapping her black apron around her waist, gesturing between me and Jenni.

"Nothing," I say, turning back to my task.

Alex throws his arm around Mariah and whispers, "Just trying to convince Will to ask Jenni out."

Mariah shrugs Alex off her shoulder. "You'll do no such thing!"

Alex holds up his hands in surrender, then turns the corner to get back to work.

"I wasn't going to," I say.

"Yeah, tell that to your dick," she mutters, coming closer.

I roll my eyes. "Come on, Mariah, it's just a bit of harmless flirting. You flirt with me all the time."

She bites the inside of her cheek. "Yeah, and it's fine because you know I'm not into dudes, and therefore, there's no way anything will ever happen."

"Alex was so disappointed when you told him that. I had to console him for weeks."

Mariah tosses her head of dark, bouncy curls from side to side, clearly amused by the information. "Well, you're both adults who can make your own decisions, so I won't say anymore about it. But I swear to God, Will, if I get a group chat notification tomorrow morning saying you fucked her, I'll be mad for a week."

I laugh. "Just a week? Seems like it could be worth it."

"Don't test me, Willan," she says, jabbing me in the arm with her index finger. "You are getting a reputation as a bit of a slut. Don't think I don't know about Priscilla."

My head drops back, exasperated. "Does everyone know about that?"

"Of course they do. If you think that girl didn't tell us every dirty detail—"

"What the fuck, Mariah?" I shout, my face turning pink.

"Oh please, you and Alex here have been drooling for months over getting an inside peek into our servers' group chat. What do you think we talk about in there? New menu items?"

I scoop handfuls of chopped lettuce into a plastic tub. "Forget it, and don't worry. I have no intention of hooking up with Jenni."

Mariah purses her glossy lips. "Mm-hmm, yeah, we'll see about that."

Heidi appears and sticks her head through the pass-through. "We're about to open up. You set up back here?"

I grumble an affirmative and Heidi leaves as Brandon walks back through the swing door.

"Wait," Alex says suddenly, "where'd the new hire go?"

Brandon scratches at his bristly beard. "Oh, she's gone. She's starting on Monday, gave her the menu to memorize on the weekend. Mariah, you good to have someone shadow you next week?"

Mariah allows a broad smile to spread across her pretty face. "Of course." She places her hands under her chin and bats her eyelashes. "You know how I love to break in the newbies."

Brandon smirks and gives Mariah a wink. "That's my girl."

Everyone disperses, but I catch Alex's eye, our wager suddenly springing to both of our minds, and we turn at the same time to ask, "What colour hair?" I clear my throat, glancing sideways at Alex. "Did the new girl have blonde or brunette hair?"

Mariah crosses her arms over her chest. "Why?"

Alex shrugs. "Friendly wager."

Brandon smirks, then leans over to whisper in Mariah's ear. Her eyes widen and she laughs as Brandon walks away and disappears back into the office.

"Well?" I ask impatiently, wondering if I'll have to pay for my own dinner tonight or if I'll get a free meal *and* get drunk.

"What did you guess, Alex?" Mariah asks.

"Blonde."

Mariah touches her finger to her chin. "And Will, you guessed brunette?"

I nod.

She cocks an eyebrow. "Sorry, boys, you're both wrong."

•———— ✳ ————•

I MANAGE to find myself in the passenger seat of Jenni's Toyota Corolla at two-thirty in the morning. She offered to drive me home after we closed the pub together, and since I wasn't in the mood to take the streetcar home at this time of night, I took her up on it. I often think about getting my own car, and I do have a few thousand dollars in savings. But the thought of driving, of getting behind the wheel after everything with my parents…it's unfathomable.

I point to the vet clinic over which Alex's and my apartment sit, and Jenni pulls her car to the side of the road.

"Thanks for the ride," I say, clutching my bag from between my legs.

She shrugs with a sweet smile. "No problem, anytime."

Jenni's brown eyes hold mine, and I watch her tongue run along her dark pink lips. There's a long pause, and I realize I've been staring at her mouth for longer than should be decent. I feel a rush of blood to my groin, and that lonely ache in my heart feels suddenly exposed. I swallow hard and clear my throat. "Do you want to come in for a bit? Watch a movie?"

"Yeah, all right." She turns off the engine and we both get out of her car and head toward the black door to the side of the clinic. I punch in the door code and lead the way up the stairs to the landing separating mine and Alex's apartment. "Alex lives there?" she whispers.

I nod as I unlock the door to my apartment, feeling suddenly desperate to feel her skin under my fingers. "Yeah."

"You must be close friends," she says as I open the door and let her in first.

I drop my bag to the floor and pull off my coat, placing it on the hook by the door. She pulls off hers, and I feel the anticipation build inside of me as I imagine what her clothes would look like piled on the floor.

"This is nice," she says, spinning.

"Want a drink?" I offer, heading toward the kitchen.

I feel her watching me. "Just water, please. I shouldn't drink if I'm driving home."

I grab a bottle of water out of the fridge and hand it to her. "You don't have to drive home if you don't want to. You could stay here."

Her eyes darken as she takes a sip from the bottle. "I guess I could, but what would we do?"

The smile tugging at the corner of her mouth tells me she wants to play.

I step toward her, shaking my hair out and letting it fall into my eyes as I push my glasses up the bridge of my nose. "I guess that depends," I say, coming close enough that she has to tilt her head back to look up at me.

She swallows. "Depends on what?"

I smirk, the slight nervous quaver in her voice making me stiffen.

"Do you want me to be a gentleman? Or," I lean over and my lips brush against the edge of her ear, "do you want me to make you come so hard you see stars?"

She turns her face to mine as the tiniest gasp escapes her throat, and I feel my adrenaline spiking as the desire to touch her floods through me. The edges of her come in and out of focus as her spearmint scented breath hits my face. Maybe this time it'll click, maybe this time it'll feel electric. Maybe this time I'll remember.

"You can try," she whispers.

I gaze into her wide, expectant eyes and smile mischievously before ducking down and grabbing her around the knees so that she falls over my shoulder. She giggles as I carry her across the living room toward my bedroom. I close the door and set her down against the wall as I stay crouched low, my fingertips gliding ever so gently up her calves, pausing for a second at the back of her knees, then up her thighs.

I'm sure it's my imagination, but it's like I can hear her voice in my head, the ghost of a whisper ringing down a long tunnel in my ears. *His hands feel so damn good.*

My fingers pause at the hem of her dress and I glance up to see her face—her teeth biting her bottom lip and her eyes half closed.

"Does that feel good?" I ask, pressing my lips against the top of her thigh.

A sharp intake of breath, then a soft whimpering. "Yes."

Her hands run through my hair, her fingers pulling on my curls as I push her dress up and over her hips, revealing her blue lace thong. I nip at the hot flesh concealed behind her panties with my teeth and feel her fingers tighten against my scalp.

Holy shit, he wasn't kidding.

Another wave of thought appears, then evaporates inside my mind as my fingers hook against the waistband of this tiny scrap of fabric. I drag it down her long, lean legs, my erection straining painfully against my jeans. I take a second to adjust myself before she notices—my hand sliding up the inside of her thigh to that gorgeous pink pussy before me.

Her shallow breaths pant above me and I look up at her face, the way it twists as my fingers slide over her sex, already soaking wet. "Look at you, so wet already."

Oh my God, I've never felt this turned on before.

That voice again. It happens with all the girls I bring home, and even though it's likely something I'm making up in my own mind, it tells me I'm touching her the way she wants.

I press one finger slowly inside of her, and she falls against the wall behind her with a gasp.

Her head tips back and her back arches, pushing her pelvis

toward my face. "Shit!" she breathes, my finger slowly sliding in and out of her.

I hook one of her legs over my shoulder, and as I curl my finger to press against the grooves of her front wall, I use my tongue to swipe against her clit.

She utters a high-pitched whine and her one leg holding her up trembles.

I continue the slow torture with my tongue and add in another finger as she thrusts against my hand and face. I move my tongue in a figure eight and her breathing becomes more and more shallow, her leg giving out.

"Hold yourself up or I won't let you come," I say, and I glance up to see her flushed, surprised face.

Who the fuck is this guy? He can tell me what to do all day long if it feels like this.

I work her into a frenzy, my fingers pumping and my tongue swirling, then I feel her tighten, her nails digging into my scalp as her leg trembles violently and she cries out loudly.

"I'm coming!"

I grin against her skin, my ego inflating with every gasp and moan that tumbles from her lips as I kiss along her pubic bone to her hip. I slowly stand, pulling her dress the rest of the way up, then over her head, where it falls to the floor with a soft thump.

Please say you're going to fuck me now.

That voice appears like vapour in my mind, and I take a moment to lavish some attention on her heaving breasts that strain against her bra. I catch a glimpse of her staring at me, and I close the distance between our mouths, a small squeak of a noise escaping as my lips devour hers. I use my free hand to skim my fingers up her back and unclasp her bra with ease, letting it fall to the floor between us.

I feel her fingers suddenly on the hem of my t-shirt, pulling it upward. I wrap my hand around the long hair of her ponytail and tug her head back, away from my face.

"I keep that on," I say simply. Her eyes shimmer with the question of why, but then I'm kissing along her jaw and down her neck, and the question dies in her throat.

I wonder what that's all about.

I've been asked about it a few times, but I have never shown anyone my scars. Not even Alex, who caught a brief glimpse of them once last summer at the beach when my shirt got stuck as I tried to remove my bag from my shoulder.

I feel her fingers instead go to my belt, the metal clicking as the muffled sound of the streetcar passes by my window. When she undoes the button on my jeans, they drop low on my hips, and I sigh with relief as my erection is almost free. Her fingertips trace along the waistband of my boxers, and I gently bite her neck.

"Tease," I whisper against her skin.

I give her ass a sharp smack with my right hand, and she gasps. I pull her away from the wall and grab both cheeks, then hoist her up onto my waist, her legs wrapping around me instinctively as I step out of my jeans and walk her to the bed. The passing lights of a car and a lone street lamp provide enough light for me to see all of her.

She falls back on the bed—me hovering over her as I take one of her nipples into my mouth. Her hand dips beneath my boxers to wrap around my cock.

Holy hell, he's big.

I try to hide my grin, and I feel my body tremble with the familiar sensation of being touched. Then, the disappointment hits. It rushes through me like a wave as I realize that everything still feels muted. Still numb, even with her lips against mine, it feels like there's a barrier between us and that gaping, longing hole in my heart spreads through me. Takes over. Possesses me.

"Are you sure you want this?" I ask as my boxers slide over my hips and my hand reaches back down between her thighs. My other hand tweaks her nipple, rolling it between my thumb and forefinger.

I wonder vaguely if they can tell. If the women I bring home can tell I'm damaged, broken. I wonder if they see the desperate loneliness freezing me inside and know they won't be able to change it.

If they do, it's not enough to back out.

Jenni nods, but that's not good enough.

"Say it out loud," I whisper.

Her eyes open and they meet mine. "Yes. Please." *My God, I want you to fuck me.*

They always do. I reach toward my side table and pull open the drawer, grabbing a condom. I tear it open with my teeth and roll it on, my free hand tracing circles up her side. Her breath hitches as I rub the tip of my cock over her clit, letting her wetness coat me before lining myself up at her entrance. I lift one of her long legs up over my shoulder, then I sink into her slowly.

"Oh my God!" Jenni cries out, her head pressing against my mattress.

Fuck, he's so big.

She grips my forearms tightly as I pull back and plunge into her again and again and again. Her whimpers turn into moans, and my name spills from her lips as I reach my hand between us to rub her clit.

If he keeps doing that, I'm going to come so hard.

Her hands press against my chest and I flinch. Her eyes widen at my reaction, but before she can say anything, I'm pushing my lips to hers and gathering her wrists in one hand. My mouth abandons hers and I hoist her hands over her head, pressing them into the mattress as I gently coax her toward another orgasm.

I can feel my release building in my groin as my stomach

muscles tighten. Her legs quiver again. I feel her walls clench and spasm around my cock and I thrust into her hard one, two, three more times, then my body stills, going rigid as I come. My hand grips her wrists tightly above her head.

I can feel the tension that leaves my body with the release, but that's all there is. Just a release, nothing else. Purely mechanical.

For a minute, I hover above her, my heart rate stabilizing and our breathing returning to normal. My glasses have slipped down to the end of my nose and everything is a blur of colour as I open my eyes. I roll off of her—our bodies slicked with sweat as we lie next to each other on my bed. I push my glasses back up onto my face and blink at the ceiling. I can feel her staring at me, so I turn to look at her. "You all right?" I ask.

She smiles. "Am I all right?" She clasps her hand to her forehead, giggling. "Yes, yes, I'm all right. Holy shit."

I smirk at her, a little bubble of pride floating to the surface, then roll over to discard the condom, tossing it into the little trash can next to my side table.

"Hey," she says as the bed creaks, "can I use your bathroom?"

I nod. "Yeah, of course, it's just across the hall."

She scoots to the edge of the bed and walks lightly to the door, glancing back at me once before heading into the bathroom.

I stoop down, grab my boxers from the floor and pull them on, propping myself up against the wooden headboard and feeling a sudden rush of guilt. Once again, I dread what happens now, when Jenni realizes I'm not interested in pursuing anything serious. How could I when I feel so apathetic toward everything?

A dull ache throbs against my temple. I'm so fucking frustrated. Why can't I feel things properly, like I know I should? All I do know is that it's not this. I can just see Mariah's face when she realizes I did fuck Jenni after all.

The toilet flushes and the light from the bathroom switches off. Jenni appears naked in the doorway, her cheeks overly pink and looking anywhere but directly at me as she searches the floor for her underwear and dress.

"I should probably go," she says, grabbing her thong and pulling it up and over her thighs.

I raise my eyebrow in surprise. "You don't have to. Stay the night if you want."

"Do you want me to?" she asks.

To be honest, it would be better if she went home now. It would avoid the awkward morning after, and whenever a girl stayed the night, I never slept very well, often tossing and turning all night. I shrug, offering the answer I know she wants. "Sure."

She glances at the empty spot next to me in the bed almost longingly, and I feel a slight pang of sadness that I can't offer her more. But then she shakes her head, her loose hair falling around her face. Maybe she *can* see how broken I am.

"No, I should go. I have class tomorrow at noon."

She pulls her dress over herself and grabs her bra from the floor.

"Oh," I say, "All right, then." I always forget most of the staff only works at the pub to put themselves through school. Even Mariah, who is working on her PhD in Sociology. I admire that Jenni's actually doing something with her life. Not like me, a pathetic twenty-four year old, minimum wage high school dropout.

I push myself up out of the bed. "I'll walk you to the door, then."

She gives me a small smile, and I brush my hand through my damp hair as I follow her down the hall and toward my door. Jenni grabs her bag and her coat, pulling them on and tucking her bra into her coat pocket.

I open the door to the stairs that lead to the street and lock eyes with Jenni as she pulls her car keys out. "This was fun," I say lamely.

She lets go a choked kind of laugh. "Yeah, it was."

The tension presses down on my shoulders as I stand there, searching for something more to say.

"When are you working next?" I ask.

"Umm, Monday, I think. I had to book the weekend off to study for an exam."

I nod and take a deep breath. "Oh, right, well, good luck."

She nods. "Thanks."

Here it is…the awkward silence. She wants me to say something, profess something, and I'm not able to do any of that. "Well, good night," I say instead.

Hurt flashes across her face for an instant, only to be replaced by a wide smile. "Good night."

She pauses for just a moment as though she wants to say something else, but then walks past me, out the door and down the stairs. She disappears out of sight and I close my door, locking it behind me. I grab a bottle of water from the fridge and make my way back to my bedroom, casting a quick glance out of my window to see Jenni getting into her car. After a few moments, she pulls out onto the nearly deserted street.

I search my floor for my jeans, pulling my cell phone out of my pocket. It's three thirty in the morning now. I set my alarm for eleven then crawl back into bed, feeling exhausted and guilty—a winning combination.

I pull my glasses off my face and set them on the table next to me. I drag my hand across my face as I inwardly curse myself. Why the fuck do I keep doing this? I think briefly about the accident and the scars, my fingers brushing along the top of my chest under my shirt for a moment, pressing on the numb, hard skin. This is what it feels like, not just physically, but everywhere. Like my whole body is damaged, even my insides. Is it possible my heart is scarred too? It would make sense, finally giving me a reason why I don't care.

My phone dings from a text message and I grab my glasses, pushing them back on my face to see who the hell is texting me at three thirty in the goddamn morning. My stomach drops when I see the text is from Mariah.

Mariah:
Hope it was worth the week of silence you've earned.
😴

·————— ✳ —————·

ALEX BURSTS through my door the morning after, making me regret giving him my spare key. He demands every detail of my encounter with Jenni, of which I tell him very little.

"What's the deal?" he asks. "You just don't like her?"

I shrug. "Didn't feel that strong of a connection."

"You know, one day," Alex says, "you're going to meet a girl that you just go crazy for, and she's not going to want to give you the time of day."

I think hard about what he said. He's probably right, so it's even more likely I'm just meant to be alone. I wonder if I've ever been in love before. I was twenty-two when the accident happened. Surely I've been in love at least once in twenty-two years. I can feel that I loved someone once and not how I loved my parents. Real romantic love. It's buried somewhere, but I can't find the memories associated with the sensation and, much like everything else in my life, it frustrates me.

2

WILL

Monday comes, and I'm dreading going to work and facing Jenni. I get dressed, make my bed, and pack my bag for work before heading out the door.

I'm suddenly staring at the red door of the pub, the peeling paint curling up near the handle. I blink at it for a moment with confusion, then I look around me, realizing I'm standing outside of the pub. I turn around fully. How the fuck did I get here? Just a second ago, I was leaving my apartment—I hadn't even gone out onto the street yet. The edges of the door blur and I push my glasses up my nose, squinting to try to focus.

The spring sun is shining through the few clouds overhead, the sound of birds chirping from a few nearby trees. I hear the rumble of an oncoming streetcar and stare at it blankly as it stops in front of me. Mariah steps off, her face friendly as she waves to someone still seated, then she spots me and rolls her eyes.

"You still have four more days, Willan," she says, pushing past me and knocking on the door to be let inside.

But I'm barely paying attention as I try and fill the gap between my apartment and getting to this spot. Did I black out? Was I daydreaming? Did I fall asleep on the streetcar?

The door opens and Heidi peers out, letting Mariah inside.

"Will, you all right?" she asks.

I turn back toward the pub and shake my head. "Uh, yeah, sorry. Just zoned out a bit, I guess."

I follow Mariah inside, my heart beating frantically in my chest as if I've just run a long distance. I stumble over my own feet, my legs trembling. My hip crashes into the hostess desk, and Heidi and Mariah look back at me.

"Will, are you sure you're okay?"

Everything turns to a blur and there's a ringing in my ears as I try to blink the world back into some semblance of focus, then I drop to the floor.

"Oh my God!" Heidi cries, her voice distant against the ringing. "Brandon! Help!"

"Will, take deep breaths!" Mariah's panicked voice reaches me, and I look around to see her blurred features to my left.

Then, someone's lifting me up from under my arms and I'm sitting on a chair, my head being pushed down between my knees. I suck in a deep breath and the ringing dissipates, the voices around me becoming clearer.

"Should we call an ambulance?" I hear Heidi ask.

I wave my hand a little. "No, no. I'm fine." Another few deep breaths and I sit up slowly, pushing my glasses up to find Mariah's concerned face level with my own, Brandon and Heidi standing behind her with their cell phones in hand.

"Will! You jerk, how dare you scare me like that," Mariah says, slapping my knee and pulling me into a hug.

I feel my scars prickle against the unfamiliar touch, then she pulls back, her dark eyes glassy.

"What happened?" Brandon asks.

I shake my head and look out the door. "I...I don't know. I just felt dizzy."

"Do you need to go home?" Heidi asks.

I push my hands against my knees and slowly stand. My heart pounds out a steady rhythm and things, while still blurry at the edges, are back to how they usually are. The ringing is gone, too. "No, I'm fine. Sorry, didn't mean to scare anyone."

Mariah sighs and rolls her eyes. "Don't be stupid. Come on then." She links her arm through mine and leads me back through the dining room, kitchen, and into the changerooms.

"You sure you're okay?" she asks again as I open my locker.

I nod and smirk at her. "You're talking to me."

She spins toward me. "I swear to Christ, if I find out that you faked all of that just to get me to talk to you again—"

I laugh and hold up my hands. "No! No, I would never. Just wasn't sure if you'd noticed."

She gives me a sly little smile. "All right, fine, I forgive you. But…" she pauses as if asking for permission.

"Go on then."

She closes her locker, holding her apron in one hand and placing her other hand on her hip. "Look, I know I tease you about sleeping around, but why do I feel like that's not necessarily what you want?"

I pull on my chef's coat and button it up. "What do you mean?"

"I've met my share of fuckboy idiot douchebags, and you, Will, are not that kind of guy. So, what's the deal?"

I shrug. "I don't know. Just don't really feel the connection I'm looking for, I guess."

Mariah blinks in surprise.

"What?" I ask.

She shakes her head. "Just not the answer I was expecting."

"What were you expecting me to say?" I ask as I shut my locker.

She shrugs. "Something stupid and jokey."

"I think you're confusing me with Alex."

Mariah laughs. "You know, if I were into dudes, I could be stupid enough to fall for you, Will."

I give her a shy smile. "How very unfortunate for me then that I have a dick."

She snorts with laughter. "And you certainly know how to use it. My God, how Jenni went on and on."

I feel my cheeks heat up and follow Mariah out of the changerooms. "Show me the chat, Mariah."

She runs ahead of me, laughing. "Absolutely not! Get away!"

Mariah tucks around the corner, heading toward the coffeemaker, and flips it on.

"Jenni's not upset, is she?"

Mariah looks back at me, her mouth pressing into a hard line. "Don't think so. I mean, it's not like you promised her anything. She knew what she was getting into."

I nod, and she winks at me before bouncing toward the dining room while I join Brandon for prep.

✴

I'D BE LYING if I said that I'm not distracted. With the weird gap in how I got here and nearly collapsing, my mind is not focused solely on work, and I cut myself twice with my knife in the process. Maybe I'm just overtired, the ache in my feet screaming at me for a break.

As three o'clock approaches, I spot Jenni passing through the swing door. Her eyes find mine and she turns pink as she waves. I smile and wave back as she heads into the changerooms. I puff out a burst of air, spotting Alex as he struts through the door. He slaps me on the back as he passes, a gigantic smile on his face.

"Ready for the newbie?"

I tilt my head. "What?"

He stares at me, dumbfounded. "New girl starts today. How did you forget?"

To be honest, I *did* forget. "Oh, right."

"Also, what's this I hear of you collapsing?"

I roll my eyes. "It was nothing, just tired, I think."

"You're not closing tonight, are you?"

I shake my head. "No, I'm first off."

"Excellent. First beer is on me, then."

He pats my shoulders, then disappears to change.

Things go blurry, and I blink rapidly to force everything back into focus. Coffee. I need coffee. Luckily, Mariah put that new pot on and I fill a large glass with ice, pouring the coffee over it and adding cream and sugar. I take a small sip, relishing in the creamy bitterness, my glasses slipping down my nose, and I turn around to head back to the line.

There's a loud sharp gasp as I collide with a small body, my iced coffee spilling all over her, right down the front of her black dress. My mouth drops open in horror at my own clumsiness, and I push my glasses back up my nose as I set the now empty glass down on the counter.

"Shit, I'm sorry—"

I look up, straight into the most brilliant pair of blue eyes I've ever seen.

"What the actual fuck?" she whispers, grabbing for a nearby stack of paper towels.

I want to help, to hand her paper towels, but I can't move as I realize just how stupid and awkward I must look right now.

Her hair is like copper fire, tumbling down over her shoulders, her pale skin in stark contrast to the black of her dress. Her face is flush with surprise and annoyance, and a constellation of freckles covers the bridge of her nose and cheeks. My gaze travels down and I can't help but stare at her small, wet chest, her skin prickling up with goosebumps from the iced coffee.

"Will, what are you doing?" Mariah calls, taking stock of the situation.

I fumble over my words, trying to shield myself from the angry energy pouring out of this woman's eyes. Like she can see straight through me. Like she wants to stab me with a knife.

"I'm so sorry," I say again, finally regaining control over my limbs and pushing paper towels into her hands. I step back with my hands raised, not sure what else to do.

The redhead rolls her eyes and waves the paper towel at Mariah. "It's all right, I'm fine, just…you know, covered in coffee now, so thanks for that." She continues to dab at the front of her soaked dress.

I feel my mouth opening and closing idiotically, trying to figure out what to say. "You were going the wrong way," I blurt out.

Mariah and the redhead stare at me.

"Will, what the fuck? It's her first day, cut her some slack."

The woman narrows her blue eyes at me. "Thanks for the pro tip," she says.

Mariah catches my eye. "Will, this is Elora. Elora…Green, right?"

Elora. What a pretty name.

Mariah stares at me expectantly as I realize she means for me to introduce myself.

"Shit, sorry. I'm Will."

I hold my hand out to shake hers. Those piercing blue eyes dilate before she glares down at my hand, but she reaches out to shake it nonetheless. I grasp her small hand and look down as I feel the slippery satin of gloves covering her hands. They're black and travel to her forearms. Like something they used to wear in old Hollywood.

My head tilts as I take her in. She's short, probably almost an entire foot shorter than me. Coffee drips from the front of her short black dress, and I can't help but stare. I can see the outline of a bra beneath the fabric and the freckles that seem to trail down her chest. I stare at the curve of her waist as it flares out over her wide hips. I lift my eyes back to her face and she's glaring at me.

"I think I've got an extra dress you can wear," Mariah says, nodding toward the changerooms.

Elora finally turns those penetrating eyes from me and transforms her sneer into a radiant smile for Mariah. "Oh, that would be amazing, thank you."

The two of them head toward the back and I'm left slightly dazed and fumbling for anything to say.

"Again, sorry!" I shout after them in a strangled voice.

As they walk away, I feel something reaching, yearning, almost grasping out of that hole in my heart. While everything else in my world is blurry and hazy, Elora is sharp, her edges so clearly defined it's like I'm finally seeing the world in high definition.

Elora is life in technicolour.

3

ELORA

I take the little black dress from Mariah and enter the bathroom, closing the door behind me. I turn toward the mirror and take in the damage, cringing at the sight of my visible bra. I tilt my head back and sigh. The embarrassment is crawling along my skin, and I try to fight off the uncomfortable shivers.

I peel my dress off and away, tossing it onto the counter next to me. I wet a handful of paper towels and quickly wipe the sticky mess off of my chest and stomach. Grabbing the dress that Mariah gave me, I pull it on. It's loose at the chest, but that is to be expected. I don't have much going on in that department, but, thankfully, it fits around the hips, my most troublesome area. I quickly fix my hair, pulling it out of the back and drawing my gloves up my arms. I take a deep breath before grabbing my wet dress off the counter and opening the door.

"That's better, right?" Mariah asks.

I smile and toss my dress into my locker. "Yes, thank you so much. God, how embarrassing."

Mariah waves her hand. "Don't worry about it, it happens all the time. The things I've found in my bra some nights when I get home," she makes a repugnant face, "gross."

I follow behind Mariah as we make our way past the prep stations, thankful that Will guy is gone for the time being. Heat creeps up the back of my neck and into my face. God, why did I have to embarrass myself in front of someone that good-looking? I feel myself flinch as the memory replays itself in my mind.

The collision, the cold liquid sliding down my chest, then looking up into a pair of magnified hazel eyes behind black glasses underneath a tumble of black curls. The way his eyes looked at me made me feel exposed, and I feel a shiver travel down my spine at the memory of it.

I follow Mariah as she greets a table and takes their orders, then she swipes her card through the computer and has me punch it all in, showing me all the different drop-down menus and how to make special changes. I follow her through the swing door again as we stop to pick up the food for another table.

"Mariah, my darling, who's this?"

A tall man with gorgeous brown skin and light green eyes is smiling at me from behind the pass-through. His arms lean against the stainless steel counter, and I can't help but smile back.

"Alex, this is Elora Green. Elora, Alex."

I reach through the opening. "Nice to meet you."

His eyes take in my glove-covered hands, and we shake. And just like everyone else constantly does, he asks, "What's with the gloves?"

I pull my hand back and tug at the top of the long silk black glove that covers me to the elbows. "I have anemia," I lie. "They keep my hands from getting too cold and uncomfortable."

"Oh," he says, "well, they look good on you. Maybe it'll be a new trend."

He winks at me, then Mariah steers me back toward the dining room.

"Come on now, stop distracting her," Mariah calls back to Alex, who scoffs.

I pull a pair of black latex gloves out of my apron and pull them over the silk. They blend well together so you can't really notice the difference and protect the fabric from any food mess, while still following the health code. I was so grateful when Brandon and Heidi said they didn't have a problem with it.

We drop the food off at its destination and after a few check-ins with other tables, we find a moment to rest.

"How are you doing? All right?" Mariah asks. She's bubbly and friendly, and I already know it'll be fun to work together.

I smile at her and sigh. "Yeah, I think so."

"I'll let you handle the next table if you're ready," she offers. "I'll just step in if you need help."

I nod. "Sure, sounds good."

"You're a fast learner," she says approvingly. "I can't believe you actually memorized the entire menu over the weekend. I still don't know half the wine list, and I've been working here for four years."

I blink at her in surprise. "Four years? Really?"

She nods. "Yup, other than Brandon and Heidi, I've been here the longest. Then Alex and Will. They both started on the same day two years ago, been inseparable ever since."

"Alex is…" I start but trail off, not sure if what I'm about to say is entirely appropriate.

Mariah immediately catches on. "Incredibly hot? I know."

"Are you dating him?" I ask.

She chuckles. "Me? Oh no, no, guys aren't my thing."

I feel confusion settle on my face for a split second before catching on. "Oh!"

She snorts with laughter. "Alex is hilarious. Total joker, never takes anything seriously but very sweet."

"What about the other one? Will? Is he always a jerk, or was that just for me?" I ask.

She raises a perfectly plucked eyebrow. "Will is…" she stares off for a moment toward the kitchen before turning back. "He's complicated. He's smart, but extremely cocky. Very protective, but also a total man whore."

I almost choke. "A what?"

"A man whore, a slut, a player…trust me, if you want to keep your heart intact, stay away."

I shake my head. "What? So he just sleeps around? With who?"

She shrugs. "Depends on the day, the week, the month. Sometimes it's a random girl who chats him up at the bar, sometimes it's one of our own."

"He sleeps with coworkers?"

Mariah smirks mischievously. "Has many times."

"Isn't that, I don't know…against the rules?" The memory of his eyes lingering on me makes my face feel hot. Was he eyeing me up as his next conquest? He's admittedly gorgeous, but the personality is a definite turnoff.

Mariah laughs out loud. "This is a pub, Elora. Aside from stealing, spitting in someone's food, and not short changing the cooks on their tip out, there aren't any rules."

"Oh." I feel incredibly naive for asking such a stupid question. I laugh it off. "Well, I'm not really into casual hook ups anyway."

"Got a boyfriend?" she asks. "Girlfriend? Other?"

I look down and straighten the pile of menus on the counter. "No, it's just me. But I'm good with that. I'm not planning on staying in the area too long anyway."

"Oh really? Why?"

I pause, my finger tracing the edge of one of the menus. "I enjoy moving around, meeting new people, not interested in getting into anything that will make me change my mind."

"Good! Keep that energy and stay away from Will. He can be quiet and keep to himself, but if he starts flirting, run far away."

I scoff. "I'm sure I can control myself."

Mariah picks up a tray as she sees one of her tables flagging her down. "They all say that, then they come crying to me when all they are to him is a one-night stand."

✴

THINGS GO WELL, shadowing Mariah the rest of the shift. She lets me serve a few tables on my own, and I feel like I'm getting the hang of it and the computer system. Mariah's right about Alex. He is funny and really cute. In fact, I find myself blushing almost every time I pass him. I'm sure he can tell because he winks or smiles at me constantly. It doesn't help that every emotion I feel is visible on my face. The perks of having fair skin, I suppose. A few times, I can feel eyes on me, and when I glance up, I see Will through the pass-through from the back station, staring at me. He looks away quickly every time, but I find myself avoiding his line of sight.

It's not that I feel unnerved by him staring. A lot of guys do, and I've gotten used to it. But it's the *way* he looks at me that makes me feel on edge. I don't know how to describe it, but he almost seems angry? Annoyed? Confused? A guy has never looked at me that way before, and I feel uncomfortable trying to sort out how to react.

A new table comes in, and Mariah lets me take it. A group of four guys in their early twenties sit at the booth and look through the menu before I head over.

"Hi, guys, how are you all doing tonight?" I ask in my friendliest voice.

They stop their conversations and I feel all of their eyes collectively scan me from head to toe, but I plaster a smile on my face and wait for their response. One of them turns his body toward me to speak for the group. "Doing good now that you're here."

How original. "I'll be your server tonight. Can I start you off with some drinks?"

"Yeah, I think we'll get a couple pitchers of Moosehead," a second guy orders.

I nod. "Right, two pitchers and four glasses?" I ask to confirm.

They all nod, and a few of them look at the menus as I turn to walk away.

"Wait!"

I turn back, the first guy summoning me back with his hand. "Yes?"

He gives me a cocky smile. "You new here?"

"Is it that obvious?"

He rubs the stubble on his chin. "What's your name?"

"Elora."

He looks me over again, and I feel that nervous energy radiate in my stomach when guys look at me like that for too long.

"Anyway," I say, trying to break the tension, "I'm just going to punch that in for you. Be right back."

I turn before any of them can call me back and let out a long breath as Mariah steps up next to me to swipe her card.

"Don't worry about them too much, they're here all the time," she says. "They like to look, but they don't touch."

I glance back in the direction of the table and the one who asked my name is still staring at me.

"Ugh, guys are so gross sometimes," I mutter as I punch in their drink orders.

Mariah flips her bouncy, dark hair, her flawless dark skin glowing from her wide smile. "I know. Why do you think I swore off all of them?"

I laugh and feel that nervousness leave the pit of my stomach.

She lowers her voice. "By the way, what's your number? I'm going to add you to our server group chat. It's good for if you need to switch a shift or need to learn which creeps to avoid. All the gossip, you know?"

"Oh, right." I laugh and give her my number, and a few moments later, I feel my phone vibrate in my apron.

I look over toward the bar and see the pitchers, so I head over to grab them. I place them down on the table, and Mariah follows behind me with glasses.

"Have you decided what you'd like to order?" I ask.

The third guy in a baseball hat speaks up this time. "Yeah, I think we're going to order a plate of nachos."

"No olives, though," the second guy says, sticking his tongue out in disgust.

I give them a small smile. "Can't say I blame you. I can't stand olives, either."

"See?" he says to his friends. "Someone who sees sense."

"I'll run and put that in for you."

I head back over to where Mariah is standing, and she swipes her card for me. "Nachos," I say, looking through the appetizer drop-down menu. I add it to the order list and click submit. "Oh, shit!" I blurt.

"What?"

"I forgot to put on the order, no olives."

Mariah doesn't seem too concerned. "Oh, no big deal. Just run back and let the kitchen know. Will's working that station tonight. Just tell him."

Fuck. "Will?"

She nods. "I'll be right back. I think that table wants their bill."

Mariah heads off toward the couple sitting at a high table as I slowly turn on my heel to the kitchen. I push through the swing door and glance around, my stomach fluttering.

I take a deep breath to calm myself and walk past the grill line in the back where I saw Will earlier. It's quieter back here, but I spot him, crouched down over a massive bin of something that looks like bags and bags of tortilla chips. I see a white and yellow chit on the counter in front of him. Likely my incorrect order.

I take a few steps closer to him. "Hey, Will?"

He jumps up suddenly, spinning around, and his elbow collides with my nose. An agonizing burst of pain shoots through my face, and I'm momentarily blinded as my eyes water. I cover my face with my hands as his gasp of surprise rings in my ears.

"Shit! Oh my God, I'm so sorry!"

I back up against the wall and force my eyes open, my lips trembling from trying to keep myself from crying. "What the hell?"

He takes a step closer to me, his hazel eyes wide behind his glasses. "I didn't mean to! You snuck up on me!"

"So, this is my fault?" I ask, and I feel something wet trickle down my face. Fuck, I think my nose is bleeding.

Will runs a hand along the back of his neck. "No! No, sorry! My eyesight is shit! Fuck, you're bleeding." He reaches out a hand toward my face.

"No!" I say, holding up a hand, and I can see the blood shining on the black latex glove. "Just stay away from me."

He grabs a box of tissues from a shelf overhead. "Here, let me help you."

I scowl at him through the pain. "I think you've done enough, thanks."

He blinks at me for a moment. "Why are you even back here?"

I feel my mouth drop open incredulously. "What?"

He pushes his glasses up on his nose. "Why are you back here?"

I suddenly remember the olives. "The nachos order I put in, I forgot to say no olives."

Will drops his shoulders. "Oh."

I can feel the blood touch my mouth, so I turn and head toward the changerooms, leaving a rather stunned and annoyed-looking Will behind. I shut myself in the bathroom and lean against the door, stifling the choked sob that crawls its vicious way up my throat.

The tears fall in earnest now. I gasp in a few shallow breaths, pull the latex gloves off, then grab a handful of toilet paper and turn to my mangled reflection in the mirror.

My heart is pounding, beating irregularly, and my legs tremble. A panic attack hits me like a freight train. *No, no, no, not now. Please, not now.* My face is swollen and red, blood trickling out of my nose and down my chin. I push the tissue paper up into my face and tilt my head back to stop the bleeding while simultaneously trying to even out my breathing. But the harder I try, the worse it gets. My skin is burning, my hands overly hot, and I drop the tissues against my nose so I can pull off my silk gloves.

I turn on the cold water in the sink and ignore the scars on my wrists and forearms as I plunge them under the tap. I sob with relief as the light above my head flickers for a moment.

The panic attack recedes as I look in the mirror again, my pale skin at odds with the swollen, bloody nose and pink eyes.

"Elora?"

Mariah's knocking on the door, and I jump at the noise.

"Are you all right? Will told me what happened."

I take a few quick breaths. "I…I'll be right out."

My heartbeat stabilizes and I splash some water over my face, trying to cool down my hot skin, washing away the blood.

Thankfully, my nose has stopped bleeding. I dry my hands, pull the gloves back on, followed by new latex ones, then quickly tuck my hair back into place.

Mariah's still there when I open the door. "Oh my God! Are you okay?"

I give her a little nervous smile and nod. She holds out her hand with a soft ice pack.

"Here, put this on your nose or it'll bruise really badly."

I shudder with relief as I press the cold pack to my throbbing nose.

"You poor thing! And on your first day!" Mariah consoles me.

"I think I'm all right. Do I look completely terrible?" I ask, raising my eyebrows at her and flinching as I remove the ice pack from my face.

She gives me a soft smile. "Let's just say, I wish I looked like that after getting elbowed in the face."

I laugh, then wince again. "Come on, then."

Mariah has taken over my table with the nachos, although they call me over at one point to ask where I disappeared to.

I point to my face. "Work related injury, I'm afraid."

There's a collective sucking in of breath and one of the guys says, "Ouch, getting hit in the nose is the worst."

"Well, I'm glad you got your food. Make sure to let me know if you need anything else."

The hours pass and the tables collectively held between Mariah, and I start to dwindle out. No one stays too late on a Monday night, and I can't wait to go home. When the guys with the nachos finally pay their bill and leave, I sit down with Mariah in an empty booth for her to show me how to close out my bills.

"How's your nose?" she asks as we count out the cash.

I graze it gingerly with my fingers. Thankfully, I didn't need to speak to Will for the rest of my shift, but again, I caught him looking at me the few times I had to go through the back. Maybe I was imagining things, but he seemed angry at me.

"I'm sure I'll survive," I mutter. "It's my dignity that's taken the worst of it."

She glances at me sideways. "Knew you were a tough cookie. Here." She puts two twenty-dollar bills down in front of me.

"What's this?"

She smirks. "Your tip from the nacho boys."

"Forty dollars?"

She leans forward. "Maybe they felt bad that you got smacked in the face."

I snort out a laugh and pocket the cash. "Maybe I'll have to come back to work on crutches."

Mariah laughs loudly. "When are you scheduled back?" she asks. "I reckon only one more day of shadowing and you can be on your own."

I perk up. "Yeah?"

She nods. "You did great tonight, all mishaps aside. Do you want to grab some dinner with us at the bar?"

As if on cue, my stomach grumbles. "Yeah, maybe."

"Here," she says, handing me the envelope full of bills and cash, "go give this to Heidi and she'll make sure it's right. Then get changed. I'll be at the bar."

I head toward the office and find Heidi counting through a tall blonde girl's envelope.

"You're all good, Jenni. See you tomorrow."

Jenni smiles at me, then heads toward the back.

"So," Heidi says, turning to me, "how'd it go?"

I shrug. "It's been an adventure."

"I heard you took an elbow to the face. Are you all right?" she asks, squinting at me.

I wince as a sharp twinge of pain rushes through me. "I'll live."

I watch as she counts through everything, making a mental note of how she does it.

"You're all good. You're back tomorrow, right?"

I nod. "Yeah, I'm shadowing Mariah again."

"All right, see you tomorrow then."

"Bye."

I head toward the changeroom, thankful that I'm going to be able to change back into my regular clothes.

"Listen, I'm sorry you feel that way, but I thought you understood that this was just a casual thing."

I pause outside of the door. The voice is deep with a slight rasp to it, and I'm pretty sure I know who it belongs to.

"I just," a female voice says, "we had such a good time, so I thought maybe we could continue."

"Is that what you want? Just a casual fuck friend?" Will asks.

There's a pause.

"Yeah, that's what I thought." He continues. "Listen, Jenni, I'm sorry if I let you think this was more than what it was, but I don't do relationships or whatever it is you want."

Mariah was right, Will really is a player. What an absolute jerk.

"Fine," Jenni says shrilly, and I move out of the way just as the door bursts open and Jenni stalks out, her blonde hair swinging behind her. It blows my mind that any guy would look at her and not want to worship at her feet.

I hear a loud sigh, then the sound of a locker slamming. I hide out of sight of the door as Will leaves, a bag slung over one shoulder and a leather jacket in his hand.

I double check to make sure the room is clear, then scurry in to change into a pair of leggings and a long t-shirt. Discarding the black latex gloves and pulling my silk ones higher up on my elbows, I grab my bag with the wet dress still inside and head out of the changerooms where I nearly run into Alex.

"Oh, hey!" he says, giving me a wide smile.

I stop short and smile back. "Hey."

"You done?"

I nod.

"How'd it go?"

I close my eyes for a long moment. "Bit of a mixed bag, if I'm honest."

He chuckles. "Fair enough. How's the nose?"

I scrunch up my face and wince from the pain. "Sore."

"Well," he says, "it's still a very cute nose."

"Oh!" A laugh escapes me. "Thanks, but I'll probably have two black eyes tomorrow. People are going to think I'm in an abusive relationship."

"Are you?"

I quirk my eyebrow at him.

"In a relationship, I mean," Alex corrects himself, his cheeks darkening.

I look away, feeling my own cheeks heat up. "No, no, I'm not."

His smile widens. "Are you joining us at the bar?"

"Umm…I haven't decided yet."

Alex's face drops, his green eyes scanning mine, then my arms, then over my gloves. I see him staring, and I pull up the ends of my gloves from where they've slipped down a little. If he sees the scars, he doesn't say anything.

"You should," he adds.

I smile slyly at him. "I'll think about it."

He passes by me, heading into the men's bathroom, and gives me another look over his shoulder. "You'll break my heart if you don't."

My cheeks heat a little, and I can't help the laugh I give out at the ridiculousness of his statement. He smirks as he disappears, so I shake my shoulders and head through the swing door to the bar.

I spot Mariah, who's sipping on a beer, and come to stand next to her.

"Everything checked out?" she asks.

I nod. "Yeah, everything's fine."

"Great, want a drink?"

My brain is at war with itself. On one hand, I'd love to just hang out and get to know Mariah and Alex better, but I'm also exhausted and sticky and reek of coffee. I'm about to say yes when Will appears next to Mariah with a beer in his hand, his jacket and bag slung over the seat next to her. He's giving me that look again, like he can't quite figure out if he's mad at me.

His gaze meets mine for a moment, and those hazel eyes give me a very distinct feeling of being X-rayed.

"Actually," I say, twisting my lips, "I think I'm going to just head home tonight. Maybe tomorrow. I'm in desperate need of a shower and a frozen pack of peas. Thanks, though."

I can feel his eyes on me as I pull my jacket from my bag.

"I'll wash your dress and bring it back for you tomorrow," I say to Mariah. "Thanks for letting me borrow it."

She waves her hand. "Of course. Always good to keep an extra, just in case."

"Thanks. Good night."

She smiles at me, and I feel Will watching as I leave.

I push open the red door and step out into the chilly April night air as I look up and down the street. I spot the sign for the streetcar and start toward it, fumbling in my coat pocket for my bus pass.

"Elora!"

I spin around. Will is jogging toward me, pulling his black jacket over his t-shirt. "What do you want?" I ask with a sigh. I hoped it might be Alex trying to convince me to stay.

"Listen," he says, pushing his glasses up his nose, "I just wanted to say sorry."

"You've said that already." I start again toward the shelter.

"Yeah…well…I guess I just wanted to say it again?"

I whip around to face him, and he nearly stumbles. "Can I ask you a question?"

His eyes dart to the side and he tucks his hands into his pockets as if surprised by my response. "Um…sure?"

"Do you spill coffee and elbow everyone in the face on their first day, or am I just extra lucky?"

He laughs a little nervously, his hand darting into the tumble of black curls.

If I wasn't so annoyed with him, I might be thinking about how utterly soft that hair looks. No, Elora, stop it.

"Look, maybe we started off on the wrong foot."

"What's the plan next? Dislocate my shoulder? Tie my shoelaces together? Hide all of my clothes while I change?"

"No, of course not—"

"It's fine," I say, cutting him off. "Thanks for the apology." I turn back toward the streetcar stop.

"Wait."

I turn back and he's closing the distance between us again.

"Can we just start over? Maybe I could take you out for coffee. I promise to keep it in the cup this time."

He smiles and I almost—*almost* melt. God, why does he have to have dimples? But Mariah's warning and the conversation I overheard with Jenni come back to me in earnest. This man is dangerous and not good for me. Even if his mouth looks positively edible. No, I'm not in a position to let some player take advantage of me right now.

"Why would you want to take me out…for coffee?" I ask with suspicion.

He shrugs. "To properly apologize."

"If that's the case, then you can just bring me one. No need to take me out." I can see his brain working through what I've said.

If it's true that he just wants to apologize, this would be acceptable. If it isn't, then he has ulterior motives. His hand flies up into his mop of hair again, pushing it off his forehead.

"Uh yeah…that could work. And maybe I can get your number?"

I roll my eyes. "I hardly think you need my number to bring me a coffee."

His cheeks redden. "I just thought that—"

"Sorry," I say, cutting him off, "but I'm not interested in being a casual fuck friend."

His eyes widen as he realizes I must have overheard his conversation. "Who says that's what I want?"

"That's what you told Jenni you want."

He purses his lips together. "That's a different situation. It's complicated."

I raise my eyebrows. "Oh, really?" I scoff. "And what exactly do you want with me, then?"

He stammers for a moment. "I…I don't know, to get to know you better?"

"Yeah, I'm going to have to say no."

He shakes his head. "Are you still pissed about earlier? Because I said I was sorry. It was an accident."

A chill wind breezes down the empty street, and I glance at the streetcar shelter, wanting to finish this conversation as quickly as possible. I pull myself up as tall as I can, even though it barely makes a dent in the gap between us. If there's one thing I've learned about men, it's that sometimes you have to resort to rudeness. "Fine, you're sorry. Doesn't mean I have to grovel at your feet now."

"I don't—"

"I'm sure you're used to girls falling all over themselves for you, but trust me when I tell you I'm *not* interested."

His hazel eyes narrow as if he's not used to being turned down. "What? Why?"

I can hear the rumbling of the streetcar approaching.

"You're not attracted to me?"

I hesitate for too long. "No."

He leans forward, his mouth quirking up at one side. "Liar."

I pull back and feel my lip curl into a sneer. "It's not a lie."

His voice drops, and something in my stomach flips over. "Then why are you blushing so hard?"

I cross my arms over my chest, enraged at my skin for betraying me. "It's probably just bruising from the elbow to the face I received earlier from an arrogant asshat."

He scoffs and tosses his head a little. "Well, aren't you just a ray of sunshine?" He takes two steps back. "Forget I said anything then. Next time, watch where you're going."

A sudden powerful gust of wind whips around us and my copper hair flies around my face as I watch him turn his collar up against the wind and head back inside.

4

ELORA

I sigh with relief when I spot the small, blue house from across the street. I make my way through the gate and unlock the door on the side of the house that opens into the narrow stairway leading to the tiny apartment upstairs. It's not fancy, but it's perfect because it's cheap and only available for six months.

When I get to the top of the stairs, there's a note taped to my door.

Dear Ms. Green,

The hot water heater is broken. Someone should be coming by on Wednesday to fix it. Unfortunately, no hot water until then.

Our apologies,

Management

My eyes close, and my head falls forward to rest against the door. The tip of my nose brushes against the hard surface, and I jump back as the pain twinges. This day is shitting on me something fierce. All I want right now is a hot shower and I can't even have that. Oh well, cold it is.

I scrunch up the note in my hand and head inside. I toss my bag onto the little grey loveseat just inside the door and flick the lights on. There is precisely one window in my entire apartment. It's all one big open room except for the small bathroom in the corner. It came furnished, which is perfect for me. I kick my shoes off as I pass the tall cubby shelf which divides the living room from the bedroom where several plants live. Picking up the remote from the river-rock-decorated coffee table, I scroll through the smart features on the TV to find a soothing playlist to listen to in the background.

Settling on a sounds-of-the-ocean playlist, I walk into the kitchen and open the freezer. Frozen dinners are usually what sustains me, so a fridge and a microwave are all I need. My stomach growls, but first I need to rid myself of the smell of coffee.

I walk into the small bathroom and turn the shower on. I pull my shirt over my head and step out of my leggings and underwear, followed by the long black gloves that I peel off my arms, tossing all of it into the hamper next to the sink. My fingers trace along the hideously scarred skin that's etched from my wrists up my forearms to nearly my elbows. It itches slightly when exposed to the air, and I try my best to resist the urge to scratch the skin raw.

When I woke up in that hospital nearly two years ago, they sent three different doctors in to interview me. I hated all of them. They all seemed convinced that I had tried to kill myself, no matter what I said. I have never felt like I wanted to die, but worse than that, I can't remember anything about my life prior to waking up there that might make that true. I know my name, how to read and tie my shoes and how to count money, but there is nothing else. Just a name and a birthdate. No memory of family, no friends, no indication of who I was before I ended up there.

One of the nurses sat with me to explain that I'd been found by some fishermen, nearly drowned under the ice of Lake Ontario. The psychologists they sent in to evaluate me concluded that whatever I'd gone through had forced some kind of fugue state or amnesia.

I look into the mirror and blink away tears. Dark purple bruising starts to appear under my eyes and across my nose. It's downright hideous. Anger floods through my veins at the thought of Will. Who just whips around like that, elbows flying! And how arrogant is he? Trying to blame me for it, then having the absolute nerve to try and ask me out after? What an absolute prick.

My heartbeat picks up again, and the scorching heat at the thought of him makes me feel like my skin is burning. I give myself one last glance in the mirror before reaching my hand into the shower. I hiss as the freezing water hits my hand and pull it back instantly.

"Well, at least it'll be refreshing and quick," I mutter, the light above my mirror flickering.

I take a few shallow breaths, building up the nerve to jump under the stream of water. "One…two…three…"

The water hits me, but it's not cold. In fact, it's the perfect temperature and I look up at the shower head, confused, as I feel the water soak my hair and run down my body. My wrists itch fiercely, so I rub my knuckles against the jagged skin to avoid hurting myself with my nails.

Maybe the hot water heater was fixed earlier than expected? Whatever the reason, I am thrilled, and I stand still as a statue for a few long minutes, letting the water wash away the coffee residue, the smell of hot oil, and the embarrassment of the day. I spend a long time in the shower, calming my mind. Every once in a while, I try to see if I can remember something, anything from before two years ago, but it's like grasping at smoke in the dark. There's just… nothing.

After my shower, I pull on a pair of pyjamas and heat up a frozen chicken dinner in my microwave. I switch the TV to some old sitcom and grab my phone from my bag as I settle in under a blanket on the couch. There's a bunch of new text messages, but I'll get to those later. First things first.

I open up the missing persons page, scanning for any new entries. It's been two years and every day I check, hoping that some picture of me will appear there. Even with an I.D. and a bank card in my pocket, the police and hospital weren't able to find anyone who might be linked to me. I can't shake the feeling that they were wrong. That there might be someone out there looking for me, wondering where I've disappeared to and desperately missing me. But there never is. At some point, I know I should just give up. If no one has bothered to find me in two years, there must be no one out there who's looking.

Maybe I *did* try to kill myself. Maybe there really is no one who cares about me, and therefore, I tried to end it all. But a part of me still refuses to believe it.

I close the missing persons page and open my social media accounts. I've made all of them public, just in case someone recognizes me. I can see there's a few new DMs in my inbox. My pulse picks up, but it's just the usual random strange men who are hoping to hook up. The first message is so lame that I scoff loudly before deleting it. The second isn't much better, so off to the trash it goes. The third, I don't even dare open. I can see it's a picture message, but I'm still recovering from the last unsolicited dick pic sent my way so it joins the others. I still hold out on the slight chance that someone I once knew will recognize me, though.

I take a quick picture of my swollen face and post it to Instagram with the caption, "First day at my new job and I get an elbow to the face. Send help."

With all of that out of the way, I open my texts to a barrage of messages, entering each new contact as they roll in.

Mariah:
Welcome, Elora, to the Flying Weasel group chat.

Don't judge us too harshly.

Mackenzie:
Yay! New girl! I'm Mackenzie. I'll meet you tomorrow.

Priscilla:
This is Priscilla. Is Elora my replacement?
You know you can never replace me, right?

Mariah:
Miss you, Cilla! It's not the same without you.
Elora, how's your face? Is it bruising yet?

Jenni:
Jenni here. What happened to her face?

Mackenzie:
Yeah, what happened?

Mariah:
Will elbowed her right in the nose.

Priscilla:
😮

Mackenzie:
OMG seriously? Ouch.

Mariah:
Yeah, and he was a total dick about it.

Priscilla:
Seriously? Why would he be a dick about it?

Lilli:
Hi! I'm Lilli.
Will being a dick? Why am I not surprised?

Priscilla:
Yeah, but what a dick, though. 😬

Mariah:
OMG eww, please, he's like my little brother. Can we try not to traumatize the newbie? Girl still has enough sense to tell him to fuck off.

Jenni:
Wish I'd told him to fuck off.

Lilli:
Jenni, you knew what you were getting into with him. From my experience, he's always been upfront about only wanting to keep things casual.

Jenni:
Doesn't mean it doesn't hurt my feelings. It was so good, though. Who the hell taught that boy to fuck like that?

Priscilla:
If you ever find out, I want to send her a thank-you card.

Wow, Will really did fuck around. The slew of messages has at least taught me one thing, and that is that I made the right decision turning Will down. I don't want to end up like this.

Pining after some guy who doesn't give a shit about me the morning after. No matter how good he is in bed.

> **Elora:**
> **Thanks for the warm welcome, everyone!**
> **My face has certainly seen better days.**

I send them the picture of my face I took for Instagram.

Mariah:
Oh dear, keep some ice to it. Take a Tylenol before bed.

Lilli:
Ouch! Hope you're OK!

Mariah:
Btw, Elora, someone was very sad you left without saying goodbye.

What follows is a picture of Alex sitting next to Mariah at the bar with a frown and big green puppy dog eyes. I look at the picture again. I can see Will in the background, his phone in his hand and looking thoroughly annoyed by his friends. Part of me wishes his annoyed look is because of what I said to him, but I doubt he gave me a second thought once I was out of his sight.

I look down at the picture again. Alex is hot, and so far, he's been nice. If he asks me out, I'll be tempted to say yes. Being in a relationship isn't really in the cards for me because I'm leaving in six months, but it might be fun to date or have some kind of companionship. But therein lies another glaring problem.

I don't know if I am ready for any kind of physical relationship. I'm not even sure if I'm a virgin. I've only kissed one person I can remember. A guy named Matt at my last job. But something about it was off, like I couldn't really feel it, like my mouth was numb. I felt so bad, too. I liked him. He was kind and patient, but something just felt off. And at the last moment, I bailed.

Elora:
Tell Alex I'll stay tomorrow as long as I don't end up covered in coffee again.

Three little dots appear under Mariah's name that tell me she's typing, followed by a picture of Alex smiling and giving me the thumbs up, and I smile to myself. I wonder if he's a good kisser. If it would feel right with him. Will isn't in the background anymore. His jacket and bag are gone, so he must have gone home.

I finish my now almost cold dinner and grab the laundry to take downstairs to the communal washer and dryer, dumping Mariah's dress and some other things into the machine. The door to my left opens and Angela, one of the tenants from the main floor of the house, nearly runs me over on her way out the door.

"Oh, hey, Elora. Sucks about the water heater, huh?"

I press my lips together in confusion. "It's already fixed."

She raises her eyebrows at me. "It is?"

I nod. "Yeah, I just had a shower, and it was fine."

She pauses. "Are you sure? I was just doing the dishes and couldn't get it above freezing."

I nod. "Yeah, I'm sure." I point at my still damp hair.

She walks to the wash basin next to the washing machine and turns on the tap to hot while I finish putting my clothes in.

Angela lets the water run for a little while then puts her fingers under the tap. "Nope, still cold as ice. Maybe you were lucky and got the last bit of hot water left in the tank?"

I reach my fingers under the faucet and feel the goosebumps scatter everywhere at the icy temperature. "Huh…weird."

I look over and notice her staring at the scars on my wrists. I quickly tuck them in against my chest after I close the lid and press start.

"Well, good night," I say and hurriedly head up the stairs as I feel her watching me.

I shut myself behind my door, leaning against it as I take deep, steadying breaths. That is why I wear the gloves, to hide the evidence of whatever had happened to me. To conceal the angry slashing scars that cover every inch of skin from my wrists to my elbows. Everyone always thinks the same thing, that they were marks inflicted from self-harm or a botched suicide attempt. No matter how hard I try to convince people it wasn't a suicide attempt, nobody ever believes me.

The first job I found once I got out of the hospital was working at Canada's favourite coffee store chain: Tim Horton's. Everyone had been friendly at first, but the moment they spotted the scars on my wrists, it was like a flip was switched. They either avoided me, turned their noses up, or looked at me with such pity I could barely stand it. So now I hide and I lie.

My scars itch again, and I rub the back of my knuckles against the skin. Exhaustion falls upon me, so I clean up my dinner mess and grab my phone before getting into bed, the light from the moon outside my window falling across the comforter as I climb in.

My body aches and I'm afraid of what my face will look like in the morning. I scroll through my phone. Mariah has added me on Instagram, and I follow her back. I look through her pictures, many of which are of her, staff members of the pub, and a few with a girl I assume is her girlfriend. There is a very cute picture of her piggybacking Alex on the beach on a bright summer's day. They are both in their swimsuits and laughing.

The next photo is of Mariah, sandwiched between Alex and Will. Will has his arm around her protectively and he is wearing swim trunks and a wet t-shirt. Why would he go swimming with a shirt on? I can tell he has a nice body from the way the thin fabric clings to his narrow waist and broad shoulders, the hint of defined muscles underneath.

I check the tags on the photo and see that Will's account is linked. I click on it and it leads me to his Instagram page. His profile picture is the same picture that led me here, the one of him, Mariah, and Alex.

The info at the top says Will Reed, 24, line cook at the Flying Weasel Pub on Queen Street East, Toronto. There are half a dozen pictures, most of which seem to be taken at the pub. There's one that looks like it's been taken in his apartment because it's a mirror selfie. His hair is much shorter than it is now and reveals a large scar above his right eyebrow I didn't notice before.

Lastly, there is a picture of him genuinely smiling. Whoever took it captured him at his best. He's sitting on what looks like a rooftop overlooking the city. His arms are wrapped around his knees and there's the biggest smile on his face, his dimples on full display, and I feel myself smiling as I stare at the photo.

There's a caption below the photo that simply says, "Happy Birthday, Mariah." It was posted almost a year ago. Mariah's birthday must be coming up soon, then. The photo has quite a few likes, mostly girls. I suck on my teeth, forcing the smile off my face, and mentally kick myself for staring far too long at Will's photo. I close the app and set my phone on the windowsill before turning over and hugging my other pillow to my chest.

Once again, I try to dig for the memories buried somewhere in my mind. For a second, I think there might be something there, a blue light over the ocean, but then it's gone, the image fading as I fall asleep.

5

ELORA

I am drowning. I'm sure of it. My skin feels like it's being stabbed by thousands of needles as I claw toward a surface I'm not even sure exists. My feet kick and my lungs burn, but there is light above me. I'm so close, close to air, close to salvation. My face breaches the surface and I gasp, my mouth inhaling the frigid air, my eyes adjusting to the darkness that seems to press in on me like a cage.

There's a shore nearby, and I push myself toward it through the water even as every muscle in my body spasms and fights against the movement. Finally, my hand grasps the muck of the shore and I haul myself up onto the snow-covered ground. My legs are still submerged, but I can't go any farther.

Ragged breaths burst out from between my lips and I can feel my hair turning to ice. I'm going to die here. I won't be able to find warmth soon enough. Would anyone even look for me here? No one would be out, it's so cold. No, this is it, this is the end.

But how did I get here? How did I end up in the water? I was searching for something, wasn't I? I push on shaking arms to look back. The lake is mostly frozen. Miraculously, I came up at a

*section where the ice splintered apart. There is something below
the surface of the ice. Is that what I came to find? A blue light
flashes briefly under the water.*

*I can hear shouting in the distance, and the blurry outlines of
two people running toward me across the ice. But that light taunts
me, flickering once again before the darkness swallows me whole.*

· ————— ✴ ————— ·

I JOLT AWAKE—the dream slipping away as the sun hits my eyes.

"No, no, no, no," I whisper, gripping the sides of my head as
if holding myself might keep the images from fading away. It's
the first time I've dreamed of anything. Water, a blue light, ice,
shouting...but nothing is clear and the harder I try to focus, the
quicker it slips away.

"Goddamn it!" I shout, slamming my hands down on either
side of me. The window rattles and a loud crash startles me as the
shelf above the TV comes loose. The little candles on top slide
down the side, falling to the floor and rolling under the coffee
table. I sigh with irritation and move my body to the edge of the
bed, my muscles aching. I rub my face to rid the sleep from my
eyes but immediately regret it when I feel the tenderness of my
nose.

I shoot out of bed and head for the bathroom. I flick the light
on and gasp. My face looks horrific, dark bruises under each eye
and across my nose, nearly making my freckles disappear.

"Shit!" I say.

I'm not even sure if makeup can cover this. Should I even go
into work? I briefly consider calling Brandon or Heidi to let them
know about my face. However, I am new and I want to finish
shadowing Mariah so I can get my own tables. I've drained most
of my savings to get this apartment, so if I don't start making

decent money soon, I'll starve. Maybe they'll stick me in the back on dishwashing duty and not let me out on the floor. How embarrassing would that be? God, the thought of working next to Will is mortifying. I'm sure Alex won't be too eager to flirt now that I look like I've lost a fight in the ring.

I check my phone and see there are some messages in the group chat. Nothing too exciting, just some of the girls asking to switch shifts for later on in the week, but then I notice the Instagram notification.

Alex Burnham started following you.

My stomach does a little jig and my finger hovers over the follow back button. Don't want to seem too eager, but I can't be sure when he did this. My profile is public so he could've spent hours looking through all my photos or maybe he didn't bother. I click the little blue follow button and land on his profile.

Alex's wide, bright smile stares up at me from almost every picture. There are dozens, a bunch of him with people I assume are his friends, possibly even family. Lots of photos at parties or concerts and even more taken at the pub. Mariah and Jenni are in a few of them, as well as Will, who always looks annoyed at having his photo taken. One particular photo is the two of them with beer boxes over their heads with holes cut out to look like helmets.

"Boys are ridiculous," I mutter, but I feel my lips curving upward. It must be nice having friends to do stupid shit with.

I eat and finish up the laundry before I head into the kitchen to wash the sink full of dishes that I just haven't had the energy to finish. I throw some sort of playlist on the TV for background noise and turn on the tap.

Nothing.

I jiggle the handles back and forth, but all I'm greeted with is the slight screeching of the taps as I twist them, the absence of rushing water filling the void. I quickly glance out the window, but there's no plumbing repair truck outside that I can see. I go back into the kitchen and try again.

A jet of water bursts out of the tap, the faucet cracking apart and water spraying everywhere. I'm instantly soaked from head to toe, the water arching as high as the ceiling and splattering all over the counters. I blink through the water, my hands coming up to shield my face as I get closer to try to turn off the tap. The kitchen ceiling light flickers and the fluorescent lights buzz over the noise.

I take a step toward the sink, trying to see if there's a way to turn the water off, but I slip on the wet tiles and my hands reach behind me to break my fall. I'm suddenly burning hot, my wrists itching wildly. Then, I see it through the strobing light from the ceiling.

A fish.

A fish made of water swims through the spray erupting from the sink. It sparkles and fans its brilliant clear fins as it makes its way toward me. Instinctively, I reach out my hand. The water from the tap stops, thousands of droplets hanging in the air around my kitchen as the little fish swims its way to my hand. My heart is beating so hard I'm sure it will burst out of my chest.

I feel the gentle touch of the fins gliding over my fingers, a cool mist breezing over my palm as it spins around in my hand. I bring it toward me until it's nearly cradled against my chest, my other hand reaching out to touch it. The light above me flickers, then dies, the water suspended in air falls, and the little fish in my palm drops to the floor with a loud splash. The light comes back on.

I sit there stupidly for a long time until the wet clothes and floor begin to make me shiver.

What the hell just happened? I feel for my head, checking to make sure I didn't fall and crack my skull against the tile floor.

Other than my unfortunate nose injury, I seem intact. My scars itch again, and I rub at them with my wet palms. Slowly, I push myself up to stand and take in the state of my kitchen. There is water everywhere.

I glance up at the steady kitchen light. Maybe it was simply a trick of the light. Maybe the elbow to the face from yesterday gave me a slight concussion and now I'm seeing things? My phone alarm rings, so I back out of the kitchen cautiously and head toward my bed, where I've left my phone.

A reminder. One hour until I have to leave for work.

"Shit," I mutter.

That means I don't have much time to clean this mess up and get ready. I grab a few towels out of the cupboard and toss them onto the wet floor of the kitchen before racing to get ready for work.

·———— ✳ ————·

I FEEL off my game when I stumble out of the changerooms, tying my apron around my waist. The strings cut into the fleshy part of my hips, but it is heavy with spare change, so there isn't much I can do about that. I find Mariah turning on the coffee pot at the end of the counter and walk over to her. "Hey!" I say, making sure I keep enough distance between us in case of another accidental coffee spill.

"Oh my goodness." Her face drops.

I cover my face with my hands. "I know! It's so bad!"

Mariah pulls my gloved hands away. "No! No, it's not that bad. Just worse than yesterday, that's all."

I sigh. "It's actually way worse, but makeup is hiding a lot of the bruising." I pull her dress out of one of the large apron pockets. "Here's your dress back."

She takes it and gives me a smile. "Thanks. Are you sure

you're all right to work? They'd understand if you wanted to stay home."

I shake my head. "No, I really want to finish up the training and get out there on my own. I need the money."

She nods. "I totally get that."

I look around the kitchen. Brandon is working the grill, and there are two guys behind the pass-through that I haven't met yet.

"He's not here today," Mariah says.

"Huh?"

She smirks. "Will. He's not here."

I sigh with relief. "Oh, good."

"I don't know what you said to him, but you must have really put him in his place. He was in a foul mood the rest of the night."

I feel a spark of triumph at that. "Good, he's such an ass." I wave a hand at my face. "And bad for my health, apparently."

Mariah chuckles before raising an eyebrow. "Alex is coming in shortly, though."

My stomach does a little tumble. "Is he?"

Mariah twists her mouth. "I think he has a little crush on you."

Heat floods my cheeks. "You think so?"

She nods. "It's actually adorable. He's not normally like that."

"Like what?"

She shrugs. "He doesn't date a lot. He had a girlfriend for a little while when he first started working here. I guess they were pretty serious, but he hasn't dated anyone that I know of since then."

This surprises me. He is incredibly good-looking with his dark skin and green eyes—surely girls are attracted to him. Maybe the ex-girlfriend broke his heart. I remember I'll be leaving in six months, and if he happens to get too attached, I'll just hurt him. Maybe it isn't such a good thing for him to have a crush on me.

"Come on, let's go check our section."

A few hours in and things are going great. Mariah introduces me to Lilli and Mackenzie, two friendly servers from the group chat. I won't lie though and say that my heart hasn't stopped thundering since Alex caught my eye as he strolled toward the kitchen to start his shift. I give him a little wave and he waves back with that broad smile.

Throughout my shift, I find excuses to grab things from the back just so I can see him.

"Hey," he says, stepping into the salad and pasta station next to the grill. "The nose doesn't look too bad."

I shrug. "The makeup is helping. Two tables already asked me if I got into a fight."

"What did you say?"

"That I won."

He laughs raucously. "You know, you may be tiny, but I bet you're scrappy."

I smile. "Just call me Mighty Mouse."

"Get any coffee spilled on you yet?" he asks.

I narrow my eyes. "No, why?"

"You said you'd stay after work if you didn't get any coffee spilled on you."

I startle, recalling the message I sent to Mariah last night. "Oh!" The fact that Will won't be around makes the idea of staying after work all the more appealing. "Yeah, sure, we can hang out for a bit."

He gives me another dazzling smile, and I spend most of the next several hours in a state of blissful anticipation. Until I spot two guys sitting down in mine and Mariah's section. It's two of the four guys from last night. The one who asked my name and his friend who hates olives. I can feel the first one staring at me, and I square my shoulders before heading over.

I smile as I approach the table, and they smile back.

"Back again so soon?" I ask.

They smile at me. "Had to make sure you hadn't ended up in the hospital. How's your nose?"

I can feel the heat of embarrassment creep up my neck. "It's been better."

The olives guy is looking through the menu while the other stares at my hips.

"Can I get you guys something to drink?" I ask, trying to pull his attention back to my face.

He shakes his head. "What's with the gloves?"

I blink. "Sorry?"

He points at my hands, covered by black satin, the black latex overtop. "The gloves. Why do you wear them? Is it some new fashion thing I've never heard of?"

He reaches out his fingers as if to touch my hand, but I pull away, tucking my hair behind my ear. "Oh, no, I have anemia. My fingers get very cold, and it helps take the edge off."

"Interesting."

I stare at him and his friend, feeling an icy bead of sweat trickle down my spine.

"It's Elora, right?" he asks.

"Yup."

"I'm Hunter, this is Dan."

"Nice to meet you."

There's an awkward moment of silence before I say, "Right… so, drinks?"

The olive hater finally looks up. "Yeah, we'll just get a pitcher of Moosehead, please."

I give him a small smile, a nod, and walk away, feeling eyes on me the whole time.

"What's up?" Mariah asks, seeing my face.

I shake my head. "Those guys from yesterday are back."

She looks discretely over her shoulder. "Hmm...guess you made an impression."

"The one guy kind of gives me creeper vibes."

"Do you want me to take over the table?" she asks me.

I shake my head. "No, I'm sure it's fine."

I do my best to stay out of their line of sight, only going by their table when necessary. Once they've both finished eating and I've dropped off the bill, I head over to take their payment.

"So, what are you doing this weekend?" Hunter asks me.

I glance at his friend, who seems preoccupied with his phone for a minute.

"Oh!" I say, scrambling for something. "Just working, really."

"Maybe I'll stop by and say hi," he says, smiling at me, as his eyes linger on my chest.

"Umm...sure, I'll probably be here."

"Thanks, Elora," he says, taking back his card. I hand him the receipt, and he gives me a wink before walking away.

Mariah leans over my shoulder. "Another forty dollars?" she asks, staring at the receipt. "They tipped you the same amount as the bill?"

I shrug, feeling queasy about the cash now in my hands. But to be fair, he hasn't asked for my number or said anything inappropriate. Really, all he's done is stare and a lot of guys do that. But there is some inherent feeling I have that makes me want to disappear around him. "Yeah," I whisper.

"Hey, listen," Mariah perks up, "it's my birthday this weekend, but because we're always so busy and most of us work late on Saturdays, I'm actually going to be having my party next week on Wednesday. Do you want to come?"

I think of the picture of Will, hugging his knees and looking over the city with that beautiful smile on his face. "Happy birthday, Mariah," it said. *No!* I scream at myself. *No, no, no. Will is bad.*

"Sure. Where are you having the party?"

"It'll be at my apartment. It's in Leslieville, so it's easy to get to, on the streetcar. I'll post the details to the group chat."

I smile. "Sounds great!"

When the last of our tables have gone, and I've closed out all of our bills, Brandon tells me I can be on my own starting Thursday, on my next scheduled shift. Mariah gives me a wink, and I order myself a chicken penne alfredo dinner with the extra money from the tip that Hunter has left me.

I sit at the bar next to Lilli, a pretty brunette with dark lipstick and a septum piercing. She's asking me about how my first few days have gone when Alex appears at my shoulder.

"Hey, Mighty Mouse," he says, "can I join you?"

I grin back at him, but my nose twinges and I end up contorting my face to tolerate the pain. Alex laughs and hops up into the bar seat, hanging his bag off the back of the chair.

"Still sore, huh?"

"Unfortunately," I say.

He removes his jacket and leans forward on the counter. "How'd it go today?"

"Much better than yesterday. Got some good tips. One table left me forty bucks."

He looks impressed. "Nice!"

"What about you? How is it working in the kitchen?"

He shrugs. "It's usually pretty boring, to be honest. It gets a bit stressful on the weekends when it's busier, but tonight was fine."

A buzzing fades into my ear and I look around as if I'll find a mosquito hovering nearby. But almost as quick as it started, it's gone, and I see Alex looking at me expectantly.

"Sorry, what?" I ask.

His eyes flicker for a moment, then he smiles.

"I asked," Alex says, bumping my shoulder with his own, "what's your deal?"

I raise my eyebrows. "My deal?"

He smirks. "Yeah. You just wander in out of nowhere, looking like Rogue from *X-Men* with the gloves, and I don't know anything about you other than you're scrappy and have an extremely large social media presence."

So he *did* spend time perusing my Instagram page. The knowledge makes my stomach flutter.

"I don't know. There's not much to know, to be honest. I move around a lot."

"Why do you move around?"

"I like seeing different parts of the province. I try not to stay in one place too long."

"Wanderlust."

I pause. "Huh?"

He laughs. "Wanderlust. Doesn't it mean, the impulse to wander?"

I laugh. "Really? Hmm…I guess that fits, doesn't it?" I like it. It sounds better than a desperately lonely girl trying to find someone who knows her, so she never stops moving, never stops searching.

"That's cool. Where did you grow up? Are you from Toronto?"

I shake my head. "No."

Alex continues the conversation, asking me about my favourite things, movies, songs. Sometimes I make things up as I go when I don't have an answer for him.

The dream I had earlier crawls back to me, replaying in my mind. The icy water, the shouting, the blue light. Then the image of the suspended water in the kitchen flashes through my mind, the memory of the little fish causing sweat to break across my skin.

"Elora?"

"Huh?" I ask.

Alex is looking at me, his eyebrows knitted together. "Are you all right?"

I shake my head. "Oh gosh, I'm sorry. I must have zoned out. I'm a bit tired."

"Hey, listen," he says, and he looks a little nervous as he leans closer to me. "I don't normally do this..."

He pauses, and I feel a smile spreading across my face as I realize what he's about to say.

"Do you—would you maybe let me take you out sometime?"

I nod enthusiastically. "Yeah, all right."

His grin widens, and he bounces in his seat. "Great. I'm not working Sunday night, are you?"

I shake my head. "Nope, I'm free."

"Do you like bowling? There's a bowling alley near my place, not far from here."

"I've never been bowling before."

His mouth drops open. "You've never been—how is that even possible? You never went to a kids' birthday party at a bowling alley before?"

I shrug and shake my head. "No."

He scratches his head and laughs. "Well, good...now I won't seem totally lame when I suck at it."

I smile again.

"Alex!"

We both turn toward Brandon, who is out of breath. "Hey, man, glad you're still here. Could you help me with something? The freezer door is stuck again."

"Yeah, I'll be right there."

I grab my bag and coat. "I should probably head home anyway."

Alex frowns, and I bite my lip to hide the grin spreading across my face.

"Well, I'll see you on Thursday, maybe?" I ask.

He nods. "For sure."

After we exchange numbers, he heads off toward the kitchen. As I head home on the streetcar, I can't keep the smile off my face.

6

WILL

I am such a fucking idiot.

My head is pounding and my eyes feel so tired and sore that I lie in bed with an ice pack over them. Being around Elora is both exciting and unsettling. Why is my vision around her so different? It's like looking directly at the sun after being in darkness for years. It's beautiful but blinding, and I can't seem to stop myself. My eyes scream at me in protest.

But, of course, I had to fuck everything up. First the coffee, then the blow to her nose. My God. Why the hell did I ask her, "What are you doing back here?" As if it was her fault. And then she overheard me blowing off Jenni. Fuck! I remove the ice pack from my face and look at my phone, the light causing my temples to throb. I open Instagram and type in her first and last name, finding her profile. It's public and, holy shit, it's…a lot.

I scroll through literally hundreds of pictures, almost all selfies. My God, is she ever beautiful, and those eyes... Even through the phone, it feels like her eyes could light my soul on fire. I feel goosebumps scatter everywhere. There are pictures of her from all over the Greater Toronto Area. Does she travel a lot? There isn't a single picture of her with anyone else. She's always alone. Doesn't this girl have any friends? Any family? A pet? Strange.

I scroll back to the top of her profile. Elora Green, 22, works at the Flying Weasel Pub on Queen Street East. Below, she's added a new photo of herself and her bruised nose with the caption, "First day at my new job and I get an elbow to the face. Send help." I groan and roll over on the bed, burying my face in my pillow. Alex's warning from the other day rings through my mind—*You know, one day, you're going to meet a girl that you just go crazy for and she's not going to want to give you the time of day.*

✳

I'M BACK *in the trees, the soft mossy earth sinking under my feet. A sharp gust of wind whips around me, the breeze rippling through my hair and up my shirt over the jagged, scarred skin.*

"Willan."

That voice calls out to me again, some familiar disembodied voice that makes my heart ache with desperate longing. Then, the familiar blue light appears again. It flickers through the trees, brighter this time, and I run for it. Run through the forest like a man possessed, the light growing brighter and brighter and brighter until...

I'm suddenly standing outside of a small blue house. There's a side gate to the left and a single window on the upper floor illuminated against the night sky. I look around. I am standing on the sidewalk opposite the house in nothing but boxers and a t-shirt, the chilly April air freezing my skin.

"What the—"

Is this a dream? Am I dreaming? I take a step toward the house. A sharp pain shoots through my bare foot. I jump back and realize I've stepped on a piece of broken glass. I hop on one foot while I look at the damage, gasping as I pull a piece of jagged glass out.

"Shit!"

Okay, so definitely not dreaming. How the hell did I get here? Where am I? The light in the window flickers, and I duck and move back toward a nearby row of hedges. I need to get out of here. Someone is going to look out their window and see some random stranger in their underwear and no shoes on their street, and think I'm some psychopath. I cross my arms over my chest against the cold and turn away toward the main road, which is only about a hundred metres away.

I take a look up at the street sign. Woodbine Avenue. I look at the surrounding area. Woodbine and…Danforth? How the hell did I make it all the way up here? What time is it? I don't have a phone or my bus pass. Fuck! How am I going to get home? It would take hours to walk and I have no shoes on, not to mention I'm now dripping blood from the cut on my foot. Thank God I fell asleep with my glasses on at least, or I'd be in real trouble. A strong gust of wind chills my skin and I turn down the alley between two stores to shield myself, my foot throbbing.

"Okay, just calm down. You can figure this out…" I mutter to myself. Maybe if I can find someone, I can borrow a cell phone and call Alex, and he can come and get me. Bring me some clothes and shoes. He has a key to my apartment, so he'd be able to get my stuff. I wonder if maybe this is all Alex's doing. Maybe it's his idea of a prank. I close my eyes, trying to remember if I used the chain lock on my apartment door. I don't think I did.

I open my eyes and…

"Whoa—"

I'm back in my apartment.

A wave of exhaustion hits me like a tidal wave and I feel myself collapse against the door, my shoulder banging into it hard. I sink to the floor, staring blankly ahead of me.

What the hell just happened? My foot is still throbbing, blood trickling out onto the wood floor. Did I just…?

The sheer idea of it is crazy. But somehow I know that's what I've done.

I need to test it, to confirm my theory consciously. I stand up, holding myself against the door to alleviate the pressure on my foot. I'm so tired. I take several long, deep breaths and close my eyes, picturing the bathroom of my apartment. There's a sharp pull along my spine and my eyes shoot open, my hazel eyes behind black glasses reflecting back at me as I now find myself standing in my small bathroom.

I watch the grin that spreads across my face in the mirror, my hands grasping the side of my head as I yell in triumph.

Teleported. I just teleported.

·————— ✳ —————·

I DON'T THINK I've ever felt more exhausted than last night, but I wake up feeling more excited than ever. This must be what happened before work the other day when I appeared outside of the pub on the street. I collapsed that time. I wonder if it's like a muscle. The more I try, the easier it'll get. With the day I have off, I plan on doing exactly that.

I practice first in my apartment, going back and forth a few times between rooms. It's tiring, and after four successful teleports, I have to rest for a while and eat something. I put the TV on in the background and grab my cell phone to check for messages. There's nothing. It's stupid, but I do a cursory teleportation Internet search. Maybe there is some information that might help, even though this is something that's supposed to be impossible. There's a few conspiracy theory sites explaining wormholes, but my eyes start to blur at the physics of it all. Really, what I'm doing is jumping from space to space. My mouth quirks. That seems like an appropriate thing to call it—Jumping. Teleporting is a mouthful, after all.

I pause for a moment. If it *was* impossible, how is it I can do this? Maybe this is all in my head, maybe I'm hallucinating. Maybe I should show someone to make sure it's real. I think briefly about calling Alex, but as my finger hovers over the call button, I think better of it. What if he freaks out and calls the cops? Would they arrest me? Would I end up in some kind of facility where they experiment on me in order to find out how I can do this? Does the government even know this is something people are capable of? If not, I don't think I want to be the one to enlighten them.

I need to keep it to myself. If nothing else, for my own safety. In order to check that I am in fact Jumping from one place to the next, and not just blacking out, I cover my shoes with flour so I can see my own footprints. I do a few more Jumps around my apartment and the lack of white floury footprints on the wood floor tells me I'm going from one room to another without walking.

Holy shit, the possibilities scroll through my mind in a blur.

All right, next challenge.

I pull my coat on and tuck my bus pass and my cellphone into my pocket just in case. I think briefly about somewhere that isn't too far, where I'm fairly sure no one will be loitering around.

The roof.

Alex and I have been on the roof of our building a bunch of times, so I know what it looks like. I close my eyes, picturing the Wi-Fi dish, the metal stairs for the back of the building. I feel that tug along my spine, then a rush of cool air. I open my eyes and spin with excitement as I look over the side of the building down onto the street.

"Yes!" I cry. Tiredness washes over me, but not nearly as strong as before. I look over the gap between my building and the next, taking in the details of the other rooftop, and mentally, I Jump without even closing my eyes. In a split second, I am standing on the other roof.

"Holy shit," I breathe, my heart begging to burst out of my chest with exertion. My glasses have gone askew, the world around me blurry, and I am sweating. I sit down for a bit of a breather against the brick rooftop wall as my eyes and temples pulse.

Why is this happening now? Was I able to do this before the accident? Is this a side effect of the accident? There are so many questions and almost no way of knowing the answer. Nothing in my life has really changed. Work is still work and life is still boring and lonely. The only new thing is…Elora.

I pull out my phone and open Instagram, finding her name and profile amongst my recent searches. She's painfully pretty. Her face bright and joyous, the freckles across her cheeks disappearing down her neck and chest. I wonder if she has freckles everywhere. What her skin might feel like under my fingers. What it might be like to kiss every freckle that lives on her skin. But the thought that she might feel just like everyone else, like a ghost, is terrifying. I can barely stand the thought of touching her and finding out it's insubstantial. That she could be so bright and I would still be numb.

I'll likely never get to find out anyway. She isn't interested, even if her blush told me otherwise. But damn, she is like the light at the end of a long, dark tunnel, a temptation I am desperate to consume. I want her.

My thoughts stray to the idea of trying to impress her. Jumping would certainly do the job. What a fucking party trick that would be. But the prospect of being imprisoned in a government facility for military research isn't something I'm at all interested in.

But what good is having a superpower if you can't tell

anyone?

⋅————— ✳ —————⋅

BY THE END of the day, I feel pretty confident in my newfound ability, even more excited to think that it's going to cut down on my commute time. I close my eyes to visualize the alley beside my local grocery store. There's a change in noise and I open my eyes, only to find myself staring directly into the face of an elderly woman with her shopping cart.

"Oh, holy shit—"

She narrows her eyes at me. "Watch your language, young man." She shakes her head, her handkerchief fluttering in the breeze, then slowly walks around me toward the back entrance of the adjoining building.

Wait. Did she not notice? How could she not see someone suddenly appearing in front of her? "I, uh, was on the ground and...wasn't watching where I was going. Sorry." She doesn't even bother to turn around but waves me off as she continues on her way, like nothing extraordinary just happened. I jog to the end of the alley, the street is busy. Maybe, just one more test...

There's a young couple walking toward me, holding hands. I Jump just in front of them, so close they have to stop.

"Hey, watch where you're going, man," the guy says. They break apart to move around me, but don't look back as they continue down the street.

"Did you not just see what I did?" I ask.

"I saw you step in front of us like an asshole," he says. He shakes his head then continues walking.

Weird. No one seems to be paying any attention to me at all. Maybe I don't have to worry about the government coming for me. Not like I'd flaunt it anyway, but it's good to know this power is going completely unnoticed.

I Jump back to the roof of my apartment and continue testing out just how far I can go. At one point, I find a stray cat and I attempt to Jump with it in my arms. Amazingly enough, it works, which opens up the possibility of being able to Jump with people. I wonder if someone would notice the Jump if they're moving with me? The thought of Jumping Alex and I to work to save on transportation time causes me to laugh so hard I end up wheezing.

•———— ✳ ————•

ALEX KNOCKS on my door sometime after midnight, so he must just be getting home from work. I take a deep breath, trying to contain myself from simply blurting out that I've turned into Nightcrawler from *X-Men* overnight.

"Hey, man," I say, opening the door for him to walk in. He hands me a paper take-out bag and I smell the cheeseburger, my mouth salivating as I realize I didn't have any dinner.

"Mistake on the order, thought you'd be hungry," he says, making his way into the apartment.

"Thanks," I say and lead the way to the couch as Alex follows.

"How was work?" I ask, opening the bag and pulling out the foil wrapped burger.

Alex is smiling in a goofy way. "It was good. Freezer door is busted again. Someone's coming in to fix it."

"Right." I cock my eyebrow at him. "Why are you in such a good mood?"

He shrugs, his smile growing even wider.

"Dude, what?" I ask.

"I have a date," he blurts.

I raise my eyebrows, surprised. Alex never goes on dates, which is strange because even I can admit he's good-looking enough to pull almost any girl he could want.

"Really?" I ask. "Who with?"

"With Elora."

I feel my stomach twist violently, and I fight hard to keep my face impassive. "Oh, really?"

"Yeah, she's gorgeous, don't you think?"

I nod. "Yeah, I guess so."

Alex continues on as if he hasn't heard me. "I mean, she is, even with the bruising on her face, compliments of you."

I roll my eyes. "It was an accident. I don't know how many more times I can apologize."

"I'm not saying it wasn't." He laughs. "I guess just not the kind of first impression you want to make."

"Yeah."

"She's pretty cool, too. We got to talking after work tonight. We're going to go out on Sunday since both of us are off."

I take another bite of my cheeseburger, though my appetite has vanished. "Right. Well, that's awesome. I hope it goes well."

"I'm kind of nervous, to be honest. It's been a while."

I suddenly feel bad for being jealous. I have had my fair share of women over the past two years, and in that time, Alex never complained or acted jealous. In fact, he often offered to be my wingman, and I was grateful. It isn't his fault that I'm so fucked up I never feel a connection with anyone.

I smile at him. "Well, I'm happy for you. What are you planning on doing?"

He looks at me sheepishly. "Bowling."

I burst out laughing. "But you're a terrible bowler! You'll just embarrass yourself."

He punches me in the arm. "Maybe she'll find it endearing? Besides, she says she's never been before, so we'll likely be equally terrible."

"Sounds like fun."

He goes silent for a few moments before finally asking, "You don't mind, do you?"

I look back at him as I stuff the last bit of cheeseburger into my mouth. "Mind what?"

"Me asking Elora out?"

Yes, I mind! That girl is fucking gorgeous and infuriating and somehow clearer to me than anything else has been in two years. "No, why would I mind?"

Alex shrugs. "Because I know you, Mr. Casanova. Figured she'd be right up your alley, but I guess the iced coffee and elbowing her in the face didn't help your cause."

I push his shoulder. "Yeah, definitely not, but no, I don't mind."

"Great," he says and stands. "You working tomorrow?"

"Yeah."

"Me too. Want to hit the gym together before?"

I nod. Can't exactly tell Alex that I've had more of a workout Jumping across rooftops than I ever could at the gym.

"Right, night then."

"Thanks for dinner," I say, and he salutes me as he walks out of the door.

After a few minutes, I turn off the TV, head into the bathroom, and turn on the shower. I'm still sweaty from earlier, and I strip down, throwing my clothes into the hamper by the door. The steam fogs up the mirror and my glasses, but before I take them off, I catch sight of something.

I wipe the steam from my lenses and step toward the mirror, my fingers tracing along circles embedded amongst the scars on my chest. I back up, flicking the extra light above the mirror on, but they're gone. I look down at myself and then into the mirror again. I'm sure I saw something, felt it even. I shake my head and get into the shower. I just learned how to teleport, circles in my scars can wait until tomorrow.

7

ELORA

My day off is as dull as they usually are. I am looking forward to going back to work on Thursday because there isn't much else to do. I don't have any friends that I keep in touch with from other jobs, finding we generally fall out of touch pretty quickly. Almost as if we were never really friends at all.

I made a quick trip to the grocery store this morning. My breath nearly stopped when I spotted a man in the line up ahead of me at the checkout with the same colour hair as me. For a moment, it felt thrilling, as if I knew him, but when he turned and smiled at me, nothing registered. I was a stranger to him, and my joy sank like a stone under water.

I did another load of laundry when I got home and cleaned up my bathroom. Clearly, I'm avoiding my kitchen. There are still towels on the floor and I'm nervous about using the sink. I think about calling my landlord to let them know there is something funny going on with it, but I also don't want them to think I broke it. I don't have the extra money to pay for a plumbing issue.

All I can think about is that little fish made of water that gently swam toward me amidst the suspended droplets of water.

I finally get up and clean the kitchen. I pile the wet towels in a basket by the door and use the mop to clean up the rest of the water from the tiles. I face the sink, looking at the tap and the pile of dirty dishes still needing to be washed. I square my shoulders and take a deep breath, squinting my eyes closed as I turn the tap on. Water gushes out in a completely normal way. I let go an enormous sigh of relief.

As lunch time approaches, I decide to make a can of soup, and when the flame ignites under the burner, my wrists itch again. I scratch at them absently, breathing deeply as the sting of my sharp nails claw at the rough skin. I turn back to the pot of soup when the flame shoots up into the air. I stumble backward, nearly crashing into the opposite wall as another burst of flame shoots upward. I reach for the dial to turn off the burner, but the stove is encased in flames, the heat of it licking against my skin as I fall backward against the counter.

I look around desperately for the fire extinguisher, but I have no idea where it is. Staring back at the menacing flames encasing the stove top, I can't help but admire the beauty of it. Mesmerizing colours of red, orange, and yellow calm my thundering heart. The dancing of the hot air whips upward and outward like something liquid and gas all at once. It's what causes me to reach out to it—to stretch my scarred hand into that flame without fear. Rather, with something like reverence.

The flames are warm as they encase my fingers, crawling up my skin, the heat like an old friend. The light above my head flickers again. I reach out my other hand—the flames jumping between my fingers like a bridge, then disappearing into the air. The flames are back to just underneath the burner and as I stare wide-eyed and amazed, there appears to be no damage.

I flop down onto the floor, the light steady again as the pulsing in my ears dissipates. What the hell just happened?

I sit cross-legged on the floor and reach my fingers back out. I envision the flames leaping toward me, and before I finish the thought, there they are again, warm little flames cradled in my hand. I flex my palm and they grow taller, wider, the size of a beach ball, then shrink again as though my mind is commanding the fire. Is that what's happening? Am *I* doing this? On purpose?

I close my palms together, and they're gone. The only sound in my apartment is the soup boiling and my heavy breathing. I stand on shaking legs. I feel tired, but my mind is alive and whirring. Spinning with the ramifications of what all of this means.

I look at the kitchen sink again.

"I wonder…"

I take a few steps toward the sink and turn on the tap—the water flowing into it and making a slurping noise as it sinks down the drain. I reach out my hand and a smile pulls up the sides of my mouth as a little clear fish made of sparkling water swims toward me, around me, brushing against my cheeks, the cool mist of it calming the flush of my skin.

"Holy shit!"

I press against the energy of the water, and it scatters into a thousand droplets hanging in the air, spinning around me. I clench my hands and flames erupt from my palms, swirling around the room and mixing through the water like some beautiful mosaic, encapsulating me in a cocoon of fire and water.

I release a breath and clench my hands as a bolt of energy radiates from my head to my fingertips. Then everything is gone. The water evaporates and the flames dissipate and I am left standing in my single room apartment in utter awe at my own power.

⋅———— ✳ ————⋅

MARIAH:

OMG, Elora, you didn't tell me you're going on a date with Alex?? 🫢

Lilli:
Seriously? My God, he is so fucking hot. So jealous.

Mackenzie:
You guys would look so cute together as a couple, though.

Mariah:
Right? He never asks girls out. He's always out here wing-manning Will and then going home alone.

Priscilla:
We can all agree that Will doesn't need a wingman. Boy just needs to be in the vicinity.

Lilli:
You're not wrong, Cilla. Even though he looks like that character from *Trailer Park Boys* with those glasses.

Mariah:
Aww, Lil, be nice! It's not his fault he's Mr. Magoo.

Priscilla:
Maybe that's why he's so good at fucking? Relies on more than his eyes?

Jenni:
Oh my God, Cilla, can you stop?

Priscilla:
Stop what?

Lilli:
Jenni's upset because she fucked Will and thought it would mean more than a one-night stand.

Jenni:
Fuck you, Lilli.

Mariah:
All right, all right. Jenni, I warned you. And him too. But does anyone listen to me? No!

Jenni:
Yeah, yeah, I know, no one to blame but myself.

Elora:
Thanks, Mariah! Alex is so sweet. He's taking me bowling! I've never been before. What do I wear?

When I wake up on Thursday morning to the slew of messages in our work group chat, I feel disoriented. It's as though the past twenty-four hours have been some wild dream, but as I lie in bed, pulling the droplets of water from the condensation on my window into a large ball of water above me, it finally starts to sink in that this is real.

As the ball of water hangs in the air, a new thought occurs to me, and I reach out my finger to touch it with utter curiosity. My skin touches the edge of the water and icy tendrils spread like veined spider webs until the ball drops into my hand, a perfect sphere of ice.

"Huh," I say, tossing the ball into the air where the icy sphere bursts apart then evaporates, tiny snowflakes falling down onto my shoulders, and I shiver as my phone vibrates on the bed.

Mariah:
You've never been bowling before? OMG adorable. Go with cute and comfy. Something to show off that fantastic ass of yours and a cute top that's easy to move around in. I'd stay away from a dress, to be honest. Also, you'll have to wear shoes that they rent you at the bowling alley, so make sure you bring socks.

Elora:
Really? Rental shoes? Gross.

Mackenzie:
That's why I haven't set foot in a bowling alley in a decade. Too traumatized.

Mariah:
It's not that bad, but they can definitely cramp your style.

Elora:
OK, noted.

Lilli:
Happy to do an outfit check for you!!

Elora:
Thanks, Lilli!

My phone vibrates and I notice there's a new Instagram message in my inbox. I smile, my stomach somersaulting with excitement when I see it's from Alex.

Alex:
Hey, just wanted to say hi and I'll see you at work later. Hope you're feeling better.

My face. I totally forgot. I jump out of bed, rushing over to the bathroom and flick the light on as I look in the mirror. My face looks…normal. There's only a bit of yellowish bruising left under each eye, but other than that, my freckles are in the right place, and my blue eyes are shining brighter than ever. I laugh as I touch my cheeks. The pain is minimal now too, and I'm sure I'll be able to cover up what's left of the bruising with makeup.

Elora:
You're sweet. I'm feeling much better. See you later.

After spending a little too long on my hair and makeup, hoping to impress Alex, I walk into the Flying Weasel around four for my first solo shift. Thursdays are busy because they're pub nights for students, so it's all hands on deck, both behind the swing door and out front. I'm wearing my most form fitting black dress today. It exposes the dip between my breasts but also shows off my waist before tightening around my hips. With my hair curled and a little more makeup than usual, I think I look quite pretty.

As I go by the pass-through, I spot Alex, who stands back and blinks at me for a second before using his lips to blow a low whistle. He leans against the counter, his strong arms apparent under his chef's coat.

"Goddamn, girl. Are you a parking ticket? Because you've got fine written all over you."

I stare for a moment, then burst into a fit of laughter. Alex smiles back, and when I finally compose myself, I ask, "Seriously? That's the line you go with? You realize I can still change my mind about that date, right?"

He holds up his hands. "I know, I know…that was lame. But seriously, you look," he takes a long pause, looking me up and down, "unbelievable."

"Oh my God, will you stop flirting and get me my burgers, please?" Lilli appears next to me with a wink, her dark lipstick and hair on point, and Alex makes a big show of promptly getting back to work, but he smiles at me again, and I feel my lips twist. Oh man, it's going to be hard to concentrate tonight.

I put my bag and coat in my locker and switch my shoes to my black flats. I pull the satin of my gloves up around my elbows, followed by the black latex ones, securing them in place, then turn to go toward the front to see what my section looks like for the night. But as I look up, the figure of the person I want to see the least is blocking the door.

Will.

"Hey there, sunshine," he says, stalking into the room like a cat who's cornering a mouse.

My stomach clenches hard. The size of his body towers over me even from several feet away. His hazel eyes widen behind his glasses and those lips make me temporarily lose the ability to think.

"Don't call me that," I mutter, and I'm sick to hear it come out sounding like a petulant child.

Will looks at me in that same strange way as that first day. Like he isn't sure whether he hates me or doesn't know where he's seen me before. He pulls his bag over his shoulder and off his chest, and I notice the slice of firm skin under the bottom of his t-shirt that peeks out at me.

"Why not?" he asks, taking a step into the small room. "I think it suits you. You're just so…what's the word? Friendly." His tone drips with sarcasm and I feel anger blush my cheeks and the back of my neck. He steps toward me, and on instinct, I step back. He stops and looks me over. "Don't worry, I'll try my very best not to elbow you in the face again," he says.

I roll my eyes as I busy myself with my apron—the strings cutting into my hips as I tie it around my waist. When I look up, he's watching me hungrily, like he's undressing me with his eyes. My mouth twists with a combination of annoyance and feeling somewhat flattered. Being under his stare makes me feel exposed. I wonder if this is how he makes all girls feel. That he's somehow blessed with the inherent ability to make women go crazy for him. I refuse to be one of them.

"Thank you," I say curtly, "and I'll be sure to stay out of your way."

Before I can move, he takes another few steps toward me, closing the gap between us and blocking my escape to the door. He pushes his glasses up his nose and I see the flecks of gold amongst the green in his earthy eyes.

"Move."

I feel a sudden swell of anger flash through me. "Excuse me?"

"Move *please*," he says, his voice a little lower, more dangerous, and I feel my legs turn to jelly at the sound of it.

"What's your problem?" I ask angrily.

"You're standing in front of my locker," he says, pointing directly over my shoulder.

I turn to look at the locker and notice the name "Will Reed" on a piece of tape on the locker behind me. I turn back around to find him smirking, and I feel like a complete idiot.

"Oh…right, sorry."

I move toward the kitchen, trying to make a quick escape.

"Are you always so defensive?"

I spin around, more flustered than ever, and stumble on my unsteady legs. How dare he make me feel this way! "Only when I'm dealing with arrogant pricks."

A sharp laugh bursts out of his mouth. "Listen, sunshine, I might be full of myself, but you're not exactly making it easy to be friends."

I make an unconscious scoffing noise and my wrists itch beneath my gloves. My God, what I would give to side swipe this asshole with a tidal wave right now.

"Also," he says, taking off his coat and tossing it into his locker, "if you're this easy to rile up, working with you is going to be so much fun."

I narrow my eyes, my brain searching for something to say, but I hear someone calling my name from up front and so with one last disdainful look at Will, I stalk off back toward the dining room. I hear him chuckling behind me, and I just know that working with Will is going to be the death of me.

When I get back into the dining room, Mariah is waving me over near the supply station.

"Hey!" I say as I approach her.

"Someone's here to see you," she says.

My heart does a full backflip layout at the words. Someone is here, for me? Maybe it is the red-headed man from the grocery store. My heart is beating so fast I feel faint.

Mariah seems to mistake the joyous panic on my face for excitement as she points toward the bar where a man is sitting on his own, staring at me.

It's Hunter. The guy I waited on the past few nights who liked to stare.

I feel that burst of excitement deflate as a shiver slithers up my spine. I try to keep my face as unchanged as possible. I should have known better than to think something so stupid—Than to have hope.

"What's he doing here?"

"Says he came here to see you," Mariah says, shrugging.

I raise my eyebrows at her. "Alone?"

"Must have," she says, then she walks off.

Hunter throws me a little wave and I push a smile onto my face before walking over to him.

"Hey there, beautiful," he says.

I feel myself inwardly cringe as his eyes travel over my body. Somehow when Hunter does it, I feel nauseous, but when Will does it…

"Hey, how are you?" I ask, trying my best to be friendly.

"Wow, your bruising is almost gone, huh? That was fast," he says, pointing to my face.

I brush my hair away. "Oh yeah, I heal quickly. Just another one of my many talents."

"I asked for a table in your section, but it's busy here on Thursdays," he says.

I look around, realizing the slight frenzy of the room and the three tables that are waiting for me to make my way to them.

"Yeah, I need to get to work. It was nice seeing you," I say.

He sticks out his palm toward me, as though hoping I'll shake his hand. He looks at me expectantly, and I feel awkward as I take his hand in mine. I feel the crinkle of paper between our palms and his pupils dilate when he realizes I've felt it.

I grip onto whatever he's given me and back away, taking a quick detour through the line to see what it is out of his sight. When I open my satin-covered palm, I realize that there's a folded up twenty-dollar bill in my hand. As I stare at it and swallow, I feel nervous bout the implications of what it means. About how uncomfortable the whole situation makes me feel.

I take a deep breath, square my shoulders, and tuck the money into my apron. I can't exactly give it back even if it's what I want to do. The thought of an awkward conversation if I return it makes me tense. What is he implying by giving me this? That he can buy my attention? That he can buy *me*?

I'm still shaken when I feel another set of eyes on me, ones that make me feel exposed and vulnerable. I look up and Will is staring at me, that same moody expression set on his face, as always.

8

WILL

Something's wrong

Elora looks unnerved. She came back onto the line for no other purpose than to collect herself. Did someone say something to her? The thought makes my anger flare like a cobra ready to strike, and the muscles of my back twitch with the urge to Jump to her—to ask if she is okay.

Her eyes meet mine from across the kitchen and she holds my gaze for a few moments. As if suddenly remembering herself, she takes a deep breath in and rolls her eyes, flips me off, then tucks whatever is in her hand into her apron, pushing her way out of the opposite swing door.

"Will, you got that Cobb salad?"

I look to Alex, who's working the grill next to Brandon. I suddenly feel guilty for the conversation I had earlier with Elora. I meant to rile her up because it's simply too easy to do. But I shouldn't be doing that, no matter how fun it is. Alex already told me he's taking Elora out on a date, and even though it's like an itch on my back I can't reach, I respect my friend and should stay out of it. He has been a good friend to me over the two years we've known each other. I'm not about to throw that away for a girl I hardly know.

Absently, I put together the salad before holding it out to Brandon. "Uh yeah, here."

He slides the grilled chicken on the plate, then places it on the pass-through shelf.

Brandon adds the steak dinner and hits the bell for a server to run it to a table. Mackenzie is there a moment later to take it to her table.

"Wait," Brandon says, staring at the salad, then turning toward me. "Will, there's no egg on that Cobb."

I blink and look at the salad on the counter.

"Oh shit, sorry. Here…"

Mackenzie passes me back the plate, and I put the egg I had already cut up onto the plate for her.

"You all right?" Alex asks me.

I nod, shifting the weight off my sore foot. It still throbs dully from where I cut it on the glass. "Yeah, fine. Just a bit distracted, that's all. Won't happen again."

But I know it might, because Elora walks back again to grab some plates and cutlery rolls for her table. She looks agitated, but I glance away before she sees me watching her.

"How's it going on your first solo shift?" Brandon asks Elora through the pass-through.

I glance up, catching her face at the edge of my vision. Her smile makes the breath catch in my throat, and I find myself jealous of Brandon as she says, "It's busy, but going well so far, I think."

Elora lingers, casting a subtle smile at Alex, who winks back at her, and I feel nauseated at the exchange. Is that what's bothering her? I know it gets busy on Thursdays because of pub night. Maybe that's it, just new job stress. Happens to the best of us.

"All right, boys, let's tighten things up a bit, yeah?" Brandon calls out to all of us.

I roll my eyes and catch sight of Alex holding up a pair of tongs behind Brandon's back, mouthing, "Yes, chef," opening and closing the tongs like some kind of crocodile's mouth.

I laugh, and Alex sticks his tongue out at me while jerking his chin toward the pass-through.

A few hours go by, and things are busy as shit. Orders are piling up, and I barely have time to think about anything other than the chits in front of me. My foot is aching from standing and hurrying around, but Alex is keeping the mood light by cracking the odd joke. A few times, Elora comes to pick something up at my spot on the line, but she doesn't make eye contact, simply stabs her chit, grabs her plates, then heads back out into the dining room. I noticed she hums under her breath while she works, and I find myself distracted whenever I hear her.

"Ugh, murder me now," I hear Mariah say as she slumps through the door and leans heavily against the counter.

"Problem?" I ask.

She looks up at me—her face annoyed. "Just this one table. Bunch of ladies complaining about how long things are taking. I'm just like…you know you came in on the busiest night of the week, right?"

"Need me to spit in their food?" I joke to her quietly enough so that Brandon doesn't hear.

She smiles. "No, but thanks for the offer. I'll let you know if I need help disposing of some bodies later, though."

I laugh as she grabs a pitcher of ice water and heads back out.

A chit pops out of the printer, and I reach for it, but as the door swings closed behind Mariah, I can see Elora standing at the bar. Even with my shitty eyesight, it's easy to spot her from how bright and clear she is. She's standing next to some guy, sitting at the bar. Some douche in a beanie who touches her arm, and she visibly flinches at the contact.

Silence presses in on my ears and the door to the dining room freezes mid-swing. I pull my eyes away from Elora to look around. A burger is hovering in mid-air above the grill, the burst of flames suspended beneath the grate. Alex is paused, pushing a plate through the pass-through toward Lilli who appears frozen, her nose crinkled in laughter at something Alex must have said. I look behind me, where a moment ago water rushed out of the tap from the sink, but is now stopped mid-stream.

"Hello?" I ask somewhat stupidly, as if someone is pranking me.

I pull my glasses off my face and clean the lenses, then cup my ears to make sure I haven't gone deaf. I take a few tentative steps toward Brandon, who doesn't move. Nobody moves. I wave my hand in front of his face. Nothing. Without even thinking, I Jump to the other side of the pass-through next to Lilli, whose face is still scrunched up with laughter. I glance up at the clock on the wall, the second hand still and unmoving.

"What the fuck…" I whisper, the silence unnerving.

I Jump out into the dining room. I spot Mariah, hovering over her table with a sour smile pressed onto her lips. Everyone is frozen. Why am I not stuck? Did I do this? Did I…stop time?

The scene I glimpse through the door brings my attention back. Elora is standing next to the man at the bar. His hand is pressed against the bare skin above her elbow. I Jump to the spot next to them. I've seen this asshole before. He's here all the time and likes to leer at the girls. Mariah always considered him harmless, but now he's decided he wants to touch something that doesn't belong to him. And while Elora doesn't belong to me either, I can see from her expression and the way her body is pulled back that she is not interested in this kind of attention from him.

He's holding a beer in his hand, so I tip the bottom of the glass upward, the liquid frozen but poised to fall right in his lap. I turn back to Elora, whose eyes are slightly glazed, her body curved in on itself out of what appears to be revulsion at the idea of being touched by this prick.

I want to punch him. I want to take his fingers and snap them like twigs for touching her without her consent. I can hardly blame him for wanting to—she is stunning. But she is interested in Alex, and the bitter sting clings to me.

Something moves outside, and I feel like I'm being watched. The hair on the back of my neck is standing up. There's a subtle shift of the light and a blur of movement through the window behind the bar. Something or someone isn't frozen. I Jump into the street, the damp night air chilling my face from the heat of the kitchens. I look up and down the street, but there's nothing there. It's quiet, the cars frozen in place, the motion of the trees halted mid-breeze. It must have been some trick of the eye. Possibly even my own reflection. But the thought that something is there watching me from the shadows crawls like bugs under my skin.

I Jump back to the kitchen and look around again, realizing I don't know how to stop this. My heart rate spikes as I start to panic. What if I'm stuck? I didn't exactly flip a switch to make it happen. It happened on its own. Maybe if I just visualize everyone moving again, it'll stop? Just like how I have to see where I'm going when I Jump across spaces. I quickly Jump back to my station, close my eyes, pressing my hands against my face. I think about the noises of the kitchen, the ticking of the clock, the laughter of my friends, the splashing of the water in the sink.

And then my ears are flooded with noise. I open my eyes and everyone is moving again. The burger falls back to the grill, Lilli laughs, and in the distance, the door swings open slightly again. Then I hear the sound of a beer falling into the lap of the douchebag who dared touch Elora Green.

ELORA SEEMS in a good mood after that, although she doesn't project that energy toward me. Why would she? It's not like I can tell her about any of this. Every time she comes into the back, she and Alex smile and flirt, and it all makes me want to crawl into a hole and die. Funnily enough, Mariah is the only one who seems to notice my bad mood.

"What's your deal tonight, Will?" she asks.

I huff out a great breath of air. "Sore."

"Oh, well, you should ask Brandon if you can be first cut," she says, gesturing toward Brandon, who is cleaning up the counter from a sauce spill.

I look over but shake my head. I'm not about to take advantage of leaving early simply because I hate seeing Elora and Alex flirt with each other or because of my sore foot. "Nah, I'm fine," I say, passing her the Caesar salad she's waiting for.

"Do you want something? Tylenol?"

I give her a small smile. "No, I'll be fine, I swear."

"Well, just let me know if you need anything," she says, turning to look at her side. "Oh, hey, El, exhausted yet?"

Elora steps up next to her. She's due to pick up a baked pasta dish from me, but it isn't ready yet.

She grabs the counter and leans back, stretching her neck from side to side, and I can't help but stare at her pale, gorgeous skin. I never thought of a neck being sexy before, but I'm hypnotized by hers.

"Yeah, I'm on my last table, though, thankfully. That Hunter guy is gone, too. He kind of gives me the creeps."

Mariah frowns. "Really? Did he do anything?"

Elora lowers her voice. "He keeps giving me money, then tries to pull me in for a hug. It's making me *really* uncomfortable."

There's a monster clawing its way through my chest as anger

spills out of every vein in my body. So that's why she had looked so distraught earlier. That asshole is trying to buy his right to touch her.

"It's fine, though. He's gone. Spilled his beer on himself, actually. Serves him right. Hopefully, he's too embarrassed to come back," she says, shaking her head.

"Ew, what a creep," Mariah exclaims. "Well, if he does, and he tries anything, don't worry. These boys have our backs. Don't you, Will?"

I look up, not expecting to be dragged into this conversation, and my eyes flick between the two of them. Elora rolls her eyes as though not convinced I would try to help her in any way ever. "Of course."

Mariah smiles, then takes off, but Elora's smile fades as she turns back to me.

She hums as she waits, and waits, and waits, her fingers drumming against the steel countertop in an irritating counter rhythm to her song.

"Is that baked pasta ready yet for 51?"

I gesture to the empty counter between us. "Do you see a baked pasta on the counter?"

"No…"

"Then, it's not ready."

Her eyes flutter closed in frustration. "You know, you don't have to be a total dick all the time."

Shit, it's simply too easy to get her going, and she just looks so damn exquisite when she's mad. "If you simply used those pretty eyes of yours, you could have answered your own question instead of bothering me."

"Yeah, well, being a dick won't make yours any bigger," she says, cocking her eyebrow as I resist the urge to let my mouth fall open. I quickly twist my lips to the side.

Where the fuck did this girl come from? I want to grab that

smart-ass little mouth of hers, press her up against the wall, and teach her some manners.

I lean forward and lower my voice so it doesn't carry. "I think you'll find that my dick is big enough for whatever job needs to be done."

Her cheeks turn bright pink, her freckles darkening across her face, and her eyes widen.

I smirk at the reaction.

"Is your job to constantly annoy me? Because your mouth does enough of that already."

I laugh. "I think you'll find that my mouth is equally talented."

I turn away from her, grabbing the finished pasta dish from the conveyor belt of the oven and setting it on the plate. I toss the garlic bread next to it and place it on the counter between us. She's still staring at me wide-eyed, lips parted.

"Close your mouth, sunshine, and hurry along, or it'll get cold," I say in a low voice. "And don't forget to come back when you need more of me."

An incredulous sharp breath escapes her, and she snaps toward the door, disappearing into the dining room.

I rub my hand against my forehead, brushing aside my slightly damp hair, and laugh through my nose. My God, it is fun to tease her. She gets so worked up and so quickly, too. My mind wanders to what that temper would bring out of her in the bedroom, and I feel my cock twitch. I clear my throat when I notice Alex moving in beside me and gulp down some air.

"What was all that about?" he asks.

I shake my head. "Nothing. Her order wasn't ready yet."

"You're being nice, right?" he asks, his eyes narrowed.

I tilt my head at him. "Of course I am. I'm always nice."

Alex grunts. "Bullshit you are. You can act like a total asshole sometimes. You seem to be particularly hell-bent on making El perfectly aware of what a jerk you can be."

"El? You've all given her a nickname now?"

Alex shrugs. "What's wrong with nicknames?"

I look away from him and wipe down my station. It's not the nickname that bothers me, it's that Alex gets to say it and not me. "Look, she's not exactly a peach herself. But I guess if you're into that…"

"I am," Alex warns.

I raise my hands. "All right, all right, I'll try to be nicer."

"Thank you."

As Alex walks away to clock out now that the rush is over, I spot Elora dropping off an armful of plates at the dishwasher. She leans forward over the edge of the sink, the back of her black dress rising to reveal more of her thighs. I can't help but stare, my body moving closer and closer down the line as I watch her. She's humming again, some beautiful, familiar tune that I can't quite seem to put a name to. I imagine Elora's pretty lips on mine, on my throat, on my…

Water suddenly hits me in the chest, the spray splashing up into my face and coating my glasses. "What the shit?" I yell. I pull my glasses off to clean them, the world falling into a blur of colour, except for the one bright thing that's laughing before me. I push them back on my face to find Elora with her one gloved hand wrapped around the dishwasher sprayer, trying very hard not to smirk.

"Whoops, sorry…it was an accident," she says in a sickly sweet voice.

The water has soaked through my chef's jacket onto the shirt underneath—the fabric clinging to my skin.

"What the hell?" I say, taking a step toward her. My jaw clenches and pressure builds between my molars, but she doesn't back up.

She tilts her head and smirks. "You seemed like you needed a cooling down anyway, so I guess it was a happy accident."

I take another step toward her, and this time, she does back up, her eyes losing their confidence as her back presses against the sink. We stand toe to toe for a moment, those blue eyes scanning my face for my next move. I start undoing the buttons of my jacket.

"What are you doing?" she asks, but her voice catches, and I know I've got her.

"You got my jacket wet," I say quietly.

"Then go change in the back."

I shake my head. "Why? Am I making you uncomfortable?" She sets her face in a frown and doesn't say anything, but her weight shifts and I notice the flush creeping its gentle way across her chest. I take another step toward her, closing the gap between us as I pull the jacket off. "Tell me to stop if you want me to."

Elora glares at me, unblinking, and for a moment, I think I may have stopped Time again. But then she bites down on her bottom lip and I have to resist the urge to use my thumb and pull it back out. I lean toward her and her eyes widen, her upper body arching back away from me as I pull down the dishwasher cover. I catch the scent of her. Vanilla and rain. I can't help but glance briefly at her mouth before stepping away.

"Careful sunshine, wouldn't want you to get *wet*."

I toss the wet jacket into the hamper next to the dishwasher and turn toward the changerooms, leaving Elora wide-eyed and breathless in my wake. The moment I'm out of sight, I take a deep breath. What am I doing? What is *she* doing? Guilt sweeps through me. God, what if Alex saw that? He deserves better than me as a friend if all I can do is continually flirt and fantasize about the girl he likes doing unspeakable things to me. No, I need to be nice and cut the flirting. But, fuck, it's going to be so hard.

· ———— ✴ ———— ·

THE NEXT MORNING, I have one mission before going to work. Figure out how to stop Time again, but unlike with Jumping, I find it's much harder to do, and I get tired quickly. Jumping is like muscle memory. Like I've always been able to do it but have simply not practiced in a while. After a few days of doing it, it's easy, barely something I even need to focus on. I can just simply do it.

But Time…that's a whole different issue. Maybe because it takes more brain power rather than something physical that my body can just do on its own, like walking. No, this is hard and frustrating and exhausting.

I spend almost all of Friday in between naps, trying to rest, and I've only managed to freeze Time once since that first time in the pub. The more I think about it, the more I convince myself it was a fluke. That I simply was just so annoyed that I've made myself believe that the cat outside my window stopped because of some super power.

It's not exactly like I can ask anyone. Yet, there was that movement I spotted outside of the bar. Was there someone else? Maybe someone who can stop Time that has been watching me? The more I think about it, the more it puts me on edge and I end up spending all of Friday night's shift on the verge of panic.

Elora doesn't have a shift tonight, which helps remove one distraction, but every time something falls or someone laughs loudly from the dining room, I feel myself flinch, as if at any moment, someone will discover me and the secret I'm hiding. Even Alex notices when he uses my spare key to barge into my apartment Saturday afternoon as I'm getting ready to leave for my closing shift tonight.

"You all right, man? You seem kind of…I don't know, on edge?"

I wave him off, grabbing some cheese from the fridge. "I'm fine."

He takes the block of cheese out of my hands. "No, you're not, and also why the hell are you limping?"

My foot has gotten worse since I'm almost always standing. "It's nothing, I stepped on some glass a few nights ago. It's just sore. I haven't had time to rest it."

"You're off tomorrow, right?"

I nod.

"Will you promise to just chill here? No running around, no going to the gym, no…whatever the fuck else you do on your days off."

"Great…sounds like a blast."

"Don't be a baby, just binge-watch something, eat junk, and lie on the couch. Fuck, where are my keys?" Alex looks around, checking his pockets.

"You know you still haven't given me your spare. If you did, this wouldn't be such an issue all the time."

Alex rolls his eyes. "I lost my spare."

"Why am I not surprised?" I mutter.

A few moments later, Alex finds his keys on my couch, holding them up to jingle them in front of me.

"Are you still going on your date with little miss Elora?" I can't help the words from spilling out of my mouth, so I turn back to the fridge, looking for something to hide my face in.

"Yes."

"Where exactly are you taking her again?"

"Bowling."

I peer over the fridge door at him. "Right. That'll definitely give you panty access."

He shrugs. "I don't know, I've got a few tricks up my sleeve. I haven't used them in a long time, but we'll see how the evening goes."

I nod and let out a breath. "Right."

"You promise you'll just chill out here Sunday to rest that foot? I really don't feel like taking you to the hospital next week and them needing to amputate your foot."

"They're not going to need to amputate it for stepping on glass."

He holds up his fingers. "Nuh uh, my uncle stepped on a nail once and did nothing about it. He kept working, kept putting on his dirty work boots every day, and it got so bad they had to remove half of his foot."

The image of a mangled foot makes my stomach heave. "All right, all right, I'll just be here Sunday doing nothing all day. Happy?"

Alex nods. "Yes, now get to work. You should've already left by now. You'll be late."

I planned on Jumping to the back alley behind the pub, so I make a big show of leaving my apartment in a hurry, as if I'm actually running late so Alex won't be suspicious. Two years working there and I've only ever been late once, and that's only because the streetcar broke down midway.

When I stroll in the front door of the pub a little while later, it's already busy. Heidi spots me from where she's taken it upon herself to serve a table before some of the other girls arrive.

"Will, can you jump on?" she calls.

I give her the thumbs up to let her know I'm on it.

I quickly change into my uniform, push my glasses up my nose and my hair back off my forehead, the scar above my eyebrow clearly visible. Then, I head out onto the line where Brandon and Raj are holding down the fort.

"Oh, Will, thank God. Can you take over here for me?" Brandon asks, pointing to the grill.

I nod while inwardly groaning. Considering my eyesight is

shit, I'll probably add a few new burns to my hands to go along with my aching foot before the end of the night.

"Hey, Elora! Can you hurry? We had a rush of people come in early," Brandon says over my shoulder.

I look up, and there she is.

Our eyes meet, and she grimaces at the realization that I am working tonight, too. She disappears for a few minutes, then reappears, passing me as she ties her apron around her waist.

"Hey, there, sunshine," I call after Brandon retreats to the prep station.

She looks at me pointedly. "I told you not to call me that."

But I have to, because if I say her name, I will tumble over that precarious edge I'm on. I'll want her name, her mouth, her taste on my tongue, always.

She has her hair up today, piled high on her head, a few copper pieces falling around her face and behind her small ears. Her cheeks are rosy, her freckles scattered across her face and down her long pale neck, disappearing under the neckline of her dress. Those hauntingly beautiful eyes are rimmed with dark liner and mascara, the contrast of the black and blue making the back of my neck feel a little too hot. She's wearing that little black dress again, the one that fits her far too well. The way it shows off every single dangerous curve makes the blood in my veins crackle.

She is the sunshine. At least to me. My eyes almost burn from looking at her straight on and, my God, does she look fucking fantastic.

Nice…I promised Alex I'd be nice. No flirting. "You look nice today." Fuck, well, that didn't last long. I don't even think I'm capable of not flirting with her.

She stands completely still, narrowing her eyes at me. "What?"

"I said," leaning forward, my hands on the counter, "you look nice today."

She tilts her head. "What is this? Some kind of stupid prank?"

I roll my eyes. "Can't you just accept a compliment?"

"From you? Hardly."

I pull my eyes away. God, she really does dislike me.

"Did Alex put you up to this?" she asks, crossing her arms over her chest.

"No," I lie.

She places her gloved hands on the counter across from me. "Whatever little game you're playing, I'm not interested."

I swallow and turn away. "Noted."

When I turn around again, she's gone and my vision goes blurry for a moment as I blink rapidly, trying to pull it back into focus, or at least as much as it can go.

Be nice, I think again. It's going to be a lot harder to be nice when she is going out of her way to push my buttons.

· ——— ✴ ——— ·

THE PUB is busy as shit and everyone is running around non-stop. Of course, I've already burned myself twice on the edge of the grill. I swear, by this point, there is probably more of my skin charred on the grill than should be legal.

My foot is aching more than ever, and I'm sweating profusely. I'm grateful that there's a slight lull in the orders, but I know it will pick up again soon.

"Hey," I say to Brandon. "Do you mind if I just pop outside for a few minutes? I need a bit of air."

He wipes his brow with the back of his sleeve. "Yeah, man, of course. Don't be long, though."

I nod and pull off my hat, shaking my hair out and brushing it back away from my face. I pass the fridges and freezer on my way toward the back door, then step out into the cool night air. I lean against the brick wall, tilting my head back and inhaling the smell of the city. There's a hint of cigarettes in the air, likely from the small smoking area by the front of the pub.

I take a few long, deep breaths and close my eyes.

The crashing sound of a trash can falling over bursts upon my eardrums, and I jolt away from the wall, looking for the cause of the noise. Someone is standing at the end of the alleyway. He's tall, and all dressed in black. His hood is up and I can't see his face, but he's staring straight at me.

"Can I help you?" I yell down, my voice echoing.

No answer.

"Hey!" I yell, taking a few steps closer. "What the hell do you want?"

He tilts his head to the side, and I can vaguely make out the white from his teeth as he smiles at me. There's something utterly menacing about that smile, but I take a few steps closer.

There's a sudden eruption of noise as the wind whips around me, leaves and debris from the alley flying up into the air to encircle me. It dissipates as quickly as it came and when I look up, the man is gone.

"Hello?" I yell.

I run down the alley toward the front of the building, but there's no one there. A chill slithers down my spine and there's sweat dripping down my back, my hands clenching at my sides.

I pull open the door to the kitchen and head back inside, glancing one last time over my shoulder at where the man stood. There's still nothing, but unease settles into the deepest part of my bones. I push my glasses up off my face and rub my eyes with my hands. In some ways, I feel like discovering my new abilities is a bit of a curse. Like somehow I'm destined to find my way into trouble simply by existing.

I walk back toward the front of the line, but there's a muffled banging sound from my right where the walk-in fridge and freezers are. I stop, trying to listen over the noisy clattering of the dishwasher and grill and fryers. There it is again, followed by a heart-stopping scream for help. In seconds, my hand is wrapping around the busted handle of the freezer, pulling, but the thick steel door is stuck. There's more banging on the door and another muffled scream on the other side.

"Don't panic!" I yell at the door. "I'll get you out, just hold on."

But whoever is stuck inside doesn't seem to be able to hear me and the banging continues, the sound of their screams ripping through my heart.

"Will, what's wrong?" Brandon appears from around the corner.

"Someone's stuck inside. The door won't open," I say, trying to get a different angle against the lever to open the door.

"Fuck, someone's supposed to be coming to fix it on Monday," he says and runs around the corner again.

The sound of a pleading voice reaches me through the door. My heart stutters and I freeze. "Elora?" I yell.

The fluorescent lights above me flicker, then go out entirely. A blood-curdling scream sounds from the inside the freezer. My heart is pounding as panic sets in. Like I'm being pulled away from the shore by a strong current and I'm going to drown. I have the fleeting thought that I could just Jump in and possibly Jump her back out, but then she might know. I still don't know if Jumping with someone else will be the same as appearing in front of strangers.

"Elora, just hold on, we're going to get you out!" I yell, my lips practically pressed against the edge of the door.

"Will, watch out!" Brandon is back with a crowbar, sticking it into the spot behind the latch of the handle.

"Here," he says, nodding his head at me, "grab the end."

I wrap my hands around the crowbar and together we push until finally there's a sharp crack like ice snapping over a frozen lake, and the door springs open. There's a moment of silence as I stare into the complete darkness of the freezer, the door opening and the air puffing out in clouds as it warms. The lights flicker back on and I spot the tiny crouched figure of Elora in the centre of the room, her bare arms wrapped around her knees, her body trembling so hard she's vibrating.

"Elora?" I say, taking a step in toward her.

She looks up sharply, those blue eyes almost glowing with intensity, her mascara smudged under each eye. She stands, and quicker than I thought she could move, she darts past me out of the door.

"Fuck," Brandon says. "Hope she's okay. I thought Heidi had put a sign on the freezer to let people know the handle is broken."

"Right," I mutter, spinning around to look at him.

"I'm going to go get one of the girls to check on her," he says, then he's gone.

I spot something black on the floor amidst a puddle of water. I stoop down to pick it up and realize they're Elora's gloves. Did she take them off in her panic? Maybe to get a better grip on the door handle? I walk back out of the freezer when I spot something odd on the wall on either side of the door frame.

These walls are covered in ice almost two inches thick, but there are two small handprints melted right through to the steel walls. I take a closer look, reaching my finger out to touch the melted outlines in the frost, and immediately yank my hand away. The heat of it burns the tip of my finger. Did she…melt ice this thick with her hands?

9

ELORA

I collapse against the bathroom door, a great shuddering sob wrenching its way out of my mouth, the pain of my raw voice causing more tears to prickle up in my eyes. I flick the light on and the fluorescents stutter into life above my head. My heart is racing, and it's difficult to catch my breath as another panic attack creeps in with every inhale. I'm not getting enough oxygen to satisfy my brain.

I snap the toilet seat lid closed and sit down harshly, lowering my head between my knees like someone told me to do at the hospital two years ago when I had my first panic attack. I feel like some giant snake has wrapped itself around my body and is slowly squeezing the life out of me.

There's sharp knock on the door.

"Elora?"

It sounds like Mackenzie's voice.

I swallow hard. "Yes?"

"Are you all right? Do you need anything?"

I take a few sharp inhales, trying to steady my voice, but it betrays me, still wavering as I say, "I just need a few minutes."

There's a pause, then a small, "Sure."

I try to envision a calm, peaceful stream. Try to imagine the sound of water as it trickles over rocks and leaves in a steady rhythm. Slowly, it helps, the vice-like grip around my chest and heart easing. I'm able to lift my head, and I lean back, resting against the cool tile wall.

Another knock at the door.

I nod, trying to force myself to get up. "I'm coming."

"Elora?"

My eyes snap open. Is that Will?

I momentarily forgot he opened the door to the freezer. The thought of that jerk seeing me terrified out of my mind and at my most vulnerable makes me feel nauseous, and I have to take a deep breath to stop the bile from rising up my throat.

When I'm sure I won't fall over, I stand up, gripping the edge of the sink with my hands. My bare hands. Fuck, where are my gloves?

"Elora?" Will calls again. "Are you okay?"

"I'm fine. I'll be out in a minute."

A pause. "I have your gloves."

I look at the door that separates us, then down at my exposed forearms and wrists. The hundreds of crisscrossing scars are vibrant against my pale skin. Shit, I don't want him to see. I know exactly what he'll think. Poor, sad, stupid Elora must have tried to kill herself. He'll probably make some joke about how I can't even do that right. It's happened before and I don't know if I can hear it again.

"Just…can you just leave them outside of the door, please?" I call, my voice trembling.

"I can, but I'd like to make sure you're okay."

I shake my head and rest my forehead against the door. Why does it have to be him?

"Just—just leave them…" my voice shakes harder, "please."

There's another long pause and a quiet, "All right."

I wait a few more minutes, then grip the doorknob. The door opens an inch, and thankfully, Will is gone. I look down and my black gloves are folded neatly on the floor. I snatch them up and shut the door again. Pulling them on immediately makes me feel better, less exposed, less vulnerable.

It was stupid to take them off in the freezer, but my hands were burning. Burning so bad I thought I might burn the fabric right off myself. And I was freezing and my emotions got the better of me. I don't really know what came over me. The frigid air sucked the courage and logic right out of me, and the darkness…

A thought pops into my head, and my eyes find themselves in the mirror. They found me crawling out of a frozen lake. The dream I had of drowning, freezing, numb—was my panic triggered by the freezer? I only went in there for a new tub of ice cream, but the moment that door wouldn't open and the air hit my skin, my brain completely shut down.

I glance at myself in the mirror, taking some tissues and trying to clean up my face where my makeup has smudged. Thankfully, my hair isn't too bad. A few more pieces have fallen around my face, but nothing too messy. I smooth out my dress and apron, then face the door and inevitably the embarrassment of getting locked in the kitchen freezer.

I walk out past the line. Brandon and Heidi are by the swing door talking.

"Oh my God, are you all right?" Heidi asks.

I pull a grin onto my face and nod. "Yeah, I'm fine. Sorry about that."

They both shake their heads. "No, no! We're sorry. The sign saying the door is broken must have fallen off. Thank God Will heard you banging on the door. It might've taken us a while to figure out where you'd disappeared to."

I blink. Will found me? I know he was there to open the door, but I didn't know he was the one who heard me screaming. Did he yell back? I thought I heard something, a whisper of someone's voice, but I can't remember now.

"It's fine, I'm fine," I say, waving my hand as if it isn't a big deal. My eyes widen. "Oh shit! My tables!"

Heidi holds her hand up. "Don't worry about it, the girls took over for you. Time to have a break, I think? What do you want to eat? It's on us."

Twenty minutes later, I'm sitting at the bar picking at the tandoori chicken dinner I ordered, compliments of Heidi and Brandon. It's delicious, but I don't have much of an appetite for anything other than the water that Ali keeps refilling for me.

Mackenzie and Lilli are sweet enough to take over my tables and still give me the tips from them, which I appreciate. I'm scheduled to close tonight, and even though Heidi offers to ask one of the girls to switch with me, I decline. I need to learn how to close, and I am feeling better now anyway. No sense throwing money away.

"Hey there, gorgeous."

I look up, and to my horror, Hunter is seating himself next to me at the bar.

"Oh!" I say simply. The hairs on the back of my neck stand on end and that nauseous feeling returns in earnest. Thankfully, I haven't eaten much.

"How are you?" he asks.

I gape at him for a moment, trying to find the right words. "I…it's been a rough night," I say, trying to give him the hint that I'd rather be alone right now. He doesn't get it, his pale eyes latching onto me invasively.

"Haven't gotten any more elbows to the face, have you?"

A nervous laugh escapes me. "No…no, thankfully not."

"Are you done for the night?" he asks, noticing my dinner plate on the bar in front of me.

I shake my head. "No, just on break. I'm closing." Shit, why did I tell him that? This night has thrown me off, and the words just tumble out like nothing.

He seems slightly put out. "Oh, right."

I notice the new group of people walking in the door looking for a table. "Right, well, I need to get back to work."

I slide off the barstool, but his outstretched hand stops me from moving. I already see the folded money tucked between his fingers. "I really should go," I say, trying to get past. I look around, hoping someone might notice the awkward interaction, but no one seems the wiser.

"Don't be rude, Elora."

I look up into Hunter's face, trying to keep the panic at bay as a dangerous thread of impatience pulls at the corners of his eyes.

I freeze as I grasp his hand—the transfer of the money into my gloved palm feels like I'm betraying myself. Alarms blare in my mind. He's dangerous, and it seems my fight-or-flight response has abandoned me. With my hand in his, he leans in and pulls me toward him, his mouth closing in on my ear.

"You look good enough to eat," he murmurs, his lips against my cheek. A wave of ice-cold shivers rush over me and I feel almost like I've been thrust back in that freezer. I pull back as he releases me, barely daring to look back at him, and head for the kitchen.

Once I'm through the swing door, my hand hovers over my cheek and I feel a jittery current spreading through me so hard that my knees tremble beneath me. I sidestep toward the dishwasher, the repetitive sloshing sound helping me remember to breathe steadily. I feel eyes on me, and I'm hardly surprised to find Will is watching me from behind the pass-through. Once again, his face is unreadable. After a moment, he blinks rapidly and rubs his eyes, like he's tired or annoyed.

I don't want him knowing I'm rattled, or at least more rattled than earlier, which, if I am honest with myself, is more than enough to want to never set foot in this building again. I walk down the line, feeling Will's gaze follow me as I grab a stack of menus and head back out into the dining room to greet my new table.

✦ ———— ✳ ———— ✦

I AM GOING to go insane. I feel like I'm constantly being watched. When I'm in the dining room, Hunter is staring at me, smiling that overly confident, menacing smile, and when I'm in the kitchen, Will's eyes always find me. Thankfully, he hasn't said much other than calling for orders to be picked up.

"Hey, El, I'm just about to finish up. Do you need anything else before I go?" Lilli pulls me out of my thoughts, her pointed, pretty face and dark lipstick still looking perfect after a busy rush.

"Oh, no, I don't think so."

"Who's the guy at the bar?" she asks.

I can practically feel the heat from Will's eyes as he listens to our conversation.

"The one in the hat. He doesn't stop staring at you. I mean, not that I blame him," she says, giggling.

I cringe. "He's just some creep. He keeps giving me unwarranted tips. It's super weird."

Lilli looks surprised. "Ew, gross. Do you want me to tell Ali to kick him out? Or if you need a ride home tonight, I don't mind waiting. I was just going to go home and study anyway."

I feel guilt wash over me. I hardly want to be the reason Lilli misses a chance to study. "No, I'll be fine. Thanks, though."

"Okay, if you're sure."

"I'm sure."

I grip the edge of the counter for a moment and take a deep breath. I am exhausted. From the panic attack and the freezer incident from earlier, but also just the long, busy shift in general. I just want to curl up in my bed and fall asleep.

"Order's up."

Opening my eyes, I spot the plates for my table sitting on the pass-through and Will wiping down the counter.

I push myself off to grab them.

"Is something wrong?"

I look up and he's studying me intensely. Once again, I feel that sensation of being X-rayed.

"I'm fine."

He rolls his eyes. "Jesus, sunshine, if I had a dollar for every time I've heard you say tonight that you're fine, I wouldn't need to work here anymore."

I'm taken aback by his response. "Well, I am!"

He leans forward. "Bullshit."

"It's not bullshit!"

"Don't lie to me," he growls. "I can see how rattled you are."

I straighten my back. "The only thing that's rattling me right now is you."

He barks out a laugh. "Believe me, if I wanted to rattle you, checking on your well-being would not be the way I'd go about doing it."

I cross my arms over my chest, my interest piqued. "Oh really? So just how exactly would you…rattle me?"

His gaze slowly travels down to my chest then back up, the movement causing heat to spread across my collarbone. He smirks and those damn dimples appear in his cheeks. "Your bra is showing."

I immediately look down, my hands flying up to cover my chest, but I'm completely covered. I look back up at him and he's shaking with silent laughter.

I narrow my eyes at him. "Oh, very funny."

"Yes, I thought so, too."

"You're an idiot," I say, grabbing the two plates and turning toward the dining room.

"What colour is it?"

I slowly turn back to him. "What?"

"Your bra," he says, still smiling, his arms stretched out to hold him up from the counter. His sleeves are rolled up and his forearms are muscular, positively drool worthy. "What colour is it?"

My stomach twists. "I'm not telling you that!"

He shrugs his shoulders. "Too bad, I was wondering if you colour-coordinate with your panties. Pink from what I can see."

My eyes widen and I immediately set down the plates on the counter to check the back of my dress, but I'm once again all covered up. The heat from my collarbone floods my face, and I turn back to Will, who's smiling wide from his place behind the counter.

Fuck, this guy sets me on edge, also was that just a lucky guess or did he actually know my underwear is pink? Maybe he does have X-ray vision.

"Too bad you'll never see it," I say sharply, picking up my plates again and feeling thoroughly rattled. Shit, I played right along with his game.

He continues chuckling. "You sure about that, sunshine?"

I turn away and say loudly, "Positive," before I walk through the door.

•————— ✳ —————•

MY LAST TABLE is almost ready to leave, and I heave a gigantic sigh. I'm also glad I told Lilli to go home because the thought of her waiting around for me makes me feel terrible. My feet are sore and my shoulders have been tense for hours. I head to the bar, where Ali is also closing out his final tabs. Hunter is still here, but thankfully, I've managed to avoid him most of the night.

"Hey," I say to Ali, leaning on the bar.

Ali gives me a friendly smile, his brown skin glistening from the busy shift. "How'd your night go?"

I let out a groan, and he chuckles. "That good, huh?"

"It's been a long night," I mutter.

"Right, I'm going to start closing down the bar. Let me know if you need any help."

I nod, but when I turn to head back into the kitchen, Hunter is standing in my path, his coat on.

"Hey, girl," he says, "you've had a busy night."

I take a step back. "Yeah, it's been pretty busy."

"Are you heading home after this?" he asks.

I think quickly. What if this guy tries to follow me to my house? "Oh no, I'm actually heading to a friend's place for the night."

He nods. "Do you need a ride? It's pretty late."

I shake my head. "No, I'm good, thanks."

He takes a step toward me and my heart rate spikes. "Well, good night then. I'll see you around."

This time, he doesn't hold out his hand, and I'm grateful until he suddenly wraps his arms around me for a hug. I barely dare to breathe as his body presses itself against mine and I feel his breath on my neck. I'm frozen, horrified, and I feel my wrists itch with a sudden burst of heat under my gloves, that electrical jittery feeling growing, growing, growing until it's almost painful under my skin. His nose touches my cheek as he pulls back, smirking.

His cold, clammy fingers linger on my bare upper arms as he backs up, but suddenly, his eyes widen and he's flailing, falling backward on his ass, a look of complete shock on his face.

I look around, thinking maybe he slipped on something, but

then my head tilts as I notice his shoelaces are tied together. How the fuck did that happen?

"Shit," I hear him mutter.

Ali is there a moment later to help him up, and I take the distraction to turn back toward the kitchen. After only a few steps, I notice Will leaning against the doorframe, watching the whole thing go down. His eyes are dark and his jaw looks tense as I approach.

His eyes follow my face as I brush past him into the kitchen, but I feel him turn to follow me.

"Are you okay?" he asks, hot on my heels.

"I'm fine."

I untie my apron and dump it on the empty counter. I pull out the receipts and bills and coins to sort through them all.

"Another dollar for me then," Will mutters.

I sigh loudly, my wrists still itching terribly and my heart racing. I close my eyes and take a deep breath. "Can you please just leave me alone?" I ask without looking at him.

The heat of his presence lingers for a moment, then it disappears, leaving me uncomfortably cold. I open my eyes and he's gone, and for the first time all night, no one is watching me. I spin around, wondering where he's disappeared to, but I don't see him anywhere.

I turn back to my counting. Why do I care? Will Reed is infuriating. *He's just making sure you are safe*, the little voice in my head whispers to me. Yeah, Alex probably asked him to keep an eye on me. Guys like Will only care about girls so they can get them into bed.

An image pops up in my mind of Will, shirtless and hovering over me on a bed, his hands exploring my bare skin. Heat pools between my legs and my pulse thrums in my core. I twist my legs together, shifting my weight. I wonder what it would be like if I actually did end up in bed with him. Is it really as good as all the other girls said it was? He rocked their worlds, apparently, and I find myself suddenly craving knowledge of what that would be like.

My own history is completely blank, forgotten. Have I ever had sex? If I have, did I enjoy it? Did I have a boyfriend? Several boyfriends? I haven't been intimate with anyone since the accident, other than that one awkward kiss. Maybe Will would be a way to discover what I'm missing out on. Surely, he'd give me a good time.

I shake my head. What the hell am I thinking? I have a date with Alex tomorrow! Alex is sweet, funny, and cute, and he likes me. Actually likes me, at least that's how it seems. Surely a kiss or being touched by Alex will be as exciting. But then, why the hell is it Will who makes me feel so goddamn hot and bothered all the time?

I finish counting out my bills and put them all into an envelope before proceeding to wipe down the counters. When I'm done, I head toward the office, where Ali is watching Heidi count through the till tray, and I drop off my envelope on the desk.

"I'm just going to go change," I say as she looks up.

She nods. "No problem."

I grab my bag from my locker, noticing that the locker labelled "Will Reed" is open and empty, but he isn't anywhere to be seen. Probably for the better if I am honest with myself. I head into the bathroom and quickly change out of my little black dress and flats, and into my jeans, sweater, and boots. I pull my gloves off and rub my knuckles against the rough, itchy skin. My sweater has long sleeves, so before I slip into my coat, I thrust my gloves into my bag along with my work shoes and dress, then head back toward the office, my bag slung over my shoulder.

Ali is sitting in the chair, but Heidi is just finishing going through my envelope. Will is standing by the office door. He's changed into his street clothes and my stomach somersaults at the sight of him. He's wearing black jeans, a white t-shirt, and a black jacket, his black curls falling effortlessly over his forehead. Butterflies drop lower and lower between my legs. It should not be legal to look that good.

I square my shoulders and walk toward the office, coming to stand right beside Will.

"You're all good," Heidi says, looking up at me. "You did good tonight," she says. "How are you feeling after earlier?"

"She's fine."

My head turns to Will, half of his mouth upturned in a crooked smirk. I glare at him.

"That was what you were going to say, wasn't it?" he asks, his head tilting to the side as he raises one dark eyebrow.

I scoff, then turn back to Heidi and Ali, who are watching us. "I *am* fine and I can say it for myself, thanks."

"Whatever," Will mutters, pushing himself away from the wall. "See you on Monday, Heidi. Later, Ali."

They wave goodbye and I watch from the corner of my eye as Will disappears out of the kitchen swing door.

"Are you okay to get home?" Heidi asks. "It's late. I don't mind driving you if you want."

I wave my hand. "No, I'm good. Thanks, though. See you next week."

"Good night."

I head out into the dining room, sure that Will is hanging around to torment me further, but he's gone. An unexpected pang of disappointment hits me, but I shake my head and make my way to the door.

The cold night air is brisk and damp. I'm glad I brought a change of clothes. I hate being cold and having to take the streetcar and buses home while cold is the worst of all. I dig my hand around in my bag for my cell phone and my bus pass. There are a few messages in the group chat from the girls, along with what appears to be information for Mariah's birthday party next week.

There is also a message on Instagram from Alex which reads:

Alex:
Hope you had a good night at work. Looking forward to tomorrow.

I smile to myself as I walk down the quiet street toward the shelter for the streetcar.

"Elora!"

I turn at the sound of my name only to find Hunter stalking toward me from the dark corner of a bakery I just passed. My smile immediately abandons my face and something ice cold slips down my spine. "Oh, hey," I say simply.

"On your way to your friend's place?" he asks.

I tilt my head with confusion and suddenly remember that I used it as an excuse that I wasn't heading home on my own.

"Oh! Yeah, on my way now. Have a good night."

I turn to continue walking, but he follows, keeping pace next to me.

"Maybe I could get your number and take you out sometime," he says.

I stop walking and turn to him. "Look, I'm really flattered, but I'm kind of seeing someone."

He gives an odd little shake of his head. "No, you're not."

My eyebrows knit together. "Um, yeah, actually, I am."

There's no trace of a smile left on his face. He steps closer, and I feel my wrists itch again.

"You know, letting me take you out on a date would be the least you could do."

"Excuse me?"

He takes another step toward me, and I feel the brick building touch my back as I try to keep the distance between us.

He leans closer, his finger reaching out to trace down the side of my face, and all the air vanishes from my lungs.

"After all the cash I've thrown your way, it's only polite."

That jolting energy floods my body as my blood boils with anger. Finally, my fight response is kicking in. "How dare—"

But Hunter is suddenly yanked away—his body whipped around to slam into the wall next to me. I side-step away along the brick as the sound of his groan reverberates into the night. Will has Hunter pinned against the wall, his hands fisted in Hunter's jacket. I stand there, shell-shocked, as Will stares menacingly at Hunter, whose eyes are popping out of his head.

"Scum," Will whispers.

I think he's about to let him go, but Will moves as fast as lightning, his hands instantly wrapped around Hunter's. There's a sickening snap that makes me jump. Hunter cries out in pain, his body doubling over as Will releases his hands and steps back.

"You think you can buy someone, you piece of shit? Touch her again, and I'll break more than your fingers." Will's chest is rising and falling fast. "Now," he says darkly, "get the fuck out of here."

10

ELORA

Hunter stumbles away, clutching his mangled hand against his chest in the other direction, his face tangled with fury. Will turns to me breathing heavily as he takes a few steps closer. "Are you hurt?" he asks.

My mouth falls open, my eyes still wide with shock and horror at what just happened. My eyes scan his face, my brain spinning and trying to put together words.

"I'm—"

"I swear to God, Elora, if you say 'I'm fine', I'm going to lose it," he barks. I flinch at the volume of his voice, and when he notices, he lowers his chin and takes a deep breath. "I'm sorry," he says quietly, his hand rifling through the mop of hair that's fallen over his forehead.

My thoughts finally click into place as air returns to my lungs.

"I…thank you," I manage, but my voice wavers.

He nods then turns to look over his shoulder where Hunter has run away with his tail between his legs.

I continue to walk toward the streetcar stop, and I hear Will walking behind me as I approach the shelter. "You don't have to follow me," I say, turning around.

"I'm not," he says.

I cock an eyebrow at him. "Then, what do you call this." I gesture between us.

He points past me in the distance where the lights of an oncoming streetcar appear. "That's my ride."

I feel the heat of embarrassment flush my cheeks. "Oh."

We stand a few feet apart, waiting as the streetcar approaches. He doesn't say anything, but I glance at him out of the corner of my eye. He's staring at something across the street. I look over where the tall, dark windows act like a mirror, and see my own reflection staring back at me.

Me, he's looking at me.

The streetcar rumbles to a stop in front of us, the doors open, and he gestures for me to lead the way. I pull myself up the stairs, flash my pass at the driver, then head toward the back, sitting down next to the window. The car is practically empty with only a few people my age who seem completely wasted on their way home from a night of too much fun.

Will pulls himself along the car and I can't help but notice he's limping a little. For a moment, I think he's going to sit down next to me in the empty seat, but he doesn't. Instead, he sits in the row behind me.

The streetcar starts moving again and my body sways with a little jolt as we chug along down Queen Street. I feel Will looking at me, my ears burning with his attention. I glance in the dark window and see his reflection. I find myself thinking about an alternate universe where I know nothing about him. Some timeline where I just randomly hop on the streetcar and sit down in front of him.

In that universe, I would be sitting here praying he'd flirt with me, thinking that his mouth looks so fucking incredible, wanting to push my fingers through his hair. He'd lean forward to start a conversation and end up flirting with me. Maybe even ask for my number and I'd give it to him. He'd flash me a smile with those dimples in his cheeks and I'd melt into a puddle on the floor.

"What's with the limp?" I ask, still staring at his reflection.

His head snaps up. "What?"

I pull my eyes from the window and turn in my seat to look at him. "You're limping. Did you get hurt?"

He squints his eyes for a moment. "Oh, no. Stepped on something a few days ago. It's just sore from standing on it for hours at a time."

"Oh," I say simply.

There's a long silence.

"Are you working tomorrow?" I ask.

He shakes his head. "Uh…no."

"Me neither."

Why is he suddenly being so quiet? I would think he'd be taking advantage of our proximity outside of work to rattle me again. I want him to rattle me.

"So," I start, "what do you do for fun on your days off?"

He looks down at his lap, a smile spreading across his face like he's remembering some private joke. "Nothing much really. Laundry, groceries, the gym…you?"

I nod. "Yeah, same."

The streetcar brakes and I grip the handle on the back of the seat to stop from sliding forward. I see Will glance at my bare fingers peeking out of the sleeve of my jacket. I look at his face and it's like he's trying to decide how to say something.

"You can ask," I say, pulling my hand away from his gaze and tucking it into my pocket.

"Ask what?"

"About why I wear the gloves," I say, shrugging.

"I wasn't going to."

I turn completely sideways, pulling my feet up and wrapping

my arms around my knees. "I don't mind really, everyone always asks."

"I figured if you wanted me to know, you'd tell me yourself."

I blink with surprise and a small laugh escapes my mouth.

"What?" he asks.

"What's with you?"

He looks around. "What do you mean?"

"Why are you behaving like this?"

"Like what?"

I gesture somewhat wildly with my hands. "I don't know... normal? Where's cocky, arrogant, can't stop annoying me Will?"

"There's more to me than just those things," he says, leaning forward in his seat.

"Like what?"

He shrugs. "Why does it matter? You've already formed your opinion of me. Why work to change it?"

"Forget it," I mutter and turn back to face the front of the streetcar.

I feel him lean forward, his lips hovering just behind my ear. "I think you like it when I'm cocky."

The sound of his voice is so fucking hot and I feel my body react to his proximity. I swallow, trying to keep my face composed.

"Hardly."

"Liar."

I turn back around in my seat and his face is so close I can make out every colour in his beautiful hazel eyes. They're darting over my face, finally landing on my mouth, and I feel betrayed by my own body as my tongue wets my lips.

The speaker overhead pulls me out of the moment, signalling my stop is next. I turn away and press the button on the pole to signal I'd like to get off.

I grab my bag and stand, faltering when Will also stands.

"What are you doing?" I ask.

He points to the door. "This is my stop."

I shake my head. "No, it's not."

He raises his eyebrows. "Yeah, it is."

The streetcar slows to a stop and the doors open. Will steps down and exits out onto the street. I follow hurriedly, the cold air hitting my face. He walks ahead of me and I have to be quick to keep up with his long legs.

"What do you think you're doing?" I ask.

He turns toward me, continuing to walk backward. "I'm going home. What are you doing?"

I stop. "You live around here?"

He stops too, then takes a few steps back toward me. "Yeah. Wait…" His fingers run across his mouth, "did you think I was following you home?"

My blush betrays me again. "No."

He smirks. "Now who's arrogant?"

I roll my eyes. "Oh, please, you're the one who can't stop flirting with me."

"According to you, I'll flirt with anyone."

I walk past him toward the end of the street and I feel him following me again.

"You know what I think, sunshine?" he asks, walking backward next to me. "I think you secretly like that I flirt with you."

I stop again. "I don't."

"You don't have to lie to me, Elora," he says, smirking. "I won't tell anyone your secret."

I glare at him, annoyed at how he sees right through me.

"Prove it," I say.

He blinks. "What?"

"Prove you live around here."

He laughs, and after a moment, he shakes his head and grabs

his wallet out of his back pocket. He pulls his driver's license out and hands it to me.

I snatch the card out of his hand and look at the picture. Damn, even his driver's license picture is gorgeous. 1737B Queen Street East, Toronto. I look quickly up at the numbers on the store fronts. Fuck…we are close by. I look back down at his I.D. "Willan? Your full name is Willan?"

He snatches the I.D. back, tucking it into his wallet. "Yeah, it is," he says, his cheeks turning red, and for once, it seems I've finally got the upper hand.

My wrists start to itch again and I absentmindedly rub at the skin with my knuckles. "Unusual name," I say.

"Not any more unusual than Elora."

I laugh. "Whatever. Good night, *Willan*."

I start to walk toward the bus stop on Woodbine Avenue.

"Wait!"

I turn around and Will is walking toward me again.

"Yes?"

"Can you do me a favour?"

My eyes scan his face. "Umm…depends what it is."

He rolls his eyes. "Can you text me when you get home?"

I narrow my eyes. "You want me to text you?"

He nods. "Yeah, after what happened with that piece of shit earlier, I'm worried you might not get home safe."

My heart constricts in my chest. He's worried about me? Or is this just another ploy to get my number?

"I don't—"

"Don't be difficult," he says looking frustrated. "We work together and you were almost assaulted earlier. Alex would kill me if I didn't make sure you got home safely."

Alex. Shit, I totally forgot about my date with Alex tomorrow.

He's staring at me expectantly. I let out a sigh and hold out my hand. "Fine, give me your phone."

He hands me his cellphone and I punch in my number with my name into his contact list. I manage to quickly glance at his contacts. There's only like a dozen people listed in his phone and almost all of them are names I recognize from the pub. Not exactly what I expected for a fuckboy. I hand him back his phone.

"Do you live far from here?" he asks.

"I live a little ways up off Woodbine at Danforth."

His eyes narrow and he tilts his head. "Really?"

"Yeah, why?"

He stares at me for a moment. "Nothing, never mind."

"Want me to prove it?" I ask teasingly.

He holds up his hands and backs away. "No. I believe you."

"Right, well. Good night then."

"Text me the moment you get in the door. I'm tired and don't want to be up all night waiting to make sure you survived the bus home."

I roll my eyes. "Fine."

I walk along the street toward the bus stop. I look over my shoulder to see if Will is watching me or following me or whatever else, but he's gone. I look up and down the street, but he's nowhere to be found. I turn back and spot the bus coming up the hill, so I run toward the stop, clutching the pass in my hands.

My phone vibrates from an incoming text message.

Will:
It's Will, get home safe. Let me know when you do.

I stare at the message for a moment as the bus comes to a stop in front of me. I notice my reflection on the doors and my breath catches at the sight of the goofiest grin spread across my face.

Oh boy…I'm in trouble.

✦

ABOUT TWENTY MINUTES LATER, I open the door to my apartment. I drop my bag onto the floor and head to the kitchen, kicking off my boots as I go. I fill a glass with water and guzzle it down before pulling my phone out of my pocket, tossing my coat onto the loveseat.

I open my texts and click on Will's message at the top. I quickly tap out a reply and hit send.

Elora:
Home now. I survived. You've completed your white knight responsibilities for the day.

I toss my phone onto my bed and go to the bathroom. I wash the makeup off my face and pull my hair down from on top of my head. I pull off my sweater and jeans and stare at myself in the mirror. I glance at my matching pink bra and underwear and a laugh bursts out of my throat before I can stop it.

That arrogant prick. How the hell did he know? Or is he just simply so experienced with women that he has some sort of intuition about underwear?

I shake my head and walk back to my bed, grabbing a shirt from my dresser.

My phone lights up with a new message, and my heart hammers in anticipation as I reach out to pick it up.

Will:
Good to know you're home safe. I was worried I might have to spend my day off as part of a search party trying to find your corpse.

I roll my eyes. I unhook my bra, discarding it before pulling the shirt over my head and climbing into bed.

Elora:
Glad searching for my dead body won't be disrupting your super important plans of doing laundry and grocery shopping.

The three little dots bubble up as he types.

Will:
Don't forget my trip to the gym. Got to stay in shape if I'm going to be rescuing chicks from freezers and scumbags.

Elora:
I'd never forgive myself if I interfered with that. I'll try not to let it happen again.

There's a pause and I feel disappointed that he hasn't said anything back. What is wrong with me? I don't like Will. He's an arrogant asshole. But my God he is hot and strong and sexy as fuck. The way he snapped Hunter's fingers like twigs. I won't lie, it was terrifying but also exhilarating.

My phone buzzes again.

Will:
So was I right?

I stare at the message, confused.

Elora:
Right about what?

Will:
Your panties.
Are they pink and do they match your bra?

My stomach flips excitedly and I know I shouldn't be doing this. I have a date tomorrow with his best friend after all.

Elora:
I guess you'll never know.

Will:
Want to play a game?

My eyebrows raise at the message and I snuggle in under the covers.

Elora:
What kind of game?

Will:
Truth or dare.

Elora:
I'm unfamiliar with the rules. Explain them to me?

I can practically hear his groan from here and I smirk as I see him typing.

Will:
You're fucking with me.

Elora:
Yes, and it's hardly the kind of game I should be playing with someone I despise.

He reads the message but doesn't respond. Fuck…did he take offence to that? I hadn't meant for it to come across as rude, but as I read it back, it definitely is. Or, maybe I'm overthinking things and he's fallen asleep.

> **Elora:**
> **Besides, I thought you said earlier that you were tired.**

He's typing again.

Will:
You're right, I am. You're probably too chicken to play anyway.

My mouth falls open. I am not too chicken. Okay, I definitely am, but I can't let him know that. An idea comes to mind that's so unbelievably cheeky that I feel myself grinning like an idiot. I push back my blanket and lift my shirt to expose my hip. I take a picture of my pink, satin underwear that curves over my hip. It doesn't give away much, just a hint of skin and fabric, but it'll prove I'm not as cowardly as he thinks I am. My fingers tremble as I hit send on the picture message.

> **Elora:**
> **You were right. Don't let it go to your head. Good night,**
> **Willan.**

Three little dots, and then,

Will:
Good night, sunshine.

11

WILL

Fuck, I am in trouble.

I open up the picture again and stare at the cropped picture of Elora's hip, the pale skin covered by pink satin panties. She really does have freckles everywhere. I've already jerked off to the thought of her lying in bed in just these panties, and I can feel myself getting hard again. Tonight has been a whirlwind. Between the stranger in the back alley of the pub to rescuing Elora from the freezer. To see *him* hugging her and caging her in.

I managed to stop Time again. Apparently, I'm only capable of it when I think of her. When that douchebag touched Elora, I wanted to snap his neck, but it's not exactly like someone could explain a suddenly dead man on the floor of the pub. Plus, it might have traumatized her, or worse, the police might have tried to pin it on her. I settled for his shoelaces instead.

I didn't think he'd be around again, though. It felt good to snap his fingers. It was almost easy. Plus, I didn't realize she lives so close to me. She said she lives off of Woodbine. I thought about the blue house I Jumped to on the night I stepped on the glass. Is it possible that she is the reason I Jumped there? I didn't know she lived there before tonight so how could I have known to Jump there unconsciously? The whole thing is very strange. Then again, I could be reading too much into it. She might not live in the little blue house at all. It seems unlikely that someone her age who just moved here would own a house. Maybe she lives with her parents? There is still so much I don't know about her.

Fuck, it's so fun to flirt with her, though. I read through our text conversation again. "This hardly seems like the type of game I should play with someone I despise."

When I first read those words, I felt so defeated. I thought that maybe everything that happened between us last night only made her hate me more. But then, she sent me that picture, and while it isn't by any stretch explicit, it is most definitely flirty. I'm walking a dangerous line. She's going on a date with Alex, and here I am texting her, asking her to play truth or dare via text message at two in the morning, and she sends me a picture of her underwear. Alex is my friend. *My best friend.* I have to stop. I look at the picture again and groan. Something about this girl makes me feel excited, electric. I don't know if it's because she hasn't fallen all over herself to get into bed with me or doesn't fall for my bullshit right away, but I'm starting to become obsessed.

I switch over to Instagram and pull up her profile. She's added two new pictures since the one of her bruises. Both are only of her. One of her outside of the pub and the other in what appears to be her bedroom. There are fairy lights strung up on the headboard and her hair tumbles down one side of her head in a way that looks like someone's just fucked her. Holy God.

This has to stop. I can't text her again. This was purely to make sure she got home safely, nothing more. I plug my phone into the charger and turn off the light on my nightstand. Tomorrow, I plan on doing a little more than just laundry and groceries. I'm going to try to stop Time again and I need a good night's rest to do it.

✳

STOP, stop, stop, stop.

I'm staring at the fan in my apartment, willing it to stop moving with my mind. It's only eleven in the morning, but already I have a splitting headache from trying to stop this damn fan.

I take my glasses off and clean the lenses with my t-shirt, then massage my temples with my fingers. I'm sure that if I don't get anywhere with this soon, I'm going to give myself a nosebleed. I try to relax the tension in my shoulders. It wasn't a conscious decision when I did it before. It really just happened. I close my eyes, listening to the whirring of the fan in front of me, feeling the breeze as it oscillates from side to side.

I think of Elora, of that asshole touching her. How uncomfortable she looked. I try to think of how I felt at that moment. Angry. Protective. Jealous, even. I hold the image of her in my mind, shadowy figures moving in on her, but I bring her into me, protecting her with my body.

There's an unusual silence that settles over my apartment, and I open my eyes to find the fan has stopped. I stand up and check the power button and the cord. It's still plugged in. A grin spreads across my face as I race to the window at the front of my apartment. Everything has stopped. A woman and her son are frozen, exiting from the streetcar. There's a dog midway through urinating on a tree. A man is texting on his cellphone as he walks along the sidewalk.

There's a car about to turn left onto the side street. The man with the cellphone is only a few steps away from stepping out right into its path.

"Shit!"

I Jump onto the sidewalk from my apartment, the sun somewhat blinding in the open space. What am I going to do?

What will happen if I move the man? Will someone notice? Will *he* notice? What if there are doomsday implications from this? I've seen a few movies with time travel enough to know that it's dangerous. But I'm not really travelling through time…I'm just stopping it, so will things really be that bad?

Can I really stand here and watch as he gets hit by a car? No.

Grabbing onto the man, I lift and move him across the sidewalk. His expression is still the same, and I can't tell if he'll even notice, but I guess I'm about to find out.

Something moves out of the corner of my range of vision. I turn toward it, letting go of the man and Jumping over to where I'm sure I saw the figure. The image of the man from last night floods my brain. Is it him? A chill races along my spine and I start to feel exposed. Vulnerable. Maybe he has been watching me. Maybe he isn't affected by the Time stop.

I look everywhere, but there appears to be no one around, and everyone, everything, is still frozen. I take one last sweeping look, glancing back at the man, then Jump back into my apartment. I stand by the window, watching the street. I close my eyes and envision everyone moving again. A moment later, the breeze ruffles my hair and the noise of the street vibrates my skull. It's suddenly so loud that it's painful after complete silence.

I watch as the man stumbles slightly. He looks around, but a second later, continues on walking.

I watch the street for a while, my head pounding. There doesn't seem to be any repercussions from my little stunt, but I'm exhausted, and even though it's only just before lunch, I lie down to take a nap. I glance at my phone, staring at the ceiling. I reread the conversation with Elora again and again, staring at the picture she sent me until I fall asleep with the phone still clutched in my hand.

✦

I FIND *myself in the forest, searching for the source of the blue light that flickers in the distance and sprint for it. It grows brighter and brighter until I'm holding my hand in front of my eyes to shield myself from the blinding light. It's like looking at a blue sun. My retinas feel scorched.*

"Willan."

The voice calls me, echoing off the trees. I look around for the origin of the voice, but find nothing. When I turn back toward the light, it's gone, and instead, a gigantic gnarled tree towers before me. It's dead. There are no leaves, just dark thick bark and spiralling limbs.

There are no other trees like it around me. I'm surrounded by birch, pine, evergreen, and maple, but this tree looks like something out of a fantasy movie.

I reach out to touch it, my fingers testing the spongy bark. I walk around it, my hand trailing behind me along the tree. The roots are enormous at the base. So large that I have to climb over them to get around it. I stop when I see that on this side, there's a hole in the trunk of the tree, like something an owl might make a home out of.

Something flickers from within, somewhere deep down the sapphire blue illumination brightens until I can't see anything but light.

"Willan."

"Will?"

There's a pounding on my door as I sit up. Who the fuck is knocking so loud? I wince as I move my legs to the side of the bed to stand up. I feel like I'm hungover…bad. My vision is blurry, my glasses have fallen off my face and I grope for them on the bed.

"Will?"

"Coming!"

It's Alex. Why the hell doesn't he just use his key, get whatever food he wants, and leave me alone?

I stumble down the hallway and find that Alex has my door partially open, but the chain lock is bolted so he can't get in. I peer around at him and he sighs.

"What the fuck, man?" I ask groggily.

Alex sighs, annoyed. "What do you mean, what the fuck? I've been calling you for over an hour. I know I told you to stay home and rest today, but I didn't expect you to just be dead to the world with your door locked."

I shake my head. "Hold on."

He steps back, and I close the door in order to unlock the chain. I open it again and Alex strolls into the apartment, heading straight for my fridge as usual.

"Don't you buy your own food?" I ask, closing the door.

"Not really, no," he mutters.

I look him up and down. He's dressed fancy. Or rather, nicer than usual, which for Alex means more than a pair of track pants and a t-shirt. Then it hits me. He has his date with Elora today. "You look nice," I murmur, sitting down on my couch.

"Thanks," he replies through chewing on an apple.

I spot my phone on the coffee table in front of me and grab it. There are six missed calls from Alex.

"All right, then, what was so important that you nearly broke down my door?" I ask.

Alex sits down next to me. "Is it true you had to bust El out of the freezer last night?"

I nod. "Yeah, actually. Who told you?"

"She did."

So, they've already spoken. Was she talking to Alex at the same time as she sent me a picture of her underwear? A flash of scorching dread creeps up my neck at the thought.

"Yeah. The sign Heidi put on the door fell down. She was pretty upset."

Alex shakes his head. "That fucking door is a menace. I had to help Brandon pry it open a few days ago."

"Well, they're going to fix it on Monday, so…"

"Were you nice?"

I glance up at him but look away. He very clearly hasn't been given any indications about anything else that happened between me and Elora.

I grab the remote for the TV and turn it on. "Yes, I was nice. Doesn't matter though, she despises me anyway."

"I hardly think—"

"She said it herself," I mutter. "She *said* she despises me." I don't know what that means because who sends a picture of their underwear to someone they hate? Fuck, she is confusing. "Anyway," I rush on, "what time are you taking her…what was it again? Bowling?"

Alex smiles. "I told her to meet me here at seven."

"Here? Why here? Shouldn't you be going to pick her up?"

He shrugs. "We're only a block away from the bowling alley, and if things go well," he wiggles his eyebrows at me, "we'll be close enough that I can suggest coming back to my place."

I try to look encouraging while I fight the urge to throw up. The idea of Alex and Elora doing anything physical together in the apartment directly next door is unthinkable. "Your place with no food. Well, good luck."

I take in his attire again—not exactly appropriate for bowling. It's too fancy, too stiff. "Why are you dressed like that for bowling?"

Alex looks down at his dress pants and shirt. "Oh, I'm meeting up with some old friends for drinks first at this swanky bar downtown, but I'll be back before seven to change."

I raise my eyebrows. "Really?"

"Yeah, some high school friends. They're in town for the weekend, so they asked if I could hangout for a bit."

My chin bobs and I turn on the Korean horror show I've been making my way through and fall back against the sofa.

"What's wrong with you?"

I turn toward Alex, who's eyeing me skeptically.

"What do you mean?"

He narrows his eyes at me. "You're in a mood. What happened?"

"I'm not in a mood."

"Yes," Alex insists, "you are."

I shift my weight. "I don't feel very good, that's all, and my foot hurts."

Alex rolls his eyes. "You're going to take it easy today, right? Stay here?"

"Fuck off, Alex, I don't need you to be my mother," I mutter.

He gives me an apologetic look. "Sorry."

I shrug. "It's fine. Now piss off."

Alex grins at me. "All right, I'm going, I'm going."

He stands up and heads for the door. "Stop locking your door, man. I'm starting to think you're getting paranoid."

I flip him off, and he laughs as he closes the door behind him. I hear his heavy footsteps going down the stairs.

I exhale and fall over sideways on the couch, covering my face with my hands. Fuck, this is not good. This has to stop. Even Alex noticed a change in my behaviour. Maybe I should just be mean to Elora. That would stop her dead in her tracks. Could I do it though? Could I be mean? Like, actually mean? I'm sure I could, but I really don't want to. I don't want her to hate me.

I spend the next little while cleaning things up around the apartment. My foot is somehow even more sore today, and when I look at it, the gash is swollen and angry-looking.

"Fuck," I mutter. I really don't want to go to the hospital. I can't stand going to the hospital after…the accident. I figure I'll hop in the shower, maybe the clean water and soap will help, then I'll plant my ass on the couch, order some delivery, and not move until morning. I grimace at the thought of potentially hearing Alex and Elora stumbling home. A horrible image of the two of them getting busy and being able to hear them through the thin walls of the apartment makes my stomach roll over.

Alex mentioned on more than one occasion how he has been woken up by my own female visitors. I suddenly wish we weren't neighbours. But the desire to flee for the night is also unappealing. If something happens between them, I want to be the first to know. Apparently, I'm a glutton for punishment.

· ———— ✳ ———— ·

A FEW HOURS LATER, my foot is up on a pillow on the coffee table in front of me, and a slasher movie is on Netflix in the background. I'm eating chow mein out of a foam container when a knocking on the door interrupts my "chill" evening. Wait…not my door. Alex's door. Elora's here. My brain short circuits for a moment, and for some reason, I duck down on my couch as if she might see me.

A few quiet moments pass, and I hear her knock again. Then again.

"Hello?"

I quietly set down my food container and try not to let my couch cushions squeak as I push myself up. I walk toward the door and lean down to peek out of the peephole. She's leaning against Alex's door, her phone in her hand. Is Alex not home yet? I check my phone, it's seven fifteen. Where the fuck is he?

She turns, and looking annoyed, knocks on his door again.

Shit, shit, shit, what should I do? Will I let my friend screw himself over? He's standing her up and I highly doubt he's doing it on purpose. Maybe he's just running late? He seemed positively smitten with her. I could let her wait here, and maybe I can get a hold of him, but having Elora in my apartment alone is a potentially dangerous situation. Especially after last night. So, what should I do? Just let her leave?

Knock, knock, knock.

I puff air into my cheeks, push my glasses up on my nose, and open my door.

She jumps and looks thoroughly confused to find me standing in the open doorway. "Will?"

It's only at this moment that I realize I'm practically wearing pyjamas, a long sleeve t-shirt and flannel pants. She looks me up and down, then back at Alex's apartment door.

"Hey," I say.

Her mouth parts, still trying to process this unforeseen change in events.

"Sorry, does Alex live here?"

I nod. "Uh yeah, that's his apartment, but I don't think he's home yet."

Her eyes dart between me and Alex's door. "And you live next door?" she asks.

I lean against the door frame. "Yeah."

She gives a slow nod of her head. She looks exceptionally pretty. Even prettier than last night. Her hair is loosely curled and tumbling around her face, her piercing blue eyes bright, and her lips a shade of brightest red. Fuck, I want to bite on that lip.

"I, um…" she says, shifting like she's unsure of herself. "I'm supposed to meet Alex here for our date at seven? Did he say anything to you about that changing?"

I shake my head. I'm not sure if I should mention he planned to go for drinks with friends from high school. "He'll probably be back any minute," I say, glancing down the stairs toward the road. "You can hang out here until he gets back?"

She looks past me into my apartment. "Hang out…with you? In your apartment?"

I shrug. "Beats sitting on the stairs, but it's your call."

She looks back down the stairs, which are covered in dust and dirt. I stand aside, already knowing her decision. She squares her shoulders, and I roll my eyes at the dramatics as she walks past me into my apartment.

She stops a few feet past the door and I see her look around appraisingly. I'm glad I cleaned up earlier. Not that it was ever too messy, but the lack of dirty dishes and clothes strewn about is a bonus.

She turns around to look at me. "This is nice."

I grin. "Thanks, sunshine."

She rolls her eyes, placing her boots by the door and her coat on the hook. When she turns around, I feel the air leave my lungs. She has on a patterned mini skirt, a crop top, and a thin black choker around her neck. Fuck, inviting her in was a bad idea.

"Just make yourself at home, I guess," I say in a strained voice. I pull my eyes away from her as she looks around, trying to decide where to sit. "I'll see if I can get a hold of Alex."

She nods. "He's not responding to my texts. I tried calling him, too."

I grab my phone from the coffee table as she sits down on the edge of my old couch and click on Alex's name in my contact list.

Ring, ring, ring, ring, ring.

He doesn't have a voicemail, so it just continues ringing.

I hang up and try texting him.

Will:
Bro, where the fuck are you? Elora's here. You're blowing it.

With my texts open, I spot Elora's name and think of the picture she sent me last night. I have to fight the blood from rushing to my groin at the thought. I turn back around. Elora's sitting straight as a rail on my couch and holding her phone in her hand.

"Do you want something to drink?" I offer.

Her head swivels to look at me. "Oh, umm…no, thank you."

I take a few steps over to sit down on the couch, wincing at the pain in my foot.

She glances down at it. "Your foot," she says quietly. "It seems worse."

I cross my arms over my chest and lean against the back of the couch. "It's fine. I just need to rest it."

We lapse into an awkward silence as the TV prattles on in the background. I see her glance at the door and periodically at me.

"You can relax, you know. I'm not going to murder you," I say, reaching forward and grabbing my food container.

She raises her eyebrow at me. "The fact that you just said that makes me think I should be worried."

I take a bite of my food. "Please," I say, smirking, "if I wanted to kill you, I would've done it last night."

She doesn't say anything, but looks down at the phone in her hands. I check mine as well. My text to Alex is still unread. I feel like I should say something. Something to make it seem like Alex not showing up isn't as bad as it is. "I'm not sure why he's not here," I say, "he's not normally like this."

"What's he normally like?"

"He's a good friend, reliable…so this is extra weird, you know? Plus, I know he has been looking forward to taking you out."

She wraps her arms around the bare part of her stomach, and I try not to count her freckles as I stare at her skin.

"I heard he doesn't date a lot of girls," she says casually.

I shake my head. "No. He had a girlfriend when we first met, but I think it was a hard breakup. I never met her, and he hasn't dated anyone since."

"What was hard about it?"

I shrug.

"He's your best friend, and you don't know why he broke up with his ex-girlfriend?"

"Look, I'd just met the guy at the time. I wasn't about to interrogate him about his personal life if he wasn't willing to share," I bite back. "I'm not in the habit of prying into people's lives."

She presses her lips together and stares at the TV for a few minutes. I take a sip of my beer as she turns toward me on the couch, pulling one leg under her. "What about you?"

"What about me?"

She waves her hand at me. "You don't do relationships now, which means you probably did them at some point."

I take another bite of my noodles. "I don't want to talk about that."

She leans against the back of the couch. "He seemed like such a good guy," she says quietly, staring at the door.

I lean forward. "He is."

She narrows her eyes at me. "If he was, he'd be here. Instead, I'm—" She stops herself and looks at me nervously.

"Instead, you're stuck with me? The one person you despise? Sorry for ruining your night."

She opens her mouth as if to say something, but then changes her mind. I guess there's not much she can really say to that.

I reach for my drink and wince as I put weight on my foot.

"I think you should see a doctor about your foot," she says, leaning forward to try and get a look at it.

I shake my head. "No...no doctors."

"You don't like doctors?" she asks.

"Doctors, hospitals, nurses, anyone in the medical profession, really."

She looks around incredulously. "Why?"

I take a sip of my drink instead of answering.

"I don't really like doctors either, to be honest."

I look at her. Our eyes meet, and I feel like she's trying to piece together some kind of puzzle. Is that what I am to her?

"Will you let me look at it?" she asks.

"Look at what?"

"Your foot, moron."

I instinctively pull my foot away from her, but I feel a sharp pain shoot up my leg and wince.

"Will, come on!"

"No way!"

She sits back, crossing her arms over her chest. "Now who's the chicken?"

Fuck.

She holds my gaze, and I twist my mouth. "Fine."

I turn to put my feet up on the couch, and she scoots forward, her gloved hands grabbing onto my ankle.

She takes a look at it, narrows her eyes, and looks back up at me. "This looks awful. You've been walking around on this for days?"

I shrug.

She presses on the skin around the wound, and I jump. "*Ow!*"

She's completely unfazed. "I think there's still something in there. What did you step on?"

Her gloved finger gently grazes the skin, and I flinch. "Glass."

She looks up. "Do you have tweezers?"

"For what exactly?" I ask, alarmed.

"For plucking my eyebrows," she says, rolling her eyes. "To get the glass out of your foot, you idiot."

I chew on the inside of my lip. "No way."

She drops my foot and I yelp in pain as it hits her leg. "Stop being ridiculous. It needs to come out and be cleaned properly."

I pull my foot away from her.

"Fine!" she says, throwing up her hands. "But don't come crying to me when it gets so infected it needs to be amputated. You would still have to go to the hospital, you know. Possibly for *weeks*."

We glare at each other, but I can't refute her logic. Damn.

"Fine," I finally say. "The tweezers are in the medicine cabinet in the bathroom."

She smirks and heads to the bathroom, swinging her wide hips in that miniskirt far too intentionally. I push my glasses up and rub the bridge of my nose. I take another swig of my beer and a few minutes later, Elora returns. She's got rubbing alcohol, bandages, and the tweezers in her arms.

She turns on the lamp at her end of the couch for better lighting, then flops down. Reaching into her purse, she pulls a pair of black latex gloves that she wears at the restaurant out of a Ziploc bag and pulls them on over her long silk gloves. She organizes everything on the coffee table between us and pats her knee.

I roll my eyes and gingerly place my foot in her lap.

She lifts it up with her glove-covered hands and picks up the tweezers. "So," she says casually, "how did you end up working at the pub?"

A sharp pain shoots through my foot and my face screws up as I try to not flinch out of her grasp. "After I got the apartment, it was the first 'now hiring' sign I spotted. I didn't even have a resume, but I walked in, no experience. Started as the dishwasher and just learned from there."

She continues poking my foot. "Where did you move from?"

"What do you mean?"

"You said you got the job after finding the apartment. Where were you living before?"

I flinch as pain flares across the sole of my foot. "With my parents."

"Parents, huh?" she says, smiling. "Are they just as lovely as you are?"

I shrug. "Not really…they're dead."

Elora freezes, the smile dropping off her face. "What?"

I close my eyes for a long moment. "They died just over two years ago."

"I…Will, I'm so sorry. I didn't know."

I blink rapidly and look over at the TV. "It's fine."

She's quiet for a few minutes as she tortures my foot. "How did they die?" she asks.

My head turns back to her. "Car accident."

"I'm sorry, that's…that's awful."

"Yeah, well, not much I can do about it now," I answer, for a lack of anything better to say. "Ow!"

I feel something sharp slide out of my foot and Elora smiles up at me triumphantly as she holds up the shard of glass she dug out.

"Got it!" she says.

She's smiling. She's smiling at me. And I have to turn away because she's too bright to look at straight on.

I feel the sting of the rubbing alcohol and gasp loudly.

"You're such a baby," she mutters.

I gesture to the bloody piece of glass. "I'm a baby? Let's see how you deal with a hunk of glass being pulled out of you."

She rolls her eyes and gently wipes down my foot. It tickles and the relief without the glass in there sweeps over me.

She presses a bandage to the sole of my foot and sets it down on her lap again.

"There, that should do it," she says while taking off the plastic gloves and placing them in a ball on the coffee table.

I flex my foot as I pull it away and put it on the floor. There's a huge difference, and I can already feel a sharp knot of tension in my shoulder blades relax.

"Thanks," I mutter, "that's actually a lot better."

She twists her lips as if trying not to smile. "See, I told you it wouldn't be that bad."

I raise my eyebrows. "I think you rather enjoyed making me squirm."

She drops her chin. "Greatly." She looks at me and she's quiet for a long time.

I watch her chest rising and falling slightly faster than before. I stare at her deliciously red mouth and my brain goes fuzzy with thoughts of just devouring her. But she didn't come here for me. She doesn't even like me, so I look away. "You should try calling Alex again," I say. "I'm starting to get worried about him."

I take a sip of my beer and see her check her phone out of the corner of my vision. I hear the phone ringing from here, but it just rings and rings and rings.

She taps out a text message, and I hear the signature whooshing noise.

"So, tell me, Will," she says, pushing her hands through her hair. She grabs my beer and takes a sip. "Who broke your heart so badly that now you 'don't do relationships'." She adds the air quotes while making a face.

I paste a big grin across my lips and turn toward her. "None of your business."

"Oh!" she says dramatically. "So someone did break your heart. Interesting. They must have been very special."

The thought presses against my memory like a thumb digging into a bruise. It hurts. I can feel it in my soul, but I don't have the details or a response for her.

"And what about you?" I say, sliding on the couch toward her.

She narrows her eyes. "What about me?"

"Why are you single, huh? Someone who looks like you must be pretty crazy if they're not shacked up with someone."

"Is that supposed to be a compliment?"

I lower my voice. "Your choice, I guess. Take it however you want."

She leans toward me, her voice quietly dangerous. "It's none of your business."

"Well, clearly, you don't mind your own, so—"

She smacks her hand down on the couch. "You are without a doubt the most infuriating person I've ever met!" she retorts, her hands gripping the sofa cushions.

I lean a little closer to her. "Likewise, sunshine."

She stands up suddenly, but so do I. Some internal instinct in me trying to match her energy. To keep her here forever. To prove I'm not who she thinks. She's about to say something, but there's a commotion on the stairs outside of the apartment, and we both look at each other before racing to the door to see what's going on. Alex is stumbling up the stairs with another girl, making out.

"Alex, what the fuck, man?" I shout.

Elora's eyes go wide, then she retreats out of my line of sight back inside my apartment. Alex blearily looks up at me, detaching his mouth from whoever this girl is.

"Oh, hey, Will! This is Sarah!" he says, slurring.

I can barely decide what to say. "Who the fuck is Sarah?" I drop my voice. "You were supposed to go out with Elora!"

Vague recognition spreads over his face. "Oh, shit, yeah. Can you cancel that for me?"

I don't think I've ever seen Alex this wasted before. It is not a good look. Sarah looks up at me, and she's equally wasted, but she looks familiar. In fact, I'm pretty sure I've seen her picture before.

"Is this your ex?" I ask in disbelief.

Alex nods. "Yeah, she came for drinks with the old crew and we were getting caught up, you know?"

He's pulling his keys out of his pocket to open his door, the two of them a tangled mess on the landing across from me. I feel something brush past me and look down to see Elora bolting down the stairs, pulling her jacket on. With a click, Alex and Sarah fall into the open door of his apartment, and without thinking, I race down the stairs after Elora.

The street is dark when I open the building's door and rain is starting to fall, the first drops hitting the pavement. I look toward the bus stop at the end of the street and spot her copper hair shining in the light from the street lamp.

"Elora!" I yell.

She stops, then turns around. Her eyelashes are damp, and she sniffs loudly as I come to a stop in front of her.

"Well, this has been fun, but I'd really like to go home now," she says as she buttons up her coat.

"I don't know what to say."

She chews the inside of her lip and nods. "It's fine. I should've known better." She turns to leave again.

"Wait!"

She stands, waiting, my brain spinning around in circles as the rain gradually gets heavier, the sound of it tapping on the ground and on her coat.

"I'm sorry. You deserve better than that."

She barks out a laugh. "No, I don't." She closes her eyes and presses her lips together. "Do you know what this night has done?" The street lamp flickers above us for a moment and her eyes darken. "All it's done is prove to me what I've known for two years. That I'm on my own. Alone. And everyone fucking sucks!"

A tear escapes her lashes and rolls down her freckled cheek.

There's a flash of lightning through the clouds and a deafening rumble of thunder. A damp wind whips around the two of us, her hair flying around her anguished face. She spins on her heel and marches off toward the bus stop. I stand there in my bare feet, trying to think of what to say, but my mind is completely blank, and the rain is pelting down on me now, soaking through my shirt. When she disappears from view, I turn back to my apartment.

When I get back inside, Alex's door is shut and I can hear talking and giggling from inside. I am so pissed off at him that I slam my hand against the door frame, dust falling from the ceiling. It doesn't seem to faze them, and I groan out loud.

I head back inside my own apartment and slam the door, locking it behind me. I turn off my TV and grab my cell phone as I sit on the couch. I pull open my text messages and tap on Elora's name.

Will:
Can you let me know when you get home? I want to make sure you get there safely.

I stare at the screen and see that she's read the message but doesn't respond. The rain is pelting against my windows as I clean up my takeout, then head to my room.

An hour later and still no response from Elora, and it makes me anxious. It also means that I can't fall asleep even though I'm tired.

Will:
Elora, tell me you've gotten home safely.

Elora:
I'm home. Please leave me alone now.

My heart sinks, and I feel like that aching hole in my chest has somehow grown—the wound fresher after seeing her so hurt. What can I possibly say? Nothing, really, she doesn't want to be comforted by me. She told me to leave her alone.

I lay on my bed on my side and stare out the window for a long time, watching the raindrops splatter against the windows with such force, the wind howling outside, the lights from the street bending from the water on the windows. I look down at my phone screen again, at her last message, and my breath halts when I see three little dots in the corner.

But then they stop. Then start again and stop. No message. I lay on my back. She wants to say something. Maybe she needs some encouragement.

Will:
Thanks for fixing my foot. Having to get it amputated would've really cramped my style.

Elora:
Well, I couldn't just let you leave it like that, but you're welcome.

An idea pops into my head, and I type the message with nervous fingers.

Will:
Truth or dare?

Elora:
Truth.

Will:
Do you really despise me?

My heart is pounding as I wait for her reply, and it feels like a century passes before my phone dings with the response.

Elora:
No.

I smile stupidly at my screen.

Elora:
Truth or dare?

I smirk. Maybe she wants to play after all.

Will:
Truth.

Elora:
How many times have you looked at that picture I sent you?

A flood of blood rushes to my groin.

Will:
Too many times.

Elora:
Why?

Will:
That's not how the game works. You've already asked your question.

Elora:
Fine.

Will:
Truth or dare?

Elora:
Dare

Will:
Send me another one.

I've pushed it too far, too quickly. I'm sure of it. And when she doesn't respond right away, I know I've blown it. I roll over and pull my pillow to my chest. The rain is easing up now and my eyes start to close, but a ding on my phone snaps them back open. Elora sent me a picture message, and I open it with a certain desperation.

The picture captures her from the chest down as if she held the camera on her collarbone. My eyes travel over the soft planes of her stomach down to her black panties—her knees up and her legs crossed at the ankle. It's the hottest thing I've ever seen, and I harden instantaneously. Alex is a fucking moron.

12

ELORA

My heart is hammering against my ribcage as I hit send on the picture message. I hear the dreaded whoosh as it flies out into space. Embarrassment and regret immediately overwhelm me. Why did I do that? Why am I even engaging in this conversation? Because he turns me on, I tell myself, and it's driving me crazy.

The picture I sent this time is way more explicit than the first one. This time it's not just a fun game, there's more to it and he'll know that. Shit. He's going to see this message and think I want to fuck him.

And I do.

The idea of him lying in bed in his apartment, looking at this picture of me while touching himself has me feeling so hot I'm almost sweating. I hear a ding and my stomach flips as I open his response.

Will:
Wow. I see I've been upgraded since yesterday.

I giggle at the message.

Elora:
Truth or dare?

Will:
Truth.

Elora:
What are you thinking right now?

The three dots bubble up a few times like he's trying to decide on his answer.

Will:
I'm thinking what an idiot Alex is for standing you up.

I smile softly. God, why does he have to be so aggravating then turn around and say something like this? Why does he have to be such a player? Is he, though? Other than his outrageous flirting, which as far as I can see, he only does with me, he hasn't directly made a move on me since that first day when he asked to take me out for coffee. In fact, it wasn't until this picture request that he's done anything at all. I'm the one who sent him the picture in the first place. Maybe he's just playing this game with me for fun. There's nothing that indicates he actually likes me. No, that's not true. There have been moments. Looks. He said it himself, he's looked at my picture too many times, so at least I know he's attracted to me. But letting myself dive too deeply into Will is dangerous.

Elora:
Good night, Willan.

Will:

Good night, sunshine.

    I wonder why he calls me that. It's such an odd thing to be called. Both demeaning and endearing depending on his inflection, and it makes me all the more confused. I have been nicknamed several things at the other places I've worked in the past two years. Most had to do with either the colour of my hair or my freckles, but this is…different. Maybe next time we play truth or dare I'll ask him. I startle at that thought, but a small smile pulls at the corners of my lips. I want to keep playing with Will.

✦

MARIAH:
How did the date with Alex go?

Lilli:
Yes! I'm dying to know!

Jenni:
I'm actually curious myself. He's so hot.

Mackenzie:
I swear if you don't spill the tea, I might die.

Elora:
Sorry to disappoint you all. The date never happened.

Lilli:
Wait, what?

Elora:

He stood me up.

Mariah:
You're fucking kidding me!

Elora:
Unfortunately not.

Mackenzie:
What happened?

Elora:
I showed up at his place at seven, but he wasn't home.
Wouldn't respond to texts or calls. Will was there and offered
to let me wait at his place. Next thing we know, Alex is
stumbling home wasted, his mouth eating some other girl's
face!

Jenni:
☺

Mariah:
OMG NO!

Elora:
It was humiliating to say the least.

Mariah:
That's it, he's not invited to my birthday party anymore.
What a dick! Was Will at least nice to you? He can be a jerk.

Elora:
He was fine, nothing I couldn't handle.

Mariah:
Wow, I'm shocked. Tell me more at work tomorrow?

Elora:
Of course 🙂

I lie in bed, still in only the underwear I was wearing when I took that picture I sent to Will. My God, what a stupid thing that was to do. He'll probably end up showing that to everyone. Maybe I should ask him to keep it to himself. Although, to be fair, it doesn't look like he has many friends. He has Alex, but I doubt he'll show him after what happened tonight. I'm not sure what his relationship is like with the other line cooks or Brandon, but he seems to keep to himself. The only other person he seems close to is Mariah.

The rain has completely stopped now, and it's well after midnight, but I can't sleep. My mind is racing and not in the way I would've expected as of this morning. All I can think about is Will, and I hate myself for it. There's just something magnetic about him, and I understand why Priscilla and Jenni jumped into bed with him. If he's able to make me feel like this while arguing with me and through flirty text messages, I'll be in real trouble if he ever decides to turn it on full force.

I imagine what his lips might feel like on mine, what his hands would feel like as they skim their way up and down my body. I think about what his mouth might feel like between my thighs, and I giggle breathlessly at the visual of his glasses going crooked while he licks me. My hand travels beneath my panties and an electric shock shoots through my body when I stroke the perfect spot.

My eyes flutter closed as I imagine running my fingers through his mess of dark curly hair as pressure starts to build in my lower abdomen. My wrists itch terribly, but I try my best to ignore it. I need this. Need this release after spending all that time in his apartment with all that tension. Need it after being stood up. My breathing hitches and my heart races to a fever pitch as my fingers circle around the bundle of nerves between my thighs and I come hard as Will's name tumbles across my lips.

I lie, gasping for breath as I come down from the high of my orgasm, a feeling of foolishness creeping over me that I thought of Will while I touched myself. I'd probably die of embarrassment if he ever found out. To be fair though, he all but admitted he touched himself while looking at my photo, and I didn't think it silly at all. In fact, it was fucking hot. Oh, God, I am in such trouble.

I go to reach for my phone charger, but it's not there. I look around and realize that something is wrong. I look over the side of my bed and scream. The bed is floating above the floor. There's a sudden whoosh and my stomach clenches as the bed drops to the floor with a crash, countless things falling to the floor of my apartment.

"Holy shit…" I whisper.

I scramble out of bed, staring at the bed frame. It's off centre now and the mattress is hanging off the frame. I approach it cautiously, as if it might bite me, reaching out my hand to touch the frame. But I stop.

The scars on my wrist are moving like they're distorted underwater. They ripple, and for a moment, I see something that wasn't there before. An image of flames, of water, of trees, and mountains and air, and I feel like my breath has left me. I fall to my knees as the image ripples and my scars fall back into place. My fingers trace over the scarred skin and a thought pierces my brain with such force I gasp.

I have more than the ability to manipulate Fire and Water. I push myself up and close my eyes, envisioning the air moving around me. My wrists itch again and when I open my eyes, the twinkle lights above my bed are flickering and there is a rush of air blowing around me. My window is closed, but it feels like I'm standing on the precipice of a cliff. The air whips through my hair, and it lifts the strands away from my neck like a gentle caress. I consciously release that energy, just like I did with Fire and Water.

There's one more element, and I search around for something I think might work. There's a little ivy plant on top of the fridge in the kitchen and I run to it. As I stare at it, the vines start to creep toward me, their movements like snakes through tall grass, and when the leaves touch my palms like it's greeting an old friend, they wind themselves around my arms, massive white blossoms erupting along the vines.

"Hello…" I whisper with a smile. The vines retreat from my arms to crawl their way up the walls of the kitchen like some gigantic, flowery spider. Turning back to the bed, I sit on the edge and flop backward, feeling alive with energy. I raise my hands and flames spark to life in one hand and a ball of water in the other. Together, they swirl around, a perfect yin and yang, and a breeze brushes against my face as a vortex pulls them together. I can feel the energy, my fingers trembling with it, my lights flickering, and my body vibrating.

It explodes outward like a shock wave. The walls and window rattling, the lights extinguishing as it throws me backward on the bed.

I lie there breathless for…I'm honestly not sure how long. Eventually, the lights come back to life, and I raise my wrists to look at them. There is a secret hidden underneath these scars. Another thought creeps into my exhausted mind that makes my stomach turn upside down. Have I always had this ability? Is this why I have the scars? To hide the truth from myself? Is that why I can't remember?

A red light flashes outside of my window. I grab my shirt from earlier, throw it on over my bra and underwear and look out over the dark street. Someone is standing on the sidewalk across from my house, staring up at me. It looks like a man, and for the briefest, craziest moment, I think it's Will. But that's ridiculous. He doesn't know where I live. A moment later, I know it's not. The stranger is dressed head to toe in black, his hood over his face, so I can't make out much more than his white teeth as he smiles up at me. I spin and hide against the wall beside the window, giving a quick glance at the door to ensure the bolt is locked.

I peek around the frame and look out of the window again, but the man is gone. I quickly scan the street, but there's no one in sight. Did I imagine it? No, that seems unlikely. Whoever it is, I'm sure they know who I am and the thought both thrills and terrifies me. I need to know who they are.

•———— ✦ ————•

I KNOW I shouldn't be nervous when I walk into work late Monday afternoon, but I am. In fact, I'm so nervous that my hands are shaking and my back is tense. I dread having to look Alex in the face. What is he possibly going to say? Will he apologize? Will he ignore me? I have no idea how this is going to play out.

Then there's Will. I'm almost more worried about seeing him. I've sent him two extremely naughty pictures since we last worked together, and I have no clue what he's thinking regarding whatever is going on between us. It's like there are two sides to him. The cocky line cook who takes pleasure in tormenting me and the flirty, protective man who likes to play truth or dare via text message.

When I enter the kitchen, both of them look up at me. Alex is on the grill and Will is at the pasta station, and the tension in the room is palpable. Alex's eyes are fixed on me and Will glances between us. He looks pissed. Have they spoken since last night? Surely they have, they live next to each other. I nod at them and walk into the changeroom, feeling their eyes on me as I pass. This is going to be a nightmare of a shift.

When I come out of the bathroom after changing, Alex is standing in the doorframe.

"El," he says softly.

I put on my most passive face. "Alex."

He takes a few steps toward me, and my wrists itch immediately. "El, I'm so sorry. I don't even know where to begin."

I throw my bag a little harder than normal into my locker and slam it shut. "Maybe you should start at the place where you stood me up only to end up coming home shit-faced with some other girl?"

He closes his eyes. "Listen—"

"What kills me, Alex, is, if I wasn't at Will's, I would've gone home and I wouldn't have seen it for myself. I would've sat at home, thinking about how I wasn't good enough or how something awful must have happened to you. Would you have tried to play it off like you got stuck somewhere? Would you have told me the truth?"

He opens his mouth, then looks me in the eyes and lowers his head. "I don't know."

"Well," I say, wrapping my apron around my waist, "I hope she was worth the cold shoulder from me." I walk toward the kitchen.

"She's my ex."

I turn around. "What?"

He runs a hand down his face. "Her name's Sarah and she's my ex from a couple of years ago."

I blink in surprise.

"I met up with old friends from high school. I didn't know she would be there. I thought it would just be a few drinks, but then we got to talking and…" He trails off, looking thoroughly upset. "She wants to try again."

I press my lips together. The anger I felt dissipates a bit at this information. She wasn't just some random girl. He loved her and now she is back. She's a memory that he can hold in his hands, and I'm jealous of him.

"I want you to know though," he says. "I like you very much. I'm sorry I hurt you in such a shitty way."

I take a deep breath and while I'm still mad, it's dissipated now to mere annoyance. "Look, I don't like to hang on to bad blood so…apology accepted." I hold out my hand for him to shake it, and he grins that brilliant smile at me as he grasps my silk-covered hand.

As I pass down the line, Will isn't there. I look around for him for a moment, but Mariah calls me from the dining room and I head out to greet her.

·———— ✷ ————·

IT'S A boring night and Jenni is first cut because there are simply not enough tables to keep all three of us busy. Alex is being overly friendly and snuck me a basket of fries to eat while I go about my shift. Of course, I also elaborated on what transpired to Mariah.

"I cannot believe that happened!" she says after meeting me at the order kiosk. "He seemed so into you!"

I shrug. "It's fine."

"It most certainly is not fine!" she splutters.

"It's his ex-girlfriend. Don't people always act stupid around their exes?"

Mariah rolls her eyes. "Yeah, I guess that's true. I know *I* do."

I smile at her.

"So you just hung out at Will's place while you waited?" she asks, raising an eyebrow.

I narrow my eyes. "Yes."

"Nothing happened?" she asks, smirking.

I shake my head. "No, of course not. He was insufferable."

"Well," she sighs, "I suppose that's for the best. Look at him over there with Jenni. Poor thing can't help herself."

My head whips around so fast my neck cricks. I rub at it angrily as I look across the pub where Jenni is perched on a barstool eating her food. Will is leaning on the bar next to her and they are very close. Closer than people who are just friends. In fact, they *are* more than friends. They're friends who casually hooked up not more than two weeks ago. He's even smiling at her with those goddamn dimples in his cheeks.

I'm such an idiot.

Here I am, playing some stupid truth or dare game via text and sending him dirty pictures of myself, and he's all over Jenni again the very next day. My God, how many girls does he have on the hook at once? Maybe there are more, more that don't even work here. I feel sick.

"You all right?" Mariah asks, noticing my silence.

I blink and force a smile. "Yeah, sorry, just zoned out for a minute. I'm looking forward to your party. Should I bring anything?"

"I'll have alcohol there, but if there's something specific you want, you can bring your own."

I nod, looking up again as Jenni leans forward and whispers something in Will's ear.

My face feels flushed and my hands are burning so hot I can barely stand it. I dash into the kitchen to calm down.

"You all right, El?" Alex asks from behind the pass-through.

"I'm fine, just need to cool down, I think."

"The freezer door's been fixed if you dare," he says, pointing his finger over his shoulder at the mass of grey metal.

I nod sharply, desperate for relief as sweat drips down my back and forehead. I pull open the door to the walk-in freezer and hurry inside. I pull off my gloves, tossing them onto the shelf in front of me, next to steel tubs of marinating meat. The light above me flickers briefly before flames erupt from my hands as my heart hammers frantically against my ribs. The warmth of the fire creates a beautiful juxtaposition between me and the cool freezer air. I pour my anger and shame into my flames, and they burn brighter, faster, until they shrink down into a single white-blue flame.

My head tilts as I stare at it. I've seen this before, felt this before. This light, this energy, this power. I feel it in my soul, like some kind of familiar song that calls to me out of the darkness of my memory.

I hear footsteps approaching and quickly clasp my hands together to extinguish the fire.

The door to the freezer opens and Will walks in. He stops when he spots me and I hastily grab my gloves, pulling them on frantically before he can see the scars.

"We have to stop meeting like this." He smirks.

My breath rises in front of my face as I struggle to regain my breath. "What?"

He walks toward me to grab a tub of frozen hamburger patties as the door swings closed. "You know, for someone who's not a cook, you spend a lot of time in the freezer."

"I just—" I say, my body trembling from the temperature. "I just needed to cool down somewhere."

He raises his eyebrow at me. "Why? Feeling…hot?"

He's flirting with me! He has some nerve. Cuddling up to Jenni in the dining room only to come back here and flirt with me? Unbelievable. I tilt my head at him. "Yes, but not for you." I start to walk past him toward the door, pulling up my gloves one last time, but he blocks me.

"What's your problem?" he asks.

"I don't have a problem."

I try to manoeuvre around him again, but he towers over me in the small space and I'm trapped, his breath rising in little clouds between us.

"Bullshit. What the fuck is going on with you?"

"Don't text me anymore."

His face pulls back. "What? Why?"

I take a deep breath and the frigid air freezes my lungs. "I think you've gotten the wrong impression of the nature of our relationship."

He leans against the metal shelf. "And what impression might that be?"

"That I actually like you."

He blinks, then narrows his eyes at me. "Hmm…I wonder how I could've gotten that impression," he says, his tone overly cheerful and mocking. "Maybe it was the panty photos you sent me?"

"That was a mistake."

"A mistake?"

"Yeah."

He raises his hand to rub his neck, turns away from me, and laughs.

"What's so funny?" I ask.

"You! You are fucking infuriating. I didn't realize it was normal behaviour to send downright pornographic pictures to someone you can't stand."

I'm at a loss for words while he stands there waiting for me to respond. I feel shame prickling up all over me. He would be the type to throw those photos in my face. I knew it. "I never should have given you my number," I whisper dangerously. "I never should've sent you those pictures or played your stupid little game!"

He takes a deep breath. "You know what you are?" He leans toward me and I shiver violently. "You're a hypocrite."

My mouth falls open with indignation. "What?"

He nods. "That's right, you're a hypocrite."

"How exactly did you come to that conclusion?"

"You are perfectly willing to forgive Alex, a guy who fucking stood you up, but you won't forgive me for an *accidental* elbow to the face?"

I blink. My face heats as his words bite into me. He's right, and it kills me to admit it. I am a hypocrite. But so is he! Flirting with Jenni and eavesdropping on my conversation with Alex. Is that why he disappeared? Is that why he was cozying up to Jenni? Why he hasn't talked to me all night? Is he…jealous?

"I regret that day, you know," he says. It's barely a whisper, his breath clouding up in front of his face in the cold air, his glasses fogging a little. I lift my gaze to meet his, and his hazel eyes are sad behind the thick glasses. "The day we met."

Disappointment rips through me like a knife, and I feel a prickle at the backs of my eyes. "Oh." I blink furiously, trying to keep the tears at bay. "Wow, I didn't realize it was such a terrible thing to have met me."

He closes his eyes and sighs. "That's not what I mean—"

"Sorry I'm such an irritating regret in your life. Why don't you have Jenni console you?"

He takes a step toward me, and I have to tilt my head back to keep eye contact. "What?"

"The two of you looked awfully cozy earlier by the bar. Just how many women do you string along for fun, Will? Thank God the worst I ever did was send you a picture of my underwear."

He shakes his head. "There's nothing going on with me and Jenni."

My teeth chatter. "Could've fooled me."

"You don't know what the fuck you're talking about," he growls at me. "Maybe if you got that pretty ginger head out of your ass for two seconds you'd realize that the whole world doesn't revolve around you!"

"And your head is so big I'm surprised you can even fit through the door!"

"Trust me, sunshine," he says, leaning down so his face is only inches from mine, "that's not the only thing about me that's big."

I feel his hot breath on my face against the shivering cold, and my body feels electrified. Goosebumps prickle up and down my arms, and I can't help but glance at his mouth. There's a small scar on the left side of his bottom lip, and I wonder for a split second how he got it. His face tilts toward me ever so slightly. I look up and his beautiful eyes are blazing as they look up from staring at my mouth.

I snap to my senses and push against his chest. "You're impossible. I could kill you," I quickly dart around him as he slowly revolves on the spot to follow me.

"And you're fun to mess with." He smirks. "My God, you really should see just how gorgeous you look when you want to stab me in the neck."

I grip the handle of the freezer door. "Well, then, you better hide all the knives."

I watch her leave, glaring at me the entire time. She throws her bag over her shoulder and with one last murderous look, she's gone.

"What the fuck is going on here?" Alex says, leaning toward me.

I turn away, tossing a rag into the laundry bin. "Nothing."

"Umm," Alex says, sidling up next to me, "that look on your face is not nothing."

"Fuck off, Alex."

He blinks at me then grins. "Holy shit, you like her!"

I turn around. "No, I don't."

He narrows his eyes at me with a knowing smile. "Yes, you do!"

I push up my glasses and rub my hand on the back of my neck. "No, I don't. She's infuriating and purposefully annoying. Not to mention she hates my guts."

Alex nods and backs up. "Whatever you say, man."

I glance up at him as he walks away and puff air into my cheeks. What a colossal fucking mess. What the hell even happened? Here I thought she was warming up to me, then she goes flying off the handle, telling me to leave her alone. I haven't even do anything except cuss Alex out for over an hour this morning about what he did.

Alex explained to me about Sarah, but holy fuck, it was still a dick move and Elora was so upset.

Secretly, I'm thrilled that Alex screwed up so spectacularly because I want her all to myself. But all this achieved is her pushing me further away. I came to work today, hoping that maybe we could patch things up. That our night-time text message games and the pictures were a sign that maybe she might give me a chance.

I barely know anything about her, but she has some kind of hold over me, and I feel like I've known her forever. Even though she looks at me like I'm a bug she wants to squash beneath her foot, I don't care, I just want to be near her.

I was surprised to find her in the freezer, even more so to see her with her long gloves off. Shit, but she looked so incredible when she was mad. Her eyes blazed as bright as blue fire, and when she was close to me, there was something there. Something in the air changed, and I almost kissed her. Her mouth looked so fucking incredible that I was hardly able to keep thinking straight. And she could deny it all she wanted, but something in her expression told me she felt something too, even if it was hidden under hatred.

I'm exhausted when I finally get home. It's been a long few days. My foot thankfully feels much better and isn't really swollen anymore. I turn on the shower and strip down while I wait for it to heat up. I briefly look at myself in the mirror, feeling repulsed by the scars covering my torso. I press my fingers along a particularly scarred ridge on my chest, the numb skin feeling rough under my touch.

I look into the mirror and jolt back. My skin looks like it's rippling, shimmering as though I'm looking at it from the bottom of a pool. And underneath, there's something…

Markings of circles and lines and numbers and letters in an intricate pattern along the skin. I look down at myself, my hands grasping at the area as if my flesh has suddenly peeled away, yet I feel nothing but scars. I look back up in the mirror and it's gone. The room fills with steam as I watch the mirror, willing the marks to reappear so I can make sense of them. I'm sure it has something to do with the abilities I've only been made aware of in recent weeks, and a strange thought occurs to me.

Am I even human?

I've seen enough science fiction movies lately to understand that there are things that sometimes can't be explained. Is this a real-life example of that? Am I an alien? I laugh out loud at the thought of being something like Clark Kent while I work in a pub kitchen. Superhero by day, fry cook by night.

"Stop it, you're being ridiculous," I mutter to myself, shaking the idea out of my head. I pull my glasses off, set them on the sink, and step into the shower. The hot water eases the tension in my neck. The tension caused by Elora, that insufferable woman. So unbelievably stubborn, but so incredibly fun. I've flirted with dozens of women, but never has it been as fun as with her. Maybe part of it is that she's totally disinterested in me and it makes me crazy. It makes me want to chase her down like a lion after a gazelle. The memory of her flushed skin and eyes blazing in that freezer makes my heart race. The amount of passion in that human excites me. Makes me think of how I can put that passion to better use.

My cock stiffens against my lower abdomen, and I stroke myself as the hot water pours down over me. I envision her on top of me, her wide, pale hips straddling me as she rides me up and down, up and down. My fingers trailing over her body and counting out the freckles scattered across her skin like the most gorgeous night sky. Would it feel different with her? I want to think so. That it wouldn't be mechanical, that it would mean something. That it just might fill in the gaping lonely hole in my chest.

My stomach muscles clench and I come hard, gasping out loud, water trickling into my mouth. I breathe deeply, allowing myself to come back down to Earth, my wet hair falling into my eyes.

After a shower, I eat a bowl of cereal and climb into bed, then I check my phone.

There's a text message from Jenni.

Jenni:
I grabbed the cake for Mariah. I think she'll love it. You know how she is with chocolate. I also got some candles with the money you gave me. She's going to be so surprised. You really are very sweet to think of doing this. I'll give you the change when I see you there on Wednesday.

Will:
Thanks, Jenni, I appreciate it.

Jenni:
By the way, I'm sorry about the other day. I knew it was just supposed to be a casual thing between us. Just want you to know that I'm cool with it. Happy to just be friends.

My chest constricts at her message.

Will:
Sorry I couldn't be more for you.

I run a hand through my hair. I'm not an idiot. I know what most of the girls at work think about me. How they think I just want to fuck around, not caring about anything. But how could I tell them the truth? That no matter how much I want to feel something for them beyond mechanical sexual impulse, it's impossible.

Of course, it spawned a reputation that I am some emotionless player, and in a way, it's true. Just not in the way they think. I shouldn't be surprised that Elora has thought the same about me. After all, I haven't exactly done much to dissuade her from thinking otherwise.

I open my text messages and stare at her name, the desire to text her so overwhelming that I have to put the phone down for a minute to stop myself. She told me not to text her anymore. I can respect that wish, but not without apologizing first.

Will:

I won't text you anymore if that's what you want, but I just wanted to apologize for calling you a hypocrite. That was uncalled for and not true.

My message is immediately read. My heart jolts at the thought that maybe she was hoping I'd message her. I wait for a few minutes, then the dots bubble up before a message comes through.

Elora:
🔪

I laugh out loud at the knife emoji she sent, not sure whether to take the message as threatening or funny, or maybe a bit of both. My thumbs hover over the digital keyboard as I decide what to do next. Maybe a skull emoji?

Will:
💀

Elora:
Good night, Willan.

I smile at the screen. Perhaps not all is lost after all. An idea springs to mind, my face spreading into a ridiculous grin as I type out a quick response.

Will:
Good night, sunshine.

◆———— ✳ ————◆

IT IS the day of Mariah's birthday party and both Alex and I have to work, however Raj has agreed to close so that we can leave early. Elora isn't working tonight, but I can't stop myself from glancing at the swing door, hoping she'll suddenly appear every few minutes. I know she'll be at the party later though, and so the hours stretch on like days before Alex and I can finally clock out.

"What's Sarah doing tonight?" I ask Alex as we step out of the pub into the misty night.

"She's working," he says simply. "Told her to come by my place later if she's up for it."

I nod. "So everything's going okay with you two?"

He smiles. "Yeah, actually. It's great. It feels like we were never apart, really. You know what I mean?"

I twist my mouth. "Not really, no."

He slaps me on the shoulder. "You will, one day."

We hop onto the streetcar, flashing our passes as it pulls up. I put mine into my pocket where the back of my fingers skim against the peace offering I got for Elora. When the idea came to me last night, I wasn't sure if I'd be able to pull it off in time, but I saw it in the window of a shop near the laundromat and thought it was perfect. Hopefully, she thinks so, too. An olive branch of sorts, or at the very least, it might garner a laugh. That would be enough.

I shake my hair out on the streetcar and we trundle along toward Jones Avenue, where Mariah's apartment is. Alex goes on and on with some story about Sarah travelling across Europe the year prior, and I feign as much interest as I can.

"Where would you go if you could go anywhere?" he asks.

I lift my eyebrows at him. "Hawaii maybe. Lazing about on those beaches would be nice. I've always liked being near the water. You?"

"Haliburton forest," he replies without hesitation. "There's something there I'd like to see again."

I want to ask him what that is, but the bell dings to signal our stop and we hop off into the cold April air. My breath rises in front of my face and the dampness seeps into my bones. We both spot Mariah's building and head for it, the moon and stars obscured above us by grey clouds. I punch in the buzzer code and we make our way to the elevators. My glasses fog with the change in temperature, and Alex laughs as I pull them off my face to wipe. The elevator opens for us and I hit the button for the fifth floor. I catch sight of myself in the mirror and shake out my hair again as I try to maneuver it into some semblance of style.

I notice Alex staring at me in the mirror. "What?"

He purses his lips together. "Who are you trying to impress?"

I shake my head. "No one."

He smirks. "Yeah, all right, then."

The elevator dings and I hear the music coming from the apartment to our left. There's a pile of shoes outside of the door on a large mat. We pull our shoes off and I open the door only to be assaulted by noise.

There must be at least forty people here to celebrate Mariah, and I can't help but grin as I see her in the living room, a large golden crown sitting on top of her dark curly hair. She spots us in the doorway and waves, smiling. Alex and I wave back, and she points to the kitchen. I've been here a few times before, so I know my way around. The apartment isn't overly large. It's one bedroom and one bathroom with a small living room and closed-in kitchen. Alex and I duck into the kitchen and the counters are covered in every kind of alcohol, along with dozens of candles in order to keep the lights dim. Vodka, rum, whiskey, tequila, Jell-O shots, and a huge cooler full of beer. There's a bunch of different bottles of mixers on the table and a stack of red plastic cups. I grab myself a beer out of the cooler and head back into the living room. I spot Jenni near the television on the wall and head over to her.

"Hey!" I speak loudly over the music.

She smiles. "Hey! I put the cake in the fridge in a paper bag so she can't see. I told her girlfriend, Lindsay, to keep her away from it, too!"

I nod. "Thanks!"

She gives me a thumbs up.

I turn around, scanning the crowd, looking for that bright copper hair. I take a sip of my beer, spotting a few other people from work like Lilli and Mackenzie.

There's a large group of people playing Beer Pong in the corner, and I spot her. She's swaying to the music, probably humming, a red cup in her hand and a slightly dreamy expression on her face. Her hips are moving rhythmically, and my imagination runs wild at what those hips could do in bed. She's wearing a green halter top and blue jeans with her usual black satin gloves that reach her elbows. Her hair is piled on top of her head in a messy bun, her beautiful pale, freckled neck exposed to the world. She shines like a lightbulb in the dark, and I'm nothing more than a moth to her flame.

I make my way around the perimeter of the room since the middle is too full of bodies until I'm directly behind her. I lean down toward her ear. She smells like vanilla and rain.

"Hello, sunshine."

14

ELORA

I whirl around in surprise, almost dropping my drink in the process, and find the magnified hazel eyes of Will Reed.

"Holy shit!" I say, startled, stumbling over my feet on account of the alcohol.

He grabs my wrist to steady me, chuckling over the music. "Whoa, easy there."

He lets me go, and I feel a sting of sadness that he's no longer touching me.

"Hi." I'm not sure what else to say. I was furious with him last night, but the anger has dissipated now. I can't seem to stay mad at him for too long. It's driving me crazy.

"What are you drinking?" he asks, gesturing to my cup.

I look down and slosh around the pink, sickly sweet liquid. "No idea," I say, "Lilli gave it to me."

He leans forward to smell my drink. "Be careful, that stuff will give you a killer hangover."

"I'll keep that in mind."

We're quiet for a few moments as I tear my eyes away from his intense gaze. I look around the room at all the people. I've never been invited to someone's house party before, not that I know of, at least. I'm not exactly sure what to do, and I don't know many people, so I've just been grooving to the music while watching everyone else.

"Do you know how to play?" he asks, breaking the silence between us.

I turn back to him. "What?"

He points at the table next to us where people are tossing what appear to be ping pong balls across the table into rows of cups of beer.

"Beer Pong," he says, "do you know how to play?"

I shake my head. "No."

"Do you want to play the next round with me?"

I think about it for a minute, the heat of his body so close to mine it makes me feel flushed and lightheaded, or maybe that's the alcohol. "On one condition."

"What's that?"

"We play against each other."

His eyes flicker with something like mischief. "All right," he says, smiling, "I'm warning you, though, I'm a pro."

I twist my mouth. "I see that big head of yours made it here all right."

He opens his mouth to speak but closes it, reconsidering. He rubs the back of his neck and laughs. "Don't worry," he says. "I'll go easy on you."

"That's hardly necessary."

The group finishes their game and we move over to the table, me at one end and him at the other. He sets down five partially filled red cups in front of me in a triangle and hands me a ping pong ball. "Ladies first."

I shake my head. "So I just…throw the ball into your cup?"

He nods. "Yeah, or you can bounce it in. But if you bounce it, I can hit it away."

I press my lips together. I hold the little plastic ball up and close one eye to aim. I toss it overhand, but it misses the table completely, and he catches it before it hits the floor.

"Nice one," he says, smiling.

Those dimples flash at me, and I feel heat flood my body. No…don't do this. He's only into you because you're not into him. But I am…I am into him. "The ball is lighter than I thought it would be," I say over the noise.

He nods and takes aim. The ball lands squarely in the second cup on my right.

I look down at it then back up.

He raises his eyebrows. "Now, you drink."

I narrow my eyes at him, grab the ball, and drink the small cup of beer. It's only a few mouthfuls, and I grimace. I wasn't overly fond of beer on the few occasions I've had it, but I'm not going to tell him that. Not when my dignity is on the line. I need to pull myself together. Losing to Will would kill me.

I put my empty cup to the side and take aim again for his cups. The shot is slightly short and bounces. Then, just before it's about to bounce right into the front cup, Will grabs the ball with his hand.

"Hey!" I exclaim.

He shrugs. "If it bounces, I can defend."

I twist my mouth with annoyance.

"What's the matter, sunshine?" he asks. His black curls fall gracefully across his forehead. He looks so hot right now, and it kills me to think he probably just woke up like that. I'm also starting to notice that most of the other females and even some of the males in the room look at him a little longer than I'd like.

He grins, and with one fluid movement, tosses the ball, which lands in another one of my cups. He leans forward on the table. "Told you I was a pro."

I drink the other cup of beer, my head feeling warm. Then I have an idea. I grab the little ball and close my eyes for a moment, feeling out the Air around us. Feeling how it moves. I open my eyes, and Will is waiting for me. "New rule," I say, "if I make this shot, you have to drink all of your cups." I'm not sure where this boldness is coming from. Must be the alcohol.

He raises an eyebrow. "And if you miss?"

I gesture to my cups. "Then I have to finish mine."

His head tilts as he thinks, then finally nods. "All right, you're on."

I smirk and hold the plastic ball up. I feel the telltale itch in my wrists and sense the ghost of a breeze flutter past my ear, over my shoulder, and down my arm. I let loose the ball and the current carries it directly into Will's centre cup. It hits the beer with a plop and Will looks up at me, startled.

"Ha!" I shout over the noise.

He looks down at the cups then back up at me, a strange expression on his face, as though he not only can't believe it, but there's something else there, too. I feel particularly smug as he picks up the little ball and settles it into the discard cup.

"Drink up," I say.

He throws back one cup after another, hardly daring to take his eyes off of me.

I take a sip of my sweet pink drink again as I watch. My head feels properly fuzzy now. I've only ever drank twice before and both times it was only a few sips of wine or beer. And it's starting to hit me like a freight train.

Will finishes his cups and walks around the table to me. "How did you do that?" he asks, his lips in a straight line.

I shrug, trying to be casual. "Lucky shot."

"No," he says leaning toward me, "no, it wasn't."

I blink. Did he see something? I only felt it. Did he feel something in the air, too? What is he implying? Did I just reveal my secret? "Are you trying to say I cheated?" I ask, pushing myself up to my fullest height.

He shakes his head and takes a step back. "No, I—"

"Hey, girl!"

I turn and see Lilli. She's holding a tray full of what appears to be little cups of Jell-O.

"Want one?" she asks, holding the tray out for us.

I look down at the differently coloured cups. "What are they?"

She grins. "Jell-O shots!"

I raise my eyebrows at her. "There's alcohol in these?"

She nods vigorously.

I grab a blue cup. "So I just swallow it?"

"Yup!"

I put the cup to my lips and sniff, it smells like raspberry. My eyes catch Will's and he's watching me intently. Holding his gaze, I tip back the cup and the Jell-O shoots down my throat in one slippery motion. I blink several times from the unusual sensation, then cough as the burn of vodka tickles my throat. "Wow," I gasp, "those are strong."

She winks and offers some to Will, but he refuses.

I'm suddenly a bit lightheaded, and the room drifts out of focus for a moment. I press my hand to my forehead, my skin burning.

"Are you okay?" Will asks.

I wave him off. "I'm fine. I'll go get some air."

"I'll come with you."

I turn to stop him, but his face is set, and I don't have the energy to argue with him tonight. We step out onto a large cement balcony, the edge damp from the moisture that seems to hang in the air. There are two people smoking by the door who nod at us as we pass them to the far side. The cold air hits my skin and I feel goosebumps prickle up all over my body, my hair instantly frizzing around my ears. I head for the far corner and lean against the inner balcony wall.

Will slowly walks up beside me. "Feel better?"

I close my eyes and nod, the cool air offering me the relief I need.

"You," he says slowly, "you look really pretty tonight."

I eye him suspiciously. "I didn't get dressed up for you, you know."

His eyes widen for a second, then he looks down. "Wow."

I immediately feel bad, my heart squeezing at his sad expression. "I'm sorry," I say, shaking my head and feeling a little dizzy. "That was a really bitchy thing to say."

He looks back up at me with a sad kind of smile. "Always so hostile."

I close my eyes for a minute, then open one to look at him, the pulsing of my heart in my ears. He pushes his glasses up the bridge of his nose, and I take an unsteady step toward him.

"My God, your eyesight must be terrible if you need glasses like Bubbles from *Trailer Park Boys*."

He stares at me in shock for a moment and barks out a laugh.

I laugh too and chug the rest of my sweet, pink drink—the sugar hurting my teeth.

"Uh," he says finally, "yeah, it's pretty bad. Even with the glasses, it's not very good."

I'm feeling exceptionally chatty now. "Is that why you accidentally assaulted me on my first day?"

He takes a step toward me. "My depth perception isn't great either. I'm always getting injured at work because of it. I guess it was only a matter of time before I caused an accident."

I purse my lips together and nod.

The two smokers leave, the door sliding open and shut. A fun beat plays over the stereo. I do a little sway and hum along to a tune that's been stuck in my head.

"What song is that?" he asks.

Damn, I forgot for a moment that I have an audience. "I uh…" I pause, trying to think, my brain working hard to try to function normally against the alcohol. "I'm not sure. It's been stuck in my head for weeks, but I can't remember where I've heard it."

His mouth turns up at the side. "It's nice. It sounds familiar, but I can't place it."

I close my eyes and spin to the tune, slipping on the damp balcony floor. I fall toward the railing, but Will's hand is once again gripping my glove-covered wrist.

"Careful," he says a little harshly.

I scoff loudly. "Okay, Mom! No need to panic." There's a crate acting like a small table with an ashtray next to the concrete wall and I step up onto it to sit on the wide ledge of the balcony. "See? I'm perfectly safe."

I wobble, and Will's face tightens. "Can you come down from there, please?"

I continue humming that strange song. This is fun. "Why?" I ask, my bare back to the open air and my heels drumming against the inside of the balcony wall.

"You could get hurt."

"I won't," I snap.

He rolls his eyes and holds out his hand to help me down. "Of course you will. You're like a walking magnet for trouble."

"Why do you care?"

He looks up at me, his eyes blazing. "Because then I'd have to start flirting with girls who actually like me. And where's the fun in that?"

My eyebrow raises, and he smirks, one of his dimples peeking out at me. Fuck. "Go ahead, I'm sure there are plenty of girls here who would be happy to go home with you, but I am not one of them."

The sliding door opens again and the music blares. Jenni comes out onto the balcony, shielding herself from the cold.

"Ready, Will?" she asks.

I turn my face back to him and narrow my eyes. "Ready for what?"

His face drops. "Listen," he says, "I'll be back in a few minutes. Can you promise to stay out of trouble until then?"

"I don't need a babysitter," I mutter, climbing down off the balcony. I realize I'm pouting, so I tuck my lip under my teeth.

He takes a deep breath and follows Jenni back into the apartment. What is going on? I grip the railing with my gloves and raindrops splatter against the material. He said there is nothing going on between him and Jenni, but what the fuck is that? What are they doing? My head spins, and I press my gloved hand to my forehead. I'm too cold now, so I head back inside. Will and Jenni are nowhere to be found. *They're probably making out somewhere*, I think angrily, as I make my way through the crowd.

On my way to the kitchen, Mackenzie spots me, her blonde hair done up in space buns on her head. "Hey! Do you need another drink?" she asks.

Perfect timing. I nod. "Yes, please."

She presses some kind of canned drink into my hand.

I sip it, and it's the best tasting thing I've had all night, and after that sweet drink, I'm crazy thirsty. "Ooh, that's good, thanks!"

Her outline blurs, and for a moment, I forget all about stupid Will and whatever secret thing he's doing with Jenni. My mind goes blank, my brain abruptly overwhelmed by a dark abyss of nothingness. My heart flutters as the beginning of a panic attack starts. "No, no, no," I whisper.

My shoulder hits something hard as I stumble into a bookcase next to the kitchen. I try to take a deep breath, but my chest constricts, and I can't get the air in. My heart beats faster and faster, like a jackhammer in my chest.

I spot the kitchen door as the music turns off and I head

through, finding the room deserted. I grab hold of the counter and lower my head, trying to focus on something, anything, to calm the panic. To keep me away from that dark abyss of loneliness and absent memory. I stare at the candle lit pattern on the linoleum kitchen floor and count the diamonds in each square.

Twenty, twenty-one, twenty-two, twenty-three…

My heart is slowing, and I try to take a deep breath. My lungs expand, and I sigh with relief. I take a few more deep breaths as my heart returns to normal. I lift my head up and open my eyes. The music in the living room has started again. I grab another red cup and fill it with water from the tap.

I hop up onto the counter, my head spinning a little from the effects of the alcohol, and take a long drink, draining it all. I lean my head back against the cupboards as the room tips sideways in the dim candlelight, my legs feeling numb as they hang, and I close my eyes, focusing on my breath for a few minutes.

"There you are."

I open one eye toward the voice and see Will entering the kitchen.

Ugh. After a panic attack, he's the last person I need, but my God, is he ever distracting to look at. The door swings shut behind him and the noise of the apartment is muffled.

"What do you want?" I ask.

He breathes out a laugh, the sound of it hitting the pleasure centre of my brain, and I feel the hairs on the back of my neck stand on end.

"Seriously?" he asks. "Always so hostile."

I close my eyes again, waving him away. "I've never been hostile in my life until I met you."

He steps closer to me. "Well, I'm sorry that I bring that out in you."

I tip my head forward and open my eyes. He's wearing dark blue jeans with a black t-shirt that matches his jacket. He's downright gorgeous, but what the hell is he doing here with me? What could he possibly want? And where is Jenni? What were they doing? More questions are circling my head, but none are making too much sense and everything is fuzzy. "Where's Jenni?"

He shrugs. "I think she's cutting up the cake for Mariah."

I feel my face scrunch up in confusion. "Cake? What cake?"

He stares at me for a long moment. "Mariah's birthday cake. I gave Jenni money to buy it on Monday." Will tilts his head at me. "Wait…did you think there was something going on with me and Jenni because I was talking to her about the cake?"

Yes, that's exactly what I thought, Will, you idiot! A flip seems to switch in my brain. I want all of his attention. I want him to try and change my mind about him, consequences be damned. "Yeah!" I say finally, "Of course I did."

He chuckles. "You're an idiot."

Something that feels like a balloon suddenly inflates in my chest. He doesn't like her, he just needed her help. Maybe I overreacted? Yeah…I overreacted. He smiles at me, and I push his shoulder. "So, you were just asking her to buy a cake?"

"Yeah."

"Oh," I say quietly, "well, I do feel like an idiot now."

The room around Will starts to spin and I put my hand down to keep myself upright.

"How much have you had to drink?" he asks.

I twist my mouth, thinking. "I'm not sure. I think I may be drunk. I've never been drunk before."

His eyes widen in surprise. "You've never been drunk before?"

I let a giggle escape my mouth, my gloved hand clamping over it as I realize what sound I made. I blink a few times, trying to focus, and when I do, Will's face looks concerned.

I tilt my head as I look over his handsome features. His sharp jaw and straight nose. His full lips with the little scar on the left side. A tingle spreads across the surface of my body as I think about what it might feel like for those lips to touch mine.

"What?" he asks.

I find myself reaching for his face, his magnified eyes darting over mine. I point to his glasses. "Can I?"

He raises his eyebrow. "Umm…yeah, sure."

I smile a little and reach forward to pull his glasses off. I turn them around and hold them up in front of my eyes. The world through the lens is just a mass of colour and it makes my eyes water.

"Jesus, Will," I say. "You weren't kidding."

I pull the glasses off my face and look back at him for the first time without the glasses. Something bright that doesn't come from the lit candles flares across his irises, and I fight against the urge to throw myself against him. To press myself into his skin and tangle each other up in knots. He's so beautiful, and I feel a gentle pulling sensation in the pit of my stomach, as though an invisible thread connects us. He's staring at me with a thoughtful expression, and even though his glasses proved he can barely see, his eyes are clear and focused on me. I swallow hard and turn the glasses back around.

"Here," I say as I push the glasses back onto his face. They're a little crooked, and I can't stop the giggling.

He straightens them, brushing the hair away out of his eyes, revealing the scar on his forehead.

"How'd you get that?" I ask.

"Get what?"

I point. "That scar."

He reaches up to run his fingers along the jagged line above his eyebrow. "Oh, it's from the accident."

"The accident?" I ask. I press my lips together as realization hits me. "The accident your parents died in?"

He nods and looks down and away from me. I feel a lump start to form in my throat.

"Yeah."

"Oh my God, Will, I didn't know…I mean, I didn't realize you were involved too."

He looks up at me, and his eyes are deep, sorrowful. Full of heart-breaking torture.

"Why…" I ask, "why didn't you say that before?"

He shrugs. "Don't really like talking about it, I guess."

My hand instinctively reaches out toward his face, wanting to comfort him, but a shiver rushes over me and I stop. Instead, I cross my arms over my chest. "And the one on your lip?"

He smirks. "That one's from a particularly kinky girl who liked to bite."

My mouth drops open in shock as my pulse throbs between my legs. "Seriously?" I ask.

He laughs. "No! It's from the accident, too."

"Oh!" I laugh.

We're quiet for a moment. His smile fades, then he blurts out, "I got you something."

I narrow my eyes. "You're not about to make some crude joke about your package, are you?"

He laughs again, and it's throaty and sultry and, fuck, it rattles me to my bones. "No, no." He digs around in his coat pocket. "Here."

He holds out a small golden dagger. It has a beautifully detailed, golden handle with a sun design on the hilt. I pull the engraved sheath off and stare at the silver blade. I turn it over and look back up into his eyes, which are staring at me expectantly.

"It's small and sharp," he says, "just like you."

I feel an ache in my chest. I smile at him, and there's a small flush that spreads across his cheeks.

"Kind of a strange gift, don't you think?"

He nods. "Yeah, well, I thought it might come in handy in case you feel the need to stab me in the neck, you know?"

I trace my fingers along the sun embossed into the hilt and my breath hitches. "There's a sun here."

"Yeah," he says, "I thought it suited your sunshiny demeanour."

I snort with laughter, and as he grins widely, I feel something around my heart melt. Fuck, this man will most likely ruin me, but I don't care. I sway on the counter again, and as I put my hand out to steady myself, my hand slips down into the sink, the dagger dropping out of my grip.

I start to fall, but Will's hand is around my forearm and pulls me back up.

"Whoa, I think you've probably had enough to drink, drunky brewster," he teases.

The room spins again, and I press my hand to my forehead, letting my eyes rest for a moment. "I'm fine," I say, hopping down off the counter into the space between the sink and Will.

There's a change in the noise level as the door of the kitchen opens, the air shifting and the candles flickering from the breeze. It slowly closes again, as though someone had opened it but changed their mind. We both look toward it, then back at each other. He's so close, and he's looking down at me, his eyes darkening. My heart pounds in my chest, my pulse echoing through my ears. Our bodies are inches from each other, so close I feel the heat radiating from his skin. He smells like citrus and spice, and it's overwhelming my already intoxicated mind. But there's something else. Something that doesn't feel right. The smell of smoke.

I sniff loudly and look around to see that flames are creeping up Will's jacket along the arm.

"Holy shit!" Will yells.

It's as if everything suddenly goes into slow motion as I stare at the flames creeping up the fabric of his jacket. I feel that telltale itch from under my gloves, and without even realizing what I'm doing, I start to pull one off my hand. On instinct, I reach toward him, toward the flames. The scars on my wrist shimmer into a picture of waves that ignite under the skin, and I feel myself smile.

"No! Don't—" I hear, but it's too late.

My palm grips his arm. Frost erupts from under my skin, spreading like snowy spider webs up and across the fiery sleeve, suffocating the growing flames. The crackle of ice forming on the surface is loud, like wood splintering apart as the flames die away. I feel a surge of power shoot through my body. The last flame fizzles out and disappears, and I remove my hand.

I feel a sudden clarity overwhelm me and I look around in fear as I realize what I've done. Will is staring at his arm, his mouth slightly open, then he looks at me. I quickly hide my bare arm against my stomach and turn to pull my glove back on.

Whatever energy I used sobers me, as if all the alcohol in my body has been burned away. I feel perfectly steady on my feet and no longer fuzzy. My mind feels so clear that it gives me a headache, like an instantaneous hangover. What have I done? Will is backing up, his fingers tracing over the frost that covers his arm, and I turn and bolt.

I burst through the door into the living room, and after spotting my jacket on one of the hooks by the door, I pull it on and head out into the hallway.

"Elora!"

I hear Will call my name, but I don't look up. I search for my shoes and lean against the wall to pull them on. Fuck, I need to get out of here. But just as I find my second shoe, Will is there, staring at me.

"Where are you going?" he asks.

I glance up at him, trying to keep my face from betraying me. "I'm going home."

"Wait," he says, his voice desperate, "what the hell just happened in there?"

I finally pull on my second shoe and stand up straight, pushing the hair off my face. "I don't know what you're talking about."

His mouth drops open, appalled by the lie.

I spot the elevator and head toward it. I need to get out of here. He needs to forget what happened. If I can get away, maybe he'll forget.

"That's bullshit, Elora. I just saw you create ice with your bare hand!"

He follows me to the elevator, and my head drops back as I try and think of something to send him away. I stab the down button with a little more force than necessary and the light over our heads flickers.

"No, I didn't, Will, you sound crazy—"

"I know what I saw."

I turn toward him, and my stomach drops with what I'm about to say. "No, you don't! You said it yourself, your eyesight is shit."

The elevator dings, the doors open, and I head inside.

"I'll go down with you. Just let me get my shoes."

"No, Will, please leave me alone."

Please, just leave me alone to figure this out. He turns to grab his shoes, and I press the button for the ground floor with urgency. I look up just in time to see the hurt on his face as the doors close.

I fall back against the mirrored elevator wall and let out a huge wracking sob of a breath. What's going to happen now? Will he tell someone? Should I go into hiding? What if he calls the police? Or what if the government tries to take me away?

The elevator doors ding and I walk through the empty foyer

out the front of the building. Rain is pouring down, and it's cold, freezing, really. I pull my coat around myself a little tighter, wishing I had an umbrella. I brace myself for the icy rain and step down the stairs that lead out onto the street.

"Elora!"

It takes me a moment, but as I turn toward the voice, my eyes widen to see Will running up to me from the outside corner of the building. How the fuck did he get down here so fast?

"How—" I turn and look at the fifth floor then back at Will, who doesn't appear out of breath at all. The rain drips down the side of his face.

"Tell me how you did it," he says in a rush.

I shiver violently as the rain soaks my hair and runs down my neck under my coat collar.

"What the hell, Will? How did you get down here so quickly?"

He squares his shoulders, standing over me, his eyes deadly serious. "I'll tell you my secret if you tell me yours."

His words run through my mind over and over again. What does that mean? Does he mean…

I feel my eyes widen. Can he do something, too? Something not…normal? But can I trust him? What if he's lying? What if I tell him…show him what I can do and he uses it against me?

"I…no," I say, turning away. "I need to go home."

"Let me take you home."

"I don't need you to do that," I say, looking around in the direction of the streetcar.

I start to walk toward it but slip on a patch of icy pavement. In one quick movement, his arm is around my waist and his face is so close to mine I feel his breath on my lips. Even in my panicked state, I realize he would only need to lean forward a few inches to kiss me.

"Will," I whisper, "stop trying to save me."

He groans. "Well, maybe if you stopped getting into situations where you need saving, I wouldn't have to."

My mouth parts, about to retort, but he cuts me off.

"Please, just let me make sure you get home safe," he says, sighing and loosening his grip on my waist. "No funny business, I promise."

I shiver, look around me, then back at him. His glasses are splattered with rain and his dark curls are plastered to his forehead. I sigh. "Fine."

He breathes a sigh of relief. "Thank you," he mutters. "Do you have a picture of your house on your phone?"

I pull my face back in surprise, not sure if I heard him right. "What?"

"Do you have a picture of what your house looks like, or your street?"

My eyes narrow, completely confused as to why this is necessary, but pull out my phone from the back pocket of my jeans anyway. I scroll through my photo gallery, him watching me the whole time. I only have one picture of the outside of the house. It's the picture from the rental listing that I happened to take a screenshot of. I turn my phone toward him so he can see. "Here," I say.

He glances at the house for a long moment and looks back up at me. "This is your house?" he asks.

I double check the picture. "Yeah, why?"

He shakes his head, water spraying everywhere. He looks around us, but with the weather, the street is empty. "Listen, I've never done this with another person before, okay?"

"What are you talking about?" I ask.

"If my theory is correct, everything will be fine. I need you to hold on tight to me," he says, "can you do that?"

I raise my eyebrow. Theory? What is he doing? Is this just

some way to get me to be close to him? As if he can hear my thought process, he rolls his eyes.

"Can you trust me this one time?" he asks, exasperated.

My eyes flutter closed and a deep shiver runs down my spine. I nod. "Fine."

He lifts my arms around his neck and wraps his around my waist, pressing our bodies together. He's muscular and warm and smells so fucking good. Shit, maybe this was a bad idea. He looks down at me and says, "All right, hold on tight, sunshine."

W hen I feel the pavement beneath my feet again and quickly glance through the rain, I know I did it. I pull back from Elora, whose warm breath caresses my neck, my fingers hovering for just a moment longer than necessary as I let go of her waist. The little blue house stands across the street from us and a nervous fluttering churns in my stomach.

I have been here before—Jumped here without even realizing what I'd done. Something led me here, to her.

"You know, if you wanted a hug, all you had to do was ask," Elora mutters.

She looks up at me, and I smile as I realize she doesn't know we've moved. I point to the house over her shoulder and she turns slowly, cautiously. I see the side of her face as she looks around, noticing the house, the street, and she whips her head back around to me, her wet hair spraying rain drops everywhere.

"Holy shit!" she exclaims.

I smirk at the look of utter surprise on her face.

"Can we go in? I'm freezing and completely soaked," I say, gesturing toward the house.

"I—I…" she stutters, taking a few tentative steps.

"You can ask whatever questions you want once we're inside," I say.

She blinks at me, pushes the strands of wet hair behind her ears, and leads the way to the side gate. I follow her up the stairs of her apartment, noting the surroundings. She opens the door with a key, then leads me inside.

It's a small bachelor style apartment. The bed is unmade and slightly rumpled in the corner, clothing strewn across the dresser. I imagine her pulling the clothes out, trying to decide on what to wear to the party, and smile. I follow behind her, my shoes squeaking against the wood floor. There's a puddle beneath both of us as we stand next to each other, not sure what to do first.

"This, umm…" she says meekly, "this is my place."

She turns to look at me, her eyes wide and questioning.

I want to tell her everything. I need someone to talk to about all of this, to try to understand it. Who would've thought it would be her?

"Elora," I start, "I know you have questions, and I have a few of my own."

She doesn't say anything, eyes still wide, so I continue.

"But would you be okay if I Jump home to change real quick? I'm soaked and I'm dripping water all over your floor. I can be back in five minutes."

A little crease forms between her brows as if she's trying to make sense of all of this.

"Umm, yeah sure," she says finally. "I should probably change myself."

I give her an encouraging smile and take a quick look again around the apartment, taking in the details so I can Jump my way back.

"Five minutes and I'll be back, all right?"

She swallows and nods again.

In the blink of an eye, I'm back in my apartment. I spend a few minutes tearing off my wet clothes and changing into dry ones. I quickly towel dry my hair and clean my glasses. I check my phone. It's been five minutes but just to double check she's ready, I send her a text message.

Will:
Ready?

Elora:
As I'll ever be.

I smile to myself and close my eyes, visualizing her apartment with the messy bed and the fairy lights. I hear a sharp gasp as I Jump to just inside her front door, and when I open my eyes, Elora is sitting on the little loveseat in front of the TV. She's taken down her hair and brushed it out so it hangs straight down her back. She's changed into what appears to be a set of pyjamas. A pair of pink cotton shorts and a black tank top. She's still wearing those black gloves up to her elbows, and she looks so unbelievably pretty at this moment that I swallow hard.

"Hi," I breathe.

"Hi," she says.

She's sitting cross-legged on the far end of the couch. She gestures to the other cushion. I take a deep breath and make my way over, sitting down next to her. Her eyes meet mine, her gaze is clear, and I wonder if whatever she did to conjure the ice sobered her up.

"So," I say tentatively, "I'm not exactly sure where to start."

Her mouth twitches at the corner. "Me neither, really."

I rub the back of my neck, and a thought comes to me. "Truth or dare?"

She smiles and pulls her knees up under her chin. "Truth."

I smile back to put her at ease, then point to her hands. "How long have you been…able to, you know…put out a fire with your hands?"

She looks at her palms for a moment. "Not long. Only a week or so."

I raise my eyebrows in surprise.

"Your turn," she says.

"Truth."

"How long have you been able to—what did you call it? Jump?" she asks.

I shrug. "Same as you, only a week."

Her eyebrows knit together. "That's so strange," she mutters. "Did you have any idea before now that you could do this?"

I shake my head. "No, no idea. You?"

She shakes her head. "Nope." She pulls a long strand of her damp hair forward and begins to twist it around her finger.

I raise an eyebrow. "Can you do anything else? You can't Jump like I can, can you?"

"No, that was…that was a shock."

I breathe out a laugh and her pink lips curve into a bright smile.

"But I can do other things," she says.

My eyes widen. "Really? Like what?"

She rubs her knuckles along the insides of her forearms absentmindedly, then gives me a nervous glance before she pulls her gloves off her arms.

I watch her intently, but as the gloves come off, I can finally see why she wears them. I've seen the back of her bare hands before, but not the inside of her forearms. The fair skin is covered in angry, jagged, crisscrossing scars like a net of pain and suffering. My heart plummets at the sight of them.

"Elora, did someone hurt you?"

She looks up at me with a sudden desperate expression, her eyes almost glowing in the dim light.

"What?" she whispers breathlessly.

I point to the scars. "Did someone do this to you?"

Her eyes suddenly well with tears, and she closes her eyes, her mouth twisting in a pained expression as tears escape, running down her freckled cheeks.

Shit, I didn't mean to make her cry. Should I apologize for what I said?

"I…no one's ever," she blinks rapidly, wiping at her face and looks back at me. "Everyone always assumes I did this to myself."

I take a sharp breath in. "What?"

She raises one of her shoulders uncomfortably. "Listen, there's something you should know."

I feel my stomach jolt nervously, like missing a step going downstairs. "What is it?"

She looks up at the ceiling for a moment. "Prior to two years ago, I can't remember anything."

The words don't register right away. "Wait, what?"

"Two years ago, I woke up in the hospital. Some fishermen had apparently pulled me out of the lake in the middle of January. They said it was miraculous I was even still alive. And I had these healed scars. They assumed from their placement that I'd tried to kill myself before, possibly multiple times. That it hadn't worked, so I tried to drown myself."

The only sound is the hammering of the rain on the little window over her bed. I feel like I can barely breathe, like I, myself, have been thrust into icy water, my lungs frozen. *Two years ago. Is it a coincidence?*

"I don't remember anything before waking up in that hospital," she whispers, looking up at me with tear-covered lashes. My fingers move as if to reach out to brush her tears away, but I stop them.

My throat feels sticky as I try to get the words out. "You don't remember anything? Not your family? Where you were born? Anything?" Surely there must be something.

She shakes her head. "No, nothing. I mean, I know how money works, and how to dress myself, what my name is, but when I try to remember, everything is just black. Like there's a wall there, or maybe even a door, and I just don't have the right key." She sighs and crosses her arms. "It's infuriating." She angrily wipes away another tear that escapes down her cheek and sniffs loudly.

"Well," I start, "for what it's worth, from what I know of you so far, you're the last person on Earth I'd ever suspect of trying to hurt themselves. You're too stubborn for that."

She breathes out a laugh. "Thanks."

We hold each other's gaze for a moment. *Tell her,* my mind screams at me. *No, not yet.*

"So," I ask, "what else can you do, then?"

She raises her eyebrow mischievously. "Ready to be amazed?"

I smile and nod. "Bring it on."

She flexes her fingers and balls them into fists. I lean forward to see, but as her hands open, flames erupt out of her palms and I jolt backward.

"Holy shit," I breathe.

She holds her arm out to the little line of candles on the crooked shelf above the TV. The flames from her hand shoot across to light the wicks, then she extinguishes the rest of the flames in her hands. This time when she opens them, there's a shimmering ball of water, the gold from the flickering candles reflecting on the surface.

Elora's fingers move and the water transforms into a little

butterfly, its wings flapping and glittering in the light as it flits over. I hold out my hand and the butterfly lands on my finger. The coolness of the water against my skin is startling. "Wow."

The next moment, it evaporates into mist, scattering over my hand as goosebumps prickle up and down my arm. She sniffles, and it seems as though her excitement to show off what she can do has called a halt to her tears. Elora reaches forward to grab something from the coffee table in front of us. It's a flat river rock. She sits back against the couch and holds it out between us. I watch in amazement as it levitates into the air.

I look past the rock to see her pink face screwed up in concentration. There's a loud crack and the stone shatters into a thousand tiny pieces like the tail of a comet. I let out a loud breath as the rock reforms before my eyes.

"Fire, Water, Earth and…" she says.

A gentle rustle of a breeze passes by my cheek, ruffling the curls on my forehead. It whips around her, her hair flying wildly around her face, then it's gone.

"And Air?" I ask.

She nods.

I huff out a breath and then suddenly remember. "So you did cheat!" I say, pointing at her. "At Beer Pong, you totally cheated!"

She presses her lips together mischievously. "To be fair, I didn't think you'd ever find out."

I laugh, and she does, too. Her laugh is beautiful and musical and full of life. The thought of her no longer on this Earth makes me feel unbearably anguished.

"So, what about you?" Elora asks. "You can Jump from place to place…can you do any of this?"

I shake my head. "No, or at least I haven't tried. But I can stop Time."

She looks at me, surprised. "Stop time? What?"

"It's harder than Jumping. Jumping is like riding a bike. Once

I knew I could do it, it was easy. But Time," I pause, "it drains me."

She raises her eyebrows. "Really?"

I nod. "I can show you, but you'll stop, too."

She glances around for a moment. "Hold on." Elora pushes herself off the couch and walks to the kitchen. She rummages in a drawer for a moment, then returns with a piece of paper and a pen. She hands them to me. "If you manage it. Write something on here, so I know."

"All right, then."

I roll my shoulders back and close my eyes. Just like before, I think about her. It's easier to do it this time with her sitting right next to me. I imagine the silence that settles down on me when everything stops, the stillness, and I hear her breathing stop. The sound of the traffic ceases, the electricity in the lights quiet. I open my eyes and she's watching me, but when I wave my hand in front of her, she doesn't react.

I take the paper and pen from between us, write a brief message for her, then place it on her lap. I briefly pause before starting Time again and just take a moment to look at her. This beautiful, powerful woman in front of me. Perhaps we were always destined to meet each other, and I laugh to myself, wishing it had been more graceful than it was. If I was destined to meet someone, I'm glad it's her.

I close my eyes again, and the noise rattles my eardrums. I blink a few times, and I instantly feel drained. Like I could curl up and fall asleep right here. I wonder why Jumping is so easy comparatively.

"Are you going to do it?" she asks.

I smirk. "Look at the paper."

Her eyes glance down to read what I wrote.

It's good to finally talk to someone about this.

She looks up and smiles. "Wow. What's it like when time stops?"

"Quiet."

She nods as if understanding. "I think the real question now is, why?"

"Why?"

"Yeah." She tucks her feet under her and shuffles closer to me like an excited child. "I mean, we can both suddenly do these seemingly impossible things. Why now? Why not always?"

"The only thing that's been different is…you."

She tilts her head. "What?"

"The only thing that's changed in my life recently," I say again, "has been meeting you."

Her eyes narrow. "You think our meeting started all of this?"

I raise my hands in surrender. "I don't know, but it's the only thing I can think of."

"Were your parents like this, that you can remember?" she asks.

I frown. "No, but…since the accident, remembering things from before is hard. Like I know I went to school, had a family, had friends, but it's all fuzzy. Like," I scoot closer to her and our knees touch, "you know Monet's paintings? Impressionist art. It's like colour and shape but nothing solid. Like I only have impressions of my memories." I sigh and rub the back of my neck with my hand. "The doctor told me it's likely a side effect of the accident. Like a brain injury or something." I pause for a long moment. "Do you think the accident has something to do with all of this?"

Her forehead creases. "I don't know. Seems strange that something happened to both of us two years ago and now we're —" She breaks off as if she's not quite sure how to classify what we can do.

"It's quite the coincidence," I add.

She nods. "I'm sorry about what happened to your parents. To you. Were you badly hurt?"

My fingers instinctively scratch at the rough scars on my chest. "I was burned pretty badly."

Her eyes turn sad, the blueness magnified by the unshed tears in her eyes. I look away, clear my throat, then I feel her hand touch mine, skin to skin. And it's as if my whole body has awakened from some kind of deep sleep. I stare down at her bare flesh on mine. She's never touched me before, not without the gloves, and it's both searing agony and the sweetest caress, and without meaning to, I let out a long, shuddering breath.

I feel like her touch has ignited something in my soul, and that desperately aching lonely hole in my heart for the first time, it feels like it might start to heal. Then, a voice echoes out of that strange place where I'm not sure if I'm imagining it or maybe somehow dreaming.

I want to let him in, but I'm worried he'll break my heart.

Will tugs at his t-shirt, and as the fabric pulls, I see the hint of scarred flesh underneath. I wonder how painful that must have been, how horrifying. And then to have the constant reminder of everything we lost on our skin every day. It's something I understood well.

I reach out and cover his large hand with my small one. I've never touched him before with my bare hands, and his skin is almost a walking contradiction, both rough and soft and the perfect temperature but also fiercely hot.

He looks at me with an expression I've never seen before. It's like euphoria, like everything suddenly makes sense to him, like he's relieved and angels have appeared to sing a chorus from the heavens.

I want to let him in, but I'm worried he'll break my heart. I pull my hand back to rest it on my knee. He stares down at his own hand, lifts it, and his fingers flex imperceptibly. Everything I thought I knew about Will has turned out to be wrong. Well, not everything. He's still cocky and arrogant and sexy as hell, but he's also caring, protective, and sweet, with a past as difficult as my own. Not to mention he can fucking teleport and stop Time. What is even happening?

His eyes dart over my face, hovering too long on my lips. I feel myself lean in toward him. Desperate for him to kiss me. Maybe with everything we've been through, it will be different for us. Maybe he'll want me longer than a night. But then what if he does want me for longer? I'll be leaving in just over five months. Will he want to follow me? Can I ask him to do that? Can I give up trying to find someone who knows me for him?

A sudden horrifying thought comes to me. Maybe there is no one out there. It can't be a coincidence that Will and I have met, suddenly developing these strange powers at the same time and both having a devastating experience two years prior.

"Will?" I ask, slightly breathless.

He blinks for a moment, then clears his throat. "Yeah?"

"Do you believe in fate?"

His brows furrow together. "What do you mean?"

"What if we were destined to meet?"

He doesn't say anything.

"I mean," I continue, "there has to be some kind of explanation for all this, right? No one should be able to do what we can do, but we happen to be in the same place at the same time by accident?"

He slowly nods. "I think it makes the most sense out of everything else going on, to be honest. And it's a bit of a relief, because *none* of this makes any sense."

A small laugh escapes me.

He watches me again for a few moments, then abruptly stands. "I should go."

His words surprise me, especially considering his reputation. Here we are in my apartment, alone. I'm being vulnerable and open—I even purposely wore my sexiest pyjamas, and he's going to leave? Is he really going to go and not even try to kiss me? Maybe I had it wrong all along. Maybe he doesn't like me after all. Or maybe he feels hesitant after my drunken behaviour earlier.

"I'm not drunk anymore," I blurt out.

He raises his eyebrow at me. "Are you implying we should drink more?"

I take a sharp breath in as disappointment quakes through me. Why am I so upset? It's for the best that he isn't hitting on me or making a move. Right? God knows at this moment, I would do anything this man asked me to do.

"No, no…of course not, I just…I didn't want you to worry about me being alone if I was."

He nods. "Oh, right. I can stay if you're worried you might need help?"

My jaw twitches. "No, it's fine. I'm completely sober. I'll just go to sleep now anyway. I'm pretty tired."

"Okay," he says, and he rubs the back of his neck with his hand. "I'll just go then."

I wait for him to head toward the door, but I remember he can teleport, or Jump, and I reach out to stop him before he goes. "Wait!"

Once again, my fingers are on his skin. His corded forearm flexes delectably under my touch, and I find myself salivating. His eyes find mine, and I feel like they can see into my soul.

I clear my throat. "Since you can Jump, and you know where I live now…"

He breathes deeply as understanding dawns on him. "Don't worry, sunshine, I won't just randomly appear in your apartment unless you ask me to." Something flickers across his face and his mouth twitches.

"Oh, no!" I yelp suddenly.

"What is it?" he asks.

I press my palm to my forehead. "Shit, I forgot the dagger at the party in the kitchen. I'm so sorry, I was trying to get out of there so fast, I for—"

Will holds out his hand, the golden dagger suddenly appearing there.

"Oh," I say, taking it in my hands, "you brought it with you?"

He shakes his head. "No, I stopped Time to go get it."

I blink up, still trying to wrap my head around what he can do.

He smirks. "Man…I shouldn't have told you about the Time powers. I could've pulled some epic pranks at work."

I roll my tongue on the inside of my cheek to keep from smirking back. "Have you? Pulled any pranks, I mean?"

The corner of his mouth turns up and a mischievous glint flares in his eyes. "Maybe."

An image of Hunter spilling his beer in his lap and falling over after his shoelaces were mysteriously tied together slams into the forefront of my mind. Will has been watching. "Hunter," I whisper, "Did you—" My mouth drops open as the pieces fall into place.

Will simply grins at me and says, "Good night, sunshine."

Then he's gone.

·————✳————·

THE TAPPING of icy rain on the window above my bed has kept me awake for over an hour now. I curl up in bed, the dagger that Will gave me on my nightstand with my phone, and I can't help but feel completely overwhelmed by everything that's happened tonight. This is absolute lunacy. Not only do I have powers, but Will does, too? Are there more people like us out there? If so, how would we even go about finding them? It's not like we can just walk up to every random stranger and say, "Excuse me, sir, can you teleport or create fire with your bare hands?"

I laugh in spite of myself and turn over. My earlier thoughts are still settling in my brain. Maybe I am alone. Maybe no one is looking for me. There is both a comfort and terror in that realization. If that is indeed the case, then I can stay here, put down some kind of roots, build a life for myself. Have actual friends, maybe even a boyfriend…

I sigh and think about Will again. About his beautiful smile, about how his hand felt under mine, about how he looked at me when I touched him. I have no sexual experiences that I can remember, other than with myself, and I've never really cared about it that much until him. And, my God, do I ever want him. The way he makes me feel simply by looking at me is positively sinful. I can only imagine what it would feel like to have his hands all over my naked skin.

But therein lies another problem. I have no idea what I'm doing in that department. I'm basically a virgin for all intents and purposes. Would he think that's okay? Would he be weirded out by that? Would it hurt? Oh my God, what if I embarrass myself? What if I'm terrible in bed? I'll have to get another job, or move away. I wouldn't be able to face it.

The sound of my phone dinging snaps me out of my thoughts. Who's texting me now? It's nearly two in the morning.

Will:
Serious problem.

I bolt upright in bed, my heart thrumming nervously. Shit! Did something bad happen? Is he okay?

Elora:
What's wrong?

A few moments, the three dots, and,

Will:
Can't sleep.

I let out a huge sigh as tension leaves my body.

Elora:
You scared me! And that hardly seems like a serious problem.

Will:
It is, though.

Elora:
Well, what exactly do you want me to do about it?

I see the little dots appear, then disappear, then appear and disappear, and it becomes obvious he is trying to think about what to say next.

Will:
I guess I just wanted to talk to you.

Elora:
You know you could've stayed if you wanted to talk.

Will:
No, it was best that I left.

Elora:
Why?

Will:
Probably would've said or done something stupid.

My heart picks up again.

Elora:
Like what?

There's a long pause, and after a few minutes, I begin to worry that maybe he finally fell asleep, but then he types again.

Will:
Listen, I know what the other girls at work say about me. And they're right.

Why would he say that? Is he trying to convince me he's no good for me?

Elora:
You're more than what they say, though, and I'm sorry I judged you before I took the time to get to know you for myself.

Will:
Thanks.

Elora:
Truth or dare?

Will:
Truth.

My fingers hover over the keyboard on my phone.

Elora:
Did you really tie Hunter's shoelaces together?

Will:
Yes.
I wanted to kill him but thought it might look suspicious if a dead body suddenly appeared in the bar.

I giggle. He's not wrong.

Not to mention it might have scared you.

Elora:
Well, thank you. I didn't realize I have a time stopping vigilante looking out for me.

Will:
Truth or dare?

Elora:
Dare.

Will:
I dare you to tell me your best pick-up line.

I let out a laugh.

Elora:
I don't have any pick-up lines.

Will:
Make one up.

My hand flies up into my now dry hair as I think. I try to remember all the cheesy things that guys have tried on me over the past two years and one in particular stands out, but maybe I can change it up a bit.

Elora:
Are you in your bed?

Will:
Yes?

Elora:
I'm in mine. Obviously, one of us is in the wrong place.

I tuck my thumbnail behind my teeth as I smile and wait for his reply.

Will:
Damn, I'll need to remember that one.

Elora:
If I catch you stealing my lines, I'll have to put this dagger to good use.

Will:
Noted.

I wonder if he's been looking at the pictures I sent him again, and my fingers tremble as they rush over the keys.

Elora:
Can I ask you for a favour?

Will:
Sure.

                Elora:
Can you not show those pictures I sent you to anyone?

He types right away, and my heart is fluttering wildly.

Will:
I would never. I don't share.

My eyes close with relief, and my stomach does a little dance.
I don't share. Maybe he wants all of my attention, too.

                Elora:
Thanks.

I try to think of what to say next, but he's typing again.

Will:
**If I didn't mess up our first meeting, and I asked you out,
would you have said yes?**

My breath halts in my chest.

                Elora:
Probably.

Will:
Good night, sunshine.

                Elora:
Good night, Willan.

———— ✦ ————

THE FREEZING WATER *penetrates me to my bones. Surely this is how I'm going to die. That strange blue light flickers below me, taunting me from the bottom of the lake.*

"Elora." The voice reaches me through the water. It's familiar, calming, and I want to follow it down into the darkness.

But there's no way to follow it. If I do, I will die. And I don't want to die. I have too much to live for, so I turn my face away from the light and toward the surface.

"Elora," it calls again, growing more and more distant, and my heart aches with the sudden thought that I'm leaving someone behind.

The ice shimmers above me, and I scramble toward it, kicking and clawing my way up to the surface. I'm confident water this cold is frozen over, blocking me in, like some icy prison. But as I rise through the depths, I see the rippling surface and my hope grows that I'll be able to get out of here.

At last, my face breaks the surface of the water and a new kind of pain finds me. The frigid air whips against my skin as I look around for an escape. Soon, the shore is under me and I lie on the rocky beach. The shouts of men running toward me echo like the sound of a distant dream. I try to raise my head, the faintest flicker of blue light like a hot flame dying under the surface of the black water.

———— ✦ ————

I WAKE UP, gasping and coughing, trying to rid imaginary water from my lungs. The dream happened again. I reach into the dark expanse of my mind, searching for anything new, but as always, there is nothing. I blink against the light filtering in through my bedroom window and the memories of last night at the party with Will come flooding back to me like a tidal wave.

I sit up in bed and pull the covers over my chest as if he might appear at any moment. No, he said he wouldn't just randomly show up. He has more respect for me than that, right?

Turning toward my phone, I see there are several messages in the group chat wishing Mariah a happy birthday, along with several pictures and a few messages asking where I went. I let them know that I'm fine, just drank a little too much too quickly, but I made it home safely.

There's also a message from Heidi asking if I can close at the pub tonight, and I respond that I am available. Thankfully, I'm not suffering from a hangover. I wonder if Will is working tonight. Maybe he'll be closing too. Maybe he'll flirt with me through the passthrough. He'll smile at me then Jump me home. Maybe I'll ask him to stay the night, and he'll touch me with those beautiful hands…

No, I can't. I'll be leaving in a few months. I shouldn't get attached, and I know myself well enough that I could never just have casual sex with someone, even if that is all he wants. I'm too starved for love.

A message dings on my phone and a grin spreads across my face when I see it's from Will.

Will:
I'm going to grab a late breakfast at the diner down the street from me. Want to join? My treat.

Is he asking me out? I mean, there's nothing to indicate that this is anything more than a casual breakfast between co-workers, maybe even friends at this point. I briefly wonder if he grabs breakfast with his other friends. Alex and Mariah, surely, but what about all the girls he randomly hooks up with? A morning after breakfast is customary. Maybe there will be a group of people. God, why am I overthinking this so much? It's just breakfast. I'm starving, and we just shared our powers with each other last night. Not to mention the thought of another bowl of Cap'n Crunch cereal has me almost gagging.

Elora:
Yeah, all right. Who else is coming?

Will:
Just me. Is that okay?

My chest inflates at the thought of being alone with him again.

Elora:
Yes, it's fine. Where should I meet you?

Will:
I can come get you in five minutes?

Oh God, he wants to just Jump here. Fuck, I probably stink of alcohol, and from the feel of it, my hair probably looks like birds have made a nest in it.

Elora:
Can you give me half an hour? I need to shower.

Will:
Sure, I'll text before I come by.

I throw myself out of bed and into the shower. After getting out, I try to choose something cute to wear to brunch. What does someone even wear? Probably something casual. Can't look too done up, right? I grab a pair of clean leggings and a crew-neck sweater and throw my hair up in a bun on top of my head. With any luck, by the time I get back later, it will be dry…wait.

My wrists itch and the lights flicker briefly as I pull on the Air in my apartment, directing it toward my head, the gentle caress of the breeze along my neck. A little added warmth from Fire and before I know it, my hair is dry. Wow, I think this is really going to cut down on my morning routine, much faster than my shitty hair dryer.

There's another ding on my phone, and I see the message from Will asking if I'm ready. I text him back that I'm just finishing up in the bathroom, so he can come by. I brush my teeth, and a few moments later, I hear him walking around the apartment. What an odd thing to never need to take the streetcar again. I stop midway through brushing my teeth.

That night after work when he helped me deal with Hunter… had he purposefully taken the streetcar with me even though he didn't even need it?

I spit out my toothpaste and rinse my mouth before walking out of the bathroom. He's standing by my bed, looking out the window, his curly black hair falling over his forehead. He's got on black jeans and a grey sweater with a flannel jacket overtop, and when he turns toward me, I feel my stomach flip as he smiles.

"Hi," he says.

I can barely keep the question contained. "Did you take the streetcar home that night after we closed together even though you could simply Jump home?"

He blinks at the accusation, then rolls his eyes. "Hi, Will, nice to see you again so soon," he says in a mildly mocking voice. "Nice to see you too, sunshine, and if I might say, always a pleasure."

I feel my cheeks flush. "Sorry, I…it just occurred to me when I was brushing my teeth, and sometimes I just blurt out—"

I halt when I notice he's silently chuckling. "Don't worry about it," he says. "I've come to expect hostility when we talk."

I cross my arms over my chest and take a deep breath. "So, did you?"

He rubs the back of his neck with the palm of his hand and takes a step toward me. "Yes."

"Why?"

He shrugs. "I wanted to make sure you got home okay. After what that creep tried to do—" He stops himself, but his jaw twitches as he takes a deep breath. "Are you mad?"

I shake my head. "No, just trying to fit all the pieces together."

He nods, looking relieved. "You ready to go?"

"I just need to grab a pair of gloves and my jacket," I say, turning toward my dresser.

"You don't have to wear those around me," he says in a rush.

I narrow my eyes. "What?"

He closes the distance between us. "I just mean…you don't have to hide them from me."

His fingers close around each of my wrists, turning them upward so my scars are fully visible in the light. My instinct is to pull them against me, but something about the way he reverently looks down at them freezes me to the spot. His body goes slightly rigid as he touches my skin, and I notice the goosebumps that prickle up all over his arms and the flush of his cheeks. Then, his thumbs lightly brush over my skin and I swear my knees start to shake as something akin to electricity floods through my body.

My throat is completely dry as I try to push the words past my lips. "It's more that I need to hide them from everyone else," I whisper, delicately pulling my hands out of his grip. "I don't like people judging me based on something they can't possibly understand."

If he looked disappointed at losing his grip on me, it was only for an instant, because he cocks an eyebrow at me questioningly.

"What?" I ask.

"Nothing," he says, "you're just a very complicated person, Elora, and I'm trying my best to figure you out."

"Any luck?"

He laughs and shakes his head. "No, but I feel like I'm getting closer."

I shove his shoulder and turn back to my dresser, where I pull on a pair of short silk gloves that tuck under the long sleeves of my sweater. I grab my jacket from the end of my bed and notice something move out of the corner of my eye. I look back and catch sight of a dark figure outside of my window on the street below.

I turn back, bracing my hands on the window frame to see the hooded figure of a man staring up at me from the street.

"Will?" I call. I turn to pull him over, but when I glance back out of the window, the figure is gone.

"What?" Will asks.

I blink rapidly. "There was a man outside. He was looking right up at me through the window."

He leans down to glance out the window. "I don't see anyone."

I crane my neck to look up and down the street. "I know I saw someone. He was dressed all in black, with a hood covering his face."

Something that looks like concern flashes across Will's face. "Are you sure?"

I nod.

"Stay here."

I go to say something, but he's gone.

A moment later, I see Will out on the street below, looking in every possible direction. He looks back up at me through the window then walks back toward the house.

"I didn't see anyone."

I spin around to find Will standing behind me. "Shit, you scared me."

"Still not used to it, huh?"

I shake my head. "I don't think I ever will be."

I look back out the window at the street below us. "I swear, I wasn't imagining it."

Will nods. "Don't worry, I believe you. I've seen him, too."

We lock eyes, and I want to ask him more, but he's close enough that I can smell him. That intoxicating scent of citrus and spice that sends a shiver down my spine, and the questions die in my throat.

"Ready?" he asks.

As if on cue, my stomach rumbles loudly and I want to die of embarrassment, but Will simply smiles and pulls my arms around his neck. Unconsciously, my fingers twist the hair at the base of his neck, and I wish I had listened to him and not worn the gloves because I bet it's soft. His fingers touch the bare skin of my back as my sweater lifts. My stomach flips and I swallow hard, and for a moment, before my apartment disappears, his eyes flare behind his glasses as though a very bright light reflects in his irises.

I didn't mean to touch her, but as her arms lifts to rest around my neck, her sweater rises and my fingers touch the bare skin of her back. I'm instantly breathless. The warmth and energy that ricochets through my body at having contact with her is intoxicating. I feel like I have too much energy, like I drank ten coffees in two minutes. And for a brief moment, I hear the gentle melody of that song she sometimes hums. My heart is racing as I Jump, intending to reappear in the alleyway behind the diner, but when I look around, we're standing on the edge of the lake on a pebbled beach, the sound of the waves crashing and lapping against the shore.

Elora looks around, then back at me with a raised eyebrow. "There's a diner here?"

I drop my hands from around her waist.

"I…sorry, I think I overshot by a bit."

She tilts her head and smiles. "A bit?"

I release a breathy laugh. "Okay, maybe a lot."

"Where are we?" she asks.

I look down the beach and see the CN Tower far in the

distance. "Still in Toronto. I think we're just too far south. I guess it's a good thing I didn't land us in the water."

But Elora has gone quiet as she looks down the pebbled shoreline.

"You okay?" I ask her.

"I think I've been here before," she says breathlessly.

"You have?"

She takes a few steps away from me and looks out over the water—the wind blowing her hair up and around her face. The rocks crunch under her feet as I take in the vast openness of the lake before us. Past the few trees on the shore, the open water stretches out with nothing but the horizon to orient you.

"I…I think this is where they found me."

The words don't quite register right away. "What?"

She turns back to me, and her eyes are wide and glistening with tears. "When they pulled me out of the lake, I think it was here…"

She turns over a large flat rock with the toe of her shoe and a tear rolls down her cheek. I feel like an idiot standing here, not sure if I should hug her, comfort her in some way. I want to grab her face and wipe the tears away and tell her everything's going to be okay.

"I don't want to be here right now," she says quietly against the noise of the waves.

"Come on, then."

She blinks and wipes at her face with her gloved fingers. She nods and reaches up to wrap her arms around my neck, pressing her face against my chest. I know she's done it so I can take us away from here, but there's something intimate in the way she leans against me, as if desperate for comfort. I take special care not to touch her bare skin this time, and the next moment, I hear the sounds of the traffic and the diner as we appear in the empty alley.

I think she'll pull away quickly and want to put some distance between us, but she stays pressed up against me, and I feel the heat of her body through my clothes. I breathe in the smell of her, vanilla and rain, and have to fight against the overwhelming desire to lift her face up to mine and kiss her.

"We're here," I whisper.

She pulls away, and I feel a sense of loss as she takes a step back, dropping her arms to her sides. "Oh."

She still looks upset. "Do you need a minute?" I ask.

She shakes her head, then rubs at her face one last time. "No, I'm fine. God, I probably look a mess, though."

I offer an encouraging smile. "No, you look stunning."

She looks up at me, her eyes and face softening.

"Come on," I say, heading toward the end of the alley and to the diner.

A few minutes later, we're seated in a red leather booth by a window in the back corner of the diner, looking over the plastic menus in front of us. I inwardly lighten at the way Elora twists her mouth as she contemplates what she might want.

The server makes her way to us, an older woman with cut up credit cards for earrings and a streak of purple through her white blonde hair.

"Drinks to start?" she asks.

"Coffee, please," I say.

Elora looks up from the menu. "Orange juice, please."

The server disappears, and I'm relieved to see Elora smile.

"I haven't had orange juice in a long time," she says, slightly giddy with excitement.

I raise my eyebrows. "Why not?"

She shrugs. "Too expensive to buy a jug at the store. Plus, I'd probably chug it all in one sitting."

I nod with understanding and spot her contemplating the menu again.

"Order whatever you like," I say. "I told you I'll pay."

"You don't have to do that," she says.

I roll my eyes. "Don't argue with me or I'll have to restrain you."

She crosses her arms and leans against the back of the booth. "I'd like to see you try. You might be able to Jump anywhere you please, but I can set you on fire."

I smirk. "You're forgetting I've already survived a fire." Without thinking, I pull down the collar of my sweater to reveal the smallest patch of scarred skin.

Elora's eyes widen with horror. "Oh my God—" she clasps her hands over her mouth. "I didn't think…shit, that was so insensitive of me."

I roll my shoulder, allowing my collar to fall back into place. "It's fine, El, don't worry about it. It was funny."

She drops her hands and stares at me, a curious crease between her eyebrows.

"What?" I ask.

"You've never called me El before."

"Oh, sorry, would you rather I not?"

She smiles. "No, it's fine."

"It's a pretty name, by the way," I say, looking away and fidgeting with the container of sugar packets on the table.

"Thanks. Guess it could be worse. I could have a name like Willan."

I glare up at her. "Ha ha."

The server comes back with our coffee and orange juice and takes our order. Elora orders French toast and a fruit salad, whereas I order what I always do when I come here, the biggest breakfast platter they have for only ten dollars.

"So," I say slowly, "how did you find yourself working at the Flying Weasel? Was it always on your bucket list to work at a dive bar?"

She snorts, and it's adorable. "First of all, it's hardly a dive bar. Believe me, I've seen far worse." She shakes her head a little as though trying to rid herself of the memory. "I saw the flyer for the job opening and I had just moved. It was close by so—"

"Wait, a flyer?"

"Yeah, it was in my mailbox."

I rub the back of my knuckle along the scar above my eyebrow. Brandon never mails out flyers for openings at the pub. In the past two years, the most I've ever seen him do is put a "Now Hiring" sign on the front door. "Are you sure you got a flyer in the mail?"

She narrows her eyes at me. "Yes…why?"

I shrug, trying not to think too much about it. It's not like Brandon's ever included me in his hiring tactics. "Sorry, it's just unusual, that's all. Brandon's never had to mail out flyers before."

Elora interlaces her fingers and leans her chin on them. "Don't believe me?"

I raise my hands. "No, I do."

She smiles. "Good. I was thinking I might have to put that dagger you gave me to good use."

"I'll keep one eye open, sunshine."

She rolls her blue eyes at me. "Why do you call me that?"

I smirk, reaching for my coffee. "That's for me to know, and you to find out."

"Should I start calling you moonbeam?"

I nearly choke on my drink. "Why moonbeam?"

"Well, you call me sunshine and you are nothing if not the opposite of that." Her eyes are alight with mischief.

I lean forward, my voice dropping. "Please, don't call me moonbeam."

A blush spreads across her cheeks, her freckles darkening, but she taps her chin with her gloved finger. "What about… moonlight? Moonface? Moonpie?"

My eyes close, feigning exasperation. "Please stop." But I can't hide my grin, and I don't want her to stop. Truthfully, this is the most fun I've had in a while.

"So," Elora says, leaning back again, "did you have fun at the party last night?"

"You could say that."

She twists her mouth. "Do you hang out at Mariah's place a lot?"

I shake my head. "No, I've only been there a few times if she has some kind of party. We usually go out or hang out at work."

"That picture she took of you is really nice," she says.

Confused, I put my coffee down. "What picture?"

"That one on your Instagram."

I tilt my head at her. "You looked at my Instagram?"

She raises her eyebrows at me. "Yes, and don't bother lying and saying you haven't looked at mine. I'm sure you were desperate for more skin exposure after those panty pictures that I never should have sent you."

I press my lips together, fighting the urge to laugh. "You can lie to yourself all you want, but you knew what you were doing when you sent me those photos."

She opens her mouth to retort, but the server arrives and sets the plates down in front of us. Elora thanks her and stares, astonished, at my meal.

"You're going to eat all that?"

I nod. "So, can I ask you a question?"

She pops a grape into her mouth, her eyes closing appreciatively as she chews. "Sure."

"What were you doing before moving here? I mean," I say, "before you started working at the pub."

She takes a sip of her juice. "When they let me out of the hospital, all I had was my ID and a bank account with a few thousand bucks. A social worker helped me find a place to live since they couldn't find any record of family or friends or a previous address."

"There was no address on your ID?"

She shakes her head. "There was, but it's an abandoned house."

I feel my eyebrows raise. "Really?"

She pushes her French toast around on her plate. "Yeah, that also didn't help the whole narrative that I was suicidal. They assumed I was homeless, living in that building, but…" She stops and her eyes glaze over.

"But you can't remember?"

She shakes her head. "It's strange because I know that it's not true, but because I can't remember…I don't know. Maybe it is true. Maybe I repressed the memories myself. Maybe there is no one out there looking for me." Her eyes flick up to meet mine and a deep crimson flush spreads across her cheeks. "Sorry, that was…I've never told anyone that before."

My heart aches, and I wish I could help her. "I'm sorry. If I knew you, and you went missing one day, I would do everything in my power to find you."

"You hardly know me."

"Does that really matter? You're still important to me."

Her eyes blaze, and once again, she's too bright to look at, so I turn away. My eyes lose focus and blur. I push my glasses up onto my forehead and rub my eyes with my fingers.

"Are you okay?" she asks.

I nod. "Yeah, just sometimes my eyes get really sensitive."

"You know," she says quietly as I readjust my glasses on my nose, "it's going to be really hard to leave here."

The noise fades into the background. "What? What do you mean? You're leaving?"

"Yeah, in five months. I only stay anywhere for six months at a time."

"Why?"

"I've tried to move around the major areas of Toronto first, since this is where they found me. Then I'll branch out. I figure if I move around, maybe someone will finally recognize me."

I stop moving entirely—the pure sadness that radiates out of that statement hitting me like a blow to the stomach. We're quiet for a few long moments.

"El—" I say but then stop myself.

"Look, I know it's stupid," she says, her eyes shining again, "but there has to be someone somewhere, right? Someone who can tell me who I am. What my life was. I mean, I didn't just appear from another world, right? I must have had parents, a family, friends…someone."

"It's not stupid," I say quietly.

She stabs her fork into her French toast. "I'm not so unlovable that no one would want me—"

"El—"

"I mean, here I am checking the missing persons page every day like some pathetic little girl—"

"Stop—"

The sound of her knife cutting through the French toast then onto the ceramic plate is shrill, but she doesn't seem to notice, her voice rising with every word.

"I'm a good person, Will, I don't deserve to end up alone like this—"

But her face has gone stony, angry, and the light above our table flickers and dies.

"Elora?" I ask.

"Is that why they don't come?" she whispers to herself.

"What are you talking about?"

A breeze ripples around us, her hair lifting off her shoulders and mine off my forehead, and there's electricity in the air as it moves.

She looks up at me sharply, her eyes practically neon with anger. "Did they abandon me because of this?"

She holds out her arms, and even though they're covered, I can sense the power buried under the fabric, under the scars, within her very skin. I grab both of her forearms with my hands, and the brightness in her eyes flickers for a moment.

"No," I say. "I don't believe that for a second."

She pulls her arms away from me. "Did they try to drown me in that lake? Did they do this to me?"

The lights in the rest of the diner flicker, the other patrons looking up over their heads as Elora stands, her hands slamming down onto the metal table.

"*Did they try to kill me?*"

Before I even realize I've done it, the sound stops, that eerie silence hovering over the room. I'm on my feet a moment later, and though I can feel that uneasy prickling sensation of someone watching me, I ignore it this time. Her face is twisted with pain and anger, crackling energy radiating out of her eyes. The power of this woman feels all-consuming and causes my blood to thrum through my veins. Elora's gloves have all but burned away from her hands, and frost has spread across the table like streaks of lightning. I quickly scan the room. No one looks at us directly, as though the impossibility of our powers is a deterrent. I need to get Elora out of here. What if she accidentally hurts someone? I drop some cash on the table, wipe the frost away, then grip Elora tightly as I Jump back to her apartment.

As soon as we're there, I free her from her frozen state, and the gentle noise of her quiet apartment floods my ears.

"El!" I cry out, and for a moment, she's disoriented, her beautiful face wild and terrifying.

Then she looks at me, and I feel a shiver run down my spine. "What did you do?" she whispers.

"I'm sorry," I say, "you were getting carried away."

Elora's eyes dart around her like a caged animal, her chest rising and falling rapidly as she tries to catch her breath. "You had no right to Jump me—"

"You don't even know what you're thinking is true! You could've hurt someone—"

"Get out," she whispers.

"El, I'm sorry, I just—"

"*Get out!*"

A shockwave radiates out of her, through the air, and I'm knocked backward off my feet. The thought of my couch springs to mind as I fall. I Jump in midair, landing hard on my old orange sofa in my apartment.

18

ELORA

I've never felt so utterly hopeless before. Even when I woke up in that hospital with nothing more than a name and the doctors insisting I had tried to kill myself, I always held onto that small glimmer of hope that had stayed alive through everything. I clung onto some foolishly optimistic idea that someone was searching for me. But now, there is a bleak emptiness that seems to stretch on before me. The possibility that there is no one coming, no one to find, that even if there is, they don't want me. And seeing the lake today. Standing on that beach was the nail in my coffin.

I can't prove it, but the idea takes hold of me with such force I can't push it away. It feels like a sledgehammer to the heart. I wasn't aware I did it, but power surged through me in my anger and it was so terrifying. Will was right to get me out of there, back here where I am safe and everyone else is safe from *me*.

Will.

I was hideous toward him, and the look on his face when I forced him to leave is etched into my soul. A new wave of despair washes over me as I realize he'll probably never want to speak to me again and it hurts all the more because after everything, he's the only one in my life who seems to care.

I look up from my place on the floor and glance out the window at the dark grey sky and the torrents of rain pelting against the house. I wipe my face of the river of tears I've shed and sniff loudly. I need another shower to help to calm down my swollen face and sinuses. I turn on the shower and catch sight of myself in the mirror. What a fucking mess. And to top it all off, I've probably just scared away forever the only person I want to see.

I hop in, the hot water running down my face and body, and the desire to keep crying overwhelms me again. My wrists itch terribly, and I lean my head back against the shower wall in frustration. I don't want this. I don't want whatever power or magic this is. I just want to know who I am and have someone want me. Is it so selfish to want that? To want someone to take care of me?

If I knew you, and you went missing one day, I would do everything in my power to find you.

Will's words shout at me through the void and my heart aches. This man hardly knows me, and other than the less than ideal first impression and his flirtatious teasing, he's only ever tried to protect me. He watched out for me with Hunter and didn't even bring it up. He looked after me at the party when I foolishly drank too much and didn't take advantage of me for his own gain. Will just removed me from a situation that was dangerous and I treated him horribly for it.

And now all I want is for him to be here. To wrap his arms around me and tell me everything is going to be okay.

You're still important to me.

The realization strikes me then as I turn the water off. I like him. Beyond a physical attraction, which has always been there, I actually like him. He's funny and charming and considerate and there is a connection between us that's tangible. But what if he doesn't feel the same way? I was so sure he would kiss me last night after the party, but he didn't.

The rain is starting to let up a bit as I get out of the shower and dress. I pick up my phone, and even though I'm not surprised, it does hurt a little to see that there is no message from Will. There are still hours to go before work and there's so much I should do, but all I want is to curl up under the covers and feel sorry for myself. So that's what I do, turning the TV on my way over so I can watch it from bed, the sitcom offering noise and laughter so my mind can digest everything that happened.

· ———— ✦ ———— ·

EVEN THOUGH I won't make much money, I'm happy to see that the pub isn't very busy when I arrive. I wave at Jenni and Mackenzie as I walk through the dining room and spot Lilli behind the bar.

"Ali off tonight?" I ask.

She nods. "Yeah, said he wasn't feeling well. No surprise there, he got wasted last night. Where did you run off to?"

I shrug. "Just went home. I'm not used to drinking."

She nods and I continue on, steeling myself as I push through the swing door into the kitchen. My eyes immediately spot him behind the pass-through and he freezes as if worried I'll explode at him. I offer what I hope to be an apologetic smile, but it probably comes out looking more like a sneer than anything else and when his expression doesn't change, I rush back toward the changerooms.

I quickly fit into the short black dress, stuffing my bag and running shoes into my locker. Emotions threaten to overwhelm me again as I realize I've probably blown it. He will never want anything to do with me again. The whacko redhead who threatened to burn a burn victim. Who got so upset that she nearly blew that diner to pieces.

"I'm a fucking idiot," I mutter, slamming the locker door shut.

"That's debatable."

His voice is like heat to a sore muscle, instant relief. I turn and there he is, his hands above him, gripping the door frame like he owns the place, and I feel my knees tremble at the way his eyes rake over my entire body from head to toe and back again.

"Hi," I say.

"Hey."

Tears threaten to spill out of my eyes again, that painful prickling forcing me to take a long, deep breath.

"Will, I'm so sorry about earlier," I say in a rush.

He's next to me a moment later. "It's all right. You don't need to apologize."

I feel his warm, strong arms wrap around me and I sink into his chest, inhaling the smell of him. For the first time, I'm not overwhelmed with my attraction to him. I simply enjoy the comfort he provides, the familiarity of someone caring enough about me to give me a hug when I need it the most.

"You were right to get me out of there," I whisper against his chest, and I feel him squeeze me tighter.

"I should've asked—"

"No...I was out of control. You did what you had to do."

I may have imagined it, but I think for a moment that maybe he kisses the top of my head.

"Oh! Sorry, I didn't realize I was interrupting," a voice announces.

Will pulls away, taking his warmth with him, and we both turn to see Alex from the doorway, looking wide-eyed between us.

"I'll be right there," Will says.

Alex looks between us one last time, then saunters back toward the line.

Will pulls at the hair at the back of his neck and chuckles. "I should get back," he says, taking a step backward toward the kitchen, his fist tapping his open palm.

I nod. "Yeah, I should get started."

"Are you closing tonight?" he asks.

"Yeah."

He smiles. "Me too."

My heart flutters with happiness at those two simple words.

"You all right, though, sunshine?" he asks, the scar above his eyebrow distorting.

I sniff and feel the smile I give him lift my cheeks. "Yeah, better now."

He leaves the room, and for the first time since my earlier crisis, I feel happy. He's done that for me.

·————✳————·

I'M OVERLY thankful that the evening didn't end up very busy. Everyone assumed that because of how terrible the rain was earlier in the day that most people decided against venturing out. I don't blame them. All I want is to curl up in a warm ball on my couch and watch some mindless TV show that will make me feel better. Or make out with Will if the opportunity presents itself.

I only have one table left after Mackenzie and Jenni have been cut, and it's well after eleven when they decide to head out. When I walk back into the kitchen to grab myself a drink, Alex is getting ready to leave.

"Hey," he says, grabbing a to-go cup and filling it with root beer.

"Heading home?" I ask.

He nods. "Yeah, not super busy tonight, was it?"

I shake my head. "No, thankfully. Kind of needed a chill shift."

"Same. Have too much fun at Mariah's last night?"

I press my lips together. "A bit. I don't really ever drink, so I guess it hit me faster than I thought it would."

"You work in the restaurant industry and you're not a big drinker? You're like a unicorn," he says, laughing.

I smile and shrug. It's not like I could tell him it wasn't a hangover, but an emotional crisis that has me needing a break. I look past his shoulder toward the back, where Will is carrying a stack of boxes out of the supply room.

"He likes you, you know."

I turn back, and Alex is smiling at me.

"What?" I ask.

"Don't worry, I'm not jealous or anything. I fucked that up, and I'm happy being back with Sarah. But…Will likes you."

I swear my heart skips a beat. "He likes a lot of girls," I say, fishing for more information. Thankfully, Alex takes the bait.

"Not like this, he doesn't," he says, pulling his bag over his shoulder, "as his best friend and neighbour, I can honestly tell you that Will has hooked up with plenty of women, but he's never looked at any of them the way he looks at you."

I feel a blush crawl across my entire face. "And what way would that be?"

"Like he's been waiting for you his whole life."

I look back at Will, who's disappearing back into the supply closet, then at Alex, who smiles at me one last time before leaving the kitchen.

I laugh to myself, pondering what Alex said. Will actually likes me?

I shake my head and walk out of the kitchen to check on my table. They've left cash and a decent tip, which I pocket and close out their bill before wiping down the table. When I head back into the kitchen, Will is standing next to the coffee maker and pouring himself a drink.

"Hey," I say, walking toward him.

He holds his hand out in front of him to stop me. "Stay back."

I freeze and frown. "What's wrong?"

"I haven't had iced coffee since I spilled mine all over this spunky redhead a few weeks ago, and I really don't want history repeating itself. I'm desperate for the caffeine."

A laugh rips past my lips, and I hold up my hands. "Fair enough. I'll stay away."

"Not forever, though, right?"

I turn back to him and I wonder if the way he's looking at me now is what Alex described to me earlier. "No, not forever, I'm just going to sit and count out my float. I don't reckon anyone else will show up before we close."

I pull off the apron from around my waist and catch Will looking me up and down, his teeth pulling on his scarred bottom lip, and I can't help but feel my lower stomach muscles clench. "You better stop looking at me like that," I say as I pull the end of my glove a little higher toward my elbow.

"Like what?"

"Like you're trying to picture me naked."

He smiles and those goddamn dimples appear. "Actually, I was trying to guess the colour of your underwear again, but I could go with naked instead."

He winks at me and walks away, and I swear I think I might melt on the spot at his nerve. Fucking hell, I would let this man ruin my life and I'd do it with a smile on my face.

19

WILL

I'm still smirking when I push the bin of trash out into the alley behind the pub. The rain has finally come to a stop, but everything is still shining and wet, the black pavement reflecting the streetlights above. And the smell of rain and fresh air fills me, reminding me once again of Elora.

Today has been such a roller coaster ride. With what happened at the diner and spending most of the afternoon stressing about how I could possibly apologize for breaching her personal space like that, I feel like I've been put through an emotional blender. Then, when she hugged me back, her small body curling in toward me like we were made to fit together, everything seemed all right with the world. How I didn't even hesitate to kiss her head, like it was an old habit, it was all so much. And then being able to flirt with her again. It's my new favourite pastime.

The sound of breaking glass makes me look up, and there, standing at the end of the alley, is the hooded man again. Watching me. Maybe if I—

Stop, stop, stop. I try to stop Time but nothing happens. It's as if he knows what I'm trying to do, the grin on his face spreading wider and wider. Then the panic sets in.

"Who are you?" I shout.

His hands explode into flame, the shock of it sending me backward against the brick wall. For a moment, I think the flames will engulf him, but even though they grow larger, they stay well controlled to his fists. I push off the bricks and Jump to the end of the alley, but when I reappear, he's gone. I feel his gaze on my back, turning around to find him where I was only a moment ago.

I Jump back, but this time he reappears above me on the roof, the flames extinguishing from his hands as he waves at me from above, then he disappears. Heat scorches my arm and I look down to see my coat sleeve on fire.

"Fuck!"

I dash back inside the kitchen and grab the first oven mitt I find to smother the flames as I wrench off the coat. I sink to the tile floor against the wall as I try to regain control of my heart, my breathing, my sanity.

I look down at the charred fabric of my chef's jacket and with shaking hands. The symbol of a spiralling eye stares back at me from where the fire burnt through the fibres. I immediately toss it away, like holding it might curse me, then scramble to my feet.

"Holy fucking shit!"

I spot Elora coming through the swing door—her face one of mild annoyance. "Come up with your guess yet?"

"We need to talk," I say, grabbing her by the arm and pulling her toward the changeroom.

"What? What's wrong?"

I pull her into the bathroom, close the door, and lock it behind me. When I turn back to face her, her eyes are wide and her face is pale.

"Will, what's going on? You're scaring me."

"Someone attacked me in the alley," I say breathlessly.

Her eyebrows knit together, her hands reaching out toward me as though she's just noticed my lack of jacket. "Oh my God! Are you okay?"

I grab her gloved hands at the wrists. "It was someone like us."

Her eyes widen, and her mouth parts. "What?"

"They could Jump like me and produce Fire like you," I say, my eyes flicking back and forth between the door and Elora's panicked face.

"Like us?" she whispers. "Well, we have to find them!"

I blink at her in shock. "What? What are you talking about?"

"If we find them, we can ask them why we're like this. They might have answers."

I shake my head. "This guy didn't want to talk—he wanted to hurt me. He set me on fire!"

"What?"

"That's not all. He burned something...a symbol...into my jacket."

"What kind of symbol?" she asks, tilting her face back.

"It was like some kind of eye. I don't know...I've never seen anything like it before."

She grasps the door handle. "Maybe it's a message!"

I grab her arm to stop her. "Or maybe it's a warning. If someone wanted to talk, why not just talk? Why stalk and intimidate?"

The logic finally seems to click, and she slowly nods. "Yeah...umm...no, you're right."

"Listen, the person you saw this morning," I say, remembering the figure she said she'd seen on her street, "what if it's the same person?"

"You think they know where I live?" she asks, crossing her arms over her chest.

I shrug. "I don't know, it's possible."

"Hang on," she says, holding up her fingers. "Why didn't you just freeze Time to find out who this person is?"

"I tried, but—" The fact that I haven't been able to stop Time when I needed to most stings. "I…I don't know. It's harder for me to do, I have to really concentrate on…" I pause, not exactly wanting to spill the beans that I always think about her when I manage to do it. "This is still all new to me. It's not like I'm some masterful Time ninja."

"All right, all right, it was just a question," she says, closing her eyes.

"Come on," I say. "Brandon's probably thinking we snuck away to fuck in the walk-in."

She stops me. "That's happened before?"

I frown. "I'm admitting to nothing."

She rolls her eyes and moves past me, back out toward the kitchen. The two of us finish our closing duties, all the while looking over our shoulders at each other, the slightest sound causing us both to flinch.

Thankfully, Brandon accepts the fact that it's been a slow night and agrees to close half an hour later.

"Man, what a terrible night. Good thing the rain stopped, though," Lilli says, pulling her coat over her work clothes and closing her locker.

"Yeah, hopefully the weekend is better," Elora says, pulling her running shoes on after changing.

"See you later."

Lilli leaves and I follow closely behind Elora as we make our way through the dark dining room, saying good night to Brandon as he locks the door behind us.

The air is still damp from the heavy rainfall, but it's not overly cold. In fact, it's the warmest it's been in weeks, but even still, the street is deserted. Elora heads toward the streetcar stop along the empty sidewalk and I follow after her as Lilli and Brandon head toward their cars.

"Where are you going?" I ask.

She turns and raises her eyebrow. "Home. Where do you think?"

I stare, openly gaping at her. "You're going home? After what happened?"

"Well, where else am I supposed to go, Will?"

But then the mysterious man is there ahead of us across the street, a blade in his hand. My panic is paralyzing. He moves so fast I can barely react before he throws the blade across the empty street, straight for Elora. Some sort of internal instinct kicks in for me to do one thing—protect her. But she's just out of my reach so I can't Jump her away from the danger. There's only one thing to do. I Jump in front of her, my eyes finding hers right before a searing pain rips through my shoulder. I let out a howl as I double over in front of her toward the wet pavement.

"Will?" Elora's voice echoes through the empty street.

My eyes sting and blur as tears of pain cloud my vision, the feeling of something hot and wet trickling down my back. Is it blood?

"Oh my God, Will!"

Elora's hands are on me, and I yelp in agony as her fingers find the source of the pain.

"What the hell is this?" she yells.

I grasp for her body in front of me when I see him. The hooded figure, his cruel smile just visible from beneath the darkness. His hands erupt into flames again and I look up just in time to see Elora's gloves burn away as her own hands burst with Fire.

My heart is hammering so hard in my chest I feel like I might die.

"Elora! Run!" I try to yell, but it comes out as more of a strangled scream.

The figure walks toward us but halts. Something is wrong. His flames extinguish and he claws at his own throat before sinking to his knees. A rattling gasp escapes from the darkness of his hood, and I realize that he's suffocating.

I look up and Elora looks like a mythical goddess. Her unearthly blue eyes practically glow in the flickering light of the street lamps, her hair lifting about her face by an invisible force, making her look like she's submerged under water. But I don't know how long she can keep this up. I need to get her out of here.

I take the momentary advantage to push myself to my feet, grab Elora around the waist and Jump. I let go of her and collapse onto the floor of my apartment, the familiar hardwood beneath my knees, ribs, and cheek. My glasses are askew and there's a flurry of movement and colour around me. I hear the drapes being pulled on the windows and the chain lock being slid into place.

"That won't help if someone who can Jump wants to get in," I mutter.

"Has he been here before?" she asks.

I shake my head as best I can and groan as I try to move my upper body. "Not that I know of."

"Well, I guess we'll find out sooner rather than later, then."

I feel her hands on my back now and see her shoes pass my line of sight across the floor.

"Will…the blood…"

"Pull it out!"

"I…no, if it's too deep, you could bleed out," she says, her voice trembling. "You need to go to a hospital."

"No!"

She huffs in annoyance. "Will, now is not the time to be stub—"

I Jump away from her to the bathroom, my eyes catching

my bloodied reflection before I yank open the cupboard for the first-aid supplies. There is no way I'm going to a fucking hospital.

"Will!" I hear Elora's voice approaching before she's pushing her way into the bathroom behind me. "Are you crazy?"

I fight the urge to cower from the anger flashing across her face. Taking as deep a breath as I can to steady my voice, I say, "Help me get it out."

"No, I already told—"

My eyes meet hers in the mirror. "Help me or go back to the living room."

She's quiet for a long moment as she holds my gaze, like she's waging an internal battle. Finally she sighs, closing her eyes and shaking her head. "Sit on the toilet," she instructs, and a small touch of relief rushes through me.

Sitting down, I close my eyes against the agony. A jolt of pain shoots down my body as her fingers brush against the blade in my back.

"Fuck!" I yell.

"Shh," she whispers, "you don't want to alert Alex."

She's right. There is no way I can explain this if he barges in knowing I'm home and he wanders in looking to raid my fridge. I know too that he'd be over in seconds if he thought I was in trouble.

I try to focus on the sound of rushing water as Elora washes her hands. Then there's snapping and crinkling of plastic as she sorts through the first-aid supplies.

"It's okay, you're going to be okay."

I peek at her reflection in the mirror as she works. Her face is smeared with blood. I look down at myself and realize my shirt is soaked, the thick liquid dripping down my arm from underneath my coat.

"Holy shit…"

"All right, Will, listen to me," she says, her voice steadier than it was earlier. "I'm…going to pull the blade out."

My knuckles crack and I clench my fists at the thought. "Hurry."

"Once it's out, I'll help you out of your coat and shirt so I can—"

"No." The scarred flesh on my chest pulls taut, and I'm suddenly the most self-conscious I've ever been. This can't possibly get any worse. If she takes my shirt off…I don't want her to see the scars. A peek of them is one thing. To have my shirt off in front of another person—in front of her—is unthinkable.

"No," I say again.

She blinks at me. "What do you mean, 'no'?"

"You can take the blade out and my coat off, but can you please leave my shirt on? Just…I don't know…tear the hole big enough that you can see without having to take it off."

She shakes her head. "Are you high? What the fuck does… that doesn't even make sense."

"Elora, please…"

"Will, you're acting crazy—"

"I don't want you to see the burns!" I shout, turning my face away from her.

She's quiet, and I dare to look into her reflection again in the mirror. Her freckled cheeks are covered in my blood and her eyes are searching mine as they glisten with moisture.

"All right," she whispers. "I'll try."

I sigh with relief, but it just causes the blade to twist angrily, and I groan again. She looks away to sort through the supplies. I'm reminded of when she fixed my foot and think how gladly I'd take that injury over this one.

"Right, I'm going to try and be as quick as possible, okay?" she says. "But if this doesn't work, I'm calling 911."

I nod. "Fine. On three?"

"Sure."

"One…two—"

A sick squelching noise echoes in my small apartment bathroom, and I nearly retch at the combination of pain and sound mixed with Elora's panicked breathing. There's a clatter of metal on the tile near the sink and she pulls at my jacket, removing it as best she can from my arms.

"Fuck…I thought we agreed on three…" I mutter.

She offers a dark little laugh. "Thought it best that you weren't expecting it."

I feel the cool rush of air against the bare skin of my arms and the soft thump of my jacket falling on the floor. There's a sharp gasp from her throat and she presses her palm against my back over the place where hot warm liquid is trickling.

"Will…" her voice catches and it sounds like she's crying, "there's too much blood. I can't see—"

I sigh, accepting the anxious torment ahead of me, and reach back with my hand to pull the shirt off. It's wet and sticks to my skin, but her fiery fingers brush against me and my breathing calms as she helps pull the shirt over and off. The t-shirt is a mangled mess of blood, and I toss it with a thick squelch to the floor.

Please let him be okay. Please, please, please…

I hear her before I realize her hands are on my skin, putting pressure on the source of all of my pain. And it confirms the suspicion I've had for over a year.

"Elora?" I ask.

"Sorry, Will, this is going to sting a bit—"

Liquid rushes over my skin and my wound throbs, the stinging causing my teeth to grind together.

Fuck, I don't even know what I'm doing! This is really bad. He needs stitches. "Sorry!" she says again. She presses her palm flat against my back as she reaches over toward the sink for something. But the pain is easing, a jittery feeling crawling across the surface of my skin, the pain slowly being replaced with a kind of numb, misty feeling.

"El, are you…using your powers?"

What is he talking about? "What? No…why?"

The pain continues to recede more and more and more, that jittery, electric feeling reaching all the way from my shoulder to my scalp and down to my toes. It's as if I can feel every cell being touched by her hand.

"It feels like it's getting better," I say. Or maybe I'm going into shock.

Her hand moves and that feeling dissipates almost instantly.

"I'm not doing anything except putting pressure on it," she says.

The pain returns in earnest. "Put your hand back."

Again the pain recedes, quicker this time, that voltage-like feeling rippling under my skin as though through every vein and artery of my body.

"I…oh my God, Will…" she whispers, "it's healing."

Her palm presses harder into my skin, a slight pinch of pain making me hiss.

"Sorry," she says, and her other hand rests lightly on my back. Warmth spreads through me at her touch, and I sigh.

"I have no idea how I'm doing this…" she says.

I chuckle. "Doesn't matter as long as it's working."

He's going to be all right. He's going to be all right.

There's a kind of choked sob from behind me as my pain narrows into a tiny point then vanishes.

"Oh!" Elora gasps. Her breath moves over my skin and a shiver runs down my spine. "It's gone," she breathes, "the wound…it's completely healed."

Something like a thumb brushes over the newly formed skin and I shudder hard, my stomach muscles contracting at her touch.

I reach my hand over my shoulder, the skin is still slick with blood, but there's no more pain, no gaping wound, just skin.

I feel the soft fabric of a towel against my arm.

"Here," her quiet voice says, "you should shower. You're covered in…blood."

I move to turn around to face her, but my chest is bare, and now that my life isn't in mortal peril anymore, I can't bring myself to let her see. Instead, I reach behind me to grasp her hand. "Thank you," my throat feels thick as I try to speak. "You'll still be here when I get out?"

I feel her hand squeeze mine. "Of course."

She drops my hand, and I see the door open and close in the mirror. A few long contemplative minutes pass before I can bring myself to move. I turn on the shower and look at myself in the mirror. I turn my back to see the trail where the blood ran down to the waist of my jeans, but the awful wound is now gone. Healed by Elora, who somehow not only has the power to manipulate all four elements but heal injuries as well. And then there's me, stabbed by a dark figure. One with powers like me and like her and who seems hell bent on attacking us.

But even with all this, there is one thing I can't get out of my head. A theory I've had for months, before ever even meeting Elora, and tonight seems to prove it. As if there could possibly be more to unravel here, I can finally say with certainty that I can read minds. Anxiety floods through me, my heart thumping wildly and my breath halting as though the admission of that is something to be feared. Something to be ashamed of. I reach out to steady myself against the sink as a terrifying thought crosses my mind. If I tell her, she may never let me touch her again.

20

ELORA

My hands are still shaking as I try to clean up the small pool of blood from Will's living room floor. There is a pile of bloody paper towels next to me by the time it's cleaned up, the sound of the shower from down the hall droning on in the background. Should I check on him? He's been in there for a while now. He did lose a lot of blood. What if he passed out? No…surely I would've heard him fall if he did. The thought of seeing him naked sends a rush of heat between my legs.

Stop it! He almost died. He almost died to save…

Will Jumped in front of me. Took that blade in his shoulder for me. My hands shake so badly that I drop the paper towels back onto the floor. The panic sets in again as I close my eyes, trying to will it away.

"Breathe…" I whisper, my grip on the edge of the kitchen sink anchoring me to reality. I try to take a deep breath, but it stutters in my chest, and I feel my eyes fill with tears again. After all this time of searching for someone, anyone who might know me, I stumble upon Will. Someone who barely knows me but cares enough to protect me. Protect me from Hunter, from that hooded stranger, from myself.

I may not have known him before I lost my memories, but I care for him so deeply that the thought of losing him like I almost did tonight causes a heartbreaking pain that I didn't realize was possible. My hand presses against the sharp ache in my chest, tears spilling from my eyes and rolling down my cheeks.

"Are you all right?"

I whip around to see Will, his curly black hair damp and hanging down over his ears and forehead to the top of his glasses. He has on a pair of sweatpants and a white t-shirt with the Flying Weasel pub logo across his chest. He's a little pale, but so handsome that I can't help but let my eyes wander, taking in every inch of him.

He takes a few steps toward me, and I hastily wipe at my face.

"You should shower," he says quietly, "you look like Carrie."

I tilt my head. "Who?"

He laughs. "Sorry, it's a character from a famous horror movie. I mean to say that you're covered in blood."

Looking down at myself again, my clothes and my hands are still covered in his blood.

"I don't have anything to change into," I say.

"I put some clean clothes on the counter in the bathroom for you."

"You did?"

He nods. "Go on." He stands aside to let me pass, and I look over my shoulder at him as I make my way down the hall.

I enter the bathroom to find Will has put away the first-aid kit and cleaned the blood from the sink and the floor. When I finally get a good look at my reflection in the mirror, I gasp at the sight. I don't know who Carrie is, but it must be a terrifying movie if the thought of her came to Will's mind at the sight of me. My hair is matted at the side where the blood has dried and my face is smeared with red, tear tracks running through it down my neck.

"Oh, God…"

I turn on the shower with shaking hands and pull off the sticky, blood-covered clothes. Not knowing exactly what to do with them, I fold them up and put them on the counter. I stare at the top half of my naked body in the mirror, my breasts hold a small smear of blood across the top and my nipples are peaked from the temperature of the room. Or maybe it's because I'm naked in someone else's house only feet away from a man who I desperately want to touch me.

And I touched him, healed him with my own hands somehow. I remember when he elbowed me in the face on that first fateful day, how quickly my bruises healed. Is this why? Do I also have some kind of healing power?

I tear myself away from the mirror to the shower—the water washing away the blood from my hand as I test the temperature. I get in and let the water wash over me for several minutes until the water on the tiles below turns clear. I pick up a bottle of shampoo from the shelf, the smell of it reminding me of Will, and I inhale and wash my hair, raking through the matted side as best as I can with my fingers. I quickly wash the rest of my skin, trying my best to make sure I haven't missed any other traces of blood before turning off the water and getting out.

I grab a nearby towel and dry off, wrapping it around myself before turning to the pile of clothes stacked on the counter for me. There is a large t-shirt and a pair of what appear to be boxers and a zip up sweater. They all feel huge on me except the boxers, which fit well over my hips. They're warm and smell like him, and I inhale deeply.

I open the door and make my way down toward the living room to find Will sitting on the couch, holding the blade I pulled out of his back. I sit down next to him, folding my bare legs underneath myself.

"Feel better?" he asks, his fingers spinning the dark metal of the blade around and around.

"Yeah, thanks for the change of clothes."

He gives me a little smile. "You look better in them than me."

I tuck my damp hair behind my ear.

"There's a symbol on the handle," he says, handing me the blade. "It's the same symbol that was burnt into my chef's jacket."

I look up and Will's hazel eyes are expectant, as if hoping I've seen it before.

"Really? I've never seen it before…at least that I know of."

He nods and takes the terrible weapon back out of my hand.

"Thank you," he says quietly.

"What?"

"For saving me, healing me…"

I shake my head. "Don't be stupid. You don't have to thank me for that. What was I going to do? Let you bleed out in the street while I went home to bed?"

He looks away but breathes a small laugh. "All the same. I'm sorry, too about being stupid over the hospital and my scars."

I blink. "Don't be. You know I understand."

I hold out my wrists—the scars crisscrossing up my forearms. His hand clenches then rests back at his side, and I wonder what's going through his mind.

"I should thank you, too," I say.

His eyebrows knit together. "For what?"

"For Jumping in front of me. For taking that blade for me. Thank you."

Will's expression softens. "I'd do it again in a heartbeat."

I feel my heart swell, a cage of butterflies escaping in my belly.

"Things are really fucked up, huh?" he says.

I laugh. "You could say that, yeah."

"Can we even go back there? My whole life depends on that place," Will says, and there's a touch of sadness to his voice. "I don't have anything else. It's like my home. My family."

"What does that guy even want from us?" I ask. "If he wants something, why not just fucking ask?"

"You were amazing, by the way," he says. "I'm not quite sure what you did, but you were winning."

I smile, feeling the blush creep across my cheeks. "Oh, thanks. I took his air away. I figure you need oxygen to make fire, but I think I went a bit overboard and sucked all the air out of his lungs, too."

His eyebrows raise at that. "Wow. Remind me not to piss you off again."

I bump my shoulder with his. "But you're so good at it, it would be a shame if you stopped."

He takes a long, deep breath. "There's something I should tell you," he blurts out, his expression turning sad.

I feel my stomach drop. "What's that?"

He rubs his hands up and down his face before clasping his hands together in front of him. "I can read your mind."

I feel like all the air has left me. "What?"

He shakes his head. "Only when we're touching, skin to skin. It's happened before, but I wasn't sure if I was imagining it or not. Tonight, when you touched my back, I could hear you."

"Well, I *was* talking—" I start to say.

"I can tell when you're talking," he says. "When I hear the thoughts, it's like I'm hearing them from one end of a tunnel. The sound is quiet and distorted."

"Test it, then," I say. "I'll think of a number between one and one hundred, and you tell me what it is."

He chuckles. "All right."

I turn to face him square on, crossing my legs in front of me and closing my eyes. I take a deep breath and think hard on the number thirty-six—the number materializing in my mind's eye.

"Got one?" I hear him ask.

I nod. "Yup."

I hold up my hand toward him, and after a moment, feel his palm against my own. That calloused yet soft skin, and it's as if the contact burns through me. *Thirty-six, thirty-six, thirty-sex… fuck! Thirty-six.* I think hard, trying to keep my thoughts in check. "Well?" I ask, opening my eyes.

His eyes are focused intently on our hands together, but there is the ghost of a smile pulling at his lips. "Thirty-six."

My eyebrows rise and heat flushes my face all the way to my ears. Oh God, did he hear me slip up? "Yes."

He smiles, his dimples appearing in his cheeks as his fingers slowly drag down my palm, his thumb brushing gently across the scars on my wrist. His touch is like fire and ice at the same time, and I want him to touch me everywhere. His throat bobs and I realize with horror that maybe he heard that and I pull my hand away, tucking it into the pocket of the oversized sweater.

"He must not know where I live for now," Will says, turning away toward the windows. "We should get some sleep and tomorrow try to come up with a plan on how to deal with this guy."

If he heard my indecent thoughts from a moment ago, he doesn't let on.

"You can sleep in my room. I'll sleep out here on the couch."

My heart drops. "Oh."

"Is that all right?" he asks.

I feel my mouth open and close as I search for the right words. What does this mean? If he heard my thoughts, this is as simple as a rejection. He knows I want him to touch me but is choosing not to. On the other hand, he said himself his power isn't always reliable, maybe he missed it or is simply trying to be chivalrous. Maybe I've misread him this whole time. Here is his second opportunity to have me next to him in a bed and he's offering to sleep on the couch.

"I can sleep on the couch instead. I'm shorter and you just had a blade pulled out of your shoulder," I try to say casually.

He smiles. "Well, considering I've been miraculously and fully healed by a super woman, it's only right that you should take the bed."

"But—"

"Don't argue with me, go on."

His eyes blaze with intensity, and I feel myself rising off the couch as if in slow motion, my wounded pride making my throat feel dry. "All right, fine," I say.

His hands are clasped in front of him, and he avoids my gaze. "Good night, sunshine."

I roll my eyes. "Good night, Willan."

Turning on my heel, I head down the hall toward the bedroom, opening and shutting the door louder than normal behind me. I check my phone. It's almost one in the morning, and I realize just how tired I am.

I assess the room. Will's room, which for a guy in his twenties, seems more orderly than I would've expected. He doesn't have much. A small dresser, a bed with a table and lamp next to it. The picture on his Instagram of him Alex and Mariah is in a frame on the dresser and I smile at it as I pick it up.

I'm surprised there aren't any pictures of his parents or any other family members, even if they aren't alive anymore. Surely there'd be a picture.

Sinking down onto the edge of his bed, I lay back against the pillow, the spicy, citrusy smell of him overwhelming me as I snuggle under the covers. The lights of a passing car reflect through the window on the ceiling. I turn over, grabbing the covers and balling them up under my chin.

I like Will. Denying it won't help me anymore. I can't stop myself from imagining his rough hands on my skin and his mouth on mine. I wonder if I would feel the scar on his lip if he kissed me. When I think about the reaction he had to me asking him to take off his shirt, a sharp pang of sadness ripples through me. Even in that life and death situation, he still wanted to hide. I feel like Will hides a lot. That cocky personality is nothing but a mask he wears to protect himself.

I should tell him how I feel. I'll just walk out into the living room, wake him up, and blurt it out before I can change my mind. I roll over onto my other side, facing the door. Surely he heard my thoughts—he must know that I want him.

No, this is a bad idea. If he wanted me, he would've made his move already. Will Reed is not a man who waits. My knee bounces idly under the covers, my fingers twisting around themselves.

What if I did tell him I want him, and he, in turn, wanted me back? What then? I don't know what a man would want me to do to get him off. I mean, I've seen some porn, but that's hardly realistic. Would it be intuitive? Somehow, I don't think so. Being good at sex is probably something you have to practice.

Okay, this is ridiculous. I *want* to have sex with him. I want it to be him. The simplest touch from him makes me crazy, and I want more—I want it all. I throw off the covers, the cool air hitting my overly warm body. Swinging my legs over the side of the bed, I sit, and sit, and sit, searching for the courage to take that first step. I take a deep breath, push myself off the bed, and march straight across the room. I grip the handle, pulling the door open, and gasp as I nearly collide with Will. His hands are gripping the door frame and his eyes snap to mine as if he is just as surprised as I am to find him there.

"Oh," I breathe.

And then his hands are cupping my face, his eyes searching mine as his body moves into the space between us. The smell of him is overwhelming, and my pulse is throbbing between my legs as his thumb brushes along my lower lip.

"I just need to ask you one question," he says, and the drop of his voice makes me feel like I'm about to fall apart.

My breath hitches as his face leans toward me and his nose touches mine.

"Can I?"

My brain practically screams yes to him, and I see the pull of a smile at the edge of his mouth, signalling that he's heard my answer before his lips crash against mine.

I leave my earthly body as the touch of his lips consumes me. My hands reach up to wrap around his neck, my fingers finally able to touch the softness of his hair, and I hear him groan low in his throat as I pull him farther into the room. We don't get far, though, before he turns me and presses me up against the wall. His one hand starts to travel down my neck, then down my arm to finally rest on my hip.

I'm dizzy and euphoric, flying as his fingers find their way to the skin of my stomach. I gasp against his mouth and he breaks away for a moment. My eyes flutter open to see him looking down at me.

"Is this okay?"

My hands drag down his back, pulling him toward me. "Yes."

I barely recognize my own voice and can't help the moan that escapes my throat as his lips come back to mine. His tongue swipes against my bottom lip, asking for permission, and I open my mouth, mine meeting his with desperation. His icy hot fingers find their place on either side of my waist, and my body ignites like a match to gasoline.

Fuck, I've never been so turned on in my entire life. Is this even really happening? His body leans into mine, pressing me against the wall, and I feel him, his strong torso, and that growing bulge in his pants. It's hard to believe that this is all for me, because he wants me, too. He was waiting outside of the room. Was he working up the nerve to come tell me he wants me like I was?

"Yes," he whispers against my mouth.

I pull back for a moment. "What?"

He's breathing heavily and his mouth is swollen, the scar on his lip slightly more visible against his darkened mouth.

"Yes, I was working up the nerve to tell you how much I wanted you—how much I *want* you…want this."

My eyes widen. I forgot he can hear my thoughts and I'm immediately horrified. Shit, what have I been thinking? What has he heard? He lowers his mouth to my jaw and kisses me gently, and my terror momentarily vanishes.

"Hearing how I make you feel is," he says, moving to kiss just below my ear, "the sexiest fucking thing," he kisses my neck and I'm about to dissolve into a puddle, "I've ever heard."

He pulls at my shirt and his teeth graze against my collarbone. I moan so gutturally that I'm shocked at the sound that comes out. He grinds his hard cock against my lower stomach and his grip on me tightens as I'm lifted, my legs wrapping around his waist instinctually. My hands twist in his hair as he moves us away from the wall and toward the bed.

Will gently lowers me down onto the mattress, the weight of his body something I've so desperately been craving. His hands push their way up my sides and my rib cage until his thumbs brush the underside of my breasts. I gasp and he pulls his face back from me, his thumbs inching so agonizingly slowly over the sensitive skin to my nipples. He's watching me, his eyes hungry as his thumbs brush over my hard nipples, and I almost pass out as my eyes roll back and my body arches up off the bed into his hands.

Nothing has ever felt this good. His rough hands are so expertly skilled, his thumbs circling the sensitive flesh of my breasts. My breathing hitches and I'm sure if he does this long enough, I'll just come from this touch alone.

"That would be a first," he breathes into my ear.

I laugh. "Your hands are magic."

He smirks. "Haven't even gotten to the best part yet."

His right hand leaves my breast and trails down my stomach to the top of the boxers I'm wearing, and I'm suddenly nervous.

"What's wrong?"

His hand has stopped, and I almost whine in protest, but I need to tell him. "I…" I pause to catch my breath. "I've never done this before."

"Done what?" he asks.

"I've never had sex."

He blinks a few times as though completely disbelieving, his eyes scanning my face. "What?"

"I mean, I've never had sex that I can remember. It's possible I did before…before two years ago, but I can't remember."

His face pulls back, looking alarmed, and I almost regret telling him anything. But he would've heard my thoughts anyway at some point. If he doesn't want to continue, it's best this stops now.

"I never said I wanted to stop," he says.

"Oh," I say, "sorry, you just seemed—"

"I'm just surprised and…nervous, now, I guess."

I place my hand on the side of his face, brushing away the

curls that fall over the tops of his glasses and running my thumb along the scar over his eyebrow.

His eyes close at my touch, and he turns his face to kiss the palm of my hand. "Are you sure you want to?" he asks, opening his eyes and looking directly into mine. "We can do other things instead."

"Yes, I want to. I want it to be you."

His hands brush the hair away from my face, the gesture so sweet. "If you want me to stop at any point, just think it or tell me and I'll stop, okay?"

I nod. "Okay."

He kisses me softly. "Don't worry," he whispers. "I'll make you feel good."

He leans down, kissing me again, and I breathe him in as his body sinks down into mine. He rolls us so I'm on top, straddling his hips, his fingers trailing up my back, the t-shirt rising higher and higher until his kiss breaks away and he's pulling the shirt off my head. I'm self-conscious of how small my breasts are and move to cover them with my arm, but he grabs my wrists in his hands and pushes my body up until I'm sitting upright over him. My whole upper body is bare before him, and he looks at me like a man dying of hunger.

"You're so beautiful," he says reverently, and I can't help the smile that curves the sides of my swollen mouth. His hips buck upward toward me, and I gasp as I feel just how hard he is. How big he is. Holy shit, how is that going to fit inside me?

"Don't worry," he says and swiftly rolls me back over so he's on top of me again. "I'll go slow."

His hands are on my breasts again as he kisses along my neck, then down between my breasts, his body sliding down over me. His hands travel down until his fingers hook into the waist of the boxers I'm wearing. I squirm underneath him as his tongue runs along my stomach, below my belly button, and I have to close my eyes against the overwhelming stimulation.

"Lift your hips for me," he says, his hot breath on my hip.

In one swift, practiced movement, the boxers and my underwear are gone, and I'm completely and utterly exposed before him.

"Will—" I breathe.

The next moment, his face is over mine, his hand against my cheek. "Do you want me to stop?" he asks.

"No," I whisper. "I want you so badly."

I reach down below me, searching for that hard length I felt but not touched, and he grabs my hands in his, pulling them up and over my head, pressing them down into the mattress. I'm completely at his mercy.

"Not yet," he says. "I have to make sure you're ready first."

With one hand, he holds my wrists, and the other skims feather-light down from my lips, over my chin, and down my throat like he's tracing me. His fingers move between my breasts, over my stomach, lower and lower until they reach that place that's been pulsing with need for too long now.

"Please," I whisper.

He kisses the side of my mouth. "Please what?"

"Please touch me."

I feel the sinful sensation of his fingers slide through my flesh and gasp loudly, eyes wide, back arching off the bed. His fingers move up and down through me, and I'm barely keeping it together. How can something feel this good?

Will's forehead drops to my shoulder, and his breathing is laboured, erratic.

"Are you okay?" I ask.

He lifts his head and nods sharply. "Yeah, you're just so wet it's making me crazy."

I sigh, then gasp again as his fingers brush over a certain spot that my own hands are well acquainted with and my hips buck hard into his hand. His fingers find that spot again and circle it around and around. There's a pressure building in the pit of my stomach and my head tips back, my eyes clamping shut against the overwhelming sensations.

"Look at me," he says.

My eyes turn to him, and he's watching me when his finger dips down, brushing against my wet opening. Back and forth and back and forth over my entrance, and I feel like I'm dying. Like he's torturing me in the best possible way. Just as I think I can't take it anymore, his finger slides in deep, and I shatter apart.

"Oh, fuck!" I cry, trying to pull free of his grasp, but he holds me in place.

He slides his finger out and back in again, his mouth capturing mine. His fingers do their extraordinary work between my legs, and I'm barely lucid. His thumb rubs circles on my clit again and my hips meet the movements of his hands.

"Ride my hand, sunshine," he whispers, "show me what you like."

He adds another finger and the invasion is only strange for a moment before the fullness of it makes the pressure build more. The pleasure I feel as he pumps and strokes me is climbing, working toward an invisible peak. The sound of his hand fucking me works me into a frenzy and I'm barrelling toward my climax, my hands desperately trying to find something to hold on to.

Then I'm crashing, writhing, trembling, and his name rips from my lips as I'm overtaken by pleasure. "Will! Oh my…fuck! Oh my God!"

I vaguely recognize that he's let go of my wrists as he peppers my face with tender kisses and I come down from an incredible high.

He rolls over on the bed and the sound of a drawer opening, then rustling. He's back a moment later, hovering over top of me.

His fingers are inside of me again accompanied by something cold.

"What's that?" I ask, trying to lift my head up to see.

"It's just lube to make it easier for you," he says.

I push myself up and catch a glimpse of him. His pants and boxers are gone, his cock free and huge, and I can see he's rolled a condom on.

"Wait, I didn't do anything to you," I protest.

He chuckles and shakes his head. "I'm going to have a hard enough time lasting any longer than a few seconds inside of you without your help first."

"Oh," I say, a small laugh bursting out.

He leans down to kiss me, and I feel the tip of him nudging up against my sex, the lube making everything that much more slippery. His tongue meets mine before he pulls back.

"Are you sure?" he asks, nudging forward a little more.

I nod, desperate to feel him inside of me. "Yes."

He reaches down, hooking one arm under my knee to pull my leg up, and I feel him press into me slowly. My head falls back and my eyes flutter closed. It doesn't hurt, but there's an unfamiliar, overwhelming pressure as he fills me slowly. Inch by devastating inch.

"Oh," I whisper.

"Fuck, El," he whispers, and his head falls to nuzzle into the space between my neck and my shoulder. My hands grip his arms, and he's trembling, his body stilling against mine.

"Will, are you all right?" I ask.

"Yeah," I hear him breathe, "I just need to get used to you for a minute."

I smile against his ear and kiss his cheek. Small kisses full of patience until he lifts his head, blinking furiously. He grabs at his glasses and tosses them aside, then he looks at me like he's never seen me before.

"I…see you," he whispers.

There's a long moment where he simply traces my face with his finger as if committing it to memory and leans down to kiss me so tenderly I feel like my heart might explode.

"I'm going to move now," his lips murmur against mine.

"I might die if you don't," I say back.

I feel his smile against my mouth, then I hear a moan burst past my lips as he pulls out and then back in.

"Oh my God—" I breathe.

The feeling of him inside of me is exquisite. I feel stretched and full and whole and so wanted. There's a familiarity in his touch, and when I open my eyes, he's looking at me like he has never seen me more clearly.

His rhythm starts to pick up and I gasp as his thumb rubs against my already overly sensitive clit, causing my body to clench and twitch under him. His mouth lowers to my breast, sucking my nipple into his mouth, his teeth gently grazing the ultra-sensitive flesh, and I'm moaning over and over again. His mouth leaves my breast for just a moment to groan through his teeth. "You feel like magic."

My God, this man will be the death of me and I will die happily as long as it's underneath him, under his touch, under his kisses. His thumb continues to circle, the feeling building again as his cock slides in and out, faster and faster. Then out of nowhere, I'm coming, and it hits me with such force I feel a jolt of electricity undulate through my body, the bed swaying underneath us as my walls clench hard around his cock.

"El, fu-ck…" he moans.

His thrusts falter in their rhythm and his muscles spasm as he comes hard, gasping for breath. His body stills and his hand leaves its place from between my legs to trace up the side of my body, up my neck to where he holds my face. His eyes gaze down at me, so beautiful, the different colours of his irises infinite, and

I'm not sure what to do with the ache in my chest at that look. A look of being wanted, being seen, being felt. He leans down to kiss me, the touch so gentle I feel like I might cry.

"You might die happily under me," he says, pushing my sweaty hair off my forehead, "but I'd die without you."

21

WILL

I can't believe those words burst out of my mouth, but I mean them. Every single syllable. If anything, I just hoped to keep my utter infatuation with Elora a bit quieter, but that seems to have gone completely out the window. Because I can see her. See everything. Every inch of my vision slammed into high definition when I pushed inside of her. My eyes burned from the sharpness of everything, and I was barely able to keep it together. It was like staring at a comet, at an eclipse, at the sun.

And I can *feel*. Feel every touch, as if my nerves have just remembered their purpose. It was almost too much. The moment I touched her, kissed her, entered her, it was like I was doing all of it for the first time. Everything about her is like the dial being turned up from negative one to eleven.

Her bright eyes look up at me, and because I don't know what else to say, I kiss her again. But, my God, does she kiss like the devil. I was like a blind man hoping to be cured, and she was my miracle.

Amazing. That was amazing.

I don't want to, but I pull out of her and immediately feel a tangible sense of loss. I don't want to let go of her body. If I do, I lose that connection to her thoughts and her feelings, but holding on to her feels invasive. So I take the moment to roll onto my back and remove the condom. When I sit up, I know there's something wrong. It's only now that I take a look around the room and my eyes narrow as I look over the edge of the bed. The ground is a couple of feet below us. Are we…floating?

"El?" I ask.

"Hmm?" her content voice reaches me.

"El, I think we're floating."

She sits up in the bed, eyes wide, and the next moment, the bed frame crashes to the floor with a hideous bang.

"Holy shit!" I yell, pulling my feet back into the middle of the bed. I look over at Elora, who covers her face with her hands and snorts with laughter. The sound of her purely joyous laugh makes my chest swell and I smile, not able to stop myself from laughing along with her.

"Did you do that?" I ask when the laughter fades.

She shrugs. "It's only happened once before."

I raise my eyebrows. "I thought you said…"

She shakes her head, and her face turns beet red. "I was by myself when it happened."

I lean forward and our noses touch. "Really? Maybe you'll have to show me how that works sometime."

She smiles shyly then sits up, looking for the clothes that I discarded in my desperation to get her naked.

"You should use the bathroom," I say.

She looks over her shoulder at me with the t-shirt in her hand. "What?"

I clear my throat. "I read once that women should…pee after sex. I thought I'd mention it in case you didn't know." I am blushing furiously.

She stares at me for a moment and I wish I had a hold of her hand so I could hear what she's thinking.

"I didn't know that. Thanks," she says, then stands. Her naked form walks away from me with the bundle of clothes in her arms.

I watch her go, then hear the bathroom door close. I turn to look around and find my boxers on the floor. I pick them up and discard the condom into the trash by my nightstand. Then, I spot my glasses up near my pillows, and I've momentarily forgotten I don't have them on. I hold them up in front of my face, my eyes squinting almost painfully as the lenses blur everything into indecipherable colour and shape. I pull the glasses away and look around again, sitting on the edge of my bed.

Everything is clear. Everything. I can see the texture of the paper blinds covering the windows and the little splashes of colour mixed into the fabric of my bedsheets. I run my hand along the place where Elora was just lying, and it's still warm.

"Missing me already?"

I turn and look toward the door. Elora is standing there back in my boxers and t-shirt, and she's never looked more gorgeous. Her hair is tangled and wild and she's practically glowing, her skin bright and flushed.

"If I said yes, would you believe me?" I ask.

She walks to me, her sexy hips swinging hypnotically. Her legs find their place between my knees as she stands in front of me, and I can't help myself, my arms wrap around her waist, hugging her body toward me, my forehead pressed against her abdomen. She smells like spice and sex, and I feel blood rush to my groin as I envision taking her again. Her fingers are pulling my hair back, the feel of her nails on my scalp causing goosebumps to appear up and down my arms.

"Right now? Yes, I would," she says, and I can almost see her smile.

I lift her up and toss her over me onto the other side of the bed. She shouts and giggles as she lands—the bed bouncing at the change in weight. Pulling her toward me, I cover us with the blankets. She rests her head on the pillow next to me and smiles a little shyly. I go to wrap my arm around her, but then remember. "Can I touch you?"

"You were just inside of me. I think asking that now is redundant," she says.

I smile, glad she hasn't lost her ability to tease me. Secretly, I always hoped the other women I slept with would leave afterwards, their presence merely a byproduct of having sex. But I feel like I would lose my mind if Elora left me.

"I just mean...I want to hold you, but I also don't want to invade your thoughts if you don't want me to hear them."

She looks away, but her hand rests on my arm, that tingling electric warmth that only she's been able to pull out of me, igniting my skin.

"You can listen if you dare."

I smirk. "Would it be that bad?"

She shakes her head. *No, it would be wonderful.* "No, but it might inflate your ego so much you'll float away."

I grin. "The fact that you levitated my bed because I made you come has already stroked my ego enough for one night."

Her face turns red, and she covers her mouth with her hand. "Oh my God, I'm so embarrassed."

I pull her hand away and entwine her fingers with mine. "Don't be. It's the best compliment I've ever gotten."

This feels different. How do I know this is different? How do I know he won't just disappear?

I feel my smile fade as I listen to her thoughts. Of course she's thinking that. My reputation is so well known I'd honestly be shocked if she wasn't.

"So," she asks, looking at our hands, "do your female guests usually sleep over?"

I rub my thumb along the back of her hand. "Sometimes they

did, sometimes they didn't. But honestly, I never cared if they stayed until now."

He cares that I stay?

"And I don't want you to think it's because it's not safe for you to go home. I want you to stay because I can't imagine another night without you next to me."

So much for playing it cool, I guess. Her eyes roam over my face and she places her other hand on my chest. My scars itch under the pressure from her hand.

I wish he knew I don't care, but I do understand wanting to hide. I can understand that better than most people.

My heart aches, and I pull her closer to me. "We should sleep. It's really late," I say.

"All right," she laughs. "I've never slept next to anyone before, but I think I might like it."

I lift my leg and pull hers closer to me, tucking them under myself. Her eyes drift closed, and I can't help but tuck her hair behind her ear, then stroke her hair softly. I hear her sigh, and I'm obsessed with the sound of it.

"Your pillow smells amazing," she says, a soft smile curling up the side of her mouth.

"Thanks."

"Can I keep it?" she jokes.

I lean forward to rest my forehead against hers. "Sure."

My hand finds its way around her waist, gliding along her velvet soft skin to splay across her back. I watch her for a while, counting the freckles on her nose like stars until her breathing deepens and her mind is quiet. And even though only a few hours earlier we were fighting for our lives, I've never felt more at peace than with her in my arms.

"Elora?" I whisper.

"Hmm," she murmurs.

"You can keep all of me if you want to."

Okay.

· ——— ✸ ——— ·

MY EYES BOLT open at the sound of the banging on my front door. There's a mass of copper hair in front of me, but I can see each strand clearly. My eyes travel down to the freckled, sleeping face of Elora, and my breath catches. She's here, she stayed. My hand still spread across the soft skin of her stomach.

"Will?" a male voice calls.

There's more knocking. It's Alex. Fuck. I don't have my phone, so I have no idea what time it is, but it's still dark outside. What the fuck could he want?

I extricate myself from the bed, trying not to wake the sleeping goddess next to me in my clothes, in my head, in my heart.

Walking as quietly as possible down the hall in my t-shirt and boxers, I reach up to unlock the chain link, but my hand pauses. The memories of what chased us last night, the memory of the pain in my shoulder causing a phantom throb to echo throughout my body, and I decide to check the peephole first.

Alex is standing outside my door, also in his boxers and a shirt. I unlock the chain, then the door and open it up.

"Alex?"

"Dude, I've been trying to get a hold of you for almost ten minutes," he says, pushing his way into the apartment. He's frantic and I'm immediately on edge.

"Why? What's wrong?"

"The pub is on fire," he says.

I freeze. "What?"

"Brandon just texted me. The fire department is there now. He got a notification on his phone that the alarms went off. He thought it might've been a false alarm but—remember a few months ago when they went off for no reason?"

I nod automatically.

"Fuck, if the place burns down...I don't want to have to look for a new job," he says.

I shake my head. "Yeah, I—"

"Will?"

Alex and I both turn to see Elora half visible out of my bedroom door, her face sleepy, her hair a gorgeous tangled mess wearing my clothes. Alex's eyes widen as he looks between the two of us, and a smirk spreads across his face.

"Hmm...seems like things were hot here too."

I shove his shoulder, but he's laughing. "Fuck off."

"Hello, my lady," Alex says, bowing deeply.

She raises her hand in greeting. "Hi, Alex."

I shake my head, and my attention turns back to him. "Should we try and do something?"

Alex shrugs. "I'm no fireman. What the hell would I do? Probably make it worse, to be honest."

I raise my eyebrows and nod, but I glance at Elora, and I don't need to touch her to be able to tell what she's thinking.

"What time is it?" I ask. It must be before dawn.

"Almost five, I think," he says.

"Listen, there's not much we can do, and it's been a really late night—"

"I'll bet it has," he says, smirking.

I roll my eyes. "So, I think we should all just go back to bed. We'll ask Brandon if we can do anything to help in the morning." I give him a poignant look as if to tell him to fuck off, I'm busy. Thankfully, he gets the hint. He always gets the hint.

"Right, well...just thought I should let you know."

"Thanks."

He nods and waves at Elora, who has crept down to the end of the hall. Then he's gone.

I immediately Jump next to her, then grab her around the waist and we're back in my room.

"I can help," she says.

"I know…here—"

I toss her a pair of sweatpants and a sweatshirt and pull on my jeans and a sweater as she dresses in the clothes over her makeshift pyjamas. Once she's bundled up, I scoop her up by the waist and kiss her. She gasps against my mouth but responds by sinking into the kiss, her arms wrapping around my neck.

"Will, your glasses—" she says, noticing as she pulls away that I'm not wearing them.

"I'll explain later," I say. "Come on."

I Jump us to the park a little way down the street, but I can already smell the smoke, see the light of the fire and hear the sirens. Thankfully, there's no one around this early in the morning, and the sky is still completely dark. Anxiety knots my stomach, the image of the hooded figure putting me on edge, my eyes scanning every alley and rooftop.

"What if it's a trap?" Elora asks, voicing my own worry.

"Keep your eyes open and don't let go of my hand." I need to be able to make a quick exit, unlike a few hours ago.

I spot a place where we can watch while remaining hidden across the street on the roof of the opposite building. "Hold on tight," I say.

I Jump us to the rooftop of a building across from the pub, then we both rush to the edge to look out at the fire. The place I found some kind of family and friends when I had nothing is engulfed in flames and smoke, crumbling into ash and embers. The firemen are overwhelmed—the flames growing even under the onslaught of their water hoses. Fire licks up the sides of the connected buildings.

"Can you—" I ask Elora, but her free hand is already outstretched and I shiver as the cool mist of water in the air brushes against my skin, like a rain cloud has been summoned directly overhead.

I watch her as mist and rain and frost creep their way through the engulfed building, accelerating the efforts of the firemen below. As the flames die, the blackened wood and brick underneath emerge. It's all charred and dead. Even if the fire is gone, the place that became my second home after my life was destroyed is gone. I feel a painful ache in my chest as the comfort this place has brought me in my darkest moments disappears.

"We should go," I say as Elora lowers her hand.

"Will, look," she says and points.

I look closer, then look back at Elora. The symbol on the door of the pub is the same one from the blade that hit me, the same one that was burned into my jacket.

"We need to go now," I say, tugging on Elora's hand and pulling her toward me. Even though we're back in my bedroom, the smell of smoke still lingers in my nose. It's on our clothes and in our hair, but we're here and we're safe.

"It was him," she says, taking a few steps away from me and turning. Her hand covers her mouth, and she looks close to tears.

"I know."

"What does he want from us?"

I shrug. "I don't know…"

"I think I need to leave Toronto," she says.

I don't say anything but stare. No, please don't leave, I finally feel whole.

I close the distance between us. "If you go, I'll go."

She shakes her head. "You said it yourself. This all started because I showed up."

"No, it's not that. It's because we're finally together. There's no going back from this now."

Her eyebrows furrow and her head tilts. "What do you—"

"I can see you, Elora. I can see everything. The moment we were connected, it's like a curtain was lifted. The doctors never knew why the prescriptions never worked for too long," I say, pointing to my face, "but I know why now."

"What are you talking about?"

I lift her hand to rest against my cheek, feeling the warmth of her skin and the tingle it sends through my entire body at the slightest touch of her against me.

"When I look at you, I can see. When I touch you…I can feel."

Her mouth opens, then closes.

"Before you, everything was fuzzy, blurry…numb. But when I saw you that first day, you were the brightest thing in the world. Sharp and clear. It almost hurt to look at you. I didn't understand why, and I hated it because you wanted nothing to do with me."

Her forehead creases, a small wrinkle appearing over her nose. "Is that…is that why you always looked so mad?"

My stomach plummets. Is that what she thought? "I looked mad?"

She nods, her eyes darting over my face, unblinking and shining.

"I wanted you so badly. From that very first moment. I was so terrified it wouldn't be like this, but when you touch me," I say, my thumb tracing along that gorgeous lower lip, "when I touch you…it's electric. For the first time, I don't feel like I'm experiencing the world through a mask."

I thought this was just physical for him. Is this really how he feels? Is this real?

"This is real. I'm yours," I say and her eyes start to shine neon blue. "I want nothing else but to belong to you, if you'll have me. I can't lose you."

A gentle sob rips past her lips. "Will—"

"Wherever you go, I want to go too, and I can take us anywhere."

Tears spill over her lashes and trail down her cheeks.

"I've been a nomad for two years," she says, looking down, "two years of searching, of waiting, of never staying anywhere long enough so I wouldn't be hurt when I had to move on. But then I met you…" *I pushed you away because I knew it would break my heart to leave you.*

My heart is hammering so fast I feel like it's going to run out of beats and I'll suddenly fall to the floor, dead.

"Maybe the person I've been waiting for, searching for this whole time…is you."

I kiss her, and the energy that radiates out of her is like a powder keg, like fire and ice consuming me.

"You're like a magnet, Will," she whispers against my mouth. "It's like my soul recognized you."

She pulls my face down and our lips touch, and she's right. It's like my soul recognized her before I did, that this was always where we were supposed to end up. Like being without her had made me blind, so when we did meet, I'd know it. Her fingers grasp the button of my jeans, grazing the skin of my abdomen, and I gasp, heat flooding down between my legs as I instantly harden.

I want you inside of me.

Her voice practically screams at me, and I'm pulling the clothes off of her as quickly as possible, trying to get to that creamy velvet skin that's usually hidden away. I want to find and kiss every freckle on her body, then do it all over again. I want to taste her and be inside of her and be everywhere for her.

Her sweatshirt and t-shirt are gone, and her nipples are already stiff as my fingers graze over them. Her head falls back, and she forgets to kiss me.

Holy fuck.

I can't help but smile as her thoughts shout at me. She unzips my jeans and they fall down my hips when her palm trails down the front of my stomach to wrap around my cock. My brain goes blank as my stomach clenches hard and I twitch in her hand.

"You need to be naked," I breathe, "right now." I pull her hands away from me to grab either side of her pants, boxers, and underwear, pulling them down her body in a rush, kneeling before her as she steps out of the pile of clothes.

"You should always be naked," I whisper, my fingers trailing up the backs of her thighs, then I trace that crease under her ass and her body bucks toward my face.

I'd never get anything done.

I can hear her laughter at the thought. "That's all right. You just need to *do* me."

This time she laughs out loud, and it's beautiful and bright. I grab her and Jump to the edge of the bed, pushing her down onto it. I step out of my pants and boxers, discarding them somewhere far away. I don't want anything in my way when I'm ready to take her. I lean down to hover over her and we kiss as I reach my hand down to my new favourite place to touch. "Are you sore at all?" I ask.

She shakes her head. "No."

"You might be after this," I smirk, and her eyes flash at me. Daring me to do it. "But first I want to taste you."

I don't need to hear her voice to know she's nervous, but she doesn't have to be. It's my favourite thing to do, and with Elora, I would gladly do it forever. "Remember, you can tell me to stop," I remind her. I run my fingers through her soaked flesh, and I have to take a deep breath to calm myself as she moans.

Don't stop.

I kiss down her body, pulling her toward the edge of the bed, then hook my arms under her legs to hold her in place. She's tense, but at the first swipe of my tongue on her sex and that shout of pleasure barrelling down at me, I don't let up. Her taste, her smell, everything is perfect, but nothing compares to the little noises she can't contain that tumble from her lips somewhere above me.

Her hands drag through my hair, and I feel ready to burst as her legs tremble and her nails scrape along my scalp.

"Oh, Will…fuck!"

She's so fucking wet I'm at risk of drowning. I press two fingers inside of her and groan at the sound of her walls pulling me in. They clench around my fingers as I fuck her, my tongue swirling on her clit.

"I'm coming! Oh my God!" she screams.

I feel the bed lift off the floor as she's pulled away from me, and I can't help but laugh as I push it back down, chuckling. "Wait for me, sunshine."

I grab a condom from my table and tear it open with my teeth before rolling it on in record time. When I turn back to her, she's sitting up, her eyes glazed over.

"Come here," she says, pulling me down on top of her to kiss her, and I hope she tastes herself on my tongue.

Her fingers sneak their way up my t-shirt toward my scars, and I pull away. "I can't," I say.

She sits up on her elbows, her legs wrapping around my waist.

"Please," she whines, and my eyes close at the thought of denying her. "I want to feel all of you against me."

I let out a long breath. "It feels awful. Rough and jagged and broken. You don't want that."

Her eyes lock on mine and she traces the scars on my eyebrow and lip with her thumb before trailing her hand down to my heart. "You're mine," she says. "All of you. Even the rough parts."

I didn't know it was possible for a heart to break from anything other than loss, but that's what it feels like now. Or maybe it was the wall I built up around my heart, cracking and crumbling down as I let her in.

I kiss her hard and nod. She pulls my shirt up and up and up and off, and I've never felt more vulnerable before. For no one but her would I do this. Her eyes travel over my torso, her face set and I flinch, thinking she's determined not to let my ugliness show in her eyes. But her hands gently glide up my arms to my shoulders, and I brace for the horror to appear in her mind.

I wish you could see how beautiful you are to me. Her hands frame my face. "I want you even more."

And before I can do anything, she's pushing me over and down onto the mattress, straddling me. She grinds her wet sex against me and she moans each time my cock rubs over her clit. I groan low in my throat when I feel her reach down to guide me to her entrance. My eyes roll back in my head as she eases herself down on top of me. She's gasping and my fingers are pressing so hard into the flesh of her hips, I'm sure it must hurt her, but even her mind is consumed by how good it feels to have me inside of her.

I can't take it anymore. I thrust my hips up sharply, filling her completely, and she screams, her eyes wide.

"Yes!"

I thrust into her again, and she cries out, falling forward over me.

"Stay up or I'll hold you there myself," I say, and her eyes dart between mine at the order.

She pushes herself back up, never tearing her eyes away from me, then that little voice that likes to play whispers at me.

Make me.

I lift my knees, planting my feet on the mattress, and thrust into her hard. She falls forward again and I can tell she tried to stay upright. My hand travels up from her navel, over her breasts, pushing her back up, and I wrap my hand around her throat just hard enough to keep her in place. I grip her hip with my other hand and thrust upward.

"Oh!"

She's so hot and wet and tight and the sounds that come out of that mouth as I fuck her should be illegal.

"Yes! Will, fuck me!"

She matches my rhythm, slamming down on me and I feel her walls grip me, and fuck, if I don't take a break, I'm going to come and I don't want this to be over yet.

I pull myself up and flip her under me, a small squeal of surprise exiting her mouth. I take a few deep breaths and she tries to sit up, but I push her back down, my hand wrapping around her throat again.

"I want you to come on my cock with my hand around your throat," I say.

Her eyes go dark and she sucks her bottom lip into her mouth. I lean down to kiss her, sucking and pulling on that lip until it's swollen and so very red and her hands clutch at my wrist, my fingers still wrapped firmly around her throat.

"Do you trust me?" I ask.

I feel her swallow beneath my palm, but she answers me with her mind.

Yes. I'll do anything you want.

"I want you to lie there and take it," I say.

I grab hold of her leg and lift it up over my shoulder, then slide into her to the hilt. She tries to keep eye contact with me, but it's too much. I can tell by the way her mind is moaning my name. Her eyes roll back and I thrust again and again as she chokes out screams from under my hand.

I'm close again, but I want her to come. I reach down with my other hand and circle her clit with my thumb and her back arches and her breasts lift and fuck if she doesn't look like the most goddamn gorgeous fucking thing I've ever seen as she takes my cock. Completely at my mercy, completely trusting in me.

"Fuck—" I groan.

Her mouth is open, and I want to fill it. My hand trails up to hook my thumb in her mouth and she instinctively sucks down on it, and that little extra does it for her. Her legs are trembling and her walls are clenching and she's sucking my thumb like her life depends on it, her tongue swirling around it.

Holy fuck, Will, I'm coming!

As though I need permission to follow her, I do too, and we're both crashing and pulsing and trembling, and I've never felt this kind of pleasure before in my entire life. I collapse onto her in a sweaty mess of limbs, my face buried in the crook of her shoulder, and I melt as her fingers trace along the muscles of my back.

Wow, as much as I hate the thought of it, Jenni and Priscilla weren't wrong about you.

"I wish it had only ever been you," I say. I feel like I need to apologize to her. For sleeping with all those other women. I don't know why I feel the need to, but I do.

"It's fine, Will," she says. "I don't care about that."

I pull out of her and roll over, vaguely aware of the bed settling back down on the floor. I discard our protection and lie down, wrapping my arms around her. "I spent two years trying to feel something, anything—with strangers, but it's always been you. I wish I knew you were coming. I would have just waited."

She smiles. "You're with me now. That's all that matters."

I push her damp hair back and away from her beautiful face. "So, what do we do now?" I ask.

She sighs. "Well, first I think I need to shower again." I grin at her. "Then, we can figure everything else out."

I stare at a hollow tree in a place I've never been before, searching for something I don't know I'm missing. That light is here again, blinking, flickering like a candle that's growing stronger as the wax burns away. And the voice calls to me again.

"Willan," it says, but the voice is so close it's as if someone said it directly in my ear. And I recognize it now. It's her voice. Elora's voice. Her voice called me out of the darkness, out of the trees, through my dreams before I even knew who she was or what she would mean to me.

And there's no longer hesitation. No longer do I wait. I grab the opening in the bark and reach inside the tree, but then I'm falling. No, I'm sinking. Lower and lower and lower and I can't breathe. I'm frozen, and the light is below me and I can hear my own voice call to her.

"Elora."

I want to dive for it, but I'll drown. It's too far down. Too far away and it's flickering out, like a flame extinguishing below me as I push for the surface, until finally my face breaks through. The frigid air hits me and I can't even take a breath because my *lungs have seized. I'm going to die. I can't die. Someone needs me.*

There's a shore, and somehow I make it there, make it to the sharp, rough pebbles. It's familiar, like I've been here before, but there's shouting and everything blurs and whirls together.

Beep, beep, beep, beep.

It sounds like a heart monitor, but I'm too afraid to open my eyes. Too afraid that I really did die, that I froze to death on that shore amongst the rocks and the roughness of the world.

"She has quite a bit of scarring it looks like," *someone says. I don't dare look.*

"Scarring? From self-harm maybe?" *the second voice asks.*

No, that's wrong. I'd never hurt myself. My life means too much to me to risk it.

"That would be my guess. Perhaps that's how she ended up in the lake in the first place," *the first voice says.*

No. No, no, no, no. No, I didn't. How could someone think that? Why can't I move? How did I get here?

"You know, like Ophelia in Hamlet. I suppose for some people, drowning could seem like a romantic way to die."

But I don't want to die. I desperately want to live. There's a reason I pushed so hard to survive in that lake. Why I left that voice behind to flicker and disappear. But I can't remember what it is. I can't remember…anything.

Someone is moving me now, touching my arms and my face and eyes, and I don't like that they touch my wrists. I don't like that they are touching me at all. There's an energy building inside of me and as it releases, I feel whoever was holding on to me let go in a hurry.

The beeping is back.

Beep, beep, beep, beep. *It's incessant.*

I'm moving.

Then rising.

Then moving again, and for a brief moment, there's a pull on my heart. Like a magnet pulling me toward something that's slowly being taken away.

No, no, no, don't go.

Please
don't
leave
me.

✳ ———— ✳ ————

I WAKE UP disoriented, to the sound of the streetcar stopping outside of my apartment. I open one eye at a time and blink away the sleep. There's a weight on my chest and I look down to find Elora, her face and one hand resting on my bare chest. The sight of her perfect skin on my scarred flesh does something to me. It makes me feel whole, and I wrap my hands around her and kiss her forehead. She stirs, her arm falling around my side to hold me closer.

Please don't leave me.

The dream. It was mine, but then…it was hers. Her drowning in that lake. She said that's where she thought they found her, almost dead. Is that what I saw? A sudden nauseous feeling turns my stomach as I remember the utter hopelessness I felt drowning in that lake. How cold, how frozen. And then to fight so hard to live only for someone to think she'd tried to die. And the light, and her voice. The same light as my dream. Maybe we're connected by more than our powers.

"El?" I ask.

Her face nuzzles farther into me.

My hand rubs up and down her arm gently, trying to wake her. "Wake up, sunshine," I say.

Her eyes open, and they're so blue they dimly glow. She lifts her head and settles her chin on my chest.

"Hi," she says, her voice thick and low.

I smile at her. "Hi."

She takes a deep breath and rubs at her face. "I had a terrible dream."

"You were drowning."

She sits up and looks down at me. "I...how do you know that?"

"I saw it," I say.

She looks down at my hand holding onto her arm. "You saw my dream?"

I push myself up to rest against my headboard, momentarily distracted by her bare chest as the covers pool around her hips.

"It started as my dream, the same one I've been having for a while now, but then it switched, and I was drowning in a frozen lake, then I was in the hospital, but I couldn't move," I tell her.

She looks past me, her eyes unfocused.

"I've never seen that part before," she says. "This was the first time. It's only ever been the lake and the light and..." She looks back at me and her eyes are wide. "And your voice. It's your voice that's been calling me."

"And your voice has been calling me in my dream."

She tucks her hair behind her ears. "What happens in your dream?"

"I'm in a forest, and I see this blue light that leads me to a hollow tree. I've never been able to see what's inside. I always wake up."

"Will, what if that's the answer to all of this? Whatever these dreams are trying to show us must be important. What if there's something there that will explain everything?"

"You think so?"

She shakes her head and shrugs. "I have no idea, but what else are we going to do? I can't go home for fear that there's someone there waiting for me. And we can't go to work—"

"Shit, the pub…I totally forgot. Stay here," I say and hop out of bed, pull on a pair of boxers and a t-shirt and head out of my room toward the living room, grabbing my phone from where I've left it on the couch.

There are a dozen missed calls from Alex, Heidi, and Brandon, and a bunch of texts from Mariah and Ali, all about the pub burning down. I head back into the bedroom. Elora is sitting on the bed in the t-shirt I'd given her yesterday and her underwear. She also has her phone in her hand.

"I wish we got there sooner," Elora says, spotting me when I enter the room to sit down next to her. "I feel so awful."

"Me too."

"This is all because of us," she whispers. "It never would have happened if that maniac wasn't following us."

I want to tell her that isn't true, that it was merely a coincidence, but the symbol on the door last night burns brightly in my mind and I know it is true. That this has happened because he knows we work there.

"We need to figure out what these dreams mean," I say finally. "Maybe if we can do that, we can deal with whoever is following us."

"And if we can't?"

I pull her small body against me and kiss the top of her head. "Then we leave. We'll go far away."

Her hands wrap around me. "I'll go anywhere as long as it's with you."

✦

WE SHOWER AND GET DRESSED. Elora is in my t-shirt and sweatshirt again, but she pulls on her jeans from last night even though there is still blood on them.

"I don't know if this will work," I say, feeling foolish now.

"Only one way to find out," she says, gripping my hand. "You told me you just need to have seen it before."

"What if it's too far? What if we get stuck there?" I say, finally voicing my concerns for this half-cocked idea that we scrambled together.

"I trust you." She pushes herself up on her toes and pulls on my neck to kiss me. I feel energy burst through me at the contact.

You can do this. She pulls her face back and wraps her arms around my neck. "Ready?"

I take one final deep breath and pull her tightly against me. "Hold on tight."

I think hard about the images I've seen in my dreams. How the forest smelled, what it sounded like, what it felt like, and the depth and age of the trees. The smell hits me first. The scent of rotting earth and damp leaves with a hint of mould. When I open my eyes, Elora is still bundled tightly against my chest.

We pull back from each other to look around. It's dark and although it's only midday, barely any sunlight reaches us through the thick canopy of the trees. The forest feels old somehow, like it's been here for thousands of years and not a soul has stepped foot inside of it until our appearance. It's unusually quiet as well, like there's no life. No birds singing, no rustling of small animals, no wind. This place feels dead.

"We should leave," I tell her.

She looks up at me. "What? Why?"

I shake my head. "Something's wrong...there's no life here."

She looks around, and as if realizing why I have my concerns, she says. "I—yeah, all right."

I reach for her waist, but her voice stops me.

Willan.

I look down at her. "Did you call me Willan?"

Her eyebrows knit together. "No…"

"I heard you…just now."

"Will, I didn't say anything."

Her face scrunches with worry, and she reaches up to touch my face, but I hear it again.

Willan.

Her mouth hasn't moved. But then I see it. Flickering through the trees like a flame growing brighter and brighter by the second. I stare at it, both terrified and intoxicated, as I watch it steadily grow brighter.

"What's wrong?"

I look down at Elora, who obviously doesn't understand what has captured my attention so profoundly. "It's here."

I feel her hand squeeze my own. "What?"

"The light, don't you see it?"

She looks around herself. "No, I don't see anything but trees."

"Come on," I say, pulling her along as I step through the spongy overgrowth.

But she's pulling me back. "Will, I think we should go. You're right, something's wrong. We shouldn't have come here."

Willan.

I can't tear my gaze away now. That magnetic pull that I only feel for Elora is here, and it's pulling me toward the light now, like a moth to the flame. And while I can feel her resistance to follow me, her hand never leaves mine, and she follows me now as I walk toward the beacon in the distance.

It's hard trekking through the trees. The ground is uneven and covered in who knows how much overgrowth. The only sounds are our breathing and the crunch of our shoes as we step gingerly along, trying to carve out some kind of path.

"Will?" Elora whispers.

"Yeah?"

"Are we getting close?" she asks.

I forgot she can't see it. "I think so," I reply, but I'm not exactly sure. Every time we have to deviate from our current path, it's like the light is suddenly farther away.

"Will, why don't you just Jump us closer?" she asks.

I stop walking. "I…I can't," I whisper. I know it before I even try. There's a film of pressure over the area now from where we came from. I grasp her hand and try to Jump but it doesn't work.

"I think we should go back," she says, gripping my arm tightly.

"No, there's something here that I'm meant to find."

I don't know why I said it, but once the words have left my mouth, I know they are true. I feel the truth of it radiating through me like a current.

We continue on and sure enough, the light grows steadier, brighter, closer with every step now.

"It's close," I whisper.

We turn past a particularly dense cluster of trees, then I see it. Set in a clearing like a monument is a gigantic hollow tree. The blue light pours out of an opening in the trunk like a diamond peeking out through a hunk of dirt. There's a warmth emanating from it, and I shiver. There's something rippling across my chest, like I've been doused in freezing water. Like somehow I've always been cold and only just realized how warm I could truly feel.

"It's there," I say. I know she's watching, but I can't tear my gaze away. It's the only thing I've ever seen as beautiful as her.

Willan.

The voice…her voice rings loud in my ears, echoing and reverberating off the trees like a gunshot.

"Stay here," I whisper. I turn to face her for the first time since I spotted the light, and I'm immediately unnerved. She looks utterly terrified, her grip on my hand tightening.

"No, please, Will! I'm scared!"

My heart aches, but I also feel like I have to do this alone. "I'm not going anywhere, but I can't hold your hand right now."

She blinks away tears that have filled her eyes.

"Trust me," I whisper.

Her hand drops from mine, and I see her fingers flex, but she nods. "Okay."

I approach the tree. Each step feels like a hundred years of existence. Whatever this is, I need it, want it, live for it. No matter what happens, I can't leave this place without it now. My hand stretches out in front of me, and I'm shivering, so cold now it might as well be snowing.

Almost there…

My fingers touch the springy rough bark, the light nearly blinding. I look back at Elora, standing with her arms wrapped around herself in the middle of the clearing, watching me so apprehensively that I can feel the nervousness pulsing in the air. I try to offer her a reassuring smile, but my face is frozen. I turn back, squinting against the bright light. It's like the sun…like her. A siren designed just for me.

I reach inside the tree, my hand groping around for a moment before grasping something that feels both hard as metal and soft as a feather. It's both heavy as stone and light as air. I wrap my fist around it and pull it from the tree. My heart is beating so fast I'm sure my ribs are about to splinter apart, my lungs barely able to keep up with it. I hold it up in front of me and open my fingers.

In the palm of my hand is a ring. A silver ring with a large brilliantly blue stone.

"Will?" Elora calls. "What is it?"

But the stone is moving as though both flame and waves are trapped beneath its surface. It glitters and spins, and it feels like

I've rediscovered an old friend. Someone I've known my entire life, my entire existence. I slide the ring onto the middle finger of my left hand.

A searing pain shoots across my torso, the scarred flesh ripping and tearing, and I think I hear Elora scream as I fall to my knees into the earth, clutching at my heart.

And then I am gone, and everything is black.

· ——— ✳ ——— ·

"IT's *the only thing I can do, the only way to save her. To save us."*

I'm standing in a small courtyard, a soft breeze and the smell of salt water in the air as the willow blows behind my parents.

My father, dark-haired like me, and my mother, her hazel eyes surrounded by her curly hair. They're alive but looking at me with such sadness. Like they know they'll never see me again.

"Don't worry," I say. "I have a plan."

· ——— ✳ ——— ·

ELORA IS STANDING *in the centre of a well. No, not a well—a court. Surrounded by eleven dignitaries. She's chained to the centre, her eyes swollen and red from crying but wide and unblinking. She's shaking so hard it looks like she's vibrating. Her copper hair hangs wildly about her face and her tears drip off the black collar around her throat.*

"We have reached the difficult decision that due to the circumstances about your nature, at this hour next week, you are to be executed."

An anguished cry like a wounded animal rips from Elora's throat as she sinks to her knees at the bottom of the court. No, that noise—it came from me.

* ——————— ✦ ——————— •

HER FACE *is in my hands, and her expression is resigned, hopeless.*

"I'm going to get you out of this," I tell her. "I won't let them hurt you."

"Will, there's nothing you can do."

Her broken, soft voice tears at my heart. "I'll convince them to change their mind. I know I can. If they kill you, they'd be killing me, too. I won't let that happen."

Her chains rustle as she turns her face to plant a kiss along the inside of my palm. "If I had to do it over," she whispers, "if I could choose a path that would save me, but it was one without you, I'd choose to die. A thousand lifetimes, and I would always choose you. No matter the consequences. My soul will always find you, Will, in every lifetime."

She smiles at me, and I pull her face into a kiss I can only describe as desperate. Desperate to save her, desperate to tell her everything I'm running out of time to say, desperate for her to know how much I love her.

* ——————— ✦ ——————— •

"WILL!"

Her hands grip me, shaking me from the cold ground.

"El?"

She lets go of a relieved breath, her arms wrapping around my body. "Will, look…" Her eyes are looking at my chest.

I forgot about the pain that burned through me, so momentarily painful I blacked out. My shirt is singed like how the hooded man imprinted that symbol on my jacket. I pull the fabric away and my heart nearly stops as I catch sight of my skin.

The burns are gone. The rough, scarred tissue of my chest is gone, and in its place is an intricate interlacing pattern of brilliantly glowing symbols. All connected like some kind of bizarre, lacey, spider web. I pull the remains of the shirt over my head and stare. There are numbers and shapes and symbols I recognize but feel like I haven't seen in a long, long time. My fingers trace the lines with familiarity.

"Wow," Elora breathes.

I look up at her face and my breath halts as our eyes meet. Eyes I remember. Eyes that were swollen and crying as she was told she would die. Eyes that had held my gaze, as I swore I would save her.

"El," I gasp, "I remember you."

"What?"

"I remember now, not all of it, but...I remember you and us. I know you. I've known you before."

Her eyes dart between mine as if she's always known this was true. I grip her face and kiss her hard. "It worked. We found each other."

A smile as bright as the sun breaks across her face.

"Well, isn't this touching." The voice splits the air like a thunder crack, and Elora and I are on our feet in an instant, our eyes scanning the trees for the source of the voice.

A dark hooded figure emerges from the trees ahead, but before I can do anything, something cold clamps around my throat a jolt of electricity surges through my body so painfully it brings me to my knees.

"Will!" Elora screams.

I can't Jump. I can't stop Time, and even though Elora is gripping me so hard it's painful, I can't hear her mind.

"Don't worry, darling, he'll live."

I know that voice. I lift my head as the hooded figure closes the distance between us through the clearing in one movement, then pulls the hood down, uncovering his face.

ELORA

"Alex?" The name tumbles out of my mouth as I grip Will in my hands. Hands that are suddenly burning, my wrists itching. I pull them away from Will and flames erupt in my palms.

"I wouldn't do that if I were you," Alex says, wagging his finger at me.

I throw a ball of flame at his smirking face, but he catches it in his hands, tossing it like a basketball onto the damp earth. The flames scatter around us in a vicious circle enclosing us in. I pull the air away and feel the shimmer of a breeze skip across my cheek. The flames dim until I hear Will yell, his body convulsing. I drop to his side and look at Alex, who is still smirking at me.

"Stop it! Please!" I beg.

Will suddenly stops and is quiet. His body twitching ever so slightly, his eyes are half closed on the ground next to me.

"Are you going to behave?" Alex asks, his face serious now.

Tears spill out of the corners of my eyes as I nod. There's nowhere for me to go, even if my brain is capable of coming up with a plan. Will is the one who can Jump. Somehow Alex made it so that Will couldn't escape once we got here, and I think whatever this thing that has been placed around his neck is repressing his ability to use his Time powers as well. Is it electricity? My fingers flex and I can feel the crackle of the current in the air against my skin. Does Alex know I can sense what it is?

"Good, this will make this a lot easier," Alex says.

"I—I don't understand," I stutter. "How—"

Alex stops, his arms crossing over his chest, and he genuinely smiles at me. "It's a fairly long story and one which unfortunately you probably won't understand because unlike our friend Will, here, your memory is still being repressed."

I blink. "My memory…"

"See?" Alex says, sounding annoyed. "That's why this has taken so long. You have no idea how frustrating it's been trying to get you both to figure it out on your own."

"Why not just tell us then? Why attack us and lure us here?" I shout. Will is stirring below me. Maybe if I'm able to get him standing, I can distract Alex and get this collar off.

"Isn't that cute? She's trying to make a plan to save him."

I spin around at a woman's voice. Sarah appears from behind a tree to my left. I feel my eyes go wide as she walks out into the clearing and wraps her arms around Alex. What the fuck is going on? Are they both—

"Atlantians?" Sarah asks. "We all are…or at least were."

Everything is spinning and the desire to suck the air out of both of them is overwhelming. Atlantians? What is she even talking about?

"Be careful," Sarah mutters darkly. "Remember what will happen to poor Willan here."

Will's fingers curl around the bare skin of my ankle, and I try to shout in my mind to him, to ask if he's all right, but something feels wrong, and I know he can't hear me.

"What do you want?" I ask through gritted teeth.

Alex and Sarah exchange glances. "It's actually pretty simple. And if you can get it for us, we'll let both of you go and never bother you again."

That deal sounds too good to be true.

"What do you want, then?"

Alex points his finger at Will's hand, where the ring with the blue stone sits shimmering with an unearthly light in the darkness.

"The ring?" I ask.

"It's a Solis," Sarah says, and her eyes look greedy as they linger on his hand.

"A what?" I ask.

Sarah smiles. "Wow, whoever repressed your memory must have been exceptionally powerful."

I shake my head. "What are you even talking about?"

Sarah rolls her eyes. "Listen, I'll give you the short version, all right? You know, in good faith. Atlantians can develop powers for the ten affinities. Alex here has Fire, I have the Mind, Willan here has Time and you, my dear," her eyes glittering with jealousy, "you are a Natural."

"A Natural?"

Alex nods. "You can control all four of the natural elements. Earth, Air, Fire, and Water."

Something rocks through my chest. Finally, I have a name for it. This bizarre thing that has changed my life so completely. It does have a name.

"You see," Alex continues, "Atlantians usually only get one each, but you, my dear, got four."

That doesn't make any sense. Will has more than Time, he can Jump—

"All males can Jump," Sarah says, waving her hand as if this was a stupid thing to say. Wait, did I say that out loud? "It doesn't count as his affinity."

I blink at her, feeling completely overwhelmed. My heart is

pounding so hard it's difficult to breathe. My mind is racing, trying to keep up with all this new information while also worrying about how Will's grip on my ankle has loosened.

"Why do you need the…what is it? Solis?" I ask.

Alex tilts his head to the side. "It's so we can go home."

"Home?"

"Yes," Sarah adds, "to Atlantis."

Atlantis? The mythological city that was swallowed by the sea? It's not real.

"It is real, actually," Sarah adds, and I'm reminded that she can read my mind. "Just not in the way that people like to theorize. You see, we were the ones who chose to be swallowed by the ocean, and we've been hiding ever since."

"But that's impossible. Someone would see an entire underwater city—"

Sarah rolls her eyes. "You know, babe, I'm getting bored. Can we just get on with this already?"

Alex kisses her temple then Jumps forward until he's mere inches in front of me.

"We want your Solis, too. We want both of them." His eyes flick down on Will again and though he tries to hide it, there is a hungry desperation in them that lets me know that this is the most important thing in the world to him.

"I don't have one," I say honestly, looking behind him at Sarah. "If you read my mind, you'll know it's true."

"Oh no, you have one. It's just missing," Sarah says. "You've seen it, though, haven't you? In your dreams?"

I cross my arms and narrow my eyes. "Surely you would know that, mind reader."

Sarah genuinely laughs. "Just because I have an affinity for the Mind doesn't mean I can access all of it. Dreams have never been something I can quite make out. It's too subconscious, like trying to see the bottom of a muddy lake."

So there are limitations to the affinities. Interesting.

Sarah's smile fades in an instant. "Just because I can't see your dreams doesn't mean I can't crush your mind like a grape."

An agonizing pain splits through my skull, and I drop to my knees next to Will. My hands clamp down on either side of my head, trying to stifle the pain. It feels like someone is taking a sledgehammer to the inside of my skull. The pain is gone as quickly as it started and I fall forward, nearly retching into the muck.

"See?" Sarah says, walking forward to kneel in front of me. "And that wasn't even the worst thing I can do. I'm actually impressed. Whoever did this to your memory must've been pissed. Is that why you were exiled? Did you piss off the Mind Master?"

I hear her words, but the lingering pain in my brain makes it hard to focus, and I fear I'm going to be sick.

"All right, Sarah, that's enough. Stay here with him until I get back," Alex says, then he grabs my shoulders to haul me to my feet. I instinctively push him away, my hands singeing holes through his shirt.

"You said you would behave," Alex says, wrestling to trap me in his arms, "or do you want Sarah to make Will forget you again? What a tragedy that would be."

The heat retracts into my hands and I stop my struggle, my head hanging and the tears silently falling down my face. Will's eyes flutter open, and my heart hammers as his gaze meets mine.

"Time to go," Alex says, and the next moment, I'm back in my apartment. Alex lets go of my body and I stumble forward toward my bed, sinking to the floor.

"Now," Alex says, clapping his hands together, "I'll make this as easy to understand given the circumstances."

I can't look at him directly—too angry and too afraid of what I might do in that anger, which would only cause Will suffering. I won't allow that. Not to mention, I have no idea where Will is or how I can get back there.

"We want your Solis."

"I already told you," I whisper, "I don't have it."

Alex kneels, and his fingers reach under my chin. I recoil at the touch and I hear his little laugh.

"How quickly things changed, huh?" he says, smiling. "You were so excited that we were going to go on a date. So excited I might touch you then."

"If you recall, you stood me up."

He smiles broadly. "I did. It worked out better than I had planned too. I had to do something to force the two of you together. After Will fucked up so bad when you first met, I thought the universe was playing a cruel joke on me."

His words cause several things to fall into place. "You did that on purpose so that Will and I would hang out together?"

He stands up again. "I won't take credit for that idea. That was all Sarah. I guess it's in the nature of women to be cruel."

My wrists itch again. I want to strangle him with my bare hands. To drown him, to take the air out of his lungs. But no, I won't risk something happening to Will.

"Anyway, I'm confident you can find your Solis," Alex says quietly. "Just do what Will did. Follow the light from your dreams. It'll lead you where you need to go."

"But, I can't Jump. I have no idea where to go. What if it's not even on this continent?"

Alex smirks. "No, it's nearby, trust me...I can tell. I can feel it."

"And if I give it to you, you'll leave us alone and never come back?"

"Exactly."

I push myself up to my feet slowly to face him.

"You're not to hurt Will in the meantime," I say resolutely. I don't have much, but if they really need this Solis thing, then I'm sure I can make some demands.

"We won't hurt him unless he tries to do something stupid and knowing him, it's always a possibility."

"You were his friend, Alex. How could you do this?"

He Jumps right in front of me again, and I stumble back, falling onto the bed. He places his arms on either side of me and leans over, caging me in. A surge of electricity pumps through my veins, the lights above my bed flickering as the urge to use my power itches horribly in my wrists.

Alex looks up at the lights for a moment, his brows lowering, but then turns his eyes back to me. Eyes that I once thought were so beautiful but are now cold and devoid of any depth.

"I think you're mistaking me for someone who gives a fuck about anything other than getting that Solis. I don't care about Will, and I don't care about you."

His body trembles with anger, and I'm frozen.

"But you care about Sarah," I whisper.

He scoffs and pushes back. "I don't care about her either. She's simply my partner. I couldn't do this alone, and she has the right affinity to accomplish it. That's all."

I blink up at him. "You mean…you don't love her?"

His eyes narrow at me. "Love is not something I'm capable of right now, and neither is she."

I try to hide my interest in that statement. A hollow, ashen look overtakes his face. He almost looks…sad.

"You have two days to find your Solis or Will dies," he says, backing up. "Oh, and just for fun…I'll have Sarah erase every last memory of you from his mind, one by one, before he does."

"Wait!" I say, scrambling off the bed. "Please! I have no idea where to even start! I have no memory of ever even having it!"

"I told you," he says coldly, "start with your dreams. Once you have it, we'll know."

Alex turns slowly to look at me and pulls the hood up over his face, his eyes and nose, disappearing into the shadow.

"Know this—if you *don't* find that Solis, I *will* kill him, and it'll be slow."

In the time it takes me to blink the tears out of my eyes, he's gone and I'm alone.

"**S**weetheart, no. We'll never see you again."

My mother's hands are grasping my face and the sting of tears burn at the back of my eyes. My mother is a saint, but I can't help but realize she's right. I might never see her again. But what is the alternative? To live here for the rest of my life with my heart in pieces as I stand idly by and watch Elora die? No, that's the unfathomable part. My parents had me for twenty-two years. Elora has the rest of me.

"Mom, you know this is bullshit. Even if I didn't love her, something has to be done. They didn't even consider alternatives, but I'm going to give them one. I know it'll work. It has to," I tell her. The Solis around her neck glows brightly before she embraces me in a crushing hug.

When she steps back, she gives me a watery smile and pushes my hair back from my forehead. "In case you never remember, I want you to know that I'm so proud of you. I've never been more proud of anything in my life."

My father pulls me away, toward the door. "You know they won't let me do the glamours myself. The Master will want to do it to make sure there's no loopholes."

I nod. "I know, but that shouldn't matter. The hardest part will be finding our Solises. After that, it should all start to come back."

My father looks at me with a terrified smile. "I'm sorry this is happening to you. To you both…"

"Me too," I say, tugging my father into a hug. "I'm sorry I can't tell you any more. It's not safe that you know, anyway."

·———— ✷ ———— ·

"WAKEY WAKEY, EGGS AND BAKEY."

My eyes flicker against the gloom. My whole body aches, every muscle tight. Someone pushes me upright from the floor. Or is it the ground? It's both soft and hard, uneven. My eyes slowly open. No, it's definitely the ground. Where am I?

And then a thousand images flash across my mind. Images of symbols instead of scars, of Elora's body under mine, of the pub on fire, of the last time I saw my parents at our small cliff side home, me pleading with the Master's council to spare Elora's life —that there was another way…

I scramble up wildly, looking around for a flash of copper hair, but it's not here. I'm not alone, though. I spot Sarah leaning against a tree a few feet away.

"Easy there, big fella," she says calmly. "I know it's probably a bit discombobulating, but if you panic, I'll have to zap you again."

I try to Jump, but the sharp sting of electricity surges through every one of my aching muscles and I drop back down to my knees.

Sarah scoffs, the sound of her feet dragging in the earth. "I told you to calm down. Each time you try to use your power, it'll zap you."

I gasp for breath as the sensation eases, my hands coming up to feel the cold metal around my neck, where sharp wires are pricking into the skin.

"An elegant solution to keep the peace in our society. Of course, it's a bitch being on the suppressing end of things. Had to make this one out of a dog collar. Took me ages to figure out how to do it."

I finally look up as my hands drop to my side. "Where's Elora?" I ask with stern impatience.

"Don't worry, Alex won't hurt her. We need her alive…for now."

My blood feels thick and boils beneath my skin. "If you touch her—"

Sarah crouches down in front of me. "You'll what? Glare at me?"

I've never wanted to hit a woman, but I'm fairly fucking close now.

She smirks. "Go ahead and hit me if you'd like. I'm a big girl."

I blink at her.

"Did you forget already?" she whispers. "Every little thought that flashes through that gorgeous head of yours is mine to see."

I blow air sharply out of my nose. "Fuck you."

She eyes me up and down. "Believe me, darling, if you asked, I would have."

My jaw is hurting from grinding my teeth together so impossibly hard I'm surprised my molars haven't cracked.

"I have to admit the thought did very often cross my mind. You are quite the generous lover. I'm exceptionally jealous of Elora, not to mention Jenni, Priscilla, Lilli, Hailey, Eden, Shanna, Joanna—"

"Shut up!" I shout, pressing my hands over my ears.

"You finally got together though, albeit it was touch and go there for a little while. Alex and I had to come up with a few tricks to get you two to see past that disastrous first meeting. Not to mention what a slut you were being."

"I said shut up!"

"Will she still feel the same once she can remember your history together before you were exiled?"

The word is like a bullet. I see Elora, collared and terrified, tears streaming down her face as she looks up at me, the blurred faces of the Masters ahead of us. The words echoing in my head as I mouth to her, *Please, don't leave me*. Breath escapes my body as I heave, trying to get air to enter my lungs, my stomach rolling and my abdominal muscles clenching so hard they feel like they're on fire.

I'm slumped over on the ground when Sarah sits cross-legged before me. She holds out a bottle of water in her hand. I glare up at her.

"I told you, I don't want to kill you. Why would I poison you now?" she says and tosses the bottle of water at my feet.

"If you don't want to kill me, then why all the knife throwing theatrics?" I mutter, my shoulder twitching with the reminder of the blade Elora pulled out of me.

Sarah rolls her eyes. "Alex was getting impatient. I told him it was a stupid idea. He figured putting her life in jeopardy would… speed up the process. He wasn't aiming to kill her, but who knew you were stupid enough to throw yourself in front of her?"

My tongue is thick in my throat. Did they know Elora could heal me?

Something flashes across Sarah's face. "We've heard stories about Naturals. That almost all of them have the added bonus of healing. When her bruising disappeared quickly, we made an educated guess she had it, too."

I look down at the bottle of water at my feet and back at her. She raises her eyebrows before I grab it and drink the water I didn't realize just how badly I needed.

"Don't make me zap you again or you'll just hurl all of that back up and I don't have any extra."

I lean back against the enormous tree trunk, my eyes closing as the sting in my throat eases.

"Listen, Willan, it's nothing personal, all right?"

I slowly open my eyes and tap the collar on my neck. "Feels a bit personal, Sarah."

She rolls her eyes. "Well, it's not. You and Elora, you're simply a means to an end."

"And what end is that?"

"Getting home."

To go home. I remember Alex saying something to Elora before he took her away. "I don't understand why you need *us* to get home."

"I guess it'll probably take time for it all to come back, huh?" Sarah says to herself. "The memory I mean. Well…I don't see any harm in telling you. The Solis is the only way to get back. Like a key to a door."

I look down at the ring on my finger, the swirling blue and white stone shining brightly in the dark. My fingers instinctively touch my chest, forgetting that the scars have disappeared. That they were never actually there.

"It was a glamour," I say, the truth of it rushing out of me so confidently I'm surprised at myself.

Sarah smirks. "Yeah, it's coming back now, isn't it? Whenever one of us is exiled, they glamour the Solis marks so those of the Other World can't see them. Only other Exiles can see what's hidden underneath. Although I guess in your case, you couldn't see them either. I wonder if it was because of your memory…" she trails off.

"That day at the beach…" I mutter, remembering how Alex had glimpsed my shirt partly off.

"That confirmed it for him, but we already had our suspicions about you. The strangest part was that your Solis was still intact and somewhere on this side. They glow, see? Both of yours are intact. I've never heard of that before. But we could tell, the energy it gives off is—" she shudders, her eyes closing as if in prayer, "addictive."

"It was you," I mutter, "whenever I stopped Time, I felt like someone was watching me."

Sarah smiles, but it's cold. "Yes…and no. I just added a little trigger to your mind that whenever you used it, you wouldn't feel safe."

"So then, why not just tell me? Why not just ask for my help? That day at the beach was over a year ago," I ask, struggling to organize my thoughts.

"Because," Sarah says, leaning forward, her eyebrow arching, "you and Elora…you're different than normal Exiles. Your memories have been modified, your affinities suppressed."

I shake my head, trying to keep up, and I look down at the ring on my finger, my thumb brushing along the top of the stone. It's neither cool nor warm, hard nor soft, and the longer I gaze at it, the harder it becomes to look away. It feels like an old friend that has finally come home. "Intact?" I ask quietly. Somehow, the thought of this stone being damaged is horrifying.

"You see, Willan," Sarah says, "when someone is exiled, they usually destroy their Solis, then chuck them out into the Other World. Meaning, they're never allowed back. Curious, don't you think, that you and Elora still have yours?"

"I…so…" the information is rushing back as though my brain is being hit by an enormous wave in the sea, "the Solis is the only way to open the portal to get back home?"

Sarah smiles, but there is no happiness behind it. It's simply hollow. "That's right. Alex and I want to go back, but we can't without a Solis each, and that's where you and Elora come in."

"Aren't you worried Alex will just take mine and leave you here?"

Sarah's pupils dilate, and her voice turns to ice. "He knows what will happen if he betrays me."

The thought of someone else handling my ring, my Solis, makes me feel so nauseated that I lean over and throw up most of the water I just gulped down. Then another thought occurs to me as Sarah's words tumble around in my head like shoes in a dryer. "My parents are alive…"

For over two years now, I've thought about them every day, about their tragic, horrifying fiery deaths. Their blurred faces were indistinguishable amongst the other random memories that never seemed to fully materialize in my mind. But they are clear now, as if they are standing before me in the dark clearing. Tears sting my eyes and I press my palms hard into my face to stop myself from crying like a fucking baby in front of someone I want to tear apart. I've been alone for so long, even more alone than I had realized. I thought Alex was my friend, but that, too, was a lie.

There is a dawning realization that I still have a family waiting for me, wondering if they'll ever seen me again. I could go home. My real home. The thought of it swells like a balloon in my chest. The need to see them again floods through me, and I blink furiously against the tears.

"I said goodbye to them. Possibly forever…for her."

The memory of tearily hugging my mother and father goodbye, seeing their agonized faces as I tried to convince them that one day we might be reunited again, floats up from the depths of my memory. Elora was sentenced to death, not exile, which is supposed to be the worst punishment you could receive. No one had been sentenced to death in Atlantis for hundreds of years. So why had Elora, of all people, received that harrowing punishment? And how did we manage to end up here instead?

25

ELORA

I pace the floor of my apartment. Back and forth and back and forth. I pull my cell phone out of my back pocket for the fourth time, as if it might actually help me somehow. But what can I do? I can't call the police. How can I possibly explain having affinities to the Toronto Police Department? I look at my text history with Will, every fibre of my being, hoping I'll see those three little dots flicker to life on my screen. But nothing. Nothing comes, and as my adrenaline rush starts to crash, I feel sick. I run to the bathroom, my empty stomach heaving into the toilet bowl.

I knew we should have left. I knew something was wrong the moment we went to that place. But would it have made any difference? Alex and Sarah knew all along. They were just waiting for us. Waiting for Will to follow his dream to that tree. To find that…Solis. The word sounds familiar, the burning desire to say it out loud.

"Solis," I whisper to myself.

I feel the energy of the word ripple over me, the fairy lights over my bed flickering briefly and my forearms itch so badly I'm horrified to find the skin red and raw as my nails scratch at it subconsciously.

"Okay…" I say, coming to stand back in the centre of my apartment. "I can figure this out. I can do this. I just need to find my Solis." Again, the word sends a shiver down my spine, goosebumps prickling up everywhere. Will is counting on me to figure this out, and for him, I would walk through fire. I take a long steadying breath, sinking to the floor to ground myself and calm my mind.

"Follow my dreams," I whisper aloud. That's what Alex told me to do. That's what Will did to find his. I let my eyes close, allowing the images to permeate my vision. My heartbeat spikes and my breaths are laboured. Before I know it, I'm choking, gasping for air, but not getting any. The feel of icy water tearing through my skin and Will's voice echoing out of the endless depth below me.

My eyes fly open.

"It's at the lake."

I scramble to my feet and with a desperate new purpose, I change into more appropriate clothes, keeping Will's sweater on under my jacket. I can't bring myself to not wear it. It smells like him and it helps to calm me. I instinctively grab a pair of gloves from the top of my dresser and pause. My fingers skimming over the silk fabric that I have grown so accustomed to over the past two years. They have hidden my biggest source of insecurity for so long, but I don't care anymore. Will doesn't care, and that's the only thing that matters to me.

I toss them back into the top drawer of my dresser and shove it closed. A loud thud echoes through the space. I turn back to the dresser, opening the drawer to see the dagger that Will gave me at Mariah's party. I reach out for it, my fingers grasping onto the filigreed hilt of the small blade. It's no bigger than a butter knife, but it's sharp.

Small and sharp like you.

I smile to myself as the memory of him offering it to me in that quiet kitchen floods my mind. Somehow it seems so long ago. My thumb brushes over the golden sun detail on the hilt, and my heart flutters at the reminder of his nickname for me. Tears threaten me again, but I sniff loudly and tuck the dagger into my boot by my ankle. It makes things uncomfortable, but I want to have something to protect myself with in case Alex or Sarah come at me with one of those collars.

I look one last time at my phone before tucking it into my back pocket, and my eyes travel around the apartment. Courage is needed now. Courage to save Will. Courage to find what I've lost and the courage to do it all with no memory of why.

✳

I SMELL the water before I see it. It's a drizzly and cold spring evening, the sun beginning its descent and the city growing darker by the minute as I trek through the walking trails toward the beach. It's really the only beach nearby and not far from where Will's apartment is. It seemed as good as any place to start looking. There is a cool breeze and my wrists itch as I warm the surrounding air to calm myself. I'm already nervous, on high alert, stressed…I don't need the chill and my chattering teeth adding to that. Not when I have the power to prevent it. And then there's the fear. The fear of the water, of finally coming face-to-face with that nightmare that always makes my heart feel like it's being torn apart.

The sound of the waves gently lapping against the sandy shore greets me. I pass a few people on my way down there. Mostly locals out walking their dogs who don't give me much notice. I wonder what it might be like. To live a normal life. No memory loss, no trauma, no scars, no powers. In another life, I wish for it.

To walk with my love hand in hand along the boardwalk with a dog as we listen to the symphony of the water. But that isn't this life.

My shoes hit the sand, my weight sinking into each step as I head toward the water. The beach is deserted, not surprising given the weather and the time of year. I look around, recognizing the city and CN Tower in the distance. I'm getting closer, I'm sure, my insides jittery with anxiety. Will immediately knew where to go. He saw the light through the trees and heard that voice call to him. My voice. There's none of that here. I was so sure that if I simply came here, something would happen.

I spot a flat rock on the shore amongst the sand, the size and shape perfect for skipping across the water. My wrists itch again as the rock rises into the air before me, landing in my upturned palm. The rock is surprisingly smooth with a warmth I can't quite define. An energy I can feel radiating through the air. I flick my wrist, releasing the stone, and watch as it skips across the surface of the water out toward the unknown. Something squeezes my heart then. A memory begging to burst through the wall of darkness. How do I know how to skip rocks? I've never done it before and in the two years since I woke up in that hospital no one has ever mentioned the pastime to me before, but here I am with a skill and no explanation.

Elora.

My whole body jumps, the sound echoing through the air. I spin around, my heart leaping into my throat as my hand flexes toward the dagger in my boot. And then there it is. A pull like a magnet behind my belly button toward the end of the beach where the sand turns to rock. I walk toward it, my legs aching from pushing through the sand until I reach the edge of the manicured beach. What lies beyond is rocky and overgrown. To my left is a steep climb up toward houses overlooking the water and to my right, the vast expanse of the lake.

The moment I step off the sand, I feel it like a weighted blanket pressing down over my skin, and I know that I'm in the right place. Perhaps I hadn't felt it before when Will accidentally Jumped here because I was just outside of the bubble. It's deadly quiet—the only sound that of the water lightly sloshing against the rocks, but there's no breeze, no birds, no noise. Just an empty hollowness. A shiver slips down my spine like ice. I close my eyes and think of Will. I need to do this, for him, for us.

Elora.

With shaky hands, I haul myself up onto the rocks toward the beach on the other side, that pull behind my navel tugging as if someone has tied a rope around my waist. I walk for what feels like an hour—the voice calling me out of the silence in Will's low, soothing tone. The houses above me on the left give way to trees and brush, but the expanse of water on my right is formidable.

I turn to look back at where I've come from, the CN Tower still way off in the distance and the beach I left behind hardly within view anymore. I recognize this place now, my throat tightening with the memory of drowning. It's where I crawled my way out of the frozen depths. The only dream I can ever remember. I try to relax, to take in air. Maybe Will bringing me here wasn't an accident after all. Maybe somehow deep within him, Will knew I needed to come here, only we didn't realize it at the time.

Elora.

The voice skitters along the still water toward me. It's like I can see it, a misty current rippling across the surface, and there it is. Flickering faintly in the distance over the water, a blue light. At the sight of it, I'm no longer afraid. A sense of complete calm washes over me, as if I'm hypnotized by what's out there. Is this what Will felt amongst the trees? No wonder he insisted we follow it. It's intoxicating, like having an adrenaline rush without any effort.

"I'm coming," I whisper aloud, my voice shattering the silence.

My wrists itch horribly as I step to the edge of the water, and without thinking, I step forward. I should be surprised, shocked by what happens, but it feels as natural as breathing as I walk across the surface of the still lake like it's cement, the water flooding the soles of my shoes. Farther and farther and farther away from the shore, the vast expanse of black water beneath me and the eerie, unnatural quiet, but all I feel is harmony as I watch the light grow brighter with every step.

I don't dare look back at the shore. I fear if I do, I might break the spell that keeps me from falling beneath the surface where the chill of the water and the darkness might swallow me whole. I keep going, step by watery step, until the light pitches forward. Beneath my very feet, a glittering diamond in a dark cave. As though my mind is working faster than I can think, the water before me starts to spin. It parts for me like watery curtains as the surface beneath my feet displaces, lower and lower, carrying me down into a well of water toward the almost blinding light below.

My feet touch the silty bottom of the lake, and I'm sure if I dared to look up, a wave of claustrophobia would crash down upon me, but nothing, not even Will's beautiful face can tear my eyes from the sight before me. A blue and white shimmering stone sits within the muck, its surface shining as though the water has no effect whatsoever upon it. My hand trembles as I reach for it, my wrists and forearms almost unbearable, as though a thousand tiny beetles are crawling beneath the skin, desperate for freedom.

My fingers close around the stone, and I raise it before me. It's like mist captured in glass, and looking at it makes my heart feel like it is exploding. Tears leak from the corners of my eyes, and I don't understand why. The overwhelming emotion I feel holding this simple, small thing makes me gasp. The stone is set in a small silver ring like Will's, and I push the band over my middle finger.

Pain tears through my arms, the scars twisting and bubbling like the skin is melting, and in that momentary slip of concentration, the well caves in around me.

·————— ✳ —————·

"You know *full well that we have the capacity to rule, and once things are set in motion, it won't take long to overthrow the other Masters."*

I stand frozen, listening in the shadows.

"I'm not denying that we have the power capable of subduing the other affinities, but what about the girl? Seems an odd coincidence that a Natural is created at the same time that we are trying to make a change," the other voice says.

A sigh. "It does present a significant problem. With what she is capable of, she's the only thing that could derail it all."

"We'll have to be careful about how we deal with her. Perhaps if we could convince her of our cause, she might—"

"She'd never go against her own affinities' ideals."

A scoff. "Which one?"

"Does it matter? All the Natural powers think the same."

"But she's young and naïve, and she is a woman…"

"What are you saying?"

"You've noticed the way she and Willan Reed watch each other, haven't you?"

My heart is hammering so hard I'm sure they can hear it. My hand presses against my mouth to quiet my desperate breaths as the voices retreat.

"Perhaps we could use their feelings for each other to our benefit."

"An interesting idea, but if she were to oppose us, there would be no stopping her. Best if we eliminate her from the equation altogether."

The sound of the door opening and slamming closed echoes through the dark empty corridors and I crumple to the floor, tears of anger streaming down my face.

✶

MY WHOLE BODY IS TREMBLING, *the metal around my neck cold. I stare through blurry eyes up at the Masters from the bottom of the court. I wonder for a moment if I'm already dead. Surely this is what death feels like. Alone and below.*

"We have reached the difficult decision that due to the circumstances about your nature, at this hour next week, you are to be executed."

An anguished cry, like a wounded animal, rips through the air, slashing against my heart. I see him then, on his knees, grasping at his chest like his heart has imploded. Will Reed breaks in that moment before me.

✶

I'M FLOATING.

The cold air is gone, and a warmth surrounds me like a hug from a mother I can't remember. I need to go somewhere, do something, but it feels so nice just floating here in the silence, in the embrace that touches every part of me. My body curls in on itself, my arms and legs weightless, like a baby in the womb— safe and secure and innocent.

But I'm not innocent. I have been forced to endure the worst.

Forced to watch Will break as my sentence was laid down by those who were sworn to protect me, protect all of us, protect my freedom. The betrayal.

I open my eyes in the murky darkness at the bottom of the lake. I lift my hands in front of me, the glowing of the Solis stone on my finger, and the scars...the scars are gone. Replaced with glowing blue designs from my palms to my elbows. Images of Fire and Earth and Air and Water. They glow so brightly and radiate such energy I'm surprised the water hasn't evaporated around me.

I know I should feel like I'm drowning, but I don't. I don't even feel the need to breathe. I look up, the shimmering surface of the lake above beckoning me with its silent call. I push off the silty floor, my toes squishing in the muck as I rise, rise, rise toward the surface. But unlike my dreams, where I clawed upward like a caged animal attempting to flee capture, now it's a heavenly ascent. Calm and joyous.

My face breaks the surface, the cold air whipping against my wet skin. I spot the shore in the distance and as I tread water, the intricate, lace-like patterns of my arms glow brightly under the surface. Propelling myself through the lake toward the shore, the element part for me so gently until my feet hit the rocky bottom. I stumble out of the lake, calling on the Air to dry and warm my clothes, but my heart sinks as the smell of Will is gone. He was the one thing that kept me calm through all of this. As the dam that kept my memories locked away from me continues to chip and crack, one singular purpose ravages through me.

Save Will.

26

WILL

When I open my eyes again, Alex is back, speaking low in Sarah's ear and watching me from his place across the clearing. I make a run for him. I want to grind him into the earth and let it swallow him. But the voltage that shoots through me the moment I move has me collapsing onto the muddy ground, my body nearing its capacity for pain.

"Can you stop, please?" Sarah asks.

"Come on, Will, I don't care if you die, but watching you wreck yourself isn't exactly fun either," Alex says, crossing his arms over his chest.

I draw in a deep breath, pushing myself back onto my knees. "Well, maybe if you let me out of this, we could settle it civilly."

Alex simply rolls his eyes. "Listen, man, it's not like I did this because I hate you. On the contrary, I think if I didn't need you for this purpose, we could've been friends."

"We were friends." My throat hurts as I try to swallow. "Did we know each other…before?"

Alex shrugs. "I never heard of you before."

"I did."

Alex and I both look at Sarah.

"I mean, we'd never met, but I knew your last name. How could I not?"

"Oh," Alex says, a strange smile twisting his face. "Right, of course."

I feel like a toddler whose older siblings are holding a favourite toy out of reach. "You going to explain to me what all that shit means?"

They look at each other, then back at me, the two speaking in unison, "No."

I sigh, aggravated. "Where's Elora?" I ask, looking down at the ground.

"I took her home," he says calmly, "told her to find her Solis for us. When she does, we'll know. Then we can get this over with."

My thoughts drift to her dream that I saw while holding her as she slept. The crushing weight of the icy water and the panic of drowning and the light, so very far down under the water. The words reach my lips to ask how she was possibly supposed to get her Solis if it was at the bottom of a Great Lake, but the image of Elora holding that little shimmering butterfly of water in her hands reminds me just how powerful she is. My eyes catch Sarah's, and she smirks at me. I hate that she can read everything that flits across my mind.

"So, remind me," I say hesitantly, "how do Solises work?"

I see the tiniest glance from Sarah toward Alex and I know instantly that they aren't telling the whole truth, but I try to cover the thought with the image of Elora exploding rocks in her living room.

Alex steps forward, clasping his hands together. "We'll use the Solises to make a portal to pass through."

I nod, and the image of a brilliant whirlpool floats to the

forefront of my mind. I've seen them before. Many times, but the last time…

"Can I ask you something?" Alex asks.

I look up at him. There is an odd expression on his face, but I try not to think about it too much. "Sure, she'll just tell you what pops into my mind once you ask anyway."

He smiles, and it looks so similar to the expression he used to flash at me every morning when he busted through my door to raid my fridge that my breath halts. "What did you two do to get exiled?"

My hand goes to my chest again, the images swirling around in my brain. For a split second, I think I see a blackened sky, but nothing solidifies just yet.

"I can't…I don't remember yet."

Alex nods and turns to walk back to Sarah.

"What did you do?" I ask, extremely curious.

Alex turns around. "I killed my father."

My mouth falls open. "You…why?"

"Because he killed my mother."

There is zero regret on his face, the truth of it practically written across his forehead, and I feel sad for him.

"I'm sorry," I whisper.

Alex shrugs. "He was a fucking hateful bastard who beat me. It's no skin off my back that he's dead. He deserved it."

"But they exiled you anyway and…" it hurts to even think the words, "destroyed your Solis."

His eyes darken.

"Do you have siblings back home?" I ask. "Other family?"

"No."

My brows pull together. "Then why go back if there's nothing for you there?"

Alex utters a dark laugh. "I don't want to go back for warm

fuzzies, Will. Do you think I'd go through all of this trouble for this long simply to go back to hang out by the seaside?"

"Then why?"

"I plan on paying a visit to the Masters."

"What for?" I ask, but somehow I already know the answer by the look on his face.

"To obliterate them all."

27

ELORA

I thought that once I retrieved my Solis and reached the beach, Alex or Sarah would suddenly appear before me, but they don't. Panic sweeps through me as I realize there isn't really any way to get ahold of them, to let them know I've been successful. But now that I've done it, the Solis ring is a familiar, comforting weight on my finger, and I'm overcome with the horrifying idea of someone taking it from me.

Once it touched my skin and the scars disappeared from my arms, it was like I was finally warm, whole. The only other feeling that came close to having the Solis back on my hand was when Will held me in his arms. The thought of handing it over to Alex or Sarah is abhorrent. I wonder if Will feels the same way. It seems a sickening thought to remove it now, nausea rolling over me as I trek back toward the sandy beach in the dark.

My skin feels alive with both power and nerves, while exhaustion weighs on my shoulders as my feet push through the sand toward the road. My mind floods with images that don't quite make sense. The memory of the Masters conspiring to get rid of me like a mooring post amongst the waves, the memories surrounding it still unclear.

I stop as my feet hit the sidewalk. If Alex and Sarah use our Solises to go back, that means that Will and I will be stranded here. Forever without this precious stone that feels like it's a part of me more integrally than my limbs, my hair, my heart.

"But Will will be safe and we will be together."

Perhaps Alex means if I make it back to my apartment with the Solis, he'll know. It's not like I can call him, right? I pull my phone from my back pocket, but it's dead. It was in my back pocket when the water crashed over me. Guess it's toast now—no bag of rice is going to bring this thing back from the dead. My socks are still soggy when I make it to Queen Street, and I riffle around in my jacket pocket for my bus pass.

"Elora?"

I spin around, but my stomach plummets into my shoes as I watch Hunter approach me from across the street. My jaw drops as he walks toward me, my eyes narrowing at the semi smile on his face, and I feel the hair rise on the back of my neck. Our last encounter was not at all pleasant and I'm happy to see that the fingers Will broke are still useless.

"What do you want?" I ask, instinctively tucking the Solis on my finger out of sight. Alex and Sarah had pulled the wool over our eyes. What if Hunter is the same as us? Atlantian. I suddenly regret not bringing a pair of gloves with me. My Solis marks are completely visible now. Solis marks? How do I know what they're called?

"Listen," he says, glancing up at me sheepishly, "I just wanted to apologize for how I behaved that night. It was shitty of me."

That is not what I expected.

"Oh, well, thank you. I appreciate the apology," I say and start toward the bus stop.

"So, are you dating that guy with the glasses?" he asks, following a few steps behind me.

I don't really know the answer to that. What Will and I have goes beyond simply dating, but I'm not about to break it down for this idiot on the street. "Yeah, I am."

"He's a lucky guy," he says.

I spin around. "Look, I appreciate the apology, but I really have to go."

He crosses his arms. "Oh, sorry. Maybe I'll see you around then."

I raise my eyebrows. "No offence, Hunter, but probably not."

Whatever repentant expression that was living on his face darkens. "What's your problem?"

I blink. "What's *my* problem?"

"Yeah! I apologized, and you're still being a gigantic bitch."

My lips press together. "Hunter, I only accepted your apology because it would've been rude not to, but the truth is that I never want to see your misogynistic face again. And if you ever see me, keep walking."

His face turns red as I turn to walk away.

"You little cu—"

His hand clasps my shoulder, his fingers digging so harshly into my skin through my coat that I yelp, but a moment later, he's on his knees, floored as voltage sweeps through my body into his. His hand leaps from me and he crumples, his hair full of static and a twitch in his arms as he lays still on the sidewalk. My eyes go wide, taking a moment to look at my hands. I didn't touch him, but the voltage is still sweeping through me, like my own personal defence mechanism.

I look around where a few people have stopped to look at me and point. A woman points at my arms, blue light peeking out from the Solis marks covered by my sweater. Can they see them? Did they see what I did to him? Without a second thought, I run. Run and run until Hunter is far behind me and I'm close to my apartment.

"Holy shit!" I pant as I fall against the wall of a building after turning the corner.

There's still something else? Something more I can do? I didn't think about doing it, but when Hunter's unwanted touch pressed into me, my body just reacted. I am starting to think there isn't anything I can't do. As far as I know, electricity isn't something Will or Alex or Sarah can do. The memory of that overheard conversation presses into my thoughts. *If she were to oppose us, there'd be no stopping her.* Is it because I'm a Natural?

I push off from the wall and keep walking. It's completely dark now, the only light from the streetlights and traffic and houses lined up along the road. I wonder what time it is as I turn the corner toward my house and stop. What if Alex or Sarah are there waiting for me? Am I ready to face them? I look down at the Solis stone on my hand and my heart aches. Now that I have it, I can hardly dare to think of giving it up. Would the few memories that have returned also disappear if it was removed?

I pull on the ring and feel resistance. Like pulling two pieces of a magnet from each other. It finally slides past the tip of my finger, chills erupting over my arms from a drop in the temperature of the air. I close my eyes, and the memories are still there, some clearer than others, but they're there. I breathe a relieved sigh and quickly push the ring back onto my hand, and it warms my body instantly.

I pull my way up the stairs to my apartment and throw myself against the back of the door as it closes, locking it for…I'm not sure why I bother. It's not like it will keep either of them out. I remove my shoes and pull my soaked socks off my frozen feet, using Fire to warm the air between my toes. The lights above my bed flicker out of the corner of my eye, and not for the first time, it's like I can feel the charge in the air. I walk to the string of fairy lights half strung up on the wall and half over my bed. My fingers touch the wire. The energy surging through the wires tickles my skin, and the pitched whine of electricity as it courses through the lights prickles at my ears, the bulbs growing brighter.

I feel like a battery soaking up a charge, practically giddy with the energy. Like someone who's been shuffling their feet across the carpet, gathering the pent-up static along their skin until they touch metal and a sharp zap releases it. I look around—my bed is metal. I reach out tentatively to touch the frame, my hair practically floating with energy. I've barely made contact when a bolt of blue electricity shoots out of my fingers toward the bed frame. The metal flares, the current streaking across every inch of the bed frame with a loud crack, and the smell of acrid smoke fills the air.

For a few moments, I can only stare. Stare between my hands and the bed while an idea starts to take shape.

28

WILL

I t's the first time I've ever been scared of Alex. A look had crossed his face as he told me about his plan for killing the Masters. That hateful, vengeful look has no place on this person, who spent the last two years being the best friend I could have asked for. Alex was funny, charismatic, happy, but this man is none of those things. How could I have been so naïve? How could I believe all of our interactions were genuine? The more I think about it, the more obvious it becomes.

Him periodically asking me about my past before the accident as if hoping to highlight how little sense the blurry memories made. That fact alone stops the breath in my chest. None of it was real. The images of my parents, friends, lovers were all planted there. Who would do that? Who would erase my life only to replace it with stock images? Why not just toss me into the Other World and destroy my Solis, punished by the awareness I'd never be able to return?

"It's an interesting question," Sarah chimes in, looking at me over Alex's shoulder.

My eyes meet hers. I keep forgetting that she can hear what she pleases.

"What is?" Alex asks, turning to look at her.

Sarah steps forward. "Why Willan and Elora's Solises are intact, but their memories were modified."

Alex stands up, his face changing to one of curiosity. "I'll admit it is extremely unusual."

"Part of the punishment is being able to remember where we come from, what we're missing out on by being cast away. But you two…they didn't want you to remember," Sarah says, her head tilting to the side.

"She…" my mouth is so dry it hurts to speak, "she was sentenced to execution, not exile."

Alex and Sarah look at each other, then back at me, wide-eyed. Obviously, this was not something they expected.

"But," Sarah says quietly, "what could they possibly have deemed worthy of an execution? There hasn't been a formal execution carried out in Atlantis in centuries."

"I think…" the words tumble out of me without thought, "I think they were afraid of her. Afraid of the power she wields."

An image of Elora surrounded by light so bright that it burned my retinas appears in my mind. Stones hovering in the surrounding air like bubbles as water swirls around, cocooning her amongst flames which lick out at everything that comes close. People scream, but Elora's face is a mixture of agony and sorrow so powerful that my heart constricts at the image. Her power drags over me like a blanket. Comforting and suffocating all at once. Even through my memory, it sears my skin and singes at the ends of my hair and clothes. She was terrifying to behold.

"What made her lose control?" I hear Sarah whisper.

The memory of the blackened sky flashes before me again, but there's nothing else. "I'm not sure."

Sarah grabs Alex's arm tightly, and they exchange a nervous look. Sarah leans in to whisper something in his ear that I can't hear, and the next moment, they are gone. I look around me, wondering if maybe they've just moved far enough away that I won't be able to hear their conversation. I go to stand, but the voltage rips through my veins, and I fall back toward the ground in a crumpled heap of sweat and mud.

"Fuck!" I shout into the eerie quiet of the woods.

I am utterly and truly trapped. I think about Elora and whether she has found her Solis yet. Perhaps that's why Alex and Sarah have disappeared. Did they go to collect her? Maybe Elora ran away. I hope she has. That she has simply packed a bag and disappeared. It feels like Elora and I have been part of someone else's plan for too long. If she had never been led to working at the pub, she could've possibly spent the rest of her life as relatively normal as possible. But would it have been normal? She would've still had the glamours on her arms, shaming her into hiding herself. Would her power have stayed repressed? Would she have found happiness with someone else eventually?

The selfish part of me hopes she wouldn't have. That no matter where she went, she'd always be mine, always long for me. Guilt rips through me. Here I've been chasing after companionship from women to no avail, while she's been alone all along. My anger boils beneath the surface as I cast my memory back, trying to remember who would've done this to us. What happened between the sentencing and when we woke up in the hospital? It seems like some of it had been my plan to save her, but surely I couldn't have done it alone. The memory is there, slowly floating to the surface out of the muck, but I can't quite grasp it yet and I feel like time is starting to run out.

Sarah reappears a moment later and while she continues to give me a look that's meant to distance herself from me, I can't help but notice that she has paled. Her eyes are shifty and her hand is jittery.

"Where's Alex?" I ask.

"Huh?" she asks, turning her sharp eyes to me.

"Alex," I say again, "where did he go?"

"She found it," Sarah says with a voice that portrays no emotion. "He's gone to collect her."

"How did you find Elora?" I ask.

Sarah tilts her head. "What do you mean?"

"You put the flyer for the opening at the pub in her mailbox, I presume. How did you know where she was so you could make sure she ended up working with me?"

"We didn't."

"What?"

Sarah and I stare at each other, and I'm trying to figure out if she's lying. But why would she?

There's a sharp snap, and the next moment, Elora is trying to wrench herself away from Alex's grip as they appear in the clearing.

"Will!" she cries out, falling to her knees. A blue shimmer on her hand catches my eye, the Solis stone ring sitting on her small, delicate finger, light emanating from it like a lighthouse in a storm.

"El!" I shout, trying to reach for her, but before I can do anything. Sarah presses the button that sends a zap through my muscles and once again I fall to the ground.

"Stop it!" she screams. "Please, we'll give you what you want! Just don't hurt him!"

If I can just touch her, just reach her somehow. Let her know it's okay. That she should run. But she's being pushed back, pushed farther away from me, and as she moves, music reverberates out of the Solis through my veins. Like a song whose melody plucks at every vulnerable heart string as it sings its tune. Elora's voice. Her voice radiates power within me, and at that moment, I realize why we are connected. Why, when she moves, I move. Why it's her who drew me to find the Solis stone, and why once we met, our affinities started to reappear. Why she has been so bright amongst the cloudy reality I've spent the past two years living in.

"You're my soulmate."

The struggle stops and the quiet presses in as the four of us collectively draw breath. I know it now. Know that's what she is. How rare it is. She is my soulmate. No matter how much distance was put between us or how much time, we would always find each other, recognize each other. I know it now just as I knew it then when I'd convinced the council of Masters to exile us instead of executing her. That they must have erased our memories and tossed us to the Other World because watching her die was the equivalent of having my own soul shattered. That if she didn't have her Solis or memory of who she was, she would no longer be the threat that everyone assumed she was.

Elora drops to her knees. "I see you."

There's a flash of movement and a shrill shriek as something black and metal clamps around Elora's throat from out of nowhere. The voltage rages through her body as she crumbles to the damp earth, and before I have a second thought, I'm running at Alex. A pain unlike anything previously administered rips through me, and I feel like my brain is exploding. My teeth grind so hard together I think my molars might burst. But then there's a different kind of pain.

A hand grips my wrist and pulls at the Solis ring, dragging it down my finger as if it weighs a hundred pounds. There's a moment of hesitation before the ring leaves my finger, then there's nothing but pain. I cease breathing, I can't see, I can't feel anything other than the pain. It's like drowning in a vat of acid, unable to discern which way is up. Mindlessly writhing in an abyss. The only other thing that grounds me to reality is her screams and the physical pain ebbs into a new horror.

My soul is in the Solis.

Alex has just taken my soul away from me. And Sarah has taken Elora's.

"Will," Alex's voice echoes as if he stands at the very far end of a long tunnel, "I'm sorry this had to happen this way."

It takes every ounce of strength I have to open my eyes. Alex and Sarah are standing between me and Elora, her twitching body on the ground, and our Solis rings sitting in the palms of their hands. Their faces alight with triumph, barely giving us a second glance. Alex reaches for Sarah, and a moment later, they are gone, abandoning us in the dark wood.

I'm not sure how much time passes. It's so dark here, there is no way to measure it other than Elora's laboured breathing from somewhere next to me. I want so desperately to touch her, but I'm so weak I can barely lift my head.

"Will?" I hear her voice croak out.

"I'm here," I murmur. "I'm sorry."

Her fingers grasp my forearm, and I can tell from her touch she's weak, too. "We need to get out of here. We need to go home."

Somehow, the strength of her voice emboldens me. "We need to get the collars off so we can Jump, but I can't…"

Elora's face appears overtop of me, her hair tickling my sweat-covered face. Her hands work at the collar around my neck, but her fingers are trembling. My eyes focus and I see her own collar is gone as mine clicks and springs open around my neck, falling to the ground.

"How?" I ask, looking up at her wide eyes.

"The collar short circuited the moment it touched my skin. The voltage, I think I can absorb it. It doesn't seem to affect me like it does you," she says, her voice still raspy. "I had to pretend it did so I could distract Sarah with false thoughts and get the key and remote away from her."

She holds up a plastic remote with red buttons and a small

black metal key. I blink at her several times, glancing between the items and her face. Her collar is smoking on the ground next to her.

"You…you tricked them?" I whisper.

She nods.

"But Elora, they took your Solis…the pain."

"I'm a big girl, Will, I survived." She grabs my face between her hands and presses her lips to mine. "I couldn't risk attacking them before you were free. They won't destroy the Solises—they need them for the portal. What I would not survive is if something happened to you."

I huff a great burst of air through my nose and pull her face to mine again. "I love you." The words tumble out like I've said them hundreds of times before, and perhaps I have, but can't remember at this moment. All I know is they're true. They are so true that saying them gives me strength when I have none.

Her eyes dart over my face as a wide grin spreads across her gorgeous mouth. "I love you too."

She kisses me again, falling over my chest as I wrap my arms around her small body. I kiss her and kiss her until once again I'm almost breathless, but this time the contact of her lips breathes life back into me. When we finally break apart, some colour has returned to her face and her grip feels stronger.

"We can find them. We'll get our souls back," she says.

"Yes," I say without a waver in my voice, "yes, we will."

✴

"How are we going to figure out where they went?"

We finally make it back to my apartment, and I collapse onto the sofa from the effort of Jumping both of us here. We're both exhausted and look like shit, but we don't know how quickly Alex and Sarah will get out of our reach.

"Do you remember how to make a portal?" I ask.

The memory is there somewhere, but it's too buried beneath the ocean floor of my mind.

"I don't remember yet," she admits. Elora closes her eyes with defeat and sinks back next to me on the couch.

The situation is dire, and the more time we spend not knowing how to proceed, the less likely it is that we will ever find them. My eyes travel to the door, still locked from the inside when we left for the forest from my dreams, not knowing it would turn into such a nightmare.

"Do you think," I say cautiously, "there might be something in Alex's apartment?"

Elora looks up at me. "Yeah, there might be."

I push myself up. "Stay here—"

"You are absolutely not going over there alone, Will," Elora says, placing her hand on my chest and glaring at me.

I chuckle at the adorable wrinkle that appears between her eyebrows when she's mad. "I only meant I don't have the energy to Jump us both past the locked door."

"Didn't he ever give you a spare key?" she asks.

I think about it for a moment. Alex barged into my apartment so often that it seemed only natural that I would give him the spare key to my place in case I ever got locked out, but every time I told him he could give me his, he ignored me. The more I think about how stupid and blind I've been about his true intentions, the worse I feel.

"No…maybe that should've been my first tip. Listen, I'll unlock it for you once I'm over there, okay?"

She nods and goes to stand by my front door.

I've only ever been inside of Alex's apartment a few times as we normally hung out here, but it's simple enough to visualize. Especially considering it is the mirror image of my place. I close my eyes and Jump. When I open them, I'm standing in a chaotic mess, as though a windstorm has rushed through. I turn toward the door and unlock it before looking around. The fridge is empty and open, with dirty dishes sitting piled up in the sink.

There is a small kitchen table covered in wires and cutters and scraps of what looks like ankle monitors. I hear the door open and glance over my shoulder to see Elora walking in. She peers around me to look at the table and she grasps an empty box from the floor.

"It's a shock collar for a dog," she says quietly. "Is that how they made—"

"Sarah mentioned she used them for parts. She definitely improved them though," I say, absentmindedly rubbing my neck. "It makes sense. We do live above a vet clinic."

Elora tosses the empty box back on the table and turns toward the living room. I follow her, stopping short at the massive pile of papers and notes on the coffee table in front of the TV. There are a few diagrams on the top of the collars that Sarah made, but it quickly becomes apparent just how under surveillance I have been over the past two years.

There are piles of notes around me. Details of conversations I've had with Alex written down with notes in the margins where Alex and Sarah were trying to figure out how much I knew. Weeks worth of my work schedules are written on a notepad, as well as a list of my most frequented stores. I spot Elora's name and a printout of her entire Instagram profile, which is extensive. There are a few pictures where they have circled something in blue sharpie. Images where her gloves had slid down on her arms a bit.

"They were trying to confirm I have Solis marks," she says, picking up the photos.

Underneath, there are photos of inside Elora's apartment and her work schedule, and just like in my case, a list of other frequented establishments.

"I don't get it," I say as Elora continues to rifle through the stacks of notes on the table. "Alex saw my Solis marks that time we went to the beach with Mariah over a year ago. Why not just explain everything to me then? Why did he have to wait?"

"I think I might know why," she says, staring at a black notebook. "Here…"

I take the book from her hands and stare down at the handwriting I've been familiar with from work for two years.

Suspicions confirmed today.

Witnessed Time affinity, Solis marks on chest and they glowed. His Solis must still be intact.

Will seems to believe the glamour that's been put on him, whatever it might be. He won't open up about it no matter how many times I ask and doesn't seem to notice the markings when they glow.

I turn the page to see notes from a few weeks later.

Proximity to another Atlantian doesn't seem to be jogging his memory either, like Sarah suggested. Perhaps it's because our Solises were destroyed? Sarah suggests at this point to flat out ask Will. Hoping Sarah can find another Atlantian and find out some more information about it.

Another page…

Asking was a bust. Whoever tampered with his memory obviously put some sort of mechanism in place that when asked about Atlantis or his Solis, he appears to have heard something completely different.

"What the fuck?" I mutter. "He did ask me directly…but I—"

I flip through the next few pages and spot Elora's name.

Possible Atlantian: Elora Green - new server at the pub. Amazingly enough, it seems her Solis is still intact like Will's. Perhaps this is what he needs to break through the fog. Would be easier if he hadn't bungled their meeting so much.

Things are happening. Will started Jumping. Sarah read his mind after he woke up out of the apartment. Looking into what affinities Elora might have. Solis marks are hard to discern since she keeps them covered at all times. No surprise there, given their placement.

Clearly, Elora and Will being in close proximity is working. Looking for ways to force proximity and see what happens. Sarah has an idea.

"Force proximity?" I whisper.

"They staged the whole standing me up scenario," she says quietly, "so we'd spend time together alone."

I scoff loudly and flip through the rest of the notebook.

"There's nothing in here about a portal," Elora says, tossing the book back down on the table.

"Keep looking here. I'm going to check out the rest of the apartment. They might have left something behind."

I turn around and head down the hallway, peering into the abandoned bathroom for a brief moment to make sure nothing in there is amiss. The door to the bedroom is ajar, and I walk into chaos. They were obviously in a hurry to pack up to leave. There are clothes and belongings strewn about, drawers left open and things hanging off of hangers in the closet. I take a step toward the dresser, and surprisingly, I find the photograph of Alex, myself, and Mariah. Mariah gave each of us a framed copy of the photo last year for Christmas. She said she was grateful to have us in her life. That she considered us brothers. My heart aches again, knowing that everything I thought I knew about Alex is a lie. The things I told him. The things he told me.

Where would you go if you could go anywhere?

He asked me that only days ago. Was it merely another attempt at trying to crack open my true memory? What did I respond with?

Hawaii, maybe. Lazing about on those beaches would be nice. I've always liked being near the water.

The irony of the conversation hits me, and I choke out a laugh. Perhaps my memories *have* been trying to break through. I can picture it so perfectly now. That home with my parents with the view of the ocean, the crash of the waves below my feet and the smell of salt in the air.

I asked him where he would want to go and out of everywhere in the world he chose...

Haliburton forest. There's something there I'd like to see again.

"Elora?"

My voice bounces off the walls of the apartment and a moment later, Elora is sprinting into the room. "What is it?"

I take a deep breath. "I think I might know where they went."

29

ELORA

We waste no time as Will wraps his arms around my body to prepare to Jump. His grip isn't as strong as it normally is and his breathing is a little shallower. The effects from the collar, as well as having our Solises removed so soon after being reunited wreaked havoc on him. I'm sure he can feel it too, that hollow ache that settled into the heart and bones now that the rings are gone. Coupled with the desperation of needing them back like we need air to breathe, it's a jittery uneasiness that only settles with the feel of his hands on my skin.

"Are you sure you can do this?" I ask, brushing my thumb along his cheek.

He exhales and nods before he pulls me to his chest.

A spark of hope flutters inside me. The smell of him sends a rush of endorphins through my veins.

"You have the collar?" he asks, leaning down toward my ear.

I pat my sweater pocket containing the one working collar we brought with us from the forest.

"Okay, here goes nothing."

The cool breeze brushes my skin, and I inhale the smell of the damp earth. I pull my face away from Will's chest as I look around. We're standing at the edge of a dense forest, a walking path just ahead of us on the right and a small cabin on the left. "Park Ranger" is written above the door and a first-aid cross is posted in the window.

"Think we should ask if they've seen them?" I suggest.

Will looks around again. "Can't hurt I suppose."

We approach the cabin and pull open the door. A burly man with a beard sits behind a desk in a green uniform. His head shoots up when we enter, his eyes narrowing in on us, and I realize what we must look like. We didn't take the time to clean ourselves up after returning from the forest where Alex and Sarah left us. Surely, I look terrible and certainly Will is not much better.

"All right?" the man asks.

"We're actually looking for friends of ours. We were wondering if you've seen them?" I offer casually.

"They lost?" he asks, standing up.

I shake my head. "No. We are actually," I lower my voice and lean toward him, "our friend is proposing and wants us to get photos, but I'm afraid we don't know which direction they went."

The man rolls his eyes. "Blonde girl?" he asks.

I nod, trying to keep my face from splitting with joy at our luck.

"Pretty sure they took trail number three. Not sure why. Nothing scenic about that route. It goes by the conservatory, though."

I give a small nod and a smile. "Oh yes, she loves the stars. That must be it. Thank you very much!"

I turn to leave, but Will is standing to the side, staring at postcards tacked up on a cork board inside the small office.

"Will?" I ask, reaching out and touching his arm.

He turns toward the man. "What's this place here? Is that close by?"

Will is pointing at an image of a tall hedge growing amongst the trees of the forest. It appears to go on forever without breaking, like some kind of gigantic green wall. It takes up the entire frame of the photo.

"Oh that? Yeah…it's maybe an hour's walk off the trail," the man says. "Strange, isn't it?"

"Yeah…" Will says, stepping closer to the pictures, "have you ever seen it in person?"

The man nods, his eyebrows pulling together. "Yeah…can't get through it, though. The hedge is too dense, and it's not like we plan on chopping it down. Just an anomaly of the forest, I guess. My coworker plans to get a drone to fly it over someday. We had one, but it malfunctioned just before we were able to have it fly over."

Will casts a subtle glance my way and I know what he's thinking. My fingers clasp on his arm. *That's where they are.*

"Do you think we could have this?" Will asks, taking the pin out and holding the photo up.

The man nods. "Sure, got plenty more where that came from."

"Thank you very much!" I say as we turn to leave.

"Good luck with your friend's proposal," he offers as the door swings shut with a loud bang behind us.

We spot the marker for trail number three and walk as quickly as we can toward it. Once we're out of sight, hidden amongst the trees, Will grabs me around the waist and we Jump. We're still on the trail but much farther into the forest. The light is scarce amongst the canopy, so I clutch Will's hand as we slowly trek over the branches and puddles. Ahead, there is another path leading toward what looks like a domed roof.

"That must be the conservatory," Will whispers.

A flicker of light catches my eye, and I turn toward the forest. In the distance, peeking out through the maze of trees, is a flicker of blue light.

"Will, do you see—"

"I see it!"

Will squeezes my hand, the two of us stepping off the trail.

We're going to need a plan.

Will eyes me as we step over a large, fallen tree trunk.

Sarah can hear our thoughts. Since we only have one collar, we should use it on her.

Will stops and nods. "All right. But what about Alex? He can Jump. What if he disappears before we can stop him?"

I look down and flex my hand, my knuckles cracking from the movement. There's a sharp tingling sensation buried beneath the skin of my fingers, and I feel it rushing to the surface as I pull on it.

"I have an idea."

· ———— ✦ ———— ·

WILL JUMPS us ahead little by little, and the light flickers and glows brighter as we chase after it like hopping across stones in a pond. Then, it appears like some great monster out of the darkness, the imposing hedge that seems to go on forever in both directions without curve or corner. The blue light filters through the dense greenery and it's quiet again. It's a dreadful, deadly silence that makes me sure there's no life other than us. The two of us raise our hands, our palms pressing against the foliage. A jolt of energy sinks into my skin and my eyes grow to the size of saucers as the Solis marks trailing from my wrists to my elbow ignite with blue light. I turn to Will, the marks on his chest glowing through the fabric of his shirt. They're so beautiful. *He* is so beautiful, his hazel eyes lit from that unearthly sapphire light below. I'm so overcome with the desire to touch him, I didn't realize he spoke.

"What?"

He grabs my hand, still outstretched toward the hedge. "I should go alone. It's not safe, and I won't be able to protect you."

I shake my head. "You're not leaving me here. I won't let them separate us again."

His eyes travel over my face before his palm rests against my cheek. My eyes close against the familiar warmth of his hand, nuzzling into that small part of him.

"El…" The sound of my name on his lips sends goosebumps prickling up and down my arms.

"You can't leave me out here. The two of them are far better practiced with their affinities than us. They will win. I'm coming with you," I say quietly.

Will sighs and finally nods, his other hand wrapping around my back to pull me forward against him, the hand on my cheek sliding back to tug behind my neck. He presses his lips to mine and I feel tiny little explosions burst all over my body and that pull tugs at me stronger than ever. With every shred of willpower I have, I push him back and shake my head. "Don't do that," I whisper.

"Don't do what?"

I look up into his breathless face. "Don't kiss me like it's the last time."

A sad smile crosses his face. "No, sunshine, I kissed you like that because you deserve to be kissed that way every single time."

A small whimper escapes my lips, but he wraps his arms around me, his face steadying and his shoulders rolling back.

"This is all going to have to go really fast," he whispers. "Where's the collar?"

I pull the metal collar from my sweater pocket and hand it to him. He carefully avoids the wires as he grips it in his fingers.

"Ready?" he asks.

I take a deep breath as his grip tightens on my waist, then we are gone.

30

WILL

Time stops. There's a pool in the centre of the space, the water as still as a mirror, reflecting the circular expanse of sky in the middle of the trees and hedge overhead. It looked like a wall from the outside, but space bends here and it circles us. It's easy this time, like it was in the pub. Perhaps it's because she's here and I know that there was never anyone watching me. And even though the world around me freezes, I can feel the threat burning against me. As though Alex's flames are reaching out to me in the invisible space between us. He is the greater threat here, and the choice to collar Sarah isn't one I readily agreed to, but I trust Elora, trust that her plan will work.

Alex and Sarah are mid turn, all of them frozen, when I release Elora. I don't give them a chance to react. The pebbled shore surrounding the pool rattles under my feet as I move toward Sarah. I hold the collar out in my hand, carefully avoiding the wires on the inside—the pulse of energy radiating into the surrounding air. If I touch it, my affinity will fail and we'll be fucked.

I manoeuvre the collar around Sarah's throat—the metal touching her skin with a barely audible zinging noise. I flip the latch, the lock clicking into place, and I exhale hard with relief. One down.

Willan.

I hear it. Hear her. The sound is like a thunderclap in the silence. That voice from my Solis calls out to me. Like it longs to be reunited, and as I hear it, I remember the feeling of being woken up after a long sleep—the feeling of being whole. I turn around, spotting the shining light of my Solis ring emanating from between Alex's enclosed fingers. My hand flexes toward it, but my other hand brushes along Sarah's exposed neck. A sharp zap shoots from my fingers and up my arm, then the silence is gone, pierced by a shrill scream.

"Will! No!"

I catch the briefest glimpse of Sarah's large eyes before she drops like an anchor in the ocean, her body convulsing with the current that travelled through to me enough to neutralize my powers. Then, there are burning hands on my skin, singeing right through the layers of my coat and shirt. There's a clatter of metal on stone and I look up just in time to see Alex's eyes meet mine, the Solis falling from his hand between us.

I try to Jump away from his hands, but Alex has me by the shirt, his fingers clawing at my exposed skin. Then, we're on the opposite side of the pool. I try to push him off me, his grip in my hair stings, and we're against the hedge, then next to Sarah, and back across the pool. The sporadic Jumps make me disoriented. If I can just stop Time again...but it's always harder to do when I can't concentrate on it. If I could just see Elora's face—I look across the pool as a fiery fist collides with my jaw.

Stars burst behind my eyelids as another scream pierces the stillness. I can feel the blisters swelling on my face from the flames and the swelling pressure from the punch. I swing my fist and it collides with skin and bone, the wet sound of blood splattering on rocks. A great groan of pain reaches my ears as

Alex slides off of me. I cough, finally catching a glimpse of Elora beside Sarah, but I can't tell what she's doing. Then, I'm burning —the air around my body too hot. So hot I can't breathe. The very air in my lungs seems to cook me from the inside out.

I grip Alex. I'm desperate to distract him, to throw his focus, so I kick out and it lands somewhere I can't see, but his groan tells me I got him somewhere good. We Jump again, landing on the side of the pool closest to Sarah. She's unconscious—her body wrapped in vines that appear to have grown out of the ground between the rocks. Where's Elora? She was there only a moment ago. My sight dims, the heat and scorching pain in my lungs becoming too great.

"*No!*" Elora screams.

There's a great rush of cool air as Alex is thrown off of me. I roll over, gasping and retching as the cool air coats my lungs and skin. Then, I see it. The Solis is between us and Alex is pushing himself up. The two of us ready to Jump toward it. I blink and I'm there, but before I can grab it, Alex collides with me. His heavy weight is on top of me and his fingers find their way around my throat, crushing my windpipe as I try to fight him off.

A howling sound blasts through my ears as if all the noise to ever exist is being sucked into a vacuum and Alex's hands slacken around my neck.

"What the fuck—" Alex whispers.

I look up through bleary eyes where Alex is staring transfixed over his shoulder. I turn my head, my eyes blinking and watering to bring the scene into focus. Elora is surrounded by a field of river stones, the pebbles from the edge of the pool rising into the air as her feet leave the ground. Her Solis marks are glowing so brightly it's hard to look at them, and her ring is back on her hand. Her hair whips around her face like she's caught in a hurricane. Streaks of light shoot between her hands like lightning caught in a bottle, and her eyes are glowing.

She looks like an angel without wings, fierce and powerful, and every inch of my skin is prickling with the strength she's pushing into the universe. A ball of sapphire energy is growing between her hands, crackling and firing.

Alex shifts off of me to stand. His eyes flick to the Solis stone, then back at Elora and he dives. I know the moment he grabs that stone he'll Jump, vanish with my soul in physical form. My hand shoots out to grab him, my fingers grasping his ankle, and I'm pulled with him as he tries to Jump, but there's nowhere to go as a streak of lightning erupts from between Elora's hands, hitting Alex squarely in the chest, the voltage transferring through my fingers and down my arm with such agony my hand releases from his leg and I fall back against the ground into darkness and smoke.

31

ELORA

There's a loud clatter as the stones and pebbles fall back to the ground, my feet retouching the earth and the wind dissipating as my hair falls. I take a tentative, shaky step forward, my shoes making a loud crunch against the shore. Step after step toward Will, his body lying crumpled on the ground by the water next to Alex.

"No, no, no, no—" I whisper, my steps quickening as I race to his side.

This isn't happening—the blast was only meant for Alex. I'd been storing that energy intending to incapacitate Alex from being able to use his affinities, but it was stronger than I ever would've thought. I'm stronger than I thought. I had to hold off because they were Jumping around together and I couldn't get a clear shot at just Alex. Then finally, the opportunity came, and I took it, knowing he was moments away from grabbing Will's Solis and disappearing possibly forever. But then Will grabbed his ankle and no, no, no, no...

"Will!" I drop to my knees next to him, my hands flitting over his face, his chest, his arms. I can barely think, barely breathe, I don't even know what to do. The Solis marks on his chest dim until they're nothing but lines indented into flesh. "No!" I sob. "Don't you dare!" I press my ear to his chest and hear the low thump of his slowing heart. "I can heal you…I…yes, it'll work," I mutter. "It'll work!"

I press the palms of my hands under his shirt and up his chest over the markings, over where the glamoured scars used to be, and pray that whatever I did that healed the knife wound in his back will work here. But will it? What if the energy I've shot at him prevents whatever healing I can manage from working?

"This has to work! Please…please, please…please don't leave me." I can't stop the tears from falling as a horrible choking sob wrenches itself from my throat. The thudding of his heart stutters and slows.

"Will! Stay with me! Don't…please, Will!"

A glimmer of blue light flashes out of the corner of my eye and I see Will's Solis ring on the ground between us and Alex. I throw myself forward, my fingers clutching at the beautiful stone, like mist under water as the pattern swirls. I sniff and swallow hard, grabbing Will's hand and pushing the ring onto his finger, my eyes wide with anticipation. This will surely help, right? It'll make him stronger, cancel out the effects of what I did. I didn't mean for it to be so strong. Oh God, I did this. This is my fault. If he dies here, it will be my fault. If he dies here, I will too.

There's a loud crunch. Hands grasp at my shoulders, and I'm wrenched backward away from Will's body, still motionless on the shore. Pain bursts from my scalp as my hair is violently tugged back. My back stings as the rocks cut through the layers to the skin of my back as Alex throws me down to the ground, his body kneeling overtop of me. His hands wrap around my throat as I look up at his face.

His eyes are madness, a soulless depth of darkness. Nothing of that beauty, that kindness, that warmth I originally thought I saw there. His lips pull back, revealing his teeth with a snarl, and his breath hisses. There's a crushing weight against my windpipe. My fingers claw at his face, at his arms, at anything, but nothing helps. I try to pull on my power, on anything, but nothing comes. Like a dead battery, I'm completely drained. I'm going to die. I've survived so much, it seems a cruel joke that this would be how it will end. Will is still unresponsive to my right. Maybe it's right that I die. If he goes, I can go with him. Maybe in another lifetime, we'll find each other again. After all, souls recognize each other, don't they?

A flex of movement and a subtle shake of his head and Will's eyes flutter but don't fully open. I want to call for him, but there's no air to give me a voice. If I can just touch him, maybe he'll hear my thoughts.

"You…bitch!" Alex hisses, the spit spraying across my face as he presses harder against my throat. The world turns hazy, my thrashing feet slowing, the dull ache against my ankle sharpening. My boot. The dagger.

With the last shred of life left in me, I bend my knee, my arm reaching for my foot. My fingers touch the warm metal hilt. I grasp it in my hand, raise my arm, and let the blade sink into his flesh wherever I can. A spurt of hot blood bursts over my face as Alex's hands release my neck to grapple at his own. A great inhale of air floods my lungs, and I fight against the darkness that threatens to pull me down. Alex's eyes are wide and terrified as a wave of blood escapes his mouth with a horrifying gurgle.

His fingers find the hilt of the dagger in his neck, his eyes latching on to mine with understanding as he tilts to the side, his body limply falling onto the blood splattered stones. The sound of blood gushing in the silence and his rattling breaths falter, and with a final twitch, it's quiet.

✦

I'M NOT sure how long we lay there, unable to move or speak, but at some point, I feel Will's fingers enclose around my wrist and I send wave after wave of thought toward him.

"El?"

Oh God, Will, I'm so sorry! I almost killed you…I killed him. It's all my fault.

"No. Elora, no, you saved me. If you hadn't blasted him, I wouldn't be here now. It was my own fault for grabbing on. I didn't think…I just acted…" He shuffles closer across the rocks and pulls me up and into his lap, holding my body against his, and my hand presses against his face like a lifeline.

I thought you were gone. I thought you left me.

His lips press against my forehead, the sound of his breath inhaling me. "I'm still here. I'm not going anywhere."

He came out of nowhere from behind me, and he was choking me, and I thought I was going to die, but…

Will squeezes me tighter. "You did what you had to do."

I want to protest, but deep down I know he's right. I was on the brink of death with no way of getting him off of me. I didn't even realize where I'd stabbed him until it was done, until it was too late. Even if killing him was necessary, it doesn't stop the guilt from suffocating me. The image of Alex's eyes realizing what I did flashes before me and the air leaves my lungs as another sob cuts through my chest.

"Shh…come on, let's go home and figure things out."

I go limp as he lifts me into the air.

But what about Sarah?

"She's still unconscious. I'll come back for her. I just need to get you safe first."

My head tips against Will's shoulder, then the light changes and the familiar scent of Will's apartment floods my nose as he lays me on the sofa before pulling a blanket over me.

"I'll be back. Just rest, all right?" Will says, stroking my hair.

I try to push myself up, but Will's hand is immediately pushing me back down onto the cushions. "No way. You stay right there until I get back."

Will, I'm fi—

"Really? You're fine?" A low chuckle escapes his lips. "Guess you owe me a dollar, sunshine."

The ghost of a smile pulls at my mouth, but it turns to a grimace at the pain in my throat.

"I'll be back soon. Sleep now," he says, his lips pressing ever so tenderly against my temple as my eyes close and my hand falls from his face. I'm exhausted.

I watch her for a moment, the blood-covered angel sleeping on my couch, before pushing myself up. My body protests my every movement, but I can't wait, this needs to be done now. I lock the door, ensuring Elora will be safe, then Jump back to the pool.

That unnatural stillness is a sharp contrast from the buzzing hum of my apartment. I smell the blood the moment I appear. The tangy metallic taste coating my tongue. I glance toward Sarah, still unconscious on the shore, then to Alex.

Alex.

I take tentative steps toward him, his body contorted in a pool of blood. An uncontrollable trembling starts from my scalp all the way to my toes as each step takes me closer to his body. Another step and another, then I'm looking down on his face, his eyes still open and vacant. The bright gleam of gold glimmers amidst the blood-covered flesh, and I see the detail of a sun on the hilt of a dagger.

The dagger I gave Elora.

She must have had it on her when we came, and I'm grateful I gave it to her. If she hadn't had it…

I close my eyes for a long moment and open them again. Alex was my best friend for two years. We did everything together. Worked together, hung out together, partied, and talked. And even though I now know he didn't care for me like I thought he did, *I* still care about *him*. He was my only constant. Him and Mariah, my only source of family. The tears sting my eyes and I let them fall as I crouch down to pull the dagger from his throat. It slides out with a thick squelching noise, and I have to fight against the bile that surges up my throat.

I should bury him, but I haven't brought a shovel and there is still Sarah to deal with. I wipe the blood off the dagger and tuck it into my back pocket as I stand. I'll come back later to deal with the body. A small moan travels across the quiet pool and my head whips around to spot Sarah, still wound up in vines with the collar around her neck. She's waking up, and I still haven't decided what I'm going to do with her. I don't want to kill her—I don't want that blood on my hands and with the collar on, she's harmless. Nothing I can't easily overpower, however she's crafty, so I take a deep breath and focus before Jumping next to her.

Her eyes flutter open as her head rocks from side to side. She opens them fully and there is a moment where she blinks at me, fear flooding her face as she pulls against her constraints.

"Sarah," I say, crouching down to grab at her bindings to hold her still, but she continues to thrash against me. "Sarah, stop!"

She settles after a moment, her chest heaving from the exertion and her eyes wide and unblinking.

"I'm not going to hurt you," I say, raising my hands off of her.

"Why should I believe you?" Her voice cracks.

I shrug. "You shouldn't, but it's the truth. I won't hurt you unless you give me a reason to."

Her eyes narrow. "Where's Alex?"

I bite the inside of my lip, my head turning to look over my shoulder, but I think better of it.

"He's dead, then."

It isn't a question, and her face shows no sign of any kind of emotional loss. Still, that doesn't stop me from what I say next. "I'm sorry."

She scoffs. "Why are you sorry? We tried to steal your Solis and leave you stranded here." She shakes her head. "You have nothing to be sorry for."

"My friend is dead."

"He was never your friend."

I nod. "He was to me."

Her head tilts. "So…what are your plans for me, then?"

I grasp her wrists and pull her up to sit. "You're going to tell me how to operate the portal, then I'm going to let you go."

Her eyes twitch slightly. "Let me go?"

I nod, and we stare at each other for a long while.

"All right, pretty boy, I'll tell you." She rolls one shoulder back and takes a deep breath. "You'll need to be here…at night."

"Why night?"

Her eyes flick upward to the open sky above the pool. "Moonlight."

I raise my eyebrows. "And that's a requirement?"

She nods and jerks her chin toward the pool. "When the moonlight touches the pool, you'll need to step onto the water. Your Solis will do the rest."

I glance down at the warm ring on my middle finger. "That's it?"

She raises her eyebrows. "Were you expecting animal sacrifice?"

I almost laugh. "No, but…how do I know you're telling me the truth?"

She smirks. "You don't, but what choice do you have?"

I nod. "Right."

We're quiet again for a long time. My fingers press against

her skin, listening for any waver in her story, but nothing stands out.

"Can I ask you something?" I whisper.

Her brown eyes focus on mine, and they're hollow and dark, no spark or light in them at all. It's unnerving. "Go on then," she says.

"What did you do? To get exiled."

Her mouth twists into a hideous smile. "I had a younger sister. She was always the favourite. Prettier, smarter, more popular…" Her nose scrunches in distaste. "I never minded much until she dug her claws into the man I loved. So I turned her brain to mush."

A wicked smile spreads across her face, followed by a sharp grimace as the collar around her neck shocks her, her body twitching as she falls over onto the stones. I stand up sharply and back away, not quite realizing just how hard I'm breathing. I know I should kill her. She's dangerous. Not just to Elora and me, but to everyone else she comes into contact with. I can't do it, though.

I scoop her up and Jump to Alex's apartment, where I place her on a chair next to the TV. Her head rolls and she looks up at me with blurry eyes.

"You have fifteen minutes to pack what you need, then I'm going to let you go," I tell her.

She blinks several times. "Why do I need to pack?"

"I never said I'd let you go *here*."

She nods once slowly. "Where will you drop me, then?"

I shrug. "Somewhere far away from here…somewhere you can start a new life."

She smiles. "Fair enough."

Sarah shakily gets to her feet, and I watch as she packs a small duffel bag with some clothes and toiletries. She opens Alex's top dresser drawer and pulls out a box full of cash.

"Where the fuck did all that come from?" I ask.

She holds it up. "The bank."

My eyes bulge. "Legally?"

She laughs out loud. "When you can Jump anywhere you please, it's easy to take whatever you want. Alex may have needed my Mind affinity to spy on you, but that male Jumping gift sure came in handy for paying the bills."

Never once did robbing a bank cross my mind since having these powers.

"Ready?" I ask as she stuffs the cash into the front pocket of her bag and slings it over her shoulder.

She takes one last look around the room, her eyes resting for a moment on the picture of Mariah, Alex, and me at the beach.

"You can take it with you if you want to remember him," I say.

She shakes her head. "No point in that. It's not like it was ever love. Purely mechanical, you know?"

I feel a dull ache in my heart at that. "Yeah…I know."

She looks up at me and takes a step forward. "It's the soul that loves, Willan. Without it, we're just robots."

The thought of going back to how it was makes my blood run cold. Feeling nothing, feeling numb, wanting so desperately to feel a connection with someone other than anything physical. It's terrifying.

"Sounds like hell," I say.

"Listen," she says quietly, "you're an idiot if you're thinking of going back."

"What do you mean?"

"Did you ever stop to think there must be a reason they exiled you here? Wiped your memories?"

The truth of her words is like a slap in the face. "I…"

"You're a bigger idiot than I thought if you don't realize how dangerous Elora is," Sarah whispers, and my eyes narrow.

"What?"

"I saw her tonight. What she can do and it—" she cuts herself off, her hand rising to her mouth. "Do you really expect a warm welcome if the Masters went through all the trouble of getting rid of you two?"

I don't say anything. I don't know what I can say. She's right. Is going back really the best idea? They wanted to kill Elora…to execute her. Somehow, I managed to convince them to exile her instead. What if they kill her if we go back?

I give my head a shake and take a step forward. "Any preferences on where you'd like to go?"

Her eyebrow arches up. "California, I think…I've got a thing for surfer dudes."

"Good bye, Sarah."

"See you later, Willan."

The noise disappears as Time freezes around me. I pull the key for the collar out of my pocket and step toward her. Her eyes don't follow me, they're fixed on the place I've just vacated as I turn the lock in the metal. A familiar clicking noise echoes in the silence. I pull the collar away where it halts in the air, waiting for Time to catch up again so it can fall. I grab both of Sarah's arms, ensuring she has her bag, then Jump.

The smell of salt water is familiar, and my feet sink into the sand on the dark beach. I look around, and there's a boardwalk not too far from here down the beach—around, there's the bright lights of what look like a restaurant on a dock over the ocean. It looks just like the picture Mariah showed me of her trip last year. I let go of Sarah's arms and back away, giving her one last look before I'm gone.

33

ELORA

The cell is dark and damp, and my toes are so cold that they are numb and purple. The dress I'm wearing does little to keep the warmth from escaping, and I can see my breath in the dim light. The raging storm outside is loud and the spray of the rain hits the stone sill of the barred window, periodically splattering my skin. My head tips back while I hum a quiet tune, the need for sleep so overwhelming but still so elusive. How can I possibly sleep when my moments are numbered?

"El?"

My head jerks up, the lights flickering on the walls just past the bars of my cell. The shadow of someone approaching quickens my heart, and I rise with a start, stumbling on my numb feet as my hands grip the stone wall behind me to stand.

A tall young man with copper hair and brilliant blue eyes rounds the corner and tears fill my eyes as I run across the space to the bars.

Brysen Green. My brother.

"El, oh my God! Are you all right?" he asks breathlessly, gripping my arms through the bars and pulling me as close as possible. The Solis marks on his bicep glimmer from the moisture in the air.

"Brys, please, it's not what you think. I didn't do what they're saying I did. Please!" The words come out strangled, and I'm trembling so hard it hurts.

"Shh," he whispers, pulling me forward again and touching his forehead to mine. "I know, I know."

The tears that I've been holding back burst out of me then, tears that I've kept inside to protect Will. To protect him from further agony of seeing me like this now. From the terrible wracking sobs that leave me breathless and heaving. We fall to the floor together and I try to get a grip on myself, but it feels useless.

"El...shh," Brysen whispers into my hair. "It's going to be okay."

I sniff hard and pull back, barely able to see him through the tears and swollen eyes. "How can you say that? How will it be okay?"

Brysen looks back over his shoulder and leans toward me. "Will has a plan. He thinks he can convince them not to execute you but to exile you instead."

I feel like my heart is being torn in half. "Exiled?"

Brysen nods.

"No," I whisper, turning away.

Brysen blinks. "What?"

I turn back to him, the metal collar around my neck cold and sharp against my sensitive skin. "I'd rather die than be exiled! To be permanently cut off from you? From Will? No…"

"Elora, listen—"

"No, you listen! I know you never approved of us, but you must understand the love Will and I share is different. What we are to each other. He's my soulmate, Brysen, and I'd rather die than be separated from him forever. To have my Solis…" I can't *even say the words. The thought of someone destroying my soul feels like a blade cutting into my skin. To turn into some emotionless, psychopathic monster—I look down at my hand where the delicate silver ring and Solis stone sit, the bright stone glowing in the dim light. The blue and white pattern swirls as if not completely solid.*

His hand gently wipes the tears from my cheeks. "I know. I know what you are to each other. But…" A loud clang in the distance makes us both jump. "Fuck, I have to go…I'm not even supposed to be here. El, we're working on a way to fix this. Please trust me."

"Brys, please tell him I'm sorry. Tell him I love him!" I plead, grasping the fabric of his shirt.

Tears are brimming in his eyes, but he nods and something presses into the palm of my hand. My eyes narrow, but he shakes his head in warning. I close my fingers around the paper he's given me and tuck it into the back of the sash around my waist.

The next moment, two guards round the corner dressed in their navy uniforms and glaring at me like they always do.

"All right, Green," the first guard says, jerking his chin at the stairwell I know is around the corner. "Figured you'd sneak down here."

"I'm going, I'm going," Brysen mutters darkly. He looks back at me and kisses my forehead again. "I love you, sis."

As Brysen stands and leaves, the small comfort of his arms leaves too, and the dreaded cold that has been tormenting me since being locked away here comes back in earnest.

"Turn out your pockets," the second guard says, turning back to me.

I look up at him, startled. "What?"

"Pull your pockets out. We need to make sure he didn't smuggle you something."

The voltage around my neck sears my skin as my Fire fights to burst out at the audacity of this man, but the shock makes me twitch and they see it. The two guards smirk as they realize I've tried to use my powers.

"Come on now, no use getting mad or you'll just zap yourself into a coma. Now turn out your pockets."

I huff out a great, angry puff of air and pull the fabric out of my pockets, showing them there is nothing there, my hands waving upward, hoping they'll be satisfied.

"Take off your bra."

I blink. "What?"

The other guard seems taken aback by the request as well. "Krew, what the fuck, man?"

"It's a perfectly reasonable request," he says, turning to the other guard. "My wife hides all kinds of shit in her bra."

The unnamed guard raises his eyebrows as if in agreement, then turns back to me, his arms folding over his chest. "Fair enough. All right, girlie, off with it, then."

It takes every ounce of self-control not to fly off the handle, but what would that accomplish? A violent shock, and they'll just do it themselves. At least if I do it, I have control over the situation. I reach behind my back and pinch the clasp. It takes my freezing fingers a few tries, but the bra finally springs apart and I pull the straps through my short sleeves, pulling the bra up through the neck of my dress. I toss it through the bars at Krew, who catches it with one hand. "Satisfied?"

He looks it over, then back to me, his eyes dark and that familiar uneasiness that sometimes follows me when I'm around men prickles at the back of my neck, sending goosebumps scattering down my arms. My nipples harden at the chill and I hastily cross my arms over my chest, but not before both guards have a good look.

"She's clean," Krew says shortly.

I sigh. "Can I have my bra back now, please?"

Krew smirks. "Why? Your tits are so small it's not like you need this anyway."

The other guard laughs as Krew tosses the bra over his shoulder like a prize, and the two of them turn to disappear around the corner and up the stairs.

I wait until the telltale clang of the metal door at the top of the stairs slams shut to scream. Scream until my lungs give out. Scream until my throat is raw. I fall sideways against the stone wall and slump back to the ground shaking, my fingers digging into my palms so hard there are little half-moon punctures in my palms.

"Fuck!"

I take a few steadying breaths, then reach behind me to pull the paper out of the sash. I'm amazed they didn't ask me to remove that, but men have their priorities, I suppose. I open up the small folded note, recognizing my brother's handwriting instantly.

Dear El,

There's a plan in the works. One where you and Will can be together. I can't tell you the details as the Mind Master might see it, but you need to know one thing. Whatever happens, you must come back to Atlantis. Whatever it takes, however long, you have to come back. I love you, sis, we all do.

Brys

P.S. Destroy this.

I look up through the bars, ensuring no one is watching me, then back down to read the note over and over, trying to understand. There is a plan. One where Will and I can be together. I have to come back...come back from where? Are they going to exile me after all? A loud bang in the distance rattles the bars, and I shove the paper into my mouth, chewing and swallowing the note down. My brother's words swirl around in my

head. Another bang as I fight against the urge to throw up.
Another and another. Bang, bang, bang…

✳

MY EYES SHOOT OPEN, a cold sweat covering my body. I'm lying on a couch that smells vaguely of citrus and spice. Will's couch. I swallow, but my throat burns, and as my fingers touch the skin there, I wince at the tenderness. Everything comes flooding back. The pool and Sarah and…Alex. The sound of the dagger piercing his flesh makes my stomach roll and I push myself up, only for my head to spin at a nauseating rate.

"El! Slow down."

It's Will. He's here, and he's holding me.

"Will." It comes out as barely more than a squeak.

"Shh," he whispers, wrapping his arms around me, "don't speak, your throat is still messed up."

I look past his shoulder to the door. There's a shovel next to it under the coats, still covered in dirt. I press my hand to his cheek.

Where were you?

He sighs. "I let Sarah go very far away from here. California, to be exact."

I feel my eyebrows rise.

"And Alex…" He glances over his shoulder at the shovel. "I buried him outside of the hedges."

A chill slides down my spine. The reality of killing a man washes over me with such uncomfortable force I want nothing more than to lie back down and go to sleep.

"Come on," Will says, pulling my hands, "you should shower, you're still…well, a mess."

It's true, I feel it all over me. Something caked onto my skin and clothes. I nod and allow Will to pull me down the hall toward the bathroom. He turns on the shower, allowing the water to run for a few minutes before he goes to leave.

"Wait," I croak out.

He stops, his hand dropping from the door handle, and I reach for it, clasping his fingers between mine.

Don't leave me alone, please.

"Do you want me to wait here?"

I start to pull my sweater and shirt over my head, stepping out of my jeans and underwear until I'm in nothing but my skin before him. His eyes darken and he swallows hard, his Adam's apple bobbing in his throat. I step over the pile of clothes at my feet toward him as the room fills with steam. My hands travel under his shirt and his stomach muscles flex at my touch, his eyelids closing for a long moment.

"El," he whispers.

I lift his shirt up over his chest, the clatter of dried dirt falling to the tile floor as he pulls it over his head. I unbutton the top of his jeans, allowing them to fall over his hips while I push his boxers down his legs. I never drop eye contact with him, and he watches me the whole time with a hungry desire burning behind his eyes. He's hard, his cock free and standing at attention as I pull him toward the shower. His beautiful face is coated in mud and blood, the same as mine.

I pull him under the hot water with me. Immediately, the Solis marks on my arms and his chest light up, the shower aglow with blue light from our bodies. Surprised, we both smile at each other, and he spins me, wrapping his arms around my waist, pulling me back to him, his length pressing against my backside. I let my head fall back against his shoulder as the water sprays over both of us, running red and brown as it washes away our sins. His hands thread through my hair, his fingers massaging my scalp as the scent of his shampoo floods my senses, letting me forget the horrors of only a few hours ago.

His hands drag across my wet skin, pressing kisses to the side of my neck. The pain there receding more and more until I feel that the bruising is gone.

"Amazing," he whispers as he kisses the side of my neck.

I push my backside against his erection and he groans against my ear, the sound setting every nerve I have on fire. I turn toward him, our chests pressing against each other. Water clings to his eyelashes, his hair dripping down his face and his eyes are lit up from his Solis marks below. I push myself up onto my toes and pull him toward me. I need to taste him, need to feel his lips against mine. I need his body to cleanse me of all the evil I've done to save us.

He plunders my mouth in earnest, his tongue as desperate as mine. Like he can't get enough of me. Hands skate down my sides as I kiss down the column of his neck, my hand moving between us to wrap around his cock. Will's body jerks against me, his head falling against mine.

"Let me have you," he whispers against the steady fall of the water.

I smile as an idea comes to me. "After."

His eyes widen, and I'm sure he can hear the thoughts in my mind as I lower myself onto the tile floor of the shower. My hand wraps around the head of his cock directly in front of me, and before I can be nervous about it, I open my mouth and swallow him down as far as I can, considering his size. Will's ensuing gasp encourages me. My tongue and lips working together with my hand as the water pours down through my hair and over my face. All I want now is to belong to him, for him to use me this way.

His hand grips the hair at the back of my head as his hips gently thrust forward, his cock reaching the back of my throat and I try my best to suppress my gag reflex by breathing through my nose, but it's difficult with the water. He pulls my head back, looking down at me on my knees before him.

"Come here," he calls. His free hand hooks under my arm to pull me to my feet. He kisses me hard, and the water turns off as he reaches behind me, the chill of no more hot water making my skin ultrasensitive to his touch, and I shiver against him. He wraps my hair around his fist and squeezes the water out with his hand as his teeth pull on my earlobe.

Please, Will.

His hands grip both of my ass cheeks and he hoists me up onto his hips, my legs wrapping around him. His erection grazes against my clit as he Jumps us soaking wet to his bedroom, sending a jolt through my body with each step. I've barely made contact with the mattress before Will is sliding down my body, his lips trailing over my hip bone, kissing so agonizingly close to the bundle of nerves between my legs.

His fingers play with me, opening me up, his thumb brushing back and forth so deliciously over my clit until I'm fisting the damp sheets.

"Will...shit..." I whisper.

Then, his tongue is on me, and if I had the vocal power to do it, I would scream out loud. But my God, that tongue of his is made for sin, shattering everything I am or ever will be as I come hard. He doesn't let up, the onslaught of his tongue and now his fingers pushing inside me, making my mind turn to dust even as I try to push him away.

Oh my God, it's too much, it's too much!

"You can give me one more, sunshine." The smile in his voice trails up at me from somewhere below. His tongue slows and his fingers curl inside of me, and that crest is building again. My fingers tangle in his wet hair, trying to ground myself, and I look down. I catch sight of this gorgeous man looking up at me with his mouth sucking on my clit and my legs tremble as I fall apart again. I breathe and breathe, trying to focus, my chest heaving.

Will watches my chest rise and fall before crawling back up

my body to take my nipples into his mouth. I try to calm myself from the relentless overstimulation.

"You ready?" he murmurs against the skin of my breast.

"Yes, please, Will," I rasp.

He moves off of me, and there's the familiar crinkle of the condom wrapper, my body trying to play catch up with my brain as the room comes back into focus. His arms snake under my back, pulling me onto him as he sits against his headboard. My legs straddle him, our faces at the same level, and without even thinking, I lift my hips up, feeling him line his cock up against my slick entrance.

"El," the sound snaps my eyes open to his, those burning hazel eyes that sparkle and reflect all the earthly colours back at me. His hand brushes my damp hair back and away from my face, his thumb brushing against my cheek. "I love you," he whispers, his nose brushing against mine.

A flood of power surges through me at the words. Every vulnerability that built itself up around my heart shatters like glass. "I love you too."

I sink down onto him slowly, his eyes closing and a guttural moan ripping from his throat as his hand grips my hip to guide me farther down.

"Jesus fucking Christ. You feel so good," he growls against my mouth, then his lips are against mine, that hard, aching need breaking me all over.

I lift myself up and down, up and down, up and down, grinding my hips against his as his hands sweep up my back, pulling me closer to him. His one hand twists my hair back to expose my healed neck, where he leaves the gentlest kisses across my throat.

His breathing becomes erratic, and his fingertips press hard into the flesh of my back. I know he's close, so I speed up as I ride him. My muscles ache, but he just feels so good filling me up. His ragged breaths pulse against my collarbone as my fingers weave through his hair, pulling on the back of his scalp to tilt his face up to mine. I pull at his bottom lip with my teeth.

"Come for me, Will," I breathe against his mouth.

His eyes burn into mine, his eyebrows knitting together, and his face contorts as I grind up and down on his cock.

"El, oh fuck!"

His hips jerk upright, his cock hitting the very end of me, and I gasp loudly. I watch his face as he comes, his eyes rolling back in his head as his eyelids flutter. The sight, utterly breathtaking and familiar. In fact, being with him like this feels so familiar, I'm sure we've been in this position before. Flashes of memories dance through my mind of our bodies together this way, answering the question I have been agonizing over for two years.

"We've done this before," he says.

My eyes search his face. "I…" my voice is strong again, "I think so."

"It's like I can see it," he says quietly, his face only inches from mine. "The memories of us before…"

My forehead rests against his and our eyes close, just taking a moment to breathe it all in. To finally have some answers. His arms hold me for several long minutes until he's finally rolling me over onto the bed. He discards our protection then turns back to me, lying down on the bed.

"Your neck is healed," he says, his fingers tracing down the hollow of my neck.

He's right, it doesn't hurt anymore.

"I asked Sarah about the portal," he whispers.

"Really?" I ask, hopeful.

He nods. "Yes…I don't know if she was lying or not, but her mind didn't waver, so I think she was telling the truth."

His fingers slide between mine absentmindedly, like he can't stop touching me even if he wanted to.

"Are you all right?" he asks.

His concerned eyes meet mine, and I shrug. "Not really, but I will be."

He nods. "El, I know what you're thinking, but…I don't know if we should go back."

I blink and push myself up. "Why not?"

"They wanted to kill you. We were lucky enough to get away once, who's to say that if we go back, they won't try it again? What if we're not so lucky next time? If something happens to you—"

He stops. There's unbearable pain in his eyes, like he's remembering it from before. The memory of him breaking down at my sentencing steals my breath away. And I have to admit, his argument makes sense. Going back is an enormous risk, especially without our memories fully restored. But Brysen's blue eyes and copper hair flash across my mind like a lighthouse in a dark sea. The note he'd smuggled me while imprisoned told me to come back no matter what. No matter how long it took, I was to make my way back.

"We have to go back," I say.

Will sits up, grasping my shoulders. "How do you know this won't be a huge mistake?"

"Brysen."

Will blinks rapidly, his eyes growing wide at the mention of my brother's name.

"Brysen…"

"Do you remember him?" I ask.

Will's face goes rigid, the muscle in his jaw twitching, but he nods.

"When I was locked up in that cell, he came to see me. He told you you had a plan to save me and he gave me a note. It said that we would be able to be together, but I had to return. I had to go back no matter how long it took." I feel tears prickling at the back of my eyes. "Plus, I just desperately miss him. My family…"

Will blows out a long breath, the fluffy curls on his forehead lifting up and revealing the scar over his eyebrow. "Then, we'll go."

I blink and grab his hands. "You don't have to come with me. You can stay here." I regret it the moment the words tumble out of my mouth. I'm too selfish to leave him now, even to keep him safe.

Will narrows his eyes. "If you think for one moment I would stay behind, I'm about to be horribly offended."

I smile and lean toward him, pressing a gentle kiss to his lips.

"We should go, then," Will says, pulling himself off the side of the bed, "I'll take you home to change and collect anything you might want to bring with you."

His arms wrap around me, and before I can even put on clothes, we're in my apartment. It's dark now, the streetlights outside the window offering the only light into my room.

"I'll come get you in half an hour," he whispers against my ear.

A jittery nervous sensation sweeps through me. This is happening, it's finally happening. I'm going home. I'm terrified.

34

WILL

I'm disoriented as I Jump back into my bedroom. I stand naked, staring at my bed for what must be at least ten minutes, not quite sure what to do with myself. I'm nervous. Nervous about going back. What if Sarah's instructions lead us right into a trap? I have a feeling that isn't the case, but that doubt is still there. Then, there's what Elora said about her brother, Brysen.

A wave of uneasiness had swept over me when she'd mentioned his name, and while I can't quite remember why, there's something about that feeling that makes me exponentially more nervous about going back. I try to remember him, remember a conversation with him. I can sense the memories are there, just out of reach.

I take a deep breath and get dressed in layers, not knowing what kind of temperature to expect if we successfully cross over. I look around my apartment, trying to think if there is anything I want to take with me, but truly, nothing stands out. It's sad, really, that I've been living this life for two years and have almost nothing to show for it. The picture on top of my dresser catches my eye, and I walk over to it. I pick up the frame in my hands, looking down on the smiling faces of myself with Alex and Mariah. This. This is what I'll take with me.

I turn the frame over and pop out the back, removing the photo. There's writing on the back with the month and year the picture was taken and a short note written in Mariah's loopy handwriting.

Love ya, Mr. Magoo. Merry Christmas xoxo, Mariah

A grin splits my face at the nickname. She hasn't called me that in a while. Then, I feel my smile sink, my heart plummeting. I'll probably never see her again. Never laugh at her jokes or be the recipient of a friendly hug or her well-intentioned nagging. And Alex…she'll never see either of us again. I can't leave without saying something. I have to say goodbye somehow.

I tuck the photo into the pocket of my hoodie and walk out into the living room, where my cellphone is still lying on the coffee table. I pick it up, ignoring the two dozen messages from everyone at work and clicking open the contacts to find Mariah's name. The sound of the phone ringing on the other end starts.

Ring, ring.

What am I even going to say? What can I say?

Ring, ring.

This is a bad idea.

Ring…

"Hello?"

My heart constricts at the sound of Mariah's voice, my mouth freezing in place.

"Will?"

"Hey," I finally splutter. "Mariah, how are you?"

A brief pause. "Will, are you okay? You always text, never call."

I sigh. "Yeah, I'm fine. Just wanted to talk to you. To hear your voice."

The sound of a small laugh echoes through the line. "Oh! Fair enough. Did you hear about the fire?"

"Yeah, I did."

There's the sound of the TV being turned down in the background, or maybe she's stepped out onto the balcony. A balcony I've sat on a handful of times. All of them, good. "You weren't there, were you? You didn't answer any of my messages —I was worried."

"No, no, I wasn't there." There's a long pause.

"Will, you sure you're all right? You sound…sad."

Tears are building up in my eyes, and I furiously try to blink them away. "No, I'm…no. Listen, I just wanted to call and tell you—"

"Tell me what?"

"I just wanted to say that I love you. You've been, like, a big sister to me the last two years and I want you to know how much you mean to me."

Another pause. "Will, you're scaring me. What's going on?"

I shake my head, a single tear escaping like a fugitive down my cheek. "I probably won't see you again for a while and I just…I need you to know how much your friendship means to me. To Alex, too." There's no need to tell her Alex's affection was all an act.

"What do you mean you won't see me for a while? Where are you going?"

I wipe at the tear angrily and sigh. "It doesn't matter."

"Where are you right now?"

I can hear her grabbing her keys, her girlfriend Lindsay in the background asking who is on the phone.

"I'm not…Mariah, you don't need to panic. I'm not going to hurt myself, Jesus."

"I don't care. I'm coming over. Where the hell is Alex?"

I feel the air leave my lungs. "I…I'm not sure. I think he's with Sarah."

I don't know if she'll ever find out the truth. Would there be an investigation when the landlord finds both of our apartments deserted? The sudden thought that I should probably burn all of those journals over at Alex's place springs to mind. It's not exactly information that should be public.

"Mariah, please, let me say goodbye."

"Will, stop, I—"

"Just say goodbye back…please."

There's a long pause, a shaky breath, then a whisper into the speaker. "Goodbye, Will. I love you. I've always considered you a brother."

"Goodbye."

I hang up, turning the phone off and removing the SIM card. My eyes clamp shut and my fingers clench so hard on the phone screen that it cracks. There's no denying it—this is going to hurt for a long time, and I hope that one day Mariah will forgive me for it.

Distracting myself by collecting all the journals and notes and other odd bits of information left at Alex's apartment, I take it up to the roof, where there's a metal bucket full of old cigarettes. I dump the notes into it and pull a lighter out of my pocket. Bending down, I touch the flame to the edge of the paper. The flame spreads, curling and licking down the edges before it catches onto the others. A bucket full of secrets and betrayal burning to ash. When there's nothing left but the glowing embers, I cast one last look over the view of the city from my roof, then Jump.

•————— ✳ —————•

ELORA IS SITTING on her bed. She's changed into a pair of black jeans, a long t-shirt, and a thick cardigan. The dagger I cleaned and gave back to her is strapped to the belt at her hips, the straps of a small backpack over her shoulders. Her hair is down and free, slightly kinked and wavy from drying while we were tangled up in each other.

She stands and crosses the room to throw her arms around me. I breathe her in, the smell of her calming my heart after the conversation with Mariah. As if she's overheard my thoughts, she whispers into my chest. "Maybe we'll come back one day."

Somehow, I know we won't. "I burned all the stuff from Alex's place. It'll be strange enough that we've all just disappeared without a trace, without that stuff lying around."

She nods, and I squeeze her a little tighter to me, kissing her forehead. "Ready?"

She pulls back, looks up at me, then around the apartment. "Yes."

A moment later, we're standing in the quiet, nearly perfect, circular hedged area at the side of the pool. Evidence of earlier events still present, the pool of blood where Alex's body was seeping into the rocky shore at the edge of the water. Elora is staring at it, her eyes glassy in the darkness.

"It's not your fault," I say.

She blinks and looks up at me. "I know...doesn't help though."

I nod and grip her hand in mine, bringing the back of her palm to my lips.

"So what do we do now?" she asks, looking at the pool.

I look up at the clear, circular expanse of dark sky above us, the moon peeking out over the edge of the horizon of trees.

"We wait for the moonlight to touch the pool. Then, we walk in. The Solis should do the rest."

Her eyebrows rise. "That's it?"

I can't help but laugh. "That's exactly what I asked. But that's what Sarah said to do."

She laughs too, then, her voice musical and vibrant against the unnatural quiet of the space. The sound seems to ripple over the surface of the unnaturally still water, like a vibrating mirror.

I can feel her trembling beside me, her hand fluctuating in temperature either from nerves, her affinities, or possibly both.

"All right, sunshine?" I ask.

She nods, then turns to look at me quizzically. "Why do you call me that?"

I feel my eyebrows disappear under my hair as they rise. "Sunshine?"

"Yeah."

Heat creeps into my cheeks. "Because from the moment I laid eyes on you, even under the iced coffee I managed to dump all over you," she chuckles, "you've been the brightest thing in my life. When you're in the room, everything else is dull by comparison."

Her face softens, her eyes locking with mine. "Really?"

"You're my soulmate, Elora. There's a reason it was your voice calling me from my Solis. I meant what I said before, you can keep all of me, have all of me forever."

Tears slide down her cheeks, but she's smiling. "I will."

The pool before us brightens as the light of the moon overhead hits the surface of the water. It starts to shimmer as the dark endless depths of the water lighten until it turns pale, almost turquoise in colour. There's a painful longing that pulls at my heart then, as if my very soul recognizes this place, knows what lies beyond it. A place I haven't been in two years, have lived as if it never existed, but here it is.

I look next to me, the expression on Elora's face the same as how I feel. We both step forward, our toes on the very edge next to the water, as if waiting for the other to take the first step.

"Will," I hear her whisper.

I squeeze her hand. "Truth or dare?"

She laughs quietly. "Truth."

"Are you scared?"

She's looking forward across the pool. "Terrified." Her eyes turn to meet mine. "Truth or dare?"

I smirk. "Dare."

"Don't let go of my hand."

"Never."

She nods, and together we step forward off the shore. The soles of our feet hit a solid surface instead of sinking through the water. The Solis rings on our hands glow brightly and our Solis marks burst with life and light. The water ahead of us starts to swirl. Like a glittering vortex, it spins and spins—the mist spraying our faces and exposed skin, our hair lifting up and around our faces. Then, it lifts, like a watery archway ahead of us reflecting not ourselves but what looks like an endless cavern. The pull is almost too much to bear now. A powerful yearning to simply step through, a power so tangible my fingers twitch.

I turn, finding Elora practically glowing, her eyes wide and unblinking.

"Ready?"

She turns and smiles. "Let's go home."

We step through the portal, and I surrender myself to wherever it takes me, as long as her hand is in mine and her light never leaves me again.

TO BE CONTINUED

WANT MORE?

Thank you for reading Where the Lights Lead, Book 1 in the Elements Series. If you enjoyed the book a review would be very much appreciated as it helps other readers discover the story. For updates on the next instalment of the Elements Series and upcoming contemporary romance novels please sign up for my newsletter via my website www.lhblake.com.

ACKNOWLEDGMENTS

It is a completely surreal feeling to be writing this section of a novel I never expected to ever finish. The idea for this story first appeared, as it does for many authors, in a dream at my family's trailer in Haliburton, Ontario in 2007. Since then it has been written and rewritten, the world has changed, the characters have evolved and gone through so many name changes it makes my head spin. But ultimately, I feel like this is the story it was always meant to be and I'm so excited to be able to share it with you.

There are so many people I want to thank but I'd like to start by thanking my husband. Phil, you have always supported my dreams and I appreciate you hanging in there with me while I stumble along on this adventure. You are my soulmate and I love you.

My three boys. I still don't know how this managed to get finished with all of your yelling and mess making, but I love you all so much in all of the many ways that make you so special.

To my parents, thank you so much for always supporting the artistic side of me and loving me enough to give me the confidence to see this through. You've never shied away from bragging about me so, even if dad never reads this, I hope you show it off to all of your friends.

To my editor, Nicolette. You definitely made this book the best it could possibly be. I've learned so much about writing and editing from your feedback and have enjoyed working together so much. Can't wait to share more of this writing adventure with you.

My beta readers. You really are the group that made me think this book could actually be something. That you enjoyed it so much gave me the courage to keep going and finally get to this moment. Thank you to Lacy P, Miriam E, Charlotte B, T.B. W, and Sarah R.

In particular, I'd like to thank Christyn W. Your comments and real time reactions really gave me an accurate sense of how a reader will react to my book and writing style. Your input was so valuable and I can't wait to show you what comes next.

Letizia L. What can I say, except that I adore you. Aside from being an amazing beta reader, now a critique partner, and one of my biggest sources of inspiration, you're also my friend. I'm so glad to have met you on this journey so you can talk me down off the ledge of insanity when things are spiralling out of control. P.S. Your airport reaction will forever live rent free in my mind.

Finally, to the reader. Thank you so much for taking a chance on this book. Thank you for supporting indie authors as we work so hard to provide entertaining stories that may otherwise have never been told. I sincerely hope you enjoyed this story and you are anxiously awaiting the next book in the series. Please feel free to leave an honest review on your preferred platform or my website - www.lhblake.com.

ABOUT THE AUTHOR

L.H. Blake is a loving wife and mother to three beautiful boys, as well as her dog Lucy. She is a full time high school teacher living in rural Ontario, Canada. An avid reader and creative writer since childhood, Blake has always loved fantasy stories, in particular fantasy romance. It has always been a lifelong dream to write and publish a novel and now that the dream has become a reality, she has no intention of stopping. Outside of books, Blake has been involved in the arts her whole life with passions for dance, musical theatre, crafting, embroidery and backyard astronomy.

Visit L.H. Blake's website: www.lhblake.com

facebook.com/lhblake.author

twitter.com/lhblakeauthor

instagram.com/lhblake.author

tiktok.com/@lhblake.author

goodreads.com/lhblakeauthor

bookbub.com/authors/lhblakeauthor

Printed in Great Britain
by Amazon

22172347R00236